GAME CHANGER

Douglas E. Richards

Paragon Press

This book is a work of fiction. The characters, incidents, and dialogues are products of the author's imagination and are not to be construed as real. Any resemblance to actual events or persons, living or dead, is entirely coincidental.

Published by Paragon Press, 2016

E-mail the author at doug@san.rr.com

Friend him on Facebook at Douglas E. Richards Author

Visit the author's website at www.douglaserichards.com

First Edition

PART 1
Revenge

"In each of us there is another whom we do not know."

—Carl Jung, Swiss psychiatrist and founder of analytical psychology

"Our unconscious brains steer our behavior. But how do our brains come to be the way they are? Why are there differences between us? To answer this we need to look one level deeper to how our brains get built. And that begins with our genes. The genes you come to the table with can have an enormous influence on your behavior. Consider this: about half of the population carries a particular set of genes. And if you have these genes your chances of committing a violent crime go up by eight hundred and eighty-two percent! The overwhelming majority of prisoners carry these genes, as does almost everyone on death row. So we can't presume that everyone is coming to the table equally equipped in terms of drives and behaviors.

"By the way, we summarize this set of genes as the Y chromosome. If you're a carrier, we call you a *male*."

—David Eagleman, Neuroscientist, Baylor College of Medicine

1

Kevin Quinn straightened the shimmering lapels of his black tux and gazed in revulsion and hatred toward the man who was dying, thirty feet or so away from him.

Quinn noted that while the man had but minutes left to live, he appeared unshaken. In command. Totally at ease.

Of course he did.

He was the most charming president since Bill Clinton. Smooth, warm, friendly. Like the highest functioning psychopaths everywhere, he could fake sincerity with absolute brilliance, plan spontaneity down to the millimeter.

And he was in the center of throngs of adoring millionaires and billionaires, who were almost sexually aroused to be mingling with someone with more power and prestige than themselves. Titans of entertainment and industry, each wanting favors, and access, and the opportunity to hobnob with the most powerful man on Earth.

A man who would finish dying, right in front of them, in a matter of minutes.

They couldn't see that it was happening, of course. For very good reason. Because Kevin Quinn hadn't begun killing him yet.

Quinn took a deep breath and adjusted the receiver in his ear that was picking up every word the president said. Every smug, misleading, charming, manipulative word uttered by Matthew Davinroy, President of the United States, and one of the most despicable monsters who had ever lived.

The mansion they were in, one of many in the wealthy municipality of Princeton, New Jersey, was situated on some of the most tranquil and scenic land on the East Coast, and encompassed thirteen thousand square feet of opulence. Chandeliers, Greek statues, fountains, marble, and fine oil paintings. Filled with men and women in the most expensive attire and wearing the most expensive jewelry.

An eclectic mix of aromas fought for dominance within the manor. Expensive perfumes and aftershaves clashed with the smell of caviar and other high-end hors d'oeuvres, continually sent around by a catering staff whose membership had been modified on this particular night. Most were seasoned waiters who had been part of the staff for years. These men and woman were in awe of the proceedings and would have paid for the privilege of being in a room with the president and numerous accomplished and famous others, even to do nothing but empty their bedpans.

But one was a Secret Service agent, wearing the same outfit as the other caterers, who had drawn a short straw, and who tried to accept being relegated to the president's personal order-taker and waiter with as much good humor as he could manage.

The buzz of conversation from dozens of small groups around the vast living room, with enough square footage to rival a small home, was ever-present, along with the clinking of cocktail glasses and crystal goblets containing fine wine and champagne.

President Davinroy was at his most charming, as he always was at these fundraising events, making sure no partygoer would regret the massive amounts of money they had donated to be there. A gala such as this being held on a Sunday night was unusual, but was dictated by the president's schedule. Most of those in attendance would have skipped their mother's funeral to be there, so this wasn't a hardship.

The president was currently surrounded by six men and women he had blessed with his presence, and would continue to bless for five or ten minutes before moving on to work the room further. Each group he joined waited patiently for their turn, and in each he held court like a queen bee in the center of a frenzy of sycophantic drones.

Just hearing Davinroy's syrupy voice made Quinn sick to his stomach. He clenched his fists and fought to weather the rage that stabbed at his insides.

With a monumental effort of will, he managed to calm himself once again. He had to be relaxed and unemotional. Dispassionate.

A president hadn't been successfully assassinated since Kennedy, and there was a reason for this. It wasn't an easy task.

He approached Jeffrey Gallup, who was standing as casually as he could near the bar, scanning the room at all times for possible threats. Quinn nodded at him. "I'm going to switch assignments with you for the next hour or so," he said. "You man the outside front, and I'll handle the bar."

Gallup shot him a disapproving look, which Quinn knew he had earned. He should have called in the switch while still outside. By walking in and basically touching Gallup on the shoulder, like he was a tag-team wrestler and not a bodyguard, he had left the outside front of the mansion unwatched for several minutes. Since Quinn was the man's superior, Gallup didn't say what was on his mind. Instead, he walked briskly to the door and out to take up his new post.

Quinn could feel the eyes of any number of partygoers lingering on him with great interest, which was common, and many didn't even bother to look away and pretend they weren't staring when he turned in their direction. When one was in direct proximity to the president, there were two facets to the experience that were irresistible. One was the opportunity to see and interact with the president, First Lady, and other celebrities. And the other was the opportunity to pick out and watch the swarm of trusty Secret Service agents, square-jawed, clean-cut Dudley Do-Right types straight out of central casting, who tried to blend in but who had no real hope of doing so.

For many women, sleeping with a Secret Service agent on the president's detail was a trophy that carried as much prestige as bagging the head of a mythical creature did for Hercules, and for years an endless stream of beautiful women threw themselves at him like confetti at a wedding.

His eyes moistened briefly as he thought of the one woman remarkable enough to have immunized him from any temptation those trying to bed him might have posed. A woman who had stolen his heart and his mind, making the thought of sex with the most beautiful and acrobatic of women seem bland and pointless by comparison. Nicole. The woman who had become his wife.

President Davinroy was standing beside his own wife, Anne, quite a celebrity in her own right, as was typical of First Ladies throughout history. She was wearing a glimmering emerald-green gown and looked to be enjoying herself. Was even she aware of what a monster she had married? Quinn thought it was impossible that she didn't suspect. But also impossible that she did.

Quinn forced himself to pretend to do his job, scanning the crowd for a possible assassin. And he found one, but only for an instant, when his own reflection materialized in a facet of a stunning crystal chandelier, and disappeared just as quickly. He was six-one, with short black hair and striking blue eyes, and he had been told he had a warm and inviting smile, although it had been so many days since he had displayed any lighthearted emotions that he wasn't sure he was still capable of them.

Finally, fifteen minutes after Quinn had assumed duty at the bar, the president ordered a drink from Special Agent Dan Oakland, who was wearing the same black vest and bow tie worn by the legitimate catering staff. Oakland worked his way through a number of groupings of partygoers and to the bar, where he delivered the order to the bartender, nodded at Quinn, and then shuffled off into the center of the crowd. He would hold his position there until Quinn indicated that he had blessed the cocktail and it was time to deliver it back to the president.

Davinroy had ordered something called a *Portuguese Nectar Vector*, a recent addition to the canon of alcoholic beverages with which Quinn was not familiar. The bartender mixed the drink and filled a cocktail glass under Quinn's watchful eye, and then, as he had been instructed, poured the excess into a separate glass, placing both on a tray and handing it to the Secret Service agent.

Quinn took a healthy drink from the bright blue liquid in the second glass, something that wasn't an absolute requirement, or deterrent, but which many agents preferred to do as an added precaution. After this was complete, while the bartender busied himself preparing the cocktails ordered by those currently encircling Davinroy, Quinn dropped an almost invisible tablet into the blue liquid in the first glass, which instantly dissolved, releasing its payload of cyanide into Davinroy's drink.

Live by the sword, die by the sword, you psychopathic asshole, thought Quinn triumphantly. There was no more fitting way for this abomination to die. Poetic justice.

Quinn nodded at the bartender and waited the few minutes it took the man to finish mixing a colorful collection of cocktails in glasses of various sizes, including one with a paper umbrella emerging, which he added to the tray that held Davinroy's beverage.

Quinn motioned Dan Oakland over to pick up the tray as hatred began to consume him once again, growing as ravenously as a magic beanstalk.

Quinn had used a new form of cyanide that was a thousand times more potent than any of its predecessors. Within seconds of the president's first sip, he would experience seizures, followed quickly by cardiac arrest and death.

Quinn only had one regret. While Davinroy's death would be painful, it would not be painful *enough*. And it would come far too quickly.

But this could not be helped.

As the agent carried the tray back toward the president, Quinn did something that he knew was a minor miracle.

He remembered.

2

There was a time—five short weeks earlier, to be exact—that Quinn had had relatively positive feelings toward Matthew Davinroy. True, their politics could not be further apart, but Quinn had thought the current president was as good a man as any politician ever was. Self-serving and narcissistic, sure, but peel away the glad-handing, the lies, and the unfair attacks on fellow politicians, and Quinn felt certain that deep down, despite his misguided policies, Davinroy was well meaning and wanted the best for his country.

But this had all changed, *profoundly*, five weeks earlier, as had Quinn's life. His world had been shattered, destroyed, by a man with no conscience or remorse.

The Davinroy family had owned a retreat in the Catskill Mountains for generations, a little over a hundred miles from Manhattan. For two weeks every summer since the president had taken office five years earlier, the resort was closed down, at least to paying customers, and it became the exclusive vacation destination for Davinroy and hundreds of guests, free of charge.

Like salmon drawn irresistibly to their spawning grounds, like Bush Senior to Kennebunkport, Bush Junior to his Texas ranch, and Barack Obama to Martha's Vineyard, Matthew Davinroy returned to the Catskill Mountains each and every year, like clockwork.

Naturally, the Secret Service came along, but twice as many as were needed. Each special agent was on duty for half of the stay, and for the other half was free to enjoy the resort as a guest.

Prior to this scheduled vacation, the president had invited all in attendance to bring their spouses for some R & R, a magnanimous gesture sure to earn him the undying thanks and loyalty of all involved. He had insisted that Quinn bring Nicole along, since she warranted an invitation on two accounts. Not only was she the wife of a man prepared to give his life to protect Davinroy's, she was also one of the president's most valued and trusted civilian advisors. In fact, Quinn had first met her during one of her frequent visits to the White House, and they had fallen in love soon thereafter.

Nicole was *perfect*, and Quinn considered himself the luckiest man alive. She wasn't classically beautiful, but her joyous personality was infectious and she brightened every room she entered like a living supernova. She was bright, funny, and full of life. Fun loving and adventurous, with an innate kindness and compassion that was unparalleled. He had quickly become so fiercely in love with this woman that at times it almost scared him.

And they were expecting their first child! A baby girl. Nicole was eight months pregnant, and Quinn was giddy over the prospect of starting a family with a woman who would be as amazing a mother as she was a wife—and this from a man who had never had an interest in marriage *or* children.

Quinn had seized upon the opportunity to have one last vacation with Nicole before their first child—whom they would name Hailey—made her grand entrance. So they had taken Davinroy up on his offer, but only after Quinn had made sure there was a hospital with a maternity ward close enough to the resort to suit their needs should tiny Hailey decide to arrive early.

Nestled inside the nearly six thousand square miles that comprised the Catskill Mountains, Davinroy's lodge was ideal. The accommodations were spacious and modern, but blended in with the surroundings. Guests were surrounded by old-growth forest and had access to a private lake on-site. In addition to boating, fishing, horseback riding, and hiking, recreational options included downhill skiing and zip-lining, just a short excursion away—not that either of these last two activities would be on the agenda for a woman deep into her last trimester, but there would still be plenty of fun to be had.

Nicole had seemed more anxious about the trip than excited, but Quinn decided this was understandable given her circumstances. Once they were there, he was certain they would have a wonderful time.

But on the very first night, the vacation Quinn was so certain would be a dream became twisted into the ultimate *nightmare*. This was the night that his cell phone had issued a piercing alarm, impossible to ignore.

Yet he *had* ignored it.

Sleep had somehow managed to cling to him and seal him inside like an impenetrable coating of shrink-wrap.

When Nicole had become pregnant, he had gotten her an elegant gold bracelet with sensors and an emergency electronic beacon hidden inside. If she pressed the bracelet in a certain way it would broadcast an alarm to his phone, along with her location. If she ever fainted or lost consciousness, not unheard of for a pregnant woman to do, the sensors would somehow know she wasn't simply sleeping and his phone would also sound the alarm. She felt silly wearing such a device, but he had teased her that she shouldn't have married a Secret Service agent if she was troubled by a man with protective instincts.

But now that her personal alarm had been triggered, this same man was failing to respond. Only the knowledge that Nicole needed him urgently—buried deep within his sleeping brain—had finally managed to unleash enough adrenaline for him to shake off his unnaturally deep, coma-like slumber, and this only after the alarm had blared for a full ten minutes.

Where was she? And what had caused her to sound the alarm?

His panic grew by the second, so much so that it became a struggle for him to even breathe. His imagination ran wild. Even the thought of her in jeopardy was unbearable, tying his stomach into knots.

What happened next was a nightmare without end, so earth-shatteringly awful that even though he could only reconstruct bits and pieces of the horror, these memories, spotty and incomplete, were utterly *devastating*.

He had stumbled through dense areas of trees and undergrowth for almost a mile, to a location deep in the woods, far from any hiking or recreational routes. There was a structure hidden within a thicket of trees and brush, the appearance and size of which he couldn't recall.

As Quinn moved toward the structure, which his phone indicated now housed his wife, a scream of pain suddenly escaped from inside and pierced the darkness.

His heart leaped to his throat.

The scream had to have come from Nicole.

The door was locked, but somehow he gained entry. How, he couldn't recall. He remembered being outside in a panic, and then being *inside*, but he had no recollection of the transition between these two realities. And despite the massive quantities of adrenaline coursing through his veins and his prolonged journey there, he still felt sluggish, still unable to fully remove the yoke of sleep.

The rest of his memories were jumbled together in a haze, evoking little clarity but immense rage and horror. He had flashes of the President of the United States delivering several savage blows to his wife's skull with a wrought iron fireplace poker. He had images of her hazel eyes, filled with anguish and horror, suddenly rolling up into her head, their light extinguished, never again to sparkle brightly in a dazzling display of intelligence and optimism. And images of his wife's lifeless body collapsing onto the bed she had been standing beside, her hands and ankles cuffed together.

All of this had happened in an instant, but the memory of it, although fuzzy, seemed eternal. Quinn had screamed and rushed forward, even before he had fully processed the absolute horror of this impossible scene, intent on killing Davinroy with his bare hands, but instead he crashed to the ground, face-first.

Davinroy had set a perimeter of nearly invisible trip wires, one of which Quinn had practically sprinted into. The next thing he could remember was being seated on a sturdy wooden chair, his ankles and wrists locked to it with plastic ties, and the chair itself strapped to a heavy bed frame.

The President of the United States stood before him with a powerful stun gun in his right hand. Quinn's body throbbed painfully from head to toe, and he had no doubt he had absorbed an unholy blast of electricity. His senses were far from a hundred percent, but it was safe to assume he had temporarily lost consciousness when his head had hit the floor, and Davinroy had then used his gun to light him up like a Las Vegas billboard, causing further disorientation and tenderizing every muscle in his body.

Nicole was now lifeless in front of him, a fate shared by his unborn daughter still locked in his wife's womb.

It couldn't be. This beautiful, wonderful woman could not be gone. The child within her could not have been snuffed out just days before her birth. *It wasn't possible.*

Nicole's face was covered in ugly welts and dark purple bruises, and both of her eyes were black and puffy, her nose broken. She had taken a beating even before her head had been staved in by a monster, and there were what appeared to be burns on her neck and arms, along with other signs of traumatic injury his mind wouldn't allow himself to fully process.

She had been so brutally tortured her death was almost a mercy.

Quinn felt as though his brain were bursting into flame, his entire being raging against the horror of what he had lost, the extraordinary, incandescent woman that Davinroy had taken from both him and the world.

"I am *so* sorry about this," said the president, with the same level of concern he might have shown had Quinn's invitation to the White House Christmas party been lost in the mail. "But Nicole did bring it on herself. She didn't leave me any choice."

Quinn didn't remember his exact response, but he was sure shouting and cursing and threatening were involved. Davinroy shot him again with the powerful stun gun.

When he stopped convulsing, the president began again. "I like you, Special Agent Quinn. You're one of my favorites. So I'm going to take the time to explain things to you. Not that this will end up mattering, but I will anyway. But I need you to not interrupt, and to show some civility, and we can avoid discharging any more electricity into you. Okay?"

Quinn was unable to respond, his paralyzed body having not yet recovered.

"First, let me say that I thought the world of your wife. You know that. Her loss is truly tragic."

He said it as though he had nothing whatsoever to do with this loss.

"*I'm going to kill you,*" croaked Quinn, the words coming out as a whisper.

His eyes flashed over the lifeless form of his wife. He held them there for just a moment, as though somehow she would stir. Somehow he would learn that this was a big mistake. Somehow divine magic would breathe life into her and she would become reanimated while he looked on. But there would be no magic on this night, divine or otherwise.

Quinn forced himself to look away as tears began streaming down his face.

"So here is what happened," said Davinroy conversationally. "Nicole stumbled on some . . . indiscretions . . . from my past that were better left buried. Long story about what aroused her suspicions, but it involved considerable bad luck and some clever deductions on her part. Fortunately, I'm a very careful man, and I learned of her activities."

"What are you *talking* about?" spat Quinn as the effects of the stun gun began to diminish.

"Turns out I have a need to inflict pain," said Davinroy with a shrug. "Not sure why, but I was born that way. As a kid, indulging these urges on small animals was enough to get my head right, but there were a few times I took this to the next level."

"You mean with humans?"

"Right. I know these urges are . . . problematic. Not exactly something voters would seek out in a president. So I keep them hidden and deny myself as much as I can. But I did have some youthful indiscretions that my family's fortune enabled me to, um . . . pave over." He sighed. "These instances were regrettable, but I control myself much better nowadays. I've pretty much been a Boy Scout since becoming president." He glanced at Nicole's body on the bed nearby and raised his eyebrows. "Well . . . for the most part."

Tears were still falling from Quinn's eyes, but these words sent him once again into a berserker rage. He threw his body toward Davinroy to strangle the life from him, ignoring the plastic straps that carved bright-red grooves into his wrists and ankles, and disregarding protests from his shoulders that they were close to dislocation.

Davinroy calmly shot him again. This time recovery took even longer, and Quinn was now too weak to even feel rage. But feelings of anguish and loss were able to thrive in the absence of more hostile emotions, and his suffering was more intense than ever.

Davinroy's horrific behavior was impossible, surreal, but maybe not to the extent that Quinn had first thought. Professional politicians all pretended to be saints, but their ranks were enriched with those who were ruthless and without a conscience. The incidence of deviant behavior among politicians was far higher than average, and scions of rich and powerful families really could get away with atrocities that would earn the average citizen a life sentence in prison.

Michael Jackson had almost certainly molested numerous boys, but his fortune had protected him from any real consequences. Senator Ted Kennedy had driven his car off a bridge on the island of Chappaquiddick, leaving a young woman in the passenger's seat to drown, returning to his hotel and not reporting the incident for over nine hours, yet he remained a senator and never served a single day in jail. Additional examples abounded. Revelations of hidden, deviant behavior in prominent people were legion.

"So Nicole was beginning to unravel some of my past I didn't want unraveled," continued Davinroy calmly. "Your wife was a regular Nancy Drew. As brilliant a detective as she was an advisor."

Quinn's thoughts and emotions had become muddled and disjointed. Not only had the light of his life been brutally murdered before his eyes, he had been repeatedly dosed with electricity and almost certainly drugged. But even though he knew he would soon be dead, something within him needed to know why. Needed to know how. Needed to understand the true nature of the evil that had destroyed him and the woman he had held so dear.

"Where are we?" he managed to whisper. "How did you slip your protection?"

"I'll explain everything, but I need to know how you found us, since I made sure to destroy your wife's phone."

Quinn told him. What did it matter at this point?

Davinroy glanced over at the bracelet on Nicole's lifeless wrist and nodded. "Nice precaution," he said approvingly. "But even so, there's no way you should be here. I dosed you with enough drug to put down an elephant for the night." He shook his head. "You must have unique genetics that make you more resistant than average."

"Are you going to answer my questions?" said Quinn.

"Certainly," said Davinroy. "About ten years ago, I had contractors build tunnels under several of the rooms out here, accessible from ingeniously hidden entrances inside closets. My room has one, which allows me to easily escape my gilded cage and get some privacy. Your room is also accessible from one of these tunnels. They all feed together and lead to various destinations, including where we are now."

"I drugged you and your wife at dinner," continued the president. "Easy to do. A dose designed to kick in after you had already fallen asleep. You Secret Service types are great at making sure that *I'm* not drugged, but you do tend to get sloppy when it comes to your own drinks. Nicole's dose was small, so I could rouse her when I needed her."

"So you came in through your tunnel and kidnapped her out of our room?"

"Exactly. She had become too suspicious to ever agree to meet with me one-on-one in a secluded location like this one. Bringing her here took some work, but I prepare well. I have golf carts and other equipment in the tunnels, which I make excellent use of whenever I'm here."

"What kind of use?"

"Mostly sexual. I pay high-end hookers big money—anonymously—to come to one of the rooms here with a tunnel entrance. I then appear and lead them underground to this location. Which you can see contains a bed. This allows me to indulge my craving, to finally engage in what you might call . . . *rough* sex. I'm only truly satisfied when the woman I'm with is terrified and in pain. I don't expect you to have any sympathy for me, but if you knew how much I suffer from suppressing these urges, I think you would. I'm the leader of the free world, with all the pressure this brings, and I'm forced to largely deny myself a primal need that is critical to my well-being. I battle against this fierce compulsion for months on end, until the pressure becomes unbearable. I only satisfy these urges the minimum amount required to keep my head on straight, so I can do the people's business."

"*Keep your head on straight?*" barked Quinn in absolute revulsion. "By killing helpless women?"

"I don't *kill* them," said the president, as though offended. "I'm not a monster. I do hurt them pretty badly, but nothing they don't recover from. And I pay them extremely well."

"Impossible. One of them would come forward, even if you *are* the most powerful man on Earth."

Davinroy smiled broadly. "Except they don't know what happened to them. America spends countless billions conducting secret research in Black laboratories across the country. In one of these labs, our best and brightest are perfecting a drug that causes total, absolute, take-it-to-the-bank, it-is-never-coming-back, memory loss. At the moment they've managed to create a pill that will wipe away the past twelve to eighteen hours of a person's life.

"I made sure to get a supply of these pills a few years back. So when I'm done with these escorts, I just deposit them a good distance away from here and feed them a pill and a sedative. No harm, no foul. They don't remember coming to my resort or their encounter with me. Not the trauma, the fear, or the infliction of pain, although it takes them a while to heal. They just know that their personal wealth has grown considerably. To be honest, if I could give them a choice, I'd bet most of them would be glad to take a beating for the kind of money I provide."

Quinn hadn't thought he could be any more horrified than he already was, but he had been mistaken. This man was a psychopathic monster in every way. How could such an abomination even exist, let alone masquerade as a human being? Davinroy looked as though he expected a humanitarian medal for improving the finances of the prostitutes he beat nearly to death, and killing Nicole and their unborn daughter hadn't troubled him in the slightest.

The idea that a monster like Matthew Davinroy could even *exist* was unthinkable, let alone rise to the presidency of the United States.

And the greatest irony of all was that Davinroy was a man who spoke out against torture in any form, all the while getting a sexual thrill from doing this with his own bare hands. He spouted nothing but pacifism, withdrawal, and peace. This had been Quinn's point of contention with the man. He was a modern-day Neville Chamberlain, the British prime minister who had famously sought appeasement with Adolf Hitler.

Davinroy's hands-off approach, his failure to engage anywhere in the world, under any circumstances, left vacuums that bad actors around the globe were only too happy to fill. Bad actors like China, Korea, Russia, and Iran. And especially terror groups like ISIS, who gladly announced their intention to commit genocide and establish a global caliphate, a worldwide Islamic government.

So Davinroy painted himself as a pacifist, when all the while he was capable of torturing and murdering a helpless woman without even *flinching*. This man—utterly ruthless, without conscience or remorse—had frequently cited Mahatma Gandhi as being his biggest inspiration, portraying himself as the exact opposite of what he really was. Here was a wolf pretending to be as peace loving as the sheep he was busy slaughtering.

But Quinn realized all of this made a macabre sense, after all. Perhaps Davinroy's refusal to truly engage against global terrorism, his call for civil rights for those who would butcher women and children, was just professional courtesy. He was just standing up for his fellow psychopaths.

If he derived sexual satisfaction from beating helpless women, perhaps he also derived satisfaction from seeing the world burn, the direct outcome of his lack of leadership and strength, but perhaps his goal all along.

"So did you rape Nicole as well?" asked Quinn, needing to know but dreading the answer, unaware that his eyes were still filling with tears.

Davinroy's lip turned up in disgust. "I find pregnant women repulsive," he replied. "And I don't *rape*. I pay handsomely for consensual sex. But the thing with your wife had nothing to do with sex. I had to find out exactly what she knew. Who she had told. Where she kept her evidence. So I tortured her for the information, killing two birds with one stone. Despite the lack of sex, I got to indulge a compulsion while getting the information I required. The good news is that it turns out she had kept her suspicions all to herself."

"You are the sickest piece of shit who ever lived!" spat Quinn. "And I know you're lying! There's no way Nicole wouldn't have told me about this. So what's really going on?"

Davinroy shook his head. "I was surprised she kept it from you myself, but she made a convincing case. And I put her under enough duress to be sure she was telling the truth. You've sworn to protect me. She didn't want to put you in an awkward or compromising position. And she couldn't really bring herself to believe that she was right about me. She hoped she was misreading the evidence. She came here searching for more. To really make a case against me, she knew the proof had to be overwhelming."

This logic was more believable than Quinn had expected. The idea of the president being a sadistic monster was extraordinary, unbelievable. And extraordinary claims required extraordinary evidence, especially when they were made against a man this powerful, this slippery.

"She didn't tell you what she was up to," continued Davinroy, "or anyone else. I have access to an advanced Artificial Intelligence program. Before I came here, I fed it comprehensive information about my indiscretions, along with Nicole's known activities during the past few weeks, and the activities of others, including you. It concluded she was operating alone, with greater than ninety-five percent confidence. And tonight I made certain this was true. I forced her to give up the password to her computer account where she kept her evidence. And I verified everything she told me."

He paused. "My interrogation technique was flawless. I guess torture really can lead to good information, after all. Although, I have to admit, once I began," he added, looking almost amused, "I got a little carried away."

Davinroy shrugged. "But my intent was to kill her tonight anyway. I had no choice. Erasing one day of memories wouldn't do the trick, since she'd been working on this for weeks. I really wish this wasn't necessary," he said with a sigh. "Disposing of her body is going to be very inconvenient for me. And she really was a good advisor."

At that instant, all the hatred and rage Quinn had been bottling up hit critical mass and exploded into a nuclear inferno. *"I'm going to kill you if it's the last thing I ever do!"* he hissed between clenched teeth. "Even if you kill me first, this won't help you. Because I promise you, I will find a way back from the grave. And I will make you *suffer!*"

"Yeah, good luck with that," said Davinroy, shaking his head in amusement.

Quinn's despair had become so great he now longed for death. Every second he remained alive was sheer agony, every instant knowing the wonderful woman he had married was lost to the world forever pure torture. "So kill me already, you psychopathic asshole!" he demanded. "*What are you waiting for?*" he screamed at the top of his lungs.

Davinroy paused for several long seconds to let total silence once again descend on the room. "I wouldn't *think* of killing you," he replied finally. "I told you, you're one of my favorite special agents. Also, as I've said, I'm truly sorry it has come to this. Truly sorry about your wife. Besides, *both* of you disappearing would just complicate things for me."

3

For almost five weeks Davinroy's plan had worked exactly as he had suggested it would.

But two days earlier flashes of memory had begun returning to Kevin Quinn.

At first Quinn thought his mind was playing tricks on him. That his grief had caused him to imagine things, or perhaps these were images and thoughts from recent nightmares, stubbornly persistent attempts by his mind to find a villain behind what had happened.

But why the President of the United States? Even for a nightmare, casting Matthew Davinroy as some impossibly evil caricature of a psychopath was beyond preposterous.

But soon the memories crystallized further. And while his recollections were still spotty, and remembered images were hazy and unrefined, the *words* Davinroy had spoken while Quinn had been tied to a chair came back to him with great clarity. And when he finally recalled Davinroy's discussion of the memory erasure drug he was about to be given, which explained the fuzziness and the gaps in his recollections, he had no doubt that the fragmentary images coming back to him were representations of reality rather than dreamscapes.

It was impossible that Davinroy could have been so calculating, so *evil*.

It was also undeniably true.

But the president had made a mistake. The memory erasure drug wasn't as foolproof as he had been led to believe. Or perhaps there was something unique in Quinn's genetics, after all, something that allowed him to fight off sedatives *and* memory agents. He investigated this possibility online, and sure enough, there were tiny genetic differences known to cause a small percentage of the population to metabolize drugs at different speeds, and sometimes in different ways, than the broader population.

As Quinn's memory returned, his mind burned once again with hatred, and he was consumed with but one mission in life: revenge. Justice would be served. He would carry out his threat or die trying.

It had required heroic effort on his part to keep the loathing he felt for the president from his face as he worked near the man the past few days. And an even greater effort to not go off half-cocked, to hold off on his attempt until he had the best chance of success.

But this fundraiser in Princeton was perfect. He would drug Davinroy the way he had been drugged.

The way *she* had been drugged.

Davinroy's scheme should have worked. Even now, much of what happened was lost to Quinn forever, or hazy and unformed, like the fleeting images of Davinroy striking his wife with a poker, and of her limp and lifeless body. But perhaps this was a mercy. Perhaps this loss of clarity wasn't due to the memory drugs at all, but instead was his psyche's way of sparing him further agony.

But the fact that he now remembered much of the incident quite well was nothing short of a miracle.

And the part he remembered most vividly of all was that he had sworn not to rest, not even in his grave, until he had personally escorted Matthew Davinroy into the bowels of hell.

And this was a promise he was now seconds away from keeping.

4

Quinn had considered going to the press, telling them what had happened, but had decided against it.

Davinroy was just too smooth, and too careful.

Ironically, politicians could be taken down by just the hint of a politically incorrect statement, but otherwise could get away with murder, literally, and a president, sitting atop the food chain, was the ultimate example of this. A president had too many connections, too many powerful friends, with too much to lose if he were taken down. The reputation of the United States itself would take too big a hit. The entire country would close ranks to protect him.

Any evidence found would be hidden from view or erased. Even if it wasn't, it would only be circumstantial. It would be Quinn's word against the president's. He was making the same calculations Nicole had made before him.

And Quinn's accusations *would* seem absurd. A grieving husband, losing his wife and child at the president's retreat in mysterious circumstances, accusing the president, so charismatic and charming, of the inconceivable atrocity of torturing and killing a trusted advisor.

And even if Quinn were able to prove it, which he thought highly unlikely, he had promised Davinroy *death*, and no lesser sentence would do. Davinroy had taken *everything* from him.

Quinn watched Dan Oakland making his way back to the group the president was in with mounting anticipation. Oakland handed each guest their cocktail of choice, including Davinroy. When the president was holding his drink and Oakland was receding into the crowd once again, Quinn allowed himself to feel a single moment of elation.

Nothing would ever bring Nicole back, true, but no one had ever needed to be erased from existence more than Matthew Davinroy.

"This is the new sensation I was telling you about, Anne," said Davinroy, nodding at his wife, his every word continuing to come through Quinn's earpiece with great clarity.

Davinroy elevated his right hand, drink included, until it was level with the First Lady's eyes. Others in the group looked on with great interest. "What would you call that color?" asked the president. "Electric neon blue?"

"Wow. That's a tough one," said the First Lady. "I can't even decide if the color is appealing," she added with a charming smile, "or just freaky."

The president grinned. "It is unusual, no denying that," he said. "But that's one of the things I like about it. But, of course, you don't choose a cocktail based on its color. It happens to also be incredibly tasty, but in a way that is so unique I can't describe it."

"I've had these myself, Mr. President," said Jessica Pospisil, president of Sony Pictures. "And I couldn't agree more." She shook her head. "Although I wish they would have chosen a more grown-up name for it than Portuguese Nectar Vector," she added in amusement.

"I can't argue with that," said the president with a warm smile. He turned to his wife once again. "Give this a try," he said. "If you like it as much as I think you will, it's yours. I can get another."

Quinn's stomach clenched as he listened to this exchange and he suddenly felt light-headed.

Impossible!

How could this be? No one's luck could be *this* good.

But even as he thought this he knew he was wrong. Adolf Hitler had survived some fourteen assassination attempts over eleven years, as lucky as he was evil.

Perhaps the most evil men in the world truly had made a pact with the Devil. How else to explain it?

Quinn rushed closer to his target and maneuvered until he found a gap in the human fence surrounding the president, giving him a narrow but clear line of sight to both Davinroy and his wife. Everything seemed to move in slow motion now as a dozen thoughts and calculations rushed across his mind at once.

The First Lady was innocent. He couldn't just let her die. And if she did, the Secret Service would seal up the house, and he would be the chief suspect. Even if he was not found responsible he would never be fully trusted again, ensuring he would never get a second chance. Davinroy would remain unscathed.

Quinn drew his weapon even before he knew he had come to a definitive decision, now only ten feet away from the first couple and their sycophants, and shot the drink from Anne Davinroy's hand just as she was raising it to her lips.

Quinn's shot was *perfect*. The sound of the gun being fired, of shattered glass, and of several screams seemed to all occur at the same instant. A shard of glass drove into the First Lady's hand, causing bright red fingers of blood to emerge, but Quinn didn't pause long enough to see it. The instant the glass shattered he changed his aim and fired once more, this time at the president, but after the first shot the president had jerked backwards, and the round barely grazed his arm.

Secret Service agents materialized from out of nowhere and tackled Davinroy like he was an NFL running back just inches from the end zone, covering him with their bodies. The First Lady received the same treatment beside him.

Quinn cursed loudly, knowing that a second shot would be useless. Moving like a predatory cat he snatched a woman nearby. In one smooth motion he spun her in front of him so she became a human shield and held his gun to her head.

The room burst into total bedlam.

Quinn backed up hurriedly into a nearby wall so he could only be approached from one direction, dragging his newfound friend with him. He had spent many years thinking on his feet, becoming expert at the tactical evaluation of rooms, people, and situations after a single glance, instantly assessing threats, weaknesses, and opportunities.

"Stop or she dies!" shouted Quinn at the top of his lungs, reacting from pure instinct, only aware of what he had said after hearing these words and discovering, to his surprise, that they had come from his own mouth.

Suddenly everyone in the room seemed to freeze, as though they had all stopped screaming, or calling out, or even breathing, and all eyes turned to him. Several of his fellow special agents had their weapons drawn and pointed at him, and had it not been for the helpless woman he now held hostage he would be dead already.

"I have no interest in harming this woman," yelled Quinn. "Or anyone else."

Still holding the gun with his right hand, he removed a cell phone from his pocket with his left, and held it out so it was easily seen. "I'm going to release this woman now," he said. "But know that I'm not wearing my bulletproof vest. Instead, I'm wearing a vest made of shaped C4. Enough to vaporize this house twice over. This phone triggers it to blow, and I've set up a dead man's switch," he explained, displaying improvisational skills that were surpassing even his own high expectations of himself. "This phone contains motion sensors. If it falls from my hand, the sensors will know it, and the explosives will be triggered automatically."

The Special Agent in Charge of the Presidential Protection Division, Cris Coffey, had been one of the agents who had tackled Davinroy, and now stood facing Quinn, with the president still on the ground and shielded by other agents behind him.

Coffey hesitated, and Quinn could tell he was trying to decide if the bomb was a bluff. Quinn guessed that the fact he had released the woman after making his threat, pushing her away from him, would be the deciding factor. Coffey would calculate that Quinn would never give up his hostage, his only hope of survival, unless his threat was real.

Other agents in the room glanced back and forth between Quinn and their boss, alert for whatever might happen next.

"Try to move Davinroy out of here and I'll trigger the C4!" barked Quinn with a snarl, and the way he uttered the president's name, the hatred and disdain and zealotry in his voice and in his expression, left no doubt that he meant it. "Don't test me, Cris!"

Coffey looked deeply into Quinn's eyes one last time and came to a decision. "Okay, we won't move him," he said quickly, striving to keep his voice as calm and soothing as he could. "But come on, Kevin. Let's not do anything rash. Let's talk this out."

"I need David Garza," said Quinn, nodding at a tall, youthful man to his left, looking dapper in a black tux and red cummerbund. *"Now!"*

Garza, a billionaire technology entrepreneur who owned the mansion they were in, took a step backwards, and the aura of command and authority he typically projected was shattered, replaced by one of primal fear.

Coffey held up his palm to Garza, indicating he should remain silent, and then turned to Quinn. "Why do you need him?" he asked.

"To lead me to his garage and give me the keys to one of his cars. I'll get the hell out of here and he'll remain unharmed. You have my word."

"You know I can't authorize that."

Quinn held out his phone toward Coffey and waved it menacingly. "What I *know* is that if this doesn't happen within thirty seconds, I'm going to blow the C4. He either does what I say, or everyone dies, *including* him."

Quinn glared at the man who had been his boss until just seconds earlier. A man he couldn't have liked or respected more. "To be honest," he continued, "I almost hope Garza *doesn't* cooperate. I'll regret the collateral damage. But at least I'll die knowing I'm taking Davinroy down with me!" he added savagely, the words spit from his mouth like a poison. "I have nothing left to lose."

Quinn had considered surrendering and doing his best to convince others of the truth, but had decided against this course almost immediately. He knew that escape would offer him a better chance to see justice done. Although, when it came to effecting an escape, and staying at large once he did, he hadn't done himself any favors.

His single-mindedness of purpose had left a glaring blind spot in his preparations. He didn't care if he lived or died after he took out Davinroy, so he hadn't planned on running. If he was ultimately caught, so be it.

But he should have planned out what he would do if his one-man operation went sideways, like it had. His rage had poisoned him to such an extent that it never occurred to him he might *fail*, an oversight that was criminally negligent. *Of course* he might fail. There were too many variables, too many moving parts, and too many eyes on the president to be certain his plan would work.

Now all he had were his wits, a gun, two hundred dollars in cash, and a small electronic device, technically illegal, that some agents carried like a rabbit's foot to help them break into cars if this ever proved necessary. This last would be most helpful of all, but its presence was just dumb luck rather than foresight, carried from force of habit alone.

He had also been lucky to have thought of the C4 bluff so quickly. He refused to hurt innocent parties, and this bluff seemed the best way to accomplish this end, as well as the best way to ensure he left the mansion with the same number of holes in his body that he had upon entering.

Now that he would be hunted and no longer with the Secret Service, killing the president would be all but impossible, but where there was life, there was hope. And if he retained his freedom, maybe he could find enough evidence, after all, for the world to know what this man really was. As long as he had breath in his body he would use it to try to bring this psychopath down.

"What's going on Kevin?" said Coffey. "Why are you doing this?"

"Because Matthew Davinroy needs to die!" he hissed. "Because five weeks ago, he tortured and killed my wife! Leaving my unborn child to die horribly within her! *That's why!*" he screamed, foaming at the mouth. "Davinroy, you sick abomination, your drug failed, and I remember. You won't get away with what you did to Nicole. I'll make sure the world knows what you've done—who you are."

Quinn turned back to Coffey. "No more explaining! I need David Garza and a pair of car keys. *Now*!" he thundered.

Davinroy and his wife were still on the ground behind Coffey and a wall of other agents, but the president spoke for the first time, whispering so that only Coffey could hear, having no idea that Quinn had arranged for his earpiece to receive the president's every word.

"For God's sake, Cris, let him leave. He's dangerous and unstable. And utterly delusional."

"And then some," Coffey whispered back.

Quinn's boss quickly turned to face David Garza. "Mr. Garza, I'm afraid I need to ask you to do what he says. We don't have any other choice."

"Damn right you don't!" shouted Quinn.

Garza took a deep breath, looking distinctly ill. He nodded at Quinn. "Follow me," he managed to croak out, motioning in the opposite direction. "The garage is this way."

"Everyone needs to clear a path!" shouted Quinn. "Anyone gets within ten feet of me and I detonate! Anyone follows us to the garage, I detonate! Understood?"

In answer, any number of guests who were between Quinn and Garza, and between Garza and the route to his garage, moved rapidly to either side, a human reenactment of Moses's parting of the Red Sea.

Quinn turned to his former boss one last time. "Cris, I don't want anyone hurt," he said almost pleadingly. "So don't let anyone follow me when I leave this place. I contingency-planned the shit out of this," he added, knowing that only his incompetence had prevented this bluff from being true. "I have an escape route ready to go, and it's heavily booby trapped."

Quinn thought this would work, would buy him time. After all, once he left, the president and First Lady were safe, which was Coffey's only concern. A hot pursuit of a man they knew was highly skilled, and one they believed to be insane, could be dangerous, not only for the agents involved but innocent bystanders along the way. Besides, Coffey was sure to think that with all of the resources at his disposal Quinn would be apprehended in record time, without need of a high-speed chase. Within fifteen minutes the military might of the entire nation would be blanketing Princeton like a swarm of locusts.

Quinn had watched Coffey's face during his exchange with the president, and he had seen his absolute certainty that Quinn had gone mad. He was shocked to see that Coffey didn't believe his accusations against the president were worth considering for even an instant, under any circumstances.

This showed Quinn exactly what he would be up against. Coffey knew him well, and knew he would never make such an accusation if it wasn't true. And Coffey was as open-minded to wild possibilities as anyone he had ever met.

And yet Quinn was certain the man had put zero credence into what he had said.

Garza led Quinn and his imaginary C4 vest and detonator into the garage without incident. More a showroom than garage, the structure was cleaner and more sparkling than some of the finest kitchens, and was immense, currently housing ten vehicles without fear of any crowding.

Quinn knew very little about elite cars, but he guessed each pristine model he saw had horsepower that approached infinity and a price tag to match. His eyes ran over a number of stunning sports cars but slowed when he came to the three sedans in the garage, a Porsche, a Jaguar, and a Maserati. This last, a model called the Quattroporte, was of particular interest.

"Give me the keys to the Maserati!" he demanded.

The Quattroporte was magnificent, but its beige color and understated grille made it the least conspicuous choice. The other cars were so flamboyant that any one of them would have stood out like a siren in a library.

After Garza gave him the keys, Quinn also demanded the billionaire hand over the cash in his wallet, which totaled six hundred and twenty dollars.

Finally, less than five minutes after his attempt on the president, Quinn left Garza and his home behind, hurtling forward in a car that felt more like a rocket ship. He slowed only for the few seconds it took to destroy his phone and fling it from the window before resuming at a speed that exceeded reckless by at least twenty miles per hour.

As Quinn sped off into the night he forced himself to remain calm and focused. No room for emotion if he was to have any chance of accomplishing his mission.

First he had to find a way to survive. Easier said than done, even for an hour or two, let alone days and weeks. Then he had to find a way to gather evidence.

Quinn would leave the president's distant past alone—for now. Instead, he would focus on the prostitutes he had beaten. They might not remember what had happened, but it would be a start. Davinroy was bound to have made at least one mistake that Quinn could use to snare him.

So Coffey didn't believe a word he said about the great Matthew Davinroy. Didn't believe the president could possibly have done what he had done.

No matter, thought Quinn. Soon the world would know what a sick, murderous abomination the president really was. Coffey's skepticism would only make him *more* determined, *more* single-minded in his goal.

As if this were even possible.

5

Quinn knew if he was still in the Maserati in twenty minutes, thirty at the very outside, he was a dead man. And this time frame would be accelerated if he remained a sitting duck among the farms and open landscape of Princeton. He needed a much better haystack to get lost within.

He sorted through a number of options, reaching a decision in seconds. There may have been better choices but he didn't have the time to search for them.

What he *did* now have was a destination—*Trenton*—twelve miles distant. He hurtled toward this city at speeds that would have launched most cars into space, but the Quattroporte somehow managed to hug the road like a constricting python.

Given the light traffic, had he adhered to speed limits, stop signs, and red lights, the trip would have taken twenty minutes. Kevin Quinn did it in nine.

Trenton, the capital of New Jersey, was urban and ghettoized, which was ideal for his needs. Although it was nearing ten o'clock on a Sunday night there were still small pockets of human activity. He had driven by the occasional group of two or more gangbangers, young males selling drugs or patrolling streets they felt they owned. There were almost forty thousand street gangs in the United States with well over a million active members, not including almost three hundred thousand in prison.

Trenton had long been fertile ground for both the Bloods and the Latin Kings, although a Guatemalan gang, aptly named GTO, for *Guatemalans Taking Over*, had come to challenge the Kings' dominance.

Like cockroaches, gangbangers preferred to come out at night.

Quinn found an isolated alleyway only four blocks from the Trenton Transit Center, a fancy name for an un-fancy train station, and parked. He exited the car and confirmed that, as expected, the alley was free from any street cameras.

Keenly aware that seconds mattered, he tore at his tux like it was on fire, stripping down to his boxer shorts and white cotton undershirt—which clung snugly to his biceps, delts, and abdomen, showing off a level of fitness even beyond that which was required for the job. Finally, he gathered up his bulletproof vest, shoes, and the various pieces of his tux, and tossed them into the trunk of Garza's car.

With this complete, Quinn drove the Maserati ten yards forward, so most of it was still hidden in the alley but enough of the front hood peeked out to be seen from more heavily trafficked areas. He left the car door open, the key fob in a cupholder, and rushed to an alley a few blocks away, where he predicted he could get the drop on three gangbangers he had spotted from his car, if he was fast enough and they hadn't changed course. He kept his right hand, which held his gun, tucked inside his boxers, against his outer leg.

For the first night of June, the air was surprisingly cool against his skin, but rapid movement heated him up to just above a comfortable temperature. The faint stench of puke and rotting garbage wafted into his nostrils periodically as he moved toward his destination.

The streets were mostly dark. Lights provided by the city were often vandalized to keep them this way, and street cameras used to see who was destroying the lights were typically targeted for destruction as well.

The darkness was punctuated only by stars, moonlight, and dim lighting from the occasional bar or tattoo parlor still open. Steel, concrete, and rust were the common themes, and graffiti and gang signs were everywhere, impossible to miss, even given the restricted visibility. Quinn could only imagine how much graffiti could be seen in the daytime.

Two helicopters streaked by, far above him, and he nodded to himself. About fourteen minutes had passed since he had left Garza's mansion. He had no doubt that additional helicopters were converging on Princeton from all sides and his photograph was now on the phones and tablet computers of every law enforcement agent in the country.

Wearing nothing but boxer shorts and socks, each sock pressing a wad of bills against one ankle, Quinn made it to his destination in time to surveil the group he was after. He circled around behind them with practiced stealth.

The group had three members, all Hispanic, heavily tattooed, and wearing gaudy gold chains and earrings. The tallest one was about Quinn's height and weight, although, like the others, his clothing was baggy and loose-fitting. The shortest wore a black baseball cap, backwards, while the third, midway in height between the other two and also ten pounds overweight, wore a gold bandana.

The colors gold and black were a common theme in their attire, the identifying colors of the Latin Kings. All three displayed these colors proudly, not exactly going out on a limb to become trendsetters in gangbang fashion.

Quinn closed the remaining distance to his three targets in a rush, silent as a tomb.

"Don't move!" he hissed when he was five feet behind them, his gun extended.

All three jumped, unable to believe they could have been surprised so completely.

The shortest of the three recovered from the shock the most quickly. "Hey, chill out, *ese*!" he said, still facing away from Quinn. "You a cop? 'Cause we 'aint done *nothing*."

"Raise your hands and turn around," said Quinn firmly. "Now!"

All three did as instructed.

"What the fuck!" said the short gangbanger, who must have been the alpha in this group, when he saw that the man holding them at gunpoint was not wearing outer clothing or shoes. "You loco, or what? Make a move against us, *underwear man*, and you buying nothing but trouble."

Quinn almost smiled at the threat. He forced them into a nearby alley to maximize privacy. He then had them place a variety of weapons on the pavement and kick them away under his watchful eye.

Quinn nodded at the tallest member of the group. "I need your clothing and shoes," he said, keenly aware of the passage of time. He then turned toward their leader, who, at about five-seven, was six inches shorter than Quinn. "And I need *your* baseball hat."

The alpha opened his mouth to respond but Quinn launched a preemptive strike. "Not a single word!" he demanded. "From now on, you speak when I *tell* you to speak. If you do what I say, you'll earn some money for your troubles. You hesitate to do what I say and I'll shoot all three of you in the head and take whatever clothing I want from your rotting corpses. Your choice."

"Slow down, ese; what's—"

"Shut up!" said Quinn, making a show of pointing a gun between the alpha's eyes. "You!" he barked at the tallest gangbanger. "Start undressing! Now! Ten. Nine. Eight . . ."

The leader of the group stared hard at Quinn, trying to take his measure. But he saw nothing but a resolve and composure that was unnerving. Quinn carried himself with an overwhelming aura of competence, as though he was military trained, had seen combat before, and had dealt death on more than one occasion. And it wasn't easy to exude this level of confidence, of *menace*, while standing in a dark alley wearing nothing but plaid boxer shorts.

Quinn's voice was matter of fact and unwavering. "*Five. Four . . .*

"Do it!" said the leader to his tall comrade, who didn't need to be told twice, moving instantly to begin undressing before the countdown reached zero.

Quinn ordered all three gangbangers to hug the pavement, facedown, while he donned his newfound clothing, which reeked of marijuana and sweat. He managed to dress quickly, despite having to maintain his vigilance and an extended gun. When he finished, he pulled the wads of money from both socks and shoved them into his new front pocket, but not before peeling off a hundred-dollar bill and dropping it on the pavement near the leader's head.

"One last thing," said Quinn, pulling the brim of his newly acquired baseball cap down to just above his eyes, "and then our business here is done."

Quinn needed an errand boy, and the choice was obvious. The short one was the leader and might try to do something stupid if he was pushed too far, afraid of losing status. The tall one was now without clothing.

But the middle one was like something out of *Goldilocks and the Three Bears*: just right. Quinn ordered this one to rise from the pavement, handed him a hundred, and told him to enter the train station a few blocks away and buy a one-way ticket to Grand Central Station in New York.

"In case you haven't guessed," said Quinn, "I'm a wanted man. I'm hotter than the center of the sun, with nothing to lose. So try anything cute and your friends die. I'd rather not kill them and attract a swarm of cops, but I'll do what I have to do." He paused. "On the other hand, come back with my train ticket and all three of you leave unharmed. You have five minutes! Go!"

Quinn watched his errand boy rush off, wondering what choice he would make.

Less than five minutes later this question was answered when Quinn's Goldilocks gangbanger returned, sweaty and out of breath, but carrying a train ticket in his grubby hand.

Quinn had him join his friends facedown on the pavement once again, and explained that if they didn't move or speak for several minutes they could go in peace. Then he vanished back into the alley without a sound, wondering how long they would lie there before realizing he had left. If they did have the guts to consider retaliation, they'd be looking for him in the train station, somewhere he had no intention of being.

6

Quinn retraced his steps back to where he had left Garza's car, allowing himself a moment of satisfaction when he saw that it was gone. With any luck, whoever took it would be breaking the sound barrier to get the vehicle as far away from Trenton as possible. Not that it would matter. Before too long they would find themselves at the center of a scene straight out of a war movie, no matter where they took it.

But regardless of any shell games Quinn might play, any feints he might orchestrate, it wouldn't be too long before the trio of punks he had just left would be discovered and interrogated. They wouldn't be inclined to help authorities, no matter what, but given the right threats or inducements they would describe what had happened. Tell those hunting for Quinn that he had been after clothing and a train ticket to Grand Central, from where countless numbers of trains departed hourly for countless destinations.

And those hunting for him would buy it, at least for a while, being forced to run down blind alleys and broaden their search parameters extensively.

Quinn carefully made his way three blocks to the other side of the train station, to a six story parking garage called *Trenton Park and Ride*, as though he had parked there and was making his way purposely toward his car. It was getting late, but trains would still be departing for several hours to come, so there were occasional cars both entering and leaving the structure.

Quinn passed an SUV parked in an area of the garage that offered a good view of most of two entire levels, and crouched beside it so he couldn't be readily seen. Five minutes later, after he watched two cars park and their owners exit the facility, a third new entrant proved to be the charm. A blue 2023 Ford Fusion. A young man in his late twenties had emerged, yanking a heavy black suitcase from the trunk.

Bingo. This man was what he wanted. Someone who would undoubtedly be staying at his destination for an extended period of time, while his car remained safely in the parking structure.

Quinn reached into his pocket and removed the device he had habitually carried while on duty but had never used, a silver disk about the size and shape of an Oreo cookie. The device was able to remotely intercept and clone signals from key fobs, now used in virtually all cars to unlock doors and start engines.

Quinn had activated his cloning device while the Ford was being parked, and a quick glance at an indicator light revealed that it had intercepted the data it needed.

The Fusion's owner began to wheel his suitcase toward the elevator and was soon out of sight. Once he was gone, Quinn quickly made his way to the Ford. Sure enough, his device worked like a charm, unlocking the Ford and signaling the car to start when he pressed on the ignition button.

Perfect. He now had transportation. With any luck, no one would know the car had been stolen for at least a few days.

He eyed the Ford's eight-inch interactive panel display and almost drooled. While he still didn't have a phone, at least he now had a way to surf the Web. He wouldn't have guessed he would miss this capability so profoundly, so quickly, but given he was on the run and in constant need of good information, the Internet was a more critical resource than ever before.

With the help of the Web, he mapped out a strategy in minutes. First, he would drive to Allentown, Pennsylvania, seventy-five miles distant, stopping in King of Prussia along the way to rob a television repair store he had identified there. Since the shop held mostly used and broken televisions, he guessed it had minimal security, which he could easily defeat. He would then take what he needed—four television remotes, a nine-volt battery, some wire, a roll of duct tape, and a small knife—and be on his way.

Once on the outskirts of Allentown he would search for a deserted but strategically located piece of land on which to park, and then sleep in his car. The longer he remained at large the more territory those after him would be forced to cover, resulting in larger gaps in their net.

He had been caught unprepared, with no contingency plan—an unforgivable sin—but he was reasonably satisfied with the progress he had made.

In the morning, he would plan ways to stay ahead of the pack, and then plot out his strategy for bringing Matt Davinroy to his knees.

7

Professor Rachel A. Howard sat at the edge of the desk with her legs dangling down, her beige flats not even close to reaching the floor of the small classroom. A heavy glass bottle of Snapple peach tea, flash-chilled just minutes earlier in her minus thirty-seven degree freezer, was open and waiting beside her, with a silver tablet computer on her lap.

Dressed in faded jeans and a light red cotton T-shirt, cut below the waist, Rachel Howard was eminently approachable and almost always cheerful, and as informal as she was brilliant. Anyone who had an encounter with her outside of Harvard University, who didn't know who she was, might think she was a homemaker, or a travel agent, or a caring, friendly social worker.

When Rachel was at a grocery store, movie, or social gathering, her appearance, style, vocabulary, and demeanor could not have been less intimidating, and none could possibly guess that this woman possessed a legendary intellect, was widely considered the foremost neuroscientist in the world, and was rumored to be on a short list for a future Nobel Prize for the groundbreaking papers she seemed to publish with astounding regularity.

In academia, business, or for that matter any human endeavor, there were two ways to get ahead. One was to know how to play the game, become skilled at sucking up to the right people, projecting the right image, playing politics, and manipulating others. Unfortunately, many of those practicing these dark arts were not highly competent in their actual jobs, and could excel only by being ruthless and unethical, stabbing colleagues in the back, poisoning their reputations for personal gain, and taking credit for the work and ideas of others.

The second way to get ahead was to be so gifted, so talented, it didn't matter how well or poorly you played politics. You could dress like a slob, be boorish or intimidating, fail to show up for mandatory cocktail parties, or even be a total asshole. Or, as was the case with Rachel Howard, you could exhibit the opposite spectrum of behavior. You could be friendly, gracious, and unassuming. You could go out of your way to bestow credit wherever it was deserved.

If you were not extraordinarily talented, these traits would get you liked, but not promoted, especially when swimming in shark-filled waters. Nice guys—or gals in this case—finished last.

Unless your competence was so great that nothing could hide it, no politicking, backstabbing, or idea theft could diminish it. Results, when they were stellar enough, could trump almost all other considerations.

There was an old joke her father, a businessman, had told her. A regional sales manager rushes into the office of the president of the company. "One of my salesmen just said that you should go jump in a lake," he reports to the president. "I assume you want me to fire him immediately."

"What an absolute jerk!" says the president. "This is intolerable. Just out of curiosity," he adds, "how are his sales numbers?"

"He's the top salesman in the region. Has been for the entire year."

The president of the company nods. "On second thought," he says, making his way out of his office, "don't fire him."

"Okay," says the subordinate in confusion. "But where are you going?"

"I'm going to find a lake to jump into," he replies happily.

Rachel smiled at this memory as the first of her students wandered into the classroom, followed within minutes by five others. All six wore casual clothing that took a cue from her well-known style, or lack thereof: jeans, yoga pants, and the like, and each had eyes that shined from the fires of an extraordinary intellect within. The Neuroscience program at Harvard was unequaled, and the graduate school had its pick of the most brilliant undergrads from around the world.

She studied the students in the class with great interest as they entered, since she was only tangentially familiar with any of them. Each sat in the front row, in uncomfortable wooden seats with large desk surfaces attached, a mere six or seven feet away from her. Several lowered steaming cups of coffee onto the desks, along with tablet computers and notepads. Given it was eight in the morning on a Monday the coffee and bleary eyes were not surprising, although Rachel habitually stuck with her Snapple, which delivered its own dose of caffeine.

Once seated, the students gazed at her with expressions she could only describe as *awestruck*, a description she was reluctant to use due to her innate humility.

The class consisted of Sanjeev Shaw from New Delhi, India; Michele Bodenheimer from Dobbs Ferry, New York; Sherry Dixon from Owensboro, Kentucky; Greg Feldman from Cincinnati, Ohio; Deb Sorensen from Basel, Switzerland; and Eyal Regev from Tel Aviv, Israel.

She had done her homework on the group before they had arrived, and the average age was twenty-four, although Deb Sorensen was only twenty, having graduated from college at the age of eighteen, and Eyal Regev was the oldest at thirty-one, only two years younger than Rachel herself. Regev was new to Harvard, having just transferred in from the grad program at Johns Hopkins. Half of the students were male and half were female, which was unusual, as most of her previous classes had been all female, or predominantly so.

No surprise there. She was an expert in all facets of neuroscience, especially learning, and knew that women had been outpacing men academically for some time, and the gap was only widening. This was a growing crisis that had received far less attention than it deserved. The disparity began in grade school, where it was increasingly difficult to get boys to read.

Research showed that boys lagged significantly behind girls across all school ages on standardized reading tests—in all fifty states. And America was not alone. In 2001, the Department of Education had conducted a massive study on fourth grade reading in forty-five countries, and the results were breathtaking: girls outscored boys in reading literacy in all forty-five.

These stats had quickly translated into college admissions, where over sixty percent of US college degrees were now awarded to women, as well as a majority of advanced degrees, and women now outnumbered men in graduate school by almost one and a half to one.

Many factors were involved. Boys were often socialized to believe that sports and other physical activities were more masculine than quiet reading. And the world was increasingly brimming with distractions: computer games, cell phones, social media, endless video entertainment, and the like, which seemed to have a slightly stronger gravitational pull for boys than girls, although both genders were becoming addicted in ever-growing numbers.

But all of this aside, boys were almost twice as likely as girls to have a reading disability like dyslexia, and brain architecture did differ between the sexes, with MRI scanning showing that the language centers in girls' brains, on average, developed faster than in boys.

Rachel considered the three male students in the class. In past generations they probably would have been considered geeky and might have struggled to find female companionship, but males on campus were now so rare she was sure they had no trouble keeping their dance cards full. Another of the endless examples of how transformative the last thirty years had been, frequently in strange and unexpected ways.

Now that the students had all settled in, Professor Rachel Howard, chair of the Harvard neuroscience department, still perched at the edge of a large desk, cleared her throat and began.

"Welcome to the summer session of Neuroscience eight twenty, *Advanced Applications*. I've been told this is considered one of the most difficult graduate courses at all of Harvard. I won't lie to you," she added with a smile, "it is. But I've also been told by many former students they believed it to be the most important course they ever took."

She paused. "While the material will be challenging, I'd also like to make this course as fun and stimulating as possible. So nothing you say will be regarded as stupid, silly, or misguided. And I welcome questions and interruptions and an open dialog at all times. If you have something to say, don't hesitate to jump right in."

She went on to explain that she would be teaching the course, but would have several of her collaborators at nearby MIT give guest lectures, who tended to be better at marrying her neurobiological discoveries with computer and electronic advances, robotics, and engineering related technology, helping to turn her theories into real world solutions.

"In this class, we're going to dive very deep into the material," she said, and then with just the hint of a smile, added, "*Very deep*."

Several students looked down nervously and others swallowed hard, visibly trying not to panic, wondering if this course would finally be a hurdle they were unable to overcome. Each had set every curve in high school and college, but now that they were together at Harvard they had finally risen to the point where everyone was as smart and hardworking as they were. Some more so. Finding themselves in a group whose members were all at their own rarified level was as *scary* as it was stimulating.

"Your knowledge of the neurological and biochemical structure of the brain will be tested greatly," continued the professor, "as will your knowledge of computers, genetically engineered synaptic modifying agents, and techniques for taking advantage of brain plasticity."

There was a pause, and Eyal Regev, the Israeli, jumped in, apparently taking her previous invitation to do so at any time at face value. "Professor Howard," he began, and was immediately stopped by a head shaking in front of him.

"Please, everyone, call me Rachel."

She knew they had heard this was her preference, but no graduate student yet had dared assume this was the case and use the familiar before being given explicit permission, out of respect for her and a certain awe at her reputation. Einstein's graduate students wouldn't have addressed him as *Albert* without being asked, even if a gun were pointed at their heads.

Regev nodded. He looked distinctly Mediterranean, with rugged, masculine features and jet-black hair. He had an accent, but it wasn't pronounced.

"Sure, um . . . Rachel," he began again, trying this name out for size and still clearly uncomfortable with it. "My name is Eyal," he added, pronouncing it *A-yall*. "Is it true that if someone distinguishes themselves in this class, you offer to hire them on as a post-doc once they've earned their PhD?"

"It is. I've done this twice in the past four years. One student joined my lab and one declined, taking a position in a lab at Stanford instead."

"The one who declined obviously wasn't as bright as you thought," said Eyal Regev with an impish grin, his brown eyes sparkling.

Rachel laughed. Just because she knew he was sucking up for all he was worth didn't mean it wasn't working. And Regev had begun his question by introducing himself, reminding her that she had forgotten to let the students do so, which she quickly rectified.

When each had the chance to say their names along with a few words about themselves, Rachel took a breath and continued with her introduction to the course. "So now that I've explained how deep we're going to go," she said, "literally to the subatomic level in some cases, I plan to do just the opposite with the first two sessions. I'd like to pull all the way back to thirty thousand feet, and examine the entire field. Examine the big picture problems we hope to solve. And not just what we *can* do, but what we *should* do. What are the possibilities? The issues? The ethics? Since we'll soon find ourselves neck deep in the trees, I think it's fitting we consider the *forest* before we begin."

The grad students appeared both relieved and intrigued. The first few sessions, at least, were going to be survivable.

"So I don't need to tell anyone in this room that we're in the right place at the right time. Neuroscience has long been considered mankind's next great frontier, the next big thing. The span from 1990 to 2000 was formally declared *the decade of the brain* by the White House. But this was only the beginning, as we are well aware. Since then, computing, medicine, genetic engineering, and brain scanning and modeling have seen exponential growth, giving us more optimism than ever.

"Most of you are so young you take these advances for granted. You don't fully appreciate just how far we've come, and how quickly, and how near we are to the achievement of miraculous things. Neuroscience is at a tipping point. You will enter this field in a transformative period, the likes of which may never be seen again.

"You're all aware of the power of exponential growth. Start with a penny and double your money every day, and in thirty-nine days you'll have over two billion dollars. But the first day your wealth only increases by a single penny, an amount that's beneath notice."

She raised her eyebrows. "On the *thirty-ninth* day, however, your wealth will increase from one billion to two billion dollars. Now *that* is a change impossible to miss. So, like a hockey stick, the graph of exponential growth barely rises from the ground for some time, but when it reaches the beginning of the handle, *watch out*, because you suddenly get an explosive rise that is nearly vertical."

She shook her head and allowed a flicker of a smile to cross her face. "Most of you, on the inside, are rolling your eyes, because you've known how exponential growth works since you were in diapers. But knowing and having an intuitive feel are two different things. And exponential growth will sneak up on you. Despite having seen this pattern over and over, scientists are still surprised by its effect. Many still have trouble taking the leap of faith that problems that seem insurmountable today will become trivial in the blink of an eye.

"When the first cell phones were practically the size of a car, who'd have foreseen modern smartphones, capable of marvels not even dreamt of just years before they came to rule the world? When Jobs and Wozniac built their first Apple computer in a garage, who could have foreseen the monumental leaps in processing power, speed, storage, and the like? The first decoding of the billions of DNA base pairs in the human genome took over a *decade*, at a cost of more than three billion dollars. A mere twenty years later, I can get my entire genome sequenced in a *day*, for less money than it takes to buy a new pair of shoes.

"This is happening in neuroscience before our very eyes. We're halfway up the handle of that hockey stick, and we'll make it all the way up from here so quickly it will surprise the most optimistic among us.

"So I want to go back to the point at which the coming revolution left the ice, so to speak, and began climbing straight up the handle of the hockey stick, about a decade ago. Have any of you heard the name Francis Collins?"

Deb Sorensen nodded. "You mean the former director of the NIH?"

"Exactly. Anyone know what he did before this?"

"Didn't he also lead the Human Genome Project?" said Michele Bodenheimer. "The one you just spoke about."

"Excellent," said Rachel. "That is correct. So Collins had seen the breathtaking pace of innovation before."

The professor lifted the tablet that had been resting on her lap and slid her fingers across it. "I thought it might be useful to read to you something he posted in 2014, when the BRAIN initiative was first announced."

She looked down at the screen and began to read:

Some have called it America's next moonshot. Indeed, like the historic effort that culminated with the first moon landing in 1969, the Brain Research through Advancing Innovative Neurotechnologies (BRAIN) Initiative is a bold, ambitious endeavor that will require the energy of thousands of our nation's most creative minds working together over the long haul.

Our goal? To produce the first dynamic view of the human brain in action, revealing how its roughly eighty-six billion neurons and its trillions of connections interact in real time. This new view will revolutionize our understanding of how we think, feel, learn, remember, and move, transforming efforts to help the more than one billion people worldwide who suffer from autism, depression, schizophrenia, epilepsy, traumatic brain injury, Parkinson's disease, Alzheimer's disease, and other devastating brain disorders.

When on May 25, 1961, President Kennedy announced plans to go to the moon by the end of the decade, most Americans (not to mention space scientists!) were stunned because much of the technology needed to achieve a moonshot didn't yet exist. Likewise, medical research today faces a wide gap between our current technologies for studying the brain and what will be needed to realize BRAIN*'s ambitious goals.*

Rachel stopped reading and faced her class once again. "There's more, but I won't go on. I just wanted to give you a flavor of where things were a decade or so ago, when many of you were in high school or even middle school. Collins goes on to detail this technology gap. But, as all of you know, ninety percent of the first draft of the brain is already done. And, as usual, it is way ahead of schedule, and has defied every expectation. When it is fully completed, and then modeled in our best computers, the power this will give us to understand the innermost workings of the human brain will be *unprecedented*. We will have a unique ability to explore ourselves, learn what makes us tick. Even with an incomplete, raw version, recent breakthroughs being made have been extraordinary. As this data grows hand in hand with advances in biotech and computer science, there is very little we won't soon be able to achieve."

Rachel Howard had been at the forefront of the field for some time, and the passion and certainty with which she delivered these words was electrifying.

After a long pause, giving her inspirational words time to marinate, she continued. "So let's go. Let's begin a big-picture discussion of such things as finding the cure for Alzheimer's. A huge and tragic disease affecting more and more of us as we extend the lifespan, and as the percentage of us who are elderly continues to increase. Let's explore findings with respect to the brain and spirituality, begging a discussion of how religion, evolution, and neurochemistry might fit together. Let's take a panoramic look at addiction research; pros, cons, issues, and ethics. And we'll want to save a good thirty minutes to discuss one of my favorite topics: research into the human sex drive, which colors every aspect of our behavior, actions, and civilization. I defy you to watch TV for ten minutes without at least one sexual reference coming up, without seeing sex being used to sell beer or hamburgers."

Rachel raised her eyebrows. "And for good reason," she said with a twinkle in her eye. "Because a strong urge to mate, to reproduce, is an absolute requirement for genes to be passed on. We can be sure of only one thing: every one of our ancestors managed to find a partner and mate, whatever that took. If not, we wouldn't be here to talk about it.

"And we'll even ask the following question," she continued, "which is stronger, the survival instinct or the sex drive? Not as obvious as it might seem at first blush. Just ask the males of certain spider species, who offer themselves up as postcoital snacks to induce females to mate with them."

Rachel couldn't help but smile at the looks of horror on the faces of her three male students. "And we'll go on to discuss a half dozen other areas that neuroscience will soon have a dramatic impact upon," she continued. "But all of this will come later in this session, or in the next. Because I'd like to begin with my two favorite topics." She paused for effect. "The first being the induction of memory loss."

The professor took a drink from her still-icy bottle of Snapple and continued. "Few would argue that restoring memory to Alzheimer's patients is a blessing. But we'll soon be able to do the opposite, as well: induce the *loss* of memory. Easily. And with surgical precision. So what do you think about this? Should we pursue this line of research? If so, for what purpose, and to what end?

"And if not, how would we stop it?"

* * *

Many miles away, a troubled man watched Rachel Howard's lecture on a large plasma monitor in fascination. She was electrifying.

The subject matter for her first two lectures was almost perfect for his needs, allowing him to garner much of what he wanted to know. These discussions would provide a window on how Rachel Howard thought about the field, what advances she had contemplated, and her take on various moral and ethical issues.

But he would also need to be careful. It would be dangerous to draw too many conclusions on the basis of public lectures. Her stance on various issues could be for the consumption of her students only, and not necessarily reflect her true opinions.

Regardless, these two lectures would illuminate the kind of issues she had pondered, her range of interests, and her recognition of what was critical and what wasn't. They would provide a framework for further analysis, further interaction. They would jump-start the process, a lucky break considering that time was of the essence.

The man turned his attention once more to the screen, where the chair of the Harvard Neuroscience department was continuing her lecture. Even knowing it was being taped, he didn't want to miss a single word or facial expression.

8

Azim Jafari, Imam of Chicago's Hamza mosque, had been in America his entire life, but had long known he was going to strike a decisive blow in the war against the West, particularly against the country of his birth. He had spent years building a reputation that would make him above suspicion, since despite any denials, Western Intelligence focused considerable attention on mosques.

And while Jafari feigned outrage over this practice, it made perfect sense. If you wanted honey, you focused on bees. Mosques had been meeting places for radicalized Islamists historically, and any number of Imams had been found to be terrorist leaders, or at the very least, terrorist sympathizers.

Although bees and honey was the wrong analogy, since his plans had nothing to do with honey. Perhaps termites and acid would be the better choice.

Some in the West had begun to question why so few peace-loving Muslims had condemned their fundamentalist, radicalized brethren, and insisted that until this happened, innocent Muslims had less reason to complain when they were painted with this same brush.

One professional cable news guest who had been particularly vocal about this over the years was a man named Abe Shapiro. He argued that TSA agents and others were fools not to use profiling. That it was the height of idiocy not to focus more on mosques and Muslims. This wasn't bigotry, he would argue, just common sense.

"I'm a short, fat Jewish guy," Shapiro had famously remarked on any number of occasions. "If scores of other short, fat Jewish guys flew planes into buildings, shot up malls, and chanted death to America, I'd expect to get closer scrutiny by the TSA. To fail to notice this pattern and keep a closer eye on me, you'd have to have your head in the sand. But I wouldn't blame the TSA agents for this scrutiny. I'd blame all the fricking short, fat Jewish guys trying to destroy civilization, who are making me look suspicious. Radicalized Muslims are the least tolerant people on Earth—especially when it comes to women, other religions, and other cultures—yet they cry the loudest at any perceived intolerance on the part of the West. And we're stupid enough to let them put us on the defensive."

Jafari had decided that these criticisms were an opportunity. He would pretend to take them to heart. Pretend to give the public what so many commentators suggested they were looking for. He would be a prominent Muslim, an *Imam*, willing to publicly condemn terrorism.

So he had made it a point to seek out cable news shows and had soon become a common presence among talking heads. He became famous for sermonizing that Islam needed to get its house in order, be more open-minded and tolerant. He shared his enlightened view on television whenever he was asked, winning praise from all quarters as a man of peace trying to effect change.

And all the while he was doing this, he searched for the perfect strategy, triggered at the perfect time, to cripple America, knowing that he was now the last Imam, and Hamza the last mosque, that would ever come under suspicion. He was so well known as a voice against radicalism that if he walked into a café with a bomb strapped to his chest, the waiter would cheerfully take his order and comment on the believability of his terrorist Halloween costume.

But even so, he instituted security precautions as though he were the *most* suspected Imam in the world. No electronic communications that would ever suggest his hatred of his country, or his love of ISIS and other such organizations. No public speeches or sermons. He made sure his mosque was routinely swept for bugs.

And now, finally, his duplicity, his patience, would pay off. Today was the day, and although it was now the crack of dawn on a Monday, he had never felt more alive.

Azim Jafari gazed out over hundreds of his hand-picked followers, from all over the country, who had made the trip to attend this special prayer meeting. His own network of sleepers. Pious believers he had carefully cultivated over many years, ready to become activated at his command. And each ready to activate their own hand-picked cells of six to eight, a multiplier effect that provided Jafari with an army of well over a thousand.

The inside of the mosque was magnificent, and the prayer hall he and his followers inhabited was the most magnificent of all, containing dozens of pairs of striking white pillars, accented with gold, leading up to a glorious blue-and-jade dome. Unlike the sanctuaries of other religions, the splendor of the architecture was not marred by the presence of pews or rows of chairs.

Two of Jafari's special congregants guarded the doors while he readied himself to begin the proceedings. He was wearing his finest white robe, and a white-and-red kufi, which could be described as either an enormous skullcap, or a round, brimless hat, shaped like a birthday cake. His dark beard was close-cropped, something that never failed to enrage him when he saw his face in a mirror.

But as much as he wanted to grow his beard longer, to please Allah, a beard that was neatly manicured was more pleasing to the mainstream, making him even more of a darling to large swaths of the American population. Sacrificing a full beard, painful though it was, was something he was willing to do for the greater good.

A hush fell over the room as Jafari made it clear he was ready to begin. He first led the assembly in prayer, humbled to be doing so for these men in particular, who were as dedicated as he was to the final elimination of infidels and the restoration of Islam to its deserved purity and glory.

Once the prayers were completed, it was finally time for him to get to the heart of the matter. Jafari drew in a deep, exhilarating breath, thrilled by the knowledge that his time had finally come, and began. "All of you are here today because you share in our righteous purpose," he said. "To bring the Great Satan to its knees. After considerable thought and preparation—considerable prayer and meditation—I have arrived at a plan I believe will do just this. A plan that will create maximum panic and havoc, with minimal operational needs." He smiled serenely. "And minimal risk of failure."

Jafari cleared his throat and looked out over his flock, a dense throng of humanity standing at attention before him, eager to learn what part they would play in his grand plan. "I call my strategy, *death by a thousand cuts*. As the name would imply, this isn't about delivering a single killing blow to the organism. This isn't about sensational attacks, about spectacle. You don't have to cut off an elephant's head to kill it. A thousand quick flicks with a razor blade will do the trick. Each, alone, not nearly fatal, but the cumulative effect deadly, causing far more trauma to the system than a single decisive blow ever could."

Jafari had arrived at the name for his operation from the form of torture and execution made famous by the Chinese, practiced from the beginning of the tenth century until 1905, when it had been banned by authorities. The Chinese had called it *ling chi*, which translated either as *death by a thousand cuts*, *the lingering death*, or *slow slicing*.

In ling chi, an executioner would use a knife to methodically remove portions of the body over an extended period of time, eventually resulting in death. According to lore, ling chi began when the torturer, wielding an extremely sharp knife, put out the victim's eyes, rendering him incapable of seeing the remainder of the torture and ratcheting up the psychological terror of the procedure.

Successive cuts removed any small body part that just happened to be sticking out, be it an ear, nose, finger, toe, tongue, or even testicle, followed by the removal of large chunks of flesh from thighs and shoulders. The entire process was said to last three days, and to total three thousand six hundred cuts, after which the butchered carcasses were paraded for the public to see.

While this lore contained extreme exaggerations—exaggerations historians and modern physicians had since corrected—there was no disagreement over the basic idea behind the executions, nor the fact that they took place. The debate centered on the question of how many mutilations, over what length of time, a victim could endure and still remain alive.

The idea of felling the Great Satan in this manner was irresistible to Jafari, and he relished the idea that *his* hand would be holding the scalpel. Yes, ISIS and others had continued to entice individuals, largely through social media, into acts of violence against America, often to great effect, but this was haphazard. Jafari's strategy would be smarter. It would be comprehensive and coordinated. And it would be infinitely more damaging.

"Once I seized upon the idea of slicing up the beast," continued Jafari, "of crippling it, forcing it to stagger around, not knowing when or where the next slice would be delivered, I put considerable effort into perfecting each and every cut. Into ordering the cuts for maximum effectiveness. At every turn I asked myself, which acts will cause the most destruction, the most terror? Which acts will push the economy toward collapse? What acts will bleed the beast the most efficiently?"

Jafari paused. "During our meeting this morning, I intend to outline our first cut. Once this phase has been completed, I will outline the next. And so on. In this way I can assess the success of each phase. I can confirm that the next cuts I have planned will still be the most effective, given the state of the beast."

This was also a security precaution. Any follower who was captured could only reveal a small portion of the plan. Jafari wouldn't insult anyone in attendance by suggesting they might provide operational details during an interrogation, but weakness happened, even in men whose hearts were in the right place. And stupidity happened. What if someone made a list that could be discovered? Allowed themselves to get drunk and then bragged about the plan?

Caution was Jafari's watchword. He would take no unnecessary chances. They would see the beauty of his full plan, the grandeur, as it slowly unfolded, like the rarest of roses revealing its beauty petal by petal.

He held out his hands, palms up, and his face glowed with an inner peace and serenity. "So it is time to announce our first move. One that could well cut the deepest of all."

He paused for effect. "This will be a cut carved by the lava-hot scalpel of *fire*," he proclaimed triumphantly.

9

Azim Jafari waited several long seconds before continuing, partly for dramatic effect, but mostly because he wanted to soak in the palpable electricity that had swept across the room, relish the heightened attentiveness of all of those standing before him in the soaring prayer hall.

"I have witnessed for myself the horrible, unparalleled *power* of Allah's fire," he continued finally. "And it is truly a power to behold. In 2007, I was living in San Diego, one of the ten most populated cities in America. In October of that year, a wildfire began to burn east of the city, heading due west. Embers from the first fire started others, and these fires grew at an incredible rate. The carnage that followed, the smoldering hell these fires created, was like something out of the *apocalypse*."

Jafari's memory of this devastation had never diminished, and he had bolstered these memories with statistics he had read afterward. He would paint his loyal followers a picture of the potential of fire to wreak terror and destruction that would be an inspiration to them.

"In a very short time," he continued, "the walls of flame were thousands of feet long, and up to eight stories tall. By the end of a single week almost eight hundred square miles of Southern California were blackened. Nearly a million residents were forced from their homes, the largest peacetime movement of civilians in America since the civil war. Before the fire was brought under control, more than three thousand structures were lost. Ash and other particulates blanketed hundreds of square miles, like the aftermath of a *nuclear war*."

Jafari paused to let this sink in, his voice now filled with awe. "During the day, the darkened sky was *eerie*. Unsettling to the depths of one's soul," he said, his prepared words now bordering on the poetic. "There was a surreal, orange cast to it, as the sun largely failed to penetrate the mass of particulates. Ash rained from the sky, turning San Diego into a sinister, coal-black version of a shaken snowglobe. Backyard pools turned from a serene blue to a sickly black as soot covered their surfaces. Residents stayed indoors, or wore surgical masks when they needed to venture outside."

He shook his head grimly. "Unless you lived through it," he continued, "no description can do it justice. The psychological impact it had was profound. There is no way to adequately convey the feelings of dread and impending doom that gripped every last resident when their entire world was covered in ash, and their sky was scorched and darkened."

Jafari could tell he now had his audience completely enthralled. "Seventeen people were consumed by the walls of flame, including five firefighters. More than a hundred more suffered injuries, not including dozens who were hospitalized due to respiratory distress. The economic impact of the fires was measured in billions of dollars. Much of the region was shut down for the entire week, including schools, universities, and businesses. Critical roads and highways were closed, and tourists and conventioneers canceled their visits. Power lines were damaged. Farms were ravaged, including more than three thousand acres of avocado groves.

"Commerce ground to a halt. For the better part of a week, one of the richest and most populous regions in the world was brought to its *knees*. San Diego suffered a *devastating* blow: physically, economically, and psychologically."

Jafari's eyes were now alive with righteous purpose. "Was a nuclear bomb needed to cause this mass destruction, this unbridled terror?" he barked to a mesmerized crowd. "The answer is *no*! Were jumbo jets needed, to smash into San Diego skyscrapers? Again, no! Did turning eight hundred square miles of a heavily populated region into a *wasteland* require expensive equipment, highly trained operatives, or complicated schemes?" He shook his head vigorously. "*A final time, no!*" he thundered.

The Imam paused, and now lowered his voice to just above a whisper. "No, this was a catastrophe that could have been brought about by a single child. A terror that could well be recreated with a few lighters and twenty dollars worth of supplies.

"Only now," continued Jafari, "the same fire would be even *more* devastating. Cities and suburbs across America are growing denser every year. Homes are closer and closer together, and civilization is encroaching more and more on the natural world. Back in 2007, Southern California was the ultimate expression of this trend. But now this situation is widespread. So our first slice into the body of *The Great Satan* will be a trial by fire."

His voice rose to a thunder once again and he held a fist out in front of him. "We will burn their forests to the *ground*! Focusing on those that straddle their densest population centers. And we won't do this in just one state, *but in forty-eight*! We will turn this country into a living, fiery *hell*, a dark, smoldering *ruin*!"

The room broke out into cheers, which were echoed and amplified by the magnificent dome above them as the Imam's followers were no longer able to contain their passion.

"Can you imagine it?" said Jafari when the prayer hall had become quiet once again. "Thousands and thousands of square miles across the entire continental United States on fire. Firefighters spread so thin they have no chance of success. A psychological, physical, and economic catastrophe that will make the San Diego fire look like a paper cut."

He leaned in toward the crowd and raised his eyebrows. "But there's more. Once firefighters have their hands full, it will be time to start even more fires. But this time not in forests. This time in buildings within the cities and dense neighborhoods themselves. The Great Chicago Fire—which raged over this very ground in 1871—started when a *single lantern* was knocked over. And it killed hundreds, and left *a hundred thousand* more homeless. And this was in 1871! I *know* we can do far better now, in the most populated cities in this country!"

The group once again broke out into cheers, and Jafari allowed himself a beaming smile for the first time. After weeks of this treatment, the United States would *wish* it had been hit with a nuclear bomb.

"We will strike in just over a month," announced Jafari. "On July 4th."

He paused to let the significance of this sink in. "On this day, Americans like to barbecue. So be it. On this day, we will barbecue *Americans*!" he shouted. "They want fireworks? We will give them *true* fireworks! They sing of rocket's red glare, we will give them all the red glare they can handle—and more. The day that heralded the birth of The Great Satan will become the day that we begin to push it over the cliff to its eventual death!"

The cheers this time were deafening, and Jafari soaked them in. The truth was, a July 4th start date was a hope, not a certainty, and he could well change it, but he didn't want to do anything to rein in their enthusiasm right now. He needed to study weather forecasts for the entire nation. Allah willing, the week surrounding July 4th would be dry across the majority of the country. If it was rainy, he would have to delay the strike until conditions were optimal.

But let them roar for a few minutes more before he continued on to the less inspiring details of the operation. Before he discussed possible changes to timing and how they would be notified of such. Before he shared his research on the most ideal locations for the fires. The most effective ways to start them, with the least manpower and materials. Cover an array of operational issues, precautions, and detailed instructions of how to proceed if caught. He had mapped out the implementation of this plan to perfection, and he needed to share all of this now with his eager audience.

Then he would set these sleepers loose.

And while America was burning to the ground, he would be busy preparing his next cut.

And then the one after that.

10

Cris Coffey sat in front of the historic Resolute desk in the Oval Office, for once not admiring the eagle and other intricate carvings cut into the oak section facing him. He was exhausted, ashamed, and anxious, dreading this meeting like the plague. An attempt on the president's life had been made—on *his* watch. Worse yet, it had been made by one of his own men. It was a black eye from which he would never recover. And now, more than eleven hours after the attack, he had yet to apprehend Kevin Quinn.

The Oval Office had famously served as the president's personal office in the White House since the days of Teddy Roosevelt. In fact, the West Wing, of which it was a part, had been rumored to be the brainchild of Roosevelt's wife, who felt the second floor of the residence, which harbored both bedrooms and offices, should be earmarked entirely as domestic space. So the West Wing was built to provide executive offices. At the time it was slated to be a temporary solution, but it soon became a permanent and indispensable addition to the president's domain.

Along with the magnificent desk, a gift from Queen Victoria in 1880, built from the timbers of the decommissioned British Arctic exploratory vessel *Resolute*, the Oval Office contained three large windows and a fireplace, along with four different exits. The east door opened to the Rose Garden, the west to a private study and dining room, the northwest to a main corridor in the West Wing, and the northeast to the office of the president's secretary.

Davinroy had motioned Coffey in but had ignored him as he finished the last page of his daily security briefing, which was delivered to his office by seven every morning. Once he finished the last sentence he turned his full attention to his visitor, now seated before him.

"Sorry to summon you at the crack of dawn," he began. "But under the circumstances . . ." He let his voice trail away, leaving the sentence unfinished.

"Of course, sir," replied Coffey. "And let me say that I can't apologize enough for what happened last night. It was a failure of epic proportions. I take full responsibility."

Davinroy shook his head graciously. "Not your fault, Cris," he said. "Not anyone's fault. Kevin Quinn just became delusional from out of nowhere. I'm not a psychiatrist, but there was no possible way for you to know that someone with this kind of access would snap like he did."

So far the president was being understanding, but Coffey knew that this would change when he learned what had really happened. Right now he thought Quinn had tried to shoot him, and failed because of the quick actions of the Secret Service.

Coffey winced, wishing he didn't have to be the one to tell him otherwise. "We worked through the night, sir," he said. "My teams had two objectives. Capture Kevin. And try to piece together what happened at Garza's mansion." He sighed. "You aren't going to like what you hear, sir, on either front."

Davinroy's eyes narrowed. "Go on," he said warily.

"I won't go into the details of our investigation, just the results. First, Kevin Quinn is still at large. Second, we've become convinced he never intended to fire a gun, or to allow himself to be exposed the way he did. Your drink," continued Coffey, glancing down at notes on his phone to make sure he got the name correct, "the *Portuguese Nectar Vector*, was poisoned. Kevin relieved the agent on bar detail, and instead of ensuring your drink was clean, he slipped a mickey into it that would have killed you within seconds of your first sip."

A horrified expression came over the president's face and he swallowed hard.

Coffey remained silent as Davinroy digested the full implications of what he had been told. As Davinroy remembered the events of the previous night, his expression became even *more* horrified. "Shit!" he said, his eyes widening. "And I gave it to *Anne* to try."

"That's right, Mr. President. We believe this is what precipitated Kevin's actions. He revealed himself so he could shoot the drink from your wife's hand, sir."

"Thank God," whispered the president.

"How *is* the First Lady, sir, if I may ask?"

Davinroy seemed lost in thought for several long seconds. Finally, he shook his head, as if to clear it, and stared at Coffey as though trying to reconstruct what he had just said. "How is Anne?" he mumbled.

"Yes, sir."

Davinroy sighed. "Given what you've just told me, it's a miracle she's still alive. So I guess she's doing well. She was gashed by the glass when it exploded. And she was terrified when the shots rang out and we were tackled. Not to mention being *horrified* after that."

"Horrified, sir?"

"Yes. Kevin Quinn accused me of an unspeakable atrocity. And even though there is no truth to what he said, no wife should have to listen to something like that. It was very upsetting."

Coffey frowned. He hadn't really thought about this, but it made perfect sense. An accusation this appalling, despite being false, would leave a foul taste in anyone's mouth. "I understand, sir."

Davinroy now looked as though he was sick to his stomach. "I should be dead," he whispered. "It was only dumb luck that saved me." He stared off into space for several long seconds, pondering what might have been—what *should* have been.

Coffey braced himself for the tirade sure to come his way. He deserved it. He had been incompetent. How could he have allowed this to happen? Instead of being heroic, as it might have appeared after the first shot rang out, Coffey and the rest of his detail had been criminally negligent. The president *should* be incensed. He or his wife could have died. And even if there had been no way to see this coming, Coffey couldn't blame the president in the slightest for condemning him, reacting emotionally, *viscerally*.

Instead, Davinroy's composure returned. "Any idea what pushed Kevin over the edge?" he asked, his expression now thoughtful.

Coffey was shocked by the president's equanimity. "None," he replied. "We've interviewed any number of people who worked with him recently, and none of them thought his behavior was out of the ordinary in any way. Two months ago he had a standard psych evaluation and passed with flying colors. This makes no sense to me at all. I have a meeting with a top psychiatrist later this morning. There may be a deep-seated reason Kevin came up with the particular delusion he did once he snapped. Perhaps he disagrees with your policies, and his mind turned you into the ultimate villain to justify killing you. I'll be interested in what the shrink says about this."

"Me too," said Davinroy. "Make sure you send me a report on the meeting."

"I will, sir. But even before my consult with the expert, it seems to me that Kevin must have snapped very recently, or he would have come after you earlier."

Davinroy nodded. "I agree," he said. Then, deciding to change gears, he added, "I read a summary of Kevin's file when he was first assigned here, but can you refresh my memory?"

"Certainly." Coffey paused for a moment, organizing his thoughts. "Kevin Quinn was a soccer and track star in high school. A tremendous athlete. He earned a black belt by the age of sixteen."

"In which discipline?"

The Special Agent thought hard for a few moments but finally shook his head. "I can't recall offhand. But I can find out for you in just a few seconds."

"No need," said Davinroy. "Go on."

"With respect to academics, he was diagnosed with ADHD, and while very bright, was a poor student. Couldn't sit still. Poor study habits. So he did ROTC in college and went right into the military. Served with distinction in a number of active theaters, including Syria, Iran, and Yemen—if I'm remembering correctly."

Coffey was tempted to call up Quinn's file on his phone, but decided that even if Quinn had served in Somalia instead of Yemen, this was close enough. And Coffey was absolutely certain he knew the precise details of the rest of Quinn's background.

"During this time he demonstrated an ability to suss out danger, think on his feet, assess complex situations, that was considered extraordinary. He possessed excellent operational awareness. He saved his fellow soldiers from springing traps during a number of missions. And when things did go south, his grasp of situational tactics, his quick thinking, and his leadership earned him very high marks. He was brave, bright, and motivated. He became an expert marksman and an expert with explosives. Ultimately, he earned two purple hearts and a number of other medals."

"Impressive," said Davinroy.

"Very," said Coffey. "And I'm not even doing his military record justice. Anyway, because of his proven skills, he was heavily recruited by the Secret Service. On paper, he was the perfect Special Agent. And it turned out that this was true in the field as well. After some lesser assignments with us, he was assigned to protect visiting heads of state. Less than a year later, he had distinguished himself so much he was put in charge of the protective detail for Awad Zahir, when Zahir came to New York to speak at the UN."

Coffey was sure the president could appreciate the trust the Secret Service had shown in Quinn by assigning him to protect this monster. As president of Syria, his invitation to speak at the UN had been highly controversial, drawing outrage and protests, and making Zahir a target of the highest order.

"I remember from here," said Davinroy. "That was only three years ago, during my first term. Kevin managed to sniff out a plot against Zahir, even though he personally despised the man, and took a bullet in the arm while protecting him."

Coffey nodded. "As you know, his involvement was never made public. We didn't want to turn Kevin Quinn into a pariah. When it came to Zahir, he would have been broadly reviled for doing the job he swore to do. I hired him for your personal detail as soon as he fully recovered."

"Good choice. I'd forgotten that Kevin was the agent involved."

"He turned out to be my best man," said Coffey. "Until now, that is," he added miserably, sickened that this man had somehow become broken.

One had to be exceptional to land a job protecting the president, especially after some of the Secret Service scandals that had erupted during the Obama administration, but Quinn was elite, even among this group. "In fact," admitted Coffey, "I planned to nominate him to be my successor when I decided to move on. He's that good."

Davinroy sighed. "This is tragic," he said. "It really is. On many levels. Kevin Quinn was an honorable man. A heroic man. He didn't deserve this. And now that he's cracked completely, who knows who he might end up hurting? He's expert with weapons and explosives. He could kill hundreds if he put his mind to it. Thousands."

The president shook his head. "And if he kills anyone, in addition to the tragedy of loss of life, this will be political poison for me, and for the Secret Service."

Coffey managed not to show his distaste at this last. He supposed that a politician couldn't help but see everything—including a mass murder, if it were to happen—through the lens of politics, but it was still disgusting. Which is why the popularity of politicians across the board had never been lower.

"You could be right," said Coffey. "Kevin could cut a swath of bodies across the country. He has the skills, and he's smart, creative, and disciplined. And he also knows the moves the team hunting him will be making."

Coffey blew out a long breath. "But I'm betting he doesn't hurt anyone. Think about this: he was willing to risk his plan, and risk his own life, to save the First Lady. Remember, before he shot at you, he made sure she didn't take a drink."

The president nodded slowly. "Good point. So this suggests he still values life. That his delusions, and the violent intentions stemming from his delusions, are centered squarely on me."

"Yes, sir. That is my thinking."

Davinroy leaned back in thought. "Maybe," he said finally. "But we can't know what's in his mind. So far the delusions are of a personal nature. But what if this changes? We can't really rely on logic here. Insane people play by their own set of rules. Yes, he risked everything to prevent Anne from being killed. But we can't be sure he won't change his colors tomorrow and go on a killing spree, targeting puppies and toddlers. So proceed with absolute caution. Don't corner him in public. Don't poke the bear. And make sure the trap is iron-clad before you spring it on him."

Coffey nodded. "Yes, sir."

"So you haven't found him yet. Do you think you're closing in?"

"I wish I could answer *yes*. But I can't. I was hoping that his psychological condition would affect his decision-making. But apparently not. He appears to be the talented man we've all come to know. He arranged to have Garza's car stolen, to keep us busy for a while. Near as we can tell now, he made his way to Trenton and then Grand Central Station. From there he could have gone anywhere. But I wouldn't be surprised to learn he never went anywhere near Grand Central Station. This could just be a ruse. He could be holed up anywhere. Or on the move anywhere. He could pick a forest and live off the land for months if he chose to, letting us spin ourselves into exhaustion out in civilization trying to find him."

Davinroy's eyes narrowed, and he looked decidedly angry for the first time. "You'll just have to up your game, Cris!" he said sharply. "I don't want to hear excuses! He's very good. You're going to have to be *better!*"

"Understood, sir."

The president glared at him for several seconds before finally relenting. "How goes the media strategy I outlined last night?" he asked.

"We invoked national security with the guests. We think the story is contained, at least for another day or two, but there is no way to be sure."

"Not good enough! If it does leak—which it will—you need to implore the media to sit on it. Once it breaks, no story will be bigger. You'll need to argue that a media circus would have an unpredictable effect on Kevin Quinn. It could well set him off further. Not to mention spooking people who might be in the path of a highly trained, psychotic killer."

"And we'd find ourselves drowning in false sightings."

"Right," said Davinroy. "Make that point also. Just be sure to make it crystal clear to all involved that media silence will give you a freer hand."

"Yes, sir."

"You do see why I want to keep this under wraps until we capture Quinn, right? This way we can unveil what happened at the same time we tie it up with a ribbon."

"Understood," said Coffey. "But no matter what, Mr. President," he added, "you can rest assured that we will not let Kevin Quinn get anywhere near you. We have to assume that his goal hasn't changed. That if he can find a way to get to you, he'll try again."

Coffey shook his head and his eyes burned with absolute resolve. "But I don't care how good he is. He won't get his chance. This time we've been forewarned. We won't be sloppy again."

"I know you won't, Cris," said the president. "But this one is personal, for obvious reasons. So I want daily updates. And I'd like to get more color on your manhunt. You can start by telling me why you think Kevin fled to Grand Central Station."

"Yes, sir," said Cris Coffey.

11

Professor Rachel Howard watched the wheels turn in the heads of her six graduate students as they considered her question: should scientists pursue research intent on erasing memory rather than restoring it?

She calmly took another swig of peach tea and readied herself for a stimulating discussion. This part of the course never failed to be fun and interesting, and often surprising, as she forced these students to flex mental muscles they rarely used, since they were typically far more experienced, and adept, at wrestling with the precision of science than they were with the imprecision of behavior and ethics.

She always began the proceedings by addressing the subject of memory erasure, which never failed to get a lively discussion going. As usual, the students looked appalled at the prospect. Each had dreamed of being the hero who found the absolute cure for Alzheimer's, not of doing just the opposite.

"This is a pretty scary thought," said Sanjeev Shaw, finally putting a voice to what they all were thinking.

Shaw's fellow students nodded their agreement.

"Scary, maybe," said Eyal Regev after a few seconds of silence had passed. "But isn't it also unstoppable? Isn't that what transformative technologies are all about? They're disruptive. And they can be used positively or negatively, for both good and ill."

Rachel nodded, impressed. "Well said," she replied. "When technology is expensive, and limited, it's easy to ensure it doesn't get into the wrong hands, that it isn't used for the wrong purposes. Genetic engineering once required multimillion dollar labs and was more of an art than a science. Computers were once bigger than houses. When this was the case, abuse was virtually nonexistent. A current example is the large hadron collider. We certainly don't have to worry about one of these being misused, simply because there *is* only one of these."

The professor leaned forward, still seated on the edge of her desk. "But once technology becomes widespread, inexpensive, commonplace, policing it becomes impossible. At that point society has to find ways to adapt to all facets of the technology, good and bad."

She paused. "So maybe it's time for the good guys to get ahead of the curve. When scientists were perfecting the computer, they never imagined that others would invent computer viruses, or that their new invention would one day be susceptible to hacking. They never guessed the computer would one day be exploited to steal money and identities, organize hate-groups, or sabotage centrifuges.

"But we've been through enough transformative technology revolutions now to know better. We don't have the luxury of pretending bad actors won't find a way to exploit new technologies. We can't stick our heads in the sand when it comes to future viruses, as it were. So while all of you, no doubt, are intent on inventing the computer, I'd urge you to at least consider pursuing research intended to *counter* the computer viruses sure to arise. Someone needs to do this. And if we're ahead of the curve this time, perhaps we can minimize the damage. This will be a recurring theme during this and the next session, as we go one by one through the broad domains that neuroscience will be able to impact in a profound way. We'll look at both the limitless promise of our coming capabilities, and their potential to cause us great peril."

Rachel hopped off the side of the desk and to her feet, standing in front of her class now for the first time. "So is it *ever* ethical to induce amnesia?" she asked.

"Yes," said Sherry Dixon without hesitation. "After traumatic events. The memories of these events can be debilitating. Their precise excision could be a cure for these people."

"While it's less clear," added Deb Sorensen, "those suffering from various phobias might also benefit from precision removal of certain memories."

"Both excellent points," said Rachel, knowing that research had been ongoing to accomplish both of these goals for many years, but not wanting to sidetrack the discussion.

"It's almost too bad there are positive benefits from this research," said Greg Feldman. "Because this gives bad actors an excuse to pursue the technology."

Regev shook his head. "That may be true," he said, "but like the professor mentioned, when research tools become as cheap and accessible as neuroscience tools are about to become, bad actors won't need an excuse, or permission, to work on whatever they want."

"Yes, but like the professor also pointed out," said Shaw, "this should give other scientists the motivation to counter this threat. To work on detecting when such memory loss drugs or techniques have been used against a person's will."

Regev looked unimpressed. "Maybe," he said. "But while knowing that this has happened is great," he pointed out, "it won't restore the memories that have been erased."

Rachel was quite pleased. She could practically feel the juices flowing in this group of students now, and these sessions would serve their purpose—get the next generation of neuroscientists out of their comfort zone. Get them to think holistically about what they were doing, and the implications, both good and bad.

"Eyal is correct," she said. "But so what? This just means there is another great research project waiting out there. The restoration of memories *after* they've been erased. A one-two punch. Detect when this technology has been used illegally, without permission, and then restore the victim's memories when it has. Why not? Computer scientists are able to restore data from hard drives that have been wiped."

"Or better still," said Regev, "find a way for the brain to block such attempts. A prophylactic drug that immunizes people against malicious memory attacks."

Rachel nodded at the Israeli. "Outstanding," she said in delight. "That would be even better."

"On the other hand," said Sherry Dixon, "I watch a lot of thrillers, and being able to permanently delete memory would save lives in certain circumstances. Suppose you're a villain, and someone stumbles on your plan, or your actual crime. Today, you'd have to kill them to keep them quiet. But if memory erasure were perfected, you could just surgically remove the offending memories, and no one would be the wiser."

Rachel grinned. "Okay, then. An upside that would only help a few people, in very specific circumstances, but an upside nonetheless. So no need to kill the guy informing on you, who is about to go into the witness protection program. Just make him forget what he knows."

Eyal Regev put on a pained expression. "No offense, Professor How—Rachel," he said in amusement, "but you should stick with your day job. You'd make a lousy criminal kingpin. I mean, the guy was going to rat you out. So you'd still have to kill him." He flashed an impish smile. "You know, to send a message."

Rachel laughed out loud. "Remind me not to get on your bad side, Eyal," she said, raising her eyebrows.

The class discussed induced memory loss for another ten minutes or so when Rachel decided to move on.

"Let's turn to another application that is near and dear to my heart," she began. "Learning. Are all of you familiar with the movie *The Matrix*?"

The movie was dated, but also somewhat iconic, and Rachel found that most of the time it was known to all of her students. She soon learned that this class was no exception.

"In my view," said Rachel, "the most extraordinary line in the entire movie was, '*I know kung fu.*' Remember that one? They zap knowledge of multiple martial arts straight into the character Neo's brain. One second he doesn't know how to fight," she continued, "and the next he's a black belt in just about every fighting discipline ever devised. Just like loading a program into a computer. Keanu Reeves, who plays Neo, says this line in equal parts shock and delight, as he realizes the knowledge of decades of intense training has just appeared magically in his mind."

"So I'm guessing your second favorite scene was on the roof with the helicopter?" said Regev.

"Good guess," she said appreciatively. "It is indeed. For those of you who don't remember it, Trinity and Neo are on a roof after being attacked. Neo sees a military helicopter that is parked there. He turns to Trinity and says, 'Can you fly that thing?' And Trinity's answer? Not yes or no, as we might expect, but simply, 'Not yet.'"

Rachel paused to give her class time to bring the memory of this scene to the surface. "I mean, it's the *perfect* response," she said enthusiastically. "Because Trinity immediately has this knowledge zapped into her brain. Less than a minute later she's an elite pilot, and away they go."

"It was truly an awesome scene," agreed Feldman, and the other five students nodded their heartfelt agreement.

"At first blush, it's not difficult to argue that this would be about the coolest capability *ever*," said Rachel, almost glowing. "And what if you didn't need to be in a matrix or have a jack in your skull? What if you could find less invasive ways to pull this off? But with the same end result: instant education. And not just education, not just superficial knowledge, but deep knowledge. Expertise."

She paused, telling herself she needed to throttle back on her enthusiasm to ensure an unbiased conversation. This was more difficult than she realized, as she had been working toward the goal of instant education for many years. And while she didn't advertise this research, and had yet to publish most of her findings, there were a number of colleagues who knew what she was trying to do, and it wouldn't surprise her if one or more of these students were aware, as well.

"Some progress toward this goal has already been made," she noted. "Enough to be fairly sure this will someday be achievable, especially now that the full map of the brain is becoming available. With luck, we'll be able to pull this off in five to fifteen years. So what are your thoughts about this?" she asked, with just the hint of a smile.

"It would be incredible!" said Sanjeev Shah in awe, and beside him, Sherry Dixon nodded her enthusiastic agreement. "The entire population of the world could be highly educated. Illiteracy would be wiped from the map."

"So does everyone agree that this would be a good thing?" asked the professor.

There was an immediate and unanimous chorus of agreement.

"Okay," said Rachel. "But there must be a downside, right? I mean, *everything* has a downside. Even a pool of the richest milk chocolate can be used to drown someone."

This example brought smiles to the faces of several students.

"Let me start us off with one possibility," said the professor. "I read a science fiction story when I was a kid. One that was many decades old even then. The Earth had been traveling through a vast region of space that, unbeknownst to us, contained some kind of invisible electromagnetic dampening field. One day the solar system and Earth finally move beyond this great cloud, and every man, woman, and child became brilliant overnight. *Beyond* brilliant. Everyone could educate themselves as fast as they could speed read. But one effect of this was that no one was willing to do menial labor. Factories stopped working. So if what I call *Matrix Learning* were perfected, isn't this one possible downside?"

"Yes," said Michele, "but this would only be temporary. Society would adjust. All of these knowledgeable people would come up with ways to eliminate menial jobs. They could create a paradise."

Rachel nodded. "I tend to agree, but it's something to tuck into the backs of our minds. So any other downsides? Is this instant education fair? You spend decades of your life, thousands and thousands of hours, struggling to cram a world-class knowledge of neuroscience into your brains. During grad school, while your friends are at the beach, you're doing all-nighter after all-nighter. Later, you work your ass off keeping up with the latest experimental literature, slaving endless hours in the lab."

She paused. "And then Matrix Learning is invented, and a day later, the guy who spent the last decade getting high and playing video games can have your same knowledge. Effortlessly. Is that fair?"

This question brought deep frowns all around.

"Yeah, that would kind of suck," said Greg Feldman.

"So in some ways," said Regev, "it would be in the best interest of those who are now highly educated to prevent this technology from happening. To protect their turf, their advantage."

"And the multibillion dollar educational system would become extinct overnight," added Sherry Dixon. "Hundreds of thousands of teachers across America would be out of work. The university system, down the drain."

"Maybe not," said Rachel. "At least not at the grade school and high school level. Maybe you'd want to limit this technology to those who are eighteen and older. Maybe you'd want to leave the current grade school and high school educational system intact. Why? Because people still need to learn how to learn. If they don't know how to learn for themselves, they won't be able to wield the knowledge that is zapped into their heads, adapt it for other applications, expand on this knowledge."

Rachel paused to let this sink in. "We have calculators that can do long division, but we still force our kids to do it the hard way. Why? So they understand the concepts behind the results. So they have the proper background for further studies."

Regev shook his head. "I hate to always be the skeptic," he said, "but banning this technology for minors will only work if you can detect when this Matrix Learning has been done. Or if preventative measures are put in place. A molecular chastity belt for the mind, that advertises when it's been violated. If not, kids will take the short cut. They can't use a calculator in class because a teacher would see it. But if they could have high school chemistry implanted into their minds, a teacher would never know it. Cheating would become rampant, and not just among kids. Many parents would be actively involved, willing to do anything to help their kids get ahead."

"Interesting point," said Rachel, pleased by the thoughtfulness of the discussion. "I tend to agree with you. So if society does agree with my point, that Matrix Learning should have restrictions, an ability to detect when someone has been the recipient of this technology will prove to be important. So cheaters can be caught. And even if we force minors to learn how to learn, I'd probably be in favor of using this at an early age, just once. To implant knowledge of how to read. To help even the playing field between boys and girls."

Several of the graduate students nodded thoughtfully.

"But moving on," said Rachel, "there can be no denying that Matrix Learning will cause social upheaval, at minimum. It's too profound a capability not to." She raised her eyebrows. "So do any other thorny issues come to mind?"

"Yes," said Deb Sorensen. "Those who prepare the Matrix Learning programs get to play God. So *who* decides what's in the programs? *Who* chooses the content of the educational package that gets, um . . . uploaded?"

"Great point, Deb," said the professor. "That would definitely be an issue. Who controls the information people are being infused with? Who decides what gets learned? When you learn the old-fashioned way, you can seek out information, try to ferret out both sides of an argument. But now, if this technology were to see widespread use, everyone would have more or less the same knowledge of a field. It's been said that history is told by the victors. So you get your history course zapped into your brain. Now you know what someone else wants you to know. But is it the truth?"

"Totalitarian regimes have always tried to control knowledge, control information," said Eyal Regev. "And even though the Internet has made that very difficult to do, kids in these countries still get indoctrinated into the regime's ideology at a young age. Matrix Learning, as you called it, would make this even easier.

"On the other hand," continued the swarthy Israeli, "an open society could make multiple versions of a history available. People could choose to download one of them, or, for a broader perspective, all of them. Just like we can choose which books to read, choosing from among those we know take conflicting positions. If there are multiple schools of thought in any field, you could get them all, and decide for yourself."

"This technology could also revolutionize the practice of democracy," noted Feldman. "The average American citizen is profoundly uninformed when it comes to politics, which makes them susceptible to lies, and to charm. But now both parties in an election could have voters upload comprehensive and complex position papers, which almost no one takes the time to read today. They could then decide for *themselves* which side they agree with."

Rachel smiled. "Very good," she said. "As Mr. Regev pointed out earlier, certain technology advances are such big leaps forward they are disruptive. In good and bad ways. In my opinion, there are few advances that would be as disruptive as Matrix Learning would be. I think you'll find that the more you think about a world in which this is possible, the more you realize there is almost no aspect of civilization that this wouldn't impact."

She paused. "Let me return to the current educational system for a moment. Sherry, you pointed out that the university system would go down the drain. What do you think the primary impact of this would be?"

"Economic," said Sherry Dixon without hesitation. "College is a multibillion dollar industry."

"Maybe," said Rachel, "but I don't think so. The professors will be busy organizing the knowledge for the Matrix Learning downloads. They'll be okay. And while they won't be giving lectures, they'll have more time to push back the frontiers of knowledge. In my view, if college were to become extinct, what would be lost is the maturing process that students undergo over four years, the social skills they hone there. Having to find a way to manage psychotic roommates and the freshman dorm insane asylum. Learning how to study when there are preferred social options, and when surrounded by chaos. No amount of Matrix Learning can teach maturity, or how to navigate complex social situations. These can only be gained through experience."

"Which brings up other Matrix Learning deficiencies," said Feldman. "What about creativity? Genius? Artistry? Knowledge alone doesn't give you higher intelligence, or magically turn you into a Rembrandt."

"Excellent," said Rachel. "There is that. But perhaps a more important consideration is this: Can knowledge without wisdom be a danger? Knowledge without experience? Knowledge won too easily?"

Rachel was about to continue when she happened to glance at a large round clock on the wall, and winced. "Wow, it appears our time was up about five minutes ago," she said. "Time flies when you're having fun. Usually, we get into several other topics during the first session, which means the discussion this time was particularly good."

The professor sighed. "And there is one additional aspect of Matrix Learning I wanted to discuss. I guess we'll just have to get to that next time."

She frowned. The discussion of the human sex drive was one of her favorites, and they would now have to go through it much faster than she would have liked. Oh well. She was confident she would find a way to make it work.

"Great session, everybody," she concluded. "See you on Thursday."

* * *

The man watching Rachel Howard and her class on a large plasma monitor leaned back in his chair and pondered all that he had heard. Fascinating. Absolutely fascinating.

He was greatly disappointed that the class had ended when it did. He was eager to learn what else she might discuss, but now he would have to wait until Thursday.

If he was willing. Every minute counted, and they would have to make their move soon, ready or not.

Time was running out.

And there was much that needed to be done.

12

Kevin Quinn remained asleep in the Ford Fusion longer than he had expected, but he was untroubled by this upon awakening. In the wee hours of the morning he had found an unpopulated stretch of geography fifteen miles beyond the outskirts of Allentown and had driven randomly for hours, literally choosing Robert Frost's *road less traveled* whenever he came to a fork.

Eventually he found himself driving up a large, wooded hill, on a secluded dirt road long forgotten by civilization, which ultimately led to an old, abandoned shack. He couldn't have asked for a more ideal location.

He had parked behind the shack, confident that he could get the sleep he so desperately needed without interruption. In fact, he suspected he could remain here for months, if not years, with little fear of being seen by human eyes.

So perhaps he had overslept, but there was certainly no urgency for him to leave. A needle hiding in a secluded, forgotten location was far safer than one traveling through the haystack of civilization, no matter how large this haystack might be. Besides, it had been a tough, long night, and he had needed to hit the reset button. Men who were sleep deprived made mistakes. He had already made one the night before, by not being properly prepared.

He couldn't afford to make another.

He was stretched out on the backseat of the car and cautiously rose to a sitting position, pausing as his eyes reached window level to take in his surroundings and ensure no one was in the vicinity. Satisfied, he exited his temporary bedroom and relieved the pressure on his bladder before returning to the back of the car to begin work on his most important project.

On the stretch of seat next to him, he carefully laid out the materials he had stolen from the TV repair shop the night before: a knife, four television remote controls, wire, duct tape, and a nine-volt battery.

Slowly, methodically, he used the tip of the knife to punch four tiny, evenly spaced holes in the front of the black baseball cap he had taken from a gangbanger in Trenton, just above the brim. He then dismantled the remotes, removed the BB-sized glass bulbs at their tips, and poked them through the holes. Finally, he wired the bulbs up to the nine-volt battery, which he taped securely to the inner brim of the hat, invisible when the hat was being worn.

He studied his handiwork, satisfied with the finished product. The tiny bulbs were almost undetectable, which had been his goal.

The rudiments of facial recognition software hadn't changed much in decades, and there remained several ways to beat these systems. Wearing a mask would do it, of course, but then you'd have to walk around in public with a *mask*, not an ideal way of warding off unwanted attention. And wearing a standard hat, a beard, or changing a hair style was useless. Facial recognition systems weren't troubled in the least by any of these measures.

What *was* effective in the battle against these algorithms was to avoid symmetry, and to obscure the area around one's eyes. A system of makeup and hairstyling had been developed many years earlier to accomplish this task, called *CV Dazzle*. The name borrowed from a technique used in World War I, also called *Dazzle*, whereby warships were painted with cubist designs, not to provide camouflage, but because these designs made it harder for the enemy to determine a ship's size, speed, and heading.

It was all about breaking up symmetry and visual continuity, which CV Dazzle did to a human face through the use of avant-garde hairstyling and makeup, strategically obscuring or modifying facial features that the recognition programs required. But this technique largely suffered from the same problem as a mask. If Quinn were to apply dark makeup to one of his cheeks, like a football player smearing black grease under his eyes, he would be anything but discreet.

Fooling facial recognition was not enough. You also had to do so while not sticking out like a neon sign.

Fortunately, cameras had more sensitive vision than humans, and this sensitivity could be used against them. Infrared LEDs could blind a camera, without registering in the visual cortex of a human being in any way. So Quinn had acquired a ball cap the night before so he could turn it into a facial recognition deterrent device.

Later he would purchase sunglasses, choosing a pair with the biggest frame he could find, which even by itself could defeat the efforts of lesser algorithms to recognize him. Combined with a hat fitted with tiny bulbs from TV remotes, which would cloak his face with camera-blinding infrared light, he would be able to operate freely.

In addition to the glasses, he would purchase a few changes of clothing that would make him look heavier than he was, platform shoes, hair dye, and black ink for selfie faux tattoos. Within a few hours he would be unrecognizable to both cameras and pursuers, and would have an ideal place in which to hole up for however long he needed.

He would secure his nest, and then he would carefully, methodically, begin planning how to destroy the President of the United States.

13

Avi Wortzman sighed loudly as the holographic presence of America's Secretary of Homeland Security, Greg Henry, vanished from his office. Henry had ended the vid-meet abruptly, even rudely, but Wortzman could hardly blame him. He would have done the same.

Wortzman was only forty-one years old, but at times like this—when crisis situations forced brutally complex, brutally consequential decisions upon him—he felt twice this age. And such times had recently begun to appear with frightening regularity.

Wortzman had distinguished himself in the military, and being an adrenaline junkie in his younger years had joined up with the special forces unit, *Shayetet 13*, the Israel Defense Forces' equivalent of the Navy Seals. From here he had graduated to Israel's most secret and fabled special operations unit, Kidon, Hebrew for *bayonet.* This group was known—at least according to an almost urban-legend mythology that had sprung up around the world—for its unequaled ability to infiltrate hostile countries and murder Israel's enemies, while barely disturbing a single blade of grass or molecule of air, leaving no trace of the op behind.

Wortzman had then served in various Intelligence capacities before finally landing in his current office, on the third floor of a famous complex in Tel Aviv. There were four Hebrew letters on the wall next to his door that read *Ramsad*, an abbreviation for *Rosh ha-Mossad.*

A rare non-Hebrew speaker—aware that the Jewish New Year, *Rosh Hashanah*, meant *head of the year*—might realize that Rosh ha-Mossad meant *head of the Mossad.* But without knowledge of this title, none would guess that Avi Wortzman held this position. There was absolutely nothing imposing about this man, or his office.

At least not on the surface.

But there were enemies of the Jewish state who had died, or had seen their best plans laid to waste, for underestimating this unassuming man.

Mossad was the Hebrew word for *Institute*, short for *HaMossad leModi'in uleTafkidim Meyuchadim*, which translated as the "Institute for Intelligence and Special Operations."

Since Avi Wortzman had taken over the reins of the Mossad five years earlier, he had saved Israel from certain destruction on more than one occasion, and had even saved the US from suffering a number of devastating blows, although Wortzman made certain that his assistance in these instances remained undiscovered.

But now, after strengthening the Institute in ways unimaginable to his predecessors, the spear he had forged and sharpened so brilliantly now threatened the stability of everything he had built. He had made a series of moves that had seemed flawless, that would leave the greatest chess grandmasters in awe, but it was collapsing in on him, backfiring.

Perhaps God had a sense of humor, or was punishing him for the hubris of believing he had finally gained the upper hand on his enemies, that there was no crisis he couldn't overcome.

Which is perhaps why he had never felt so weary, so ancient. Why the thick, black hair that had so proudly served him during harrowing special operations missions had recently abandoned ship, leaving his head as bald as a light bulb. And why he now took blood pressure medication on a regular basis.

He had thought the heavy lifting was all but over, but the weight of the world had returned to his shoulders with a vengeance, more crushing than ever before.

As the head of Mossad, he was the caretaker of an entire country, an entire *people*. The stress was backbreaking, the demands incomprehensible, even to those commanding other such agencies around the world.

Because no country was a greater underdog, at least on paper, than the biblical land of milk and honey. The fact that Israel still even *existed* was a miracle of biblical proportions, surrounded as it was by a sea of hostile countries—many whose leaders publicly avowed to annihilate the tiny island of democracy and march any remaining Jews into the sea, to finish the job that Hitler had started, even while denying the holocaust had ever happened.

It might have been accurate to compare Israel's survival to the story of David and Goliath, but only if David had been pitted against a *hundred* Goliaths.

The country Wortzman was responsible for defending was so minuscule that almost *five hundred* Israels could fit inside the United States, and Israel's entire population was greatly exceeded by the population of *North Carolina* alone.

Israel bordered Syria, Jordan, Egypt, and Lebanon, four countries that collectively outnumbered the Jewish state fifteen to one. And while these four countries were all next-door neighbors—just in case *their* hatred of Israel wasn't virulent enough—the neighbors just down the block included such tolerant and open-minded peace lovers as Iraq, Iran, Somalia, Yemen, Sudan, Kuwait, Libya, Turkey, Saudi Arabia, Pakistan, and Afghanistan.

One of Wortzman's predecessors, Meir Dagan, who had headed the Mossad for eight years, from 2002 until 2010, had hung a framed black-and-white photo of his grandfather on his office wall. The man was shown surrounded by jeering Nazis who would shoot him minutes later, along with thousands of other Jews in Lokov, Ukraine. The photo was taken by a non-Jewish neighbor of the victim, at the request of the proud Nazi butchers.

Dagan would tell visitors that he displayed this photo, not just to remind himself of history, of what was at stake, but to remind him to take the threats of those who vowed to destroy the Jews with utter sobriety, and that the barbarism inside the human soul could be unleashed far more easily than any modern, civilized citizen of the world could truly comprehend.

In 1961, the Yale psychologist Stanley Milgram demonstrated experimentally what had been demonstrated in the real world all too often throughout history: that human beings were pliable, and could easily be goaded into acts of great cruelty by those they considered to be in authority.

The famous Milgram study asked volunteers to shock unseen subjects, behind a wall, for a pretend memory experiment, whenever the pretend subjects failed to remember a word pair from a list, with the intensity of the shock increasing with every wrong answer. If at any time a volunteer wanted to stop the experiment, stop pressing a button they believed was delivering electricity and agony to test subjects, they were given a verbal prod by the man they had been told was in charge. First they were simply told to *please continue*. If they later wanted to halt, they were told, *the experiment requires that you continue*. After this, *it is absolutely essential that you continue,* and finally, *you have no other choice; you must go on.*

Despite actors on the other side of the wall screaming in agony, complaining of a heart condition, and begging for the experiment to be stopped, fully sixty-five percent of the volunteers could be encouraged to advance all the way to the highest level of electric shock. A result that had *stunned* the world. And a result that had since been verified by so many researchers, in so many countries, it had become indisputable.

The only part of this result that had stunned Avi Wortzman was that anyone had been surprised. It seemed to him that even a cursory glance at human history, filled with butchery, war, slavery, and genocide, would make this result utterly predictable.

So Wortzman had followed Dagan's lead. Behind his sturdy oak desk, Wortzman had hung a painting he had commissioned, depicting, not just the holocaust, but numerous other instances in which the Jewish people were persecuted throughout history. Since the religion had become the first to believe in a single, abstract god, rather than idols, its adherents had faced a never-ending barrage of hatred and violence.

While Christianity was able to quickly win the battle for monotheistic souls, rather than show good will toward the religion their savior had practiced, European Christian populations throughout the centuries had held *all* Jews responsible for the death of Christ. They had spread accusations that Jews routinely kidnapped and murdered Christian children, so their blood could be used in religious rituals. When the Black Death wiped out more than half the population of Europe in the fourteenth century, it was no surprise that Jews were blamed, and untold thousands were put to death, many burned alive.

This virulent anti-Semitism had erupted decade after decade, century after century, resulting in multiple pogroms, forced conversions, expulsions, and mass murders. France, Germany, Italy, England, Russia: none were immune from this hatred.

So Wortzman had hung a painting, a montage, depicting any number of these atrocities, with the words, "Never Again!" spelled in black wooden Hebrew letters attached to the wall above it. But he had not stopped there.

Wortzman was well aware that while his power as the head of Mossad was immense, so was his responsibility, and that the ethics of almost every decision he made had become hideously complex. So, while he hung the words, Never Again! above his montage, below it he hung a silver frame containing a famous quote. A quote written by, of all people, Friedrich Nietzsche, the German philosopher many mistakenly believed to be the godfather of Nazism and Fascism. Nietzsche had strongly and unambiguously denounced both nationalism and anti-Semitism, but after his death in 1900, his sister had reworked his unpublished writings to comport with her own beliefs, bastardizing many of his views.

Wortzman displayed Nietzsche's words to remind him of the need to cling to his own humanity as tightly as he could, despite the temptations to do otherwise. He turned toward them now, re-reading them as he had done on so many occasions.

Battle not with monsters,
Lest ye become a monster.
And if you gaze into the abyss,
The abyss gazes back into you.

Wortzman blew out a heavy sigh. *Battle not with monsters*. The problem, of course, was that he had no choice but to do this. In fact, *battling with monsters* could well have been his job description. And as much as he strived to heed Nietzsche's warning about the likely consequences, he wondered how many people would think he had long since crossed this line, had long since become a monster in his own right.

The Mossad leader was torn from his reverie as Yaron Hurwitz burst through the door, breathless. "I'm too late, aren't I?" he said in Hebrew after taking a single glance at his boss.

Wortzman motioned for him to sit down but didn't reply.

"You already supplied the intel to Greg Henry, didn't you?" said Hurwitz as he pulled a chair close to Wortzman's desk.

Hurwitz's official title was deputy director, but most in the Institute thought of him simply as Wortzman's indispensable right hand. Like his boss, Hurwitz had come up through the military and intelligence ranks, but his expertise was long on signal, electronic, and computer intelligence, and short on work in the field.

Wortzman nodded. "I insisted on an emergency vid-meet with Henry the second after I alerted you. Got off the call five minutes ago."

Hurwitz whistled, calculating that the entire call couldn't have lasted for more than three or four minutes. "That was one efficient vid-meet," he said.

He shook his head in disapproval. "I wish you would have waited just a little longer until I could get here. I could have been a sounding board. Two heads are better than one—even when one of those heads is *yours*."

"I had no choice. Nothing you could have said would have changed my decision. We would just have wasted precious minutes. What would you have me do, say nothing about Jafari's plans and then watch while America burned to the ground a few weeks or months later?"

"Of course not. We had to stop this. But we could have delayed just a bit to make sure our friends in DHS got the intel through anonymous channels. Hard to pretend the intel didn't come directly from us when, you know, the intel came directly from us." Hurwitz frowned deeply. "Or we could have kept track of everyone in Jafari's meeting and taken them out ourselves in the days to come."

Wortzman shook his head, unable to believe what he had just heard. He wasn't the only one being affected by lethal doses of stress. "Jafari had *hundreds* of men in that mosque," he said. "And we're so shorthanded, we could recruit a thousand agents and still be understaffed. The last thing we need to do is try to assassinate hundreds of zealots in the States, especially when the US authorities believe they're innocent."

"Yeah, okay," said Hurwitz dourly, but then quickly broke out into a broad grin. "I have to admit, that may be the dumbest thing I've ever said."

"Just proves that you're human, Yaron. Given everything that's going on, we're both under a lot of pressure."

"So what about my first thought?" pressed Hurwitz. "Why wouldn't you route the intel so it came in their door anonymously?"

"No time. My guess is Jafari's meeting will only last another few hours, if that. Even for us, this would leave little time to green-light a neutralization plan. And the US is a much larger, slower animal." He shrugged. "Look at it this way, by coming out of the closet on this, they'll owe us one."

Hurwitz rolled his eyes at his boss's last statement. "Yeah, the pressure is definitely getting to us."

This time it was Wortzman's turn to smile at his own stupidity. It had been a feeble attempt at finding a silver lining. And a misguided one. The Mossad already seemed far too competent for its own good, which is why they had long since perfected means to feed intel to the Americans in ways that were either anonymous, or made it appear the Americans themselves had discovered it.

The Mossad had already raised far too many eyebrows, had pulled far too many rabbits out of the hat. By showing their hand here, they were sure to attract additional unwanted attention, and further arouse the suspicions of the Americans.

The relationship between Israel and the US, and their respective Intelligence services, was complicated at the best of times. And these weren't the best of times. So a better description of the relationship would be *treacherously* complicated.

Yes, the two countries were strong allies, but US agencies had taken endless heat for their unwillingness to share intelligence, sources, and methods with their own sister departments. And the seventeen intelligence gathering agencies in the US were closer to each other than mere allies, they were appendages of the very same organism. If sister agencies refused to share with each other, Israel could hardly be blamed for its own reluctance to do so.

"Given how severely depleted our resources are right now," noted Hurwitz, "it's lucky Jafari decided to trigger his sleeper cells when he did."

"Very," agreed Wortzman. "I was just about to redeploy our meager remaining assets." He paused. "Were you able to listen to any of his Thousand Cuts speech on the way over here?"

"Yes. I'll want to run some computer simulations on his fire strategy, but my instincts tell me Jafari is on to something, and that such an attack would be devastating. Nice to get this *Ben-Zonah* removed from the board," he said, using an Arabic epithet that translated into *son of a whore*. "Even if we did have to show our hand."

Hurwitz frowned. "Speaking of which, what exactly did you tell Greg Henry?"

"I just gave him a few sentence introduction to the crisis and then fed him the video feed from the Chicago mosque, backed up to when Jafari was describing his death-by-fire plan. I told Henry the footage was courtesy of an agent we had on the inside."

"Did he ask how the hell we managed to place an agent there while he was busy pulling on his schlong?"

"No, he was in too big of a hurry. But he *will*, you'd better believe it. Just as soon as this situation has been handled. And he'll be asking why we're fielding agents on US soil without their knowledge. We have to come up with a plausible story."

Wortzman paused. "I told him not to factor our man into his planning, by the way. That he had an escape route mapped out, and would be gone before they took any action."

"After they've taken out Jafari, they'll be wondering how our man could vanish so completely."

Avi Wortzman nodded. "I guess we'll just have to be at our most creative."

His second-in-command blew out a long, tired breath. "*Ma nishtanah halailah hazeh*?" he mumbled under his breath, tilting his head toward the ceiling as if beseeching an overly demanding deity. This was a well-known passage from the Passover service that translated roughly into, *Why is this night different from all other nights?*

Wortzman squinted in confusion. "I didn't quite catch that."

"*Of course* we'll have to outdo ourselves on this one, Avi," he replied with a weary shrug. "What else is new?"

14

Kevin Quinn gently placed the black baseball cap he had augmented on the passenger's seat of the Ford and exited the vehicle once again. He would soon make a trip into town for disguise and supplies, but he first needed to recon the shack and his surroundings.

The shack was made of wood slats that had seen much better decades, and the coloration of the mottled structure varied from gray to brown to rust, all displeasing to the eye. The entire structure was about twice the size of a three-car garage, and was bereft of windows or openings of any kind, save for a dingy door that was splintered around the periphery and hung slightly ajar.

Quinn took a deep breath and entered, propping the door open for better illumination.

The inside of the shack made the outside look like *Buckingham Palace*.

It smelled of decay, mold, and dirt. The floorboards were eaten away by insects and weather, and several of the slats were broken or had gaps to the ground a foot below. Quinn had hoped there might be something useful inside, but his hope was quickly dashed as he glanced around. The roof had several gaping holes and the morning sunshine left a mottling of light and dark.

A rusted-out bed frame rested against the corner of the structure, and a torn, moldy mattress that looked like it had been to hell and back could be found nearby. Other than this, and the encroachment of weeds and vegetation in several places, nothing remained.

Quinn refused to conjecture as to why the structure had been built in the first place, and by whom. It could have been a staging area for a hunter, a place for a would-be Unabomber to write his demented manifesto, or a butcher shop used by a long-ago mass murderer. This didn't matter now.

The important thing was that with a concerted effort, Quinn wouldn't have too much trouble fixing it up enough to suit his needs. The structure would keep wildlife out, and with some makeshift repairs, the roof could be made to keep weather out as well. He could get an inflatable mattress and a battery-powered camping refrigerator, which he could recharge using both solar power and the Ford's battery.

He would wait a suitable length of time and then he would take his first step. He would contact police and hospitals in the vicinity of Davinroy's resort, seeking reports of battered women with no memory of how they came to be this way. Once he identified a few, he would meet with them, reconstruct events as much as possible, and show that these mysterious beatings all took place when Davinroy was nearby.

After that he would make a trip to Davinroy's resort and find his tunnel system, including entrances inside several of the rooms, which must have been exquisitely well hidden for them to remain undiscovered this long. He would expose this system of passageways and describe to the media how the president had used them to beat up prostitutes, and to torture and kill the love of his life.

He had little doubt that Davinroy would find a way to slime out of these accusations yet again, to issue creative explanations for the tunnel system, and contend that when he had confided their existence to Quinn, it had fueled his growing psychosis. But even so, the revelation of this subterranean maze and battered prostitutes would infuriate Davinroy and raise suspicions. And some would dig deeper, possibly making additional discoveries or raising additional questions for the president to answer.

And Quinn would keep digging. If Nicole had found exposed threads, he would also. No matter how microscopic they were, he would pull at them relentlessly until Davinroy's ball of deceit and atrocity was completely unraveled.

And he would have all the time he needed up here on *horrid-shack hill*. Or maybe horrid-shack *mountain*, since he was either on a very large hill, or a very small mountain. There were only two paved roads that led anywhere near this location, and only one road, unpaved, that led to the summit. The best off-road vehicles might make the trip, but not without difficulty, and not without advertising their presence.

There was an expanse of un-forested ground at the summit, all to the north side of the shed, but the terrain was strewn with enough large rocks, fallen tree branches, and thick vegetation to make landing a helo right next to the shed impossible. A sneak attack on foot might take him by surprise, but once he added a few cameras and sensors at strategic locations, this, too, would become impossible.

An assault force could rappel from helos, but Quinn could always escape into the woods on the south side, which the shack abutted, if this were to occur. Later today he would set up some booby traps around his perimeter, and steal an all-terrain motorcycle, which he would hide nearby in the woods. He would then plot out a foolproof escape route in the unlikely event the authorities ever did come for him here.

He had neglected to plan for failure at the Garza fundraiser, but he was proud of the moves he had made since. As long as he remained careful, he could use this mountain, and this shack, as his base of operations for *months* if he had to, without anyone being the wiser.

A floorboard creaked behind him, causing his heart to jump to his throat.

He wheeled around, raising his gun as he did so, but he was too late. Two men were behind him, both with guns already extended in his direction.

"Don't move!" commanded the taller of the two. "Drop the gun! Hands in the air!"

Quinn did as instructed.

On second thought, he decided, it was possible that his assessment of how long he could remain here without being discovered was just a *trifle* too optimistic.

15

"Erge," said DHS Secretary Greg Henry the moment he ended the connection with Wortzman, panic in his voice. "I need you to set up a *priority alpha* vid-meet *immediately*. Attendees are me, President Davinroy, and Deputy Secretary O'Malley. Get Davinroy first, and don't wait for O'Malley."

"Working to establish vid-meet now," replied his digital assistant, Erge, whose soothing, feminine voice wouldn't have changed in cadence one iota if the room were on fire.

Less than three minutes later holographic images of two men appeared in front of Greg Henry, almost flawlessly rendered, so much so that only a prolonged study would reveal that they weren't actually in the room. The software displayed a small text window that hovered just beside each man's right shoulder, indicating the identity of each and that they were both actually seated in the Oval Office of the White House. Simultaneously, Henry's holographic image had joined them *there*. In this way, vid-meet technology ensured that each side experienced the meeting as though it were taking place at their own location.

The appearance of Cris Coffey next to the president took Henry by surprise, but just for a moment. Given that Henry and other high-ranking members of the intelligence community had been notified of the attempted assassination the previous night, the presence of the head of Davinroy's security detail made sense.

Henry knew it was bad form not to ask how the president was faring after the attack, but he had no time to spare—had possibly run out of time already.

"What is this about?" demanded Davinroy.

Henry glanced suggestively at Coffey. "This is for your ears only," he said, as a holographic version of his second-in-command, Matthew

O'Malley, popped into existence in the offices of both Henry and the president, while a display window beside O'Malley's head indicated that he was actually at Fort Bragg, where he had gone to meet with a general.

"Nonsense," said the president, giving the slightest nod to acknowledge the newcomer who had just teleported into his presence. "Cris is cleared to hear whatever you have to say." He shrugged. "Since he happens to be here with me, he can lend his considerable expertise to the proceedings."

Henry had no time to argue. Besides, Cris Coffey just might add perspective, at that. He had come up through the shadowy world of Black Ops, rising to the very highest levels. Not only was Coffey still revered in this world, he continued to consult with many of his old colleagues, keeping his fingers in many Black Ops pies and retaining considerable clout.

Henry could only imagine what Coffey had seen and done, and the power he had once wielded. He was considered to be exceedingly smart and skilled. But he had become jaded, had begun to burn out, and had been looking for an exit door.

The previous Secretary of Homeland, Kristen Brennan, had worked with Coffey early in her career—Coffey had saved her life, in fact—and she had seized on the opportunity to bring him on to head up Davinroy's security detail. The Secret Service, once under the province of Treasury, was now part of DHS, so Greg Henry was technically Coffey's boss. Given all of this, even if Henry had time for it, making a compelling argument to exclude Coffey from the proceedings would not be easy, and he decided against it.

"We have an ongoing situation in the Hamza mosque in Chicago," said Henry, his eyes locked onto the president's, which the vid-meet software would ensure was the case in the Oval Office as well. "While I was waiting for you to join the vid-meet," he added, "I activated a strike team and instructed them to get to an isolated staging area a few minutes helo flight from the mosque. They'll wait there for my orders."

"The name of that mosque rings a bell," said Davinroy.

Henry drew in a deep breath and nodded. "I'm not surprised. It's led by an Imam who you know well," he said, not relishing giving the president the bad news. "Azim Jafari."

President Davinroy had cited this Imam on several occasions, singing his praises for being a devout Muslim with the courage to speak out against extremism, to preach for tolerance and peace between peoples and nations. Two years earlier he had even invited Jafari to be his guest at a State of the Union Address, asking Jafari to rise as he thanked him for being such a fine representative of the peace-loving religion of Islam.

Talk about rubbing salt into the president's wound. Kevin Quinn, a trusted special agent, had just tried to kill him, and now Henry had to tell the man that his favorite Imam was an extremist, after all. Not a good twelve hours for President Davinroy when it came to betrayals.

"Jafari is about to unleash hundreds of sleepers, even as we speak," explained Henry, "on a coordinated mission to . . ." he paused, searching for the best, quickest way to get his point across. "Well, to basically burn down this country. Each sleeper will recruit others, and together will set forests ablaze, and then cities, using a variety of fire accelerants. I have footage of Jafari inside the mosque ordering this attack, but there's no time for you to see it now."

"You're certain there is no mistake?" said the president in disbelief. "That Jafari is directly behind this plot?"

"I am, sir."

"Shit!" thundered Davinroy. "God *damnit*!" The president was angrier than Henry could ever remember. "How is it that you had Jafari under surveillance, *and you didn't notify me*? Are you an idiot, Greg! You know I've used him as a positive example. You don't think I'd want to know he was under suspicion?"

"He wasn't," said Henry, swallowing hard. "The tip and the footage came to us courtesy of our friends in Israel. Wortzman at Mossad."

"How the hell did *they* get it?" snapped the president.

I only wish I knew, thought Henry. Aloud he said, "With all due respect, sir, we need to make some immediate decisions. I can give you a more comprehensive briefing later."

"And you trust this intel absolutely?"

Henry thought about this for a brief moment. "I do, sir. Mossad intel tends to be . . ." he paused. What? The best in the business? Flawless? "Extremely sound, sir," he finished.

Henry knew that this was an understatement. The Mossad was magic. Precise, thorough, and as far as he could tell, never wrong. How could they be so damn good? Their intel was *uncanny*.

It was also embarrassing.

The US Intelligence Community consisted of seventeen separate agencies, employing over two hundred thousand operatives. Including the many Black projects and agencies, the total intelligence budget was nearing eighty billion dollars a year, although not even Henry knew the exact figure. No one really did, since the government routinely used accounting practices that would get corporate CEOs thrown in jail.

Almost thirteen hundred government organizations and two thousand private companies were tasked with intelligence, operating from over ten thousand locations spread across the country, and well over a million Americans held top-secret security clearances. In Washington and surrounding areas alone, thirty-three building complexes for top-secret work had been constructed since 2001, occupying seventeen million square feet—three times that of the biggest office complex in the world: the Pentagon.

And yet tiny Israel, fly-speck Mossad, using less than one percent of these resources, routinely ate the lunch of the gargantuan US intelligence apparatus. Henry had gone mad trying to figure out how they were doing it. Their reputation had always been impeccable, but for many years now they had upped their game even further.

Rumor had it that they had somehow derailed the Iranian nuclear program, which had proceeded apace, despite a nuclear agreement with the US that the entire world knew would not be honored. DHS suspected that Israel had somehow dismantled the North Korean program as well, before the psychotic Korean leader could do any damage, although there was no concrete evidence to that effect.

Part of the Mossad's success was that it was lean and efficient, while the US system was bloated, redundant, and uncoordinated. More didn't always mean better, sometimes it just meant more complicated, more bureaucratic, and more prone to paralysis. Vast incompetence could hide out within the US system without ever being weeded out. Not so in the Mossad.

And Israeli intelligence had to be nearly perfect. Mossad had to work smarter, with more creativity, and to think outside of the box. Because Israel depended on this agency to ensure its very survival.

When you're an eight-hundred-pound gorilla you don't have to be smart or well trained. But when you're an eighty-pound weakling, *surrounded* by eight-hundred-pound gorillas, the three pound mass between your ears had to be used to its fullest—and then some.

The Mossad was also blessed with top drawer civilian resources to draw upon. Israel had long been a science and technology mecca, harboring the second highest concentration of hi-tech companies in the world, behind only Silicon Valley. These companies were founded and driven by talented members of a population with the highest percentage of PhDs, MDs, scientists, engineers, and technicians on the planet.

Davinroy was now seething. Clearly, the fact that the intel had come from Israel had poured salt in his wounds. Or maybe acid. "Recommendations?" he barked.

"I recommend breaching the mosque with gas," said Henry. "Knocking them out and then mopping up."

"Jesus Christ, Greg!" snapped the president. "You want to assault a mosque? Yeah, that will do wonders for our country's relationship with Muslims."

"I'm aware of the optics," said Henry. "But there are too many of them, in too heavily populated of an area, to let them disperse. They're radicalized and unpredictable, which makes them too dangerous to take any chances with."

"I agree with Greg," offered Cris Coffey. "It's the only way."

"And the probability of success?" said the president.

"Very high," replied Henry. "The assault team I scrambled is already preparing for such a breach, awaiting my final order. They're studying the video the Israelis provided and holographic blueprints of the mosque right now. These are my best men, with our most advanced equipment."

"Okay, do it," said the president dourly, his expression conveying just how little he wanted to make this decision.

"I suggest we clear a perimeter around the mosque first," said Deputy Secretary O'Malley. "Just in case."

"I agree," said Henry. "See to it," he instructed his second-in-command. "Order the breach. Give the team a green-light the moment a six-block radius has been cleared. Be sure they come up with some reasonable excuse for the evacuation. Gas leak, imminent meteor strike, something. Just make sure the exodus is done quietly and doesn't tip off the jihadists."

"Roger that," said O'Malley, blinking out of existence to attend to these details.

Once O'Malley had vanished, the president also dismissed Cris Coffey, leaving him alone with Greg Henry.

"As if an assault on a mosque isn't bad enough," said Davinroy the moment Coffey had exited the room, "Jafari's involvement makes this an even bigger nightmare. If it gets out that he was the ringleader, it will convince the haters out there to mistrust Islam even more. We can't have that."

Henry had worked with Davinroy too long not to be able to read between the lines. The man only cared about himself and politics. What he meant was, if it got out that Jafari was the ringleader, he, Davinroy, would look like a gullible idiot. *That* is what he couldn't tolerate.

"It's an unfortunate turn of events," said Henry. "But there's nothing we can do about it."

"Maybe," said Davinroy. "Maybe not. No one would *have* to know of Jafari's involvement. We could bottle up all details, citing national security. And we could announce that the terrorists chose this mosque because of Jafari's heroic stance, and kidnapped him so he was forced to be in attendance. Out of hatred for him and what he stood for."

Henry was unable to hide the look of disgust that flashed across his face. Presidents of old had distorted events in this manner before, but this practice was getting more audacious and commonplace with each subsequent administration. Truth and reality had come to mean very little when compared to political correctness and political expediency.

"Do you have a problem with this, Greg?" demanded the president. "You do understand that there are times when you have to hide the truth for the greater good. Which is why we don't tell the public about all the terrorist threats we stop. If they knew about some of the disasters we've narrowly averted, and how often new threats emerge, no one in America would be able to sleep at night. In this case, why sour the country's relations with Muslims any further? Enlightened people know that Islam is a religion of peace. Is the truth worth hate crimes breaking out? Does it matter who is responsible, as long as we stop the attack? What if telling the truth about one man results in the eventual deaths of hundreds, as misunderstandings between religions grow?"

Henry said nothing. He had heard these arguments before. Sometimes history had to be whitewashed. Sometimes the public had to be protected from the truth, like a small child whose dog had passed away. Better to invent the fiction of sending Spot off to a farm where he could be happy and run free, rather than introducing the concept of death to a four-year-old.

But was this the proper analogy? Were American citizens little more than sheltered children? Sometimes it did seem that way.

But in Henry's opinion, the more clear-eyed the public was about the true nature of a threat, the better. Davinroy would argue, *had* argued, that only key power players in government and the military needed to be clear-eyed. That as long as the chess masters knew the endgame, why scare the pawns unnecessarily, even if they did tend to be on the front lines.

"It doesn't matter what I think of this," said Henry. "Because it won't work. Jafari and his followers will be proud of this attempt. They'll all want to be sure he gets credit for it. No way they'll let us rewrite history so Jafari is a victim rather than a mastermind."

Davinroy frowned deeply and tilted his head. "It would work if there were no survivors," he said after several long seconds of thought.

"What?"

"No survivors means our narrative could be whatever we chose it to be," replied Davinroy. "The knockout gas you're planning to use," he continued. "Is it flammable?"

"I'm not sure."

"*Make sure it is.* Jihadists tend to embrace their own deaths. If we try to take them alive, but they happen to light a match in the midst of a flammable cloud of gas, there is nothing we can do about that. Correct?"

Henry's mouth had dropped open but he didn't respond.

"We just have to be sure to stay ahead of the story. To make it clear that we tried to take them peacefully, and were careful not to do any damage to the mosque. That it was *their* choice to martyr themselves." The president shrugged. "They planned to burn down the entire country. The least we can do is let them burn down one mosque."

"Are you ordering me to kill them all, sir?" asked Henry.

"Of course not!" said Davinroy, pretending to be offended. "How can you even ask that? That would be an unlawful order. All I want you to do is make it clear to your team leader to choose a knockout gas that is highly flammable. And that if the extremists inside decide to martyr themselves for their cause, to literally go out in a blaze of glory . . ." He raised his eyebrows. "Well, just let your man know that we think this would definitely be the best outcome for all concerned."

16

The two men holding Kevin Quinn at gunpoint stepped forward from the darkness, having stationed themselves in a corner of the shed not illuminated by the door or the gap in the ceiling. Quinn's eyes flickered across every inch of them as they fully emerged into the light, like Sherlock Holmes desperately searching for an obscure clue with which to seize an advantage.

How had he been found? *It just wasn't possible.* He was certain he had covered his tracks.

Both men were fit and had assumed a stance indicating they were highly trained. But they were both dressed in short-sleeved knit shirts, and the shorter, thicker one, about five-eleven, had a small diamond in each of his earlobes, and long hair tied back into a ponytail. If these visual clues weren't enough, seconds had gone by since Quinn had raised his hands and they had yet to identify themselves as Secret Service, FBI, police, or any other authority, which they were required to do if they were legitimate.

And he didn't hear further commotion outside of the shack, or the whip of helicopter blades. For a target as high-value as he now was, enough armed men to field a football team should be charging toward them right now, as a backup to the two men who had entered the shack.

"Hold out your hands, wrists together," barked the taller man as his partner approached with white plastic zip-tie handcuffs.

Quinn calculated his chances of survival if he attacked before his hands were bound, and didn't like the result. He was very good, but it didn't take a mathematician to know his chances would be one in twenty, at best. And it was important to factor into the equation that they wanted him to remain alive, at least for a while. Had they wanted him dead, he'd be dead already.

Quinn offered no resistance as the short, powerfully built assailant slipped the plastic strips around his wrists and zipped them tight. Seconds later the man made a chain of linked zip-ties and bound Quinn's ankles, leaving enough play in between for him to take short steps, so he could waddle forward like a duck. The man also relieved Quinn of his gun and the small electronic device that cloned key fobs, his expression making it clear he knew exactly what it was, and shoved both into his pocket.

Finally, he backed away, made a show of looking Quinn up and down to take in the clothing he had stolen in Trenton, and shook his head. "The Secret Service's dress code is really slipping," he said with a smirk. "Or have they begun hiring gangbangers?"

"How did you find me?" said Quinn, lowering his outstretched arms to a resting position in front of him.

The taller man shrugged. Unlike his partner, he was clean-cut and impeccably groomed. "We didn't," he replied pleasantly. "The man who hired us told us where to find you and how to make our approach, and we took it from there."

Quinn's agile mind dissected this information from every angle, knowing his survival might depend on how quickly he could make sense of what was happening.

"No interest in knowing who we are?" asked the man who had bound Quinn, his gun now extended once again. "Would've thought that would be your first question."

Quinn shook his head dismissively. "Would you have told me?"

"Not a chance. But I thought you'd ask."

"No need. You're both American, military trained. But just as clearly, no longer in the military. Your partner didn't say your *boss* told you where to find me, or your CO. He said *the man who hired us*. So I'm guessing you two are freelance. Probably began work at a PMC. Until recently, that is, when you decided to go even *more* freelance."

Quinn could tell from the glances they exchanged that he had scored a direct hit. Private Military Corporations, or PMCs, were organizations of mercenary soldiers who performed ops in numerous countries engaged in hostilities, most often at the behest of the US government. These businesses had grown so quickly over the past two decades that their membership now dwarfed that of the entire US military.

"So what PMC were you with?" continued Quinn. "Probably one of the best. Blackwater? Kroll? Sandline?" he guessed. "You worked at one of these for a time and then got an illegitimate offer you couldn't refuse." He shook his head in disgust. "And here you are," he added in contempt, "like trained dogs."

"Really?" said the pony-tailed mercenary, shaking his head in amusement. "You're giving *us* the Boy Scout speech? You think your attempt to assassinate the President of the United States gives *you* the moral high ground?"

Quinn ignored him. "So the question isn't who you are. The question is: who do you work for? And more importantly, what do you want with me?"

"Nice analysis, Agent Quinn," said the clean-cut merc. "You're even sharper than I thought you'd be. As to who we work for, I can't tell you. As to what they want with you, all I can tell you is that our instructions are to capture you and babysit until our employer gets here." He shrugged. "Apparently, he's eager to meet you."

"Why?" asked Quinn reflexively, knowing he wouldn't get an answer.

What was going on? How had he been found so easily? And what could anyone want with him now? Why capture and hold the most wanted man in America if you had no interest in bringing him to justice?

Quinn's ability to imagine plots and ambushes others might have hatched was nearly unequaled, but he couldn't come up with a single idea of what this might be about. He considered that Davinroy was behind it, but ruled this out immediately. After all, if this were the case, Quinn would be dead already.

Whoever was responsible had gone to a lot of trouble and expense to capture and hold him. And no matter how good they were, they were taking quite a risk getting anywhere near someone as scorching hot as he now was.

While Quinn was deep in thought, the tall mercenary had been busily manipulating his phone, ignoring Quinn's question as expected. "I just notified our employer that you are safely in our hands," he announced.

"How soon until he arrives?" asked Quinn.

"We were told we might have to babysit you for two or three days," answered the taller merc, who seemed to be the one in charge. "It all depends on when he can get here."

"Why not take me to *him*?"

The man laughed. "Good one, Agent Quinn. This must be your version of an idiot test. Okay, I'll play. Because he can move about freely, and you can't. See, he didn't just try to assassinate President Matthew Davinroy."

After a short pause, the mercenary's grin turned into a frown. "Speaking of which," he said to his partner, who still had his gun trained on Quinn, despite his captive's state of immobility, "now that he's secured, we need to take precautions so we aren't surprised by a group trying to arrest him."

He ordered Quinn to sit cross-legged on the filthy, eroding wooden slats that passed for the shack's floor. The zip-ties binding Quinn's legs left just enough freedom of motion for him to comply with this demand, albeit with some difficulty. In this position, the two mercenaries could turn their backs on him for several seconds if they wanted without fear of attack.

The mercenary in charge ordered his phone to call up public domain satellite imagery and display a topographical map of the area, centered on their current GPS coordinates and extending out for four miles in every direction. He set the phone on the floor and it began projecting a red, holographic map, as instructed, about five feet on a side.

Both mercenaries walked around the floating 3-D image of the elevated ground they were now on, giving it careful study. After several minutes of this the man in charge turned to his partner and said, "I'll watch Quinn. You put up cameras and sensor alarms here, here, and here," he instructed.

These would cover the dirt road that snaked up to the summit they were on, along with the two paved arteries that led to the dirt road. He then chose six other locations for the placement of surveillance devices, giving the two men visibility on all likely ground assaults.

Quinn noted with interest that they had set up the surveillance exactly the way he was planning to do once he had obtained the proper supplies.

"I'll need three or four hours to get everything installed," said the stocky mercenary.

"Understood."

"So what if the people hunting for him do close in before our guy gets here? What then?"

"If that happens, our orders are to kill him," responded his partner, looking down at Quinn and shooting him an apologetic look. "And then to get the hell out of here. Sorry, Quinn. But our employer must not want you *that* bad."

He smiled. "On the other hand, if you're half as good as I think you are, these precautions are just a formality. No one will find you. And my employer tells me that, at least at the moment, no one looking for you has the faintest idea where you are."

Quinn's eyes narrowed in thought. Who could possibly be behind this? Who could find him with seemingly effortless efficiency while at the same time having insight into the efforts of the multitudes now hunting for him? This was perhaps the most impenetrable mystery he had ever encountered.

The stocky mercenary left the shack to carry out his surveillance mission while his partner killed the map and retrieved his phone. He then spent several minutes absorbed by his electronic companion, leaving Quinn alone with his thoughts.

"I need to make a short trip outside," said Quinn, breaking the long silence. "Nature calls."

The mercenary hesitated.

"If you don't mind watching me pee," said Quinn, "I don't mind peeing while you hold a gun on me."

Without waiting for permission, Quinn uncrossed his legs and managed to rise to a standing position. He nodded toward the zip-ties around his ankles. "Or are you worried I'll sprint away from you? I'm pretty sure I can reach speeds of a tenth of a mile an hour, maybe more."

"After you," said the man with the gun, gesturing toward the open door.

Quinn began to waddle forward. As he reached the point closest to his captor, he pretended to trip. The mercenary instinctively moved forward to try to catch him and Quinn acted, launching himself at his adversary with all of his might. Both men crashed to the floor, barely missing the jagged edge of a broken floorboard. The merc recovered and rose to a standing position while Quinn flailed at the man's arms, scratching and clawing for all he was worth.

The mercenary was an experienced soldier and made sure to keep his gun beyond the reach of his bound prisoner, who was no match for him in his restrained state. He shoved Quinn back to the floor, kicking him savagely several times in the side and chest.

"*What are you thinking?*" he demanded.

Quinn groaned in pain and rolled onto his back.

"You had no chance!" continued the mercenary in contempt. "For someone who's supposed to have elite skills, you're a major disappointment. This is the best you can do? Embarrass yourself by trying to scratch me like a pathetic *little girl?*"

Quinn pushed himself to a seated position. "I didn't *try* to scratch you," he said calmly. "I *did* scratch you. Notice that you're bleeding."

The man looked down at several millimeter-thin red lines on his left arm, where Quinn had just managed to break the skin with his nails. He shook his head and laughed. "Well, in that case," he said sarcastically, "I stand corrected. You should be proud."

"Oh, I am," replied Quinn. "*Very*. I don't know what you know about last night, but I never planned to use a gun on Davinroy. I tried to *poison* him first." He raised his eyebrows. "I slipped an ultra-pure form of cyanide into his drink. Had the bastard actually taken a sip, he would have died a million times over. I knew this would leave just the faintest traces of cyanide on my fingertips and under my nails, but I figured I'd have plenty of time to scrub it away afterward."

The merc's eyes widened in alarm.

"Turns out I never did get the chance to wash up," continued Quinn. "Go figure. And while this trace residual amount isn't enough to be deadly if ingested, I managed to deposit it directly into your *bloodstream.* My guess is that you now have between two and five hours before paralysis and heart failure set in."

Quinn glared at the merc with a feral intensity. "But sorry my attack was such a disappointment to you," he said icily.

17

The tall mercenary stood at a boundary of light and darkness in the dingy structure and glanced down at the scratches on his arm once again, and then back at his prisoner, studying him. His panic of a moment before had given way to a calm resolve. "You're bluffing," he said.

Quinn laughed. "Sure I am."

"You tried to *shoot* the president. Even my sources know that much. This poisoning fiction is just the product of a desperate mind."

"Keep telling yourself that if it makes you feel better. But if you want to live, cut me loose now. The guy I got the poison from told me about a simple antidote. But one you won't find by searching online. If we leave now, we could be at a drug store in an hour, and I can give you what you need with time to spare."

"Just cut you loose?" said the merc in amusement. "I suppose you'll want your gun back too?"

Quinn smiled. "As a matter of fact, yes. And I'll want *your* weapons as well. You'll be driving, while I hold a gun on you."

"You have balls the size of Texas, Agent Quinn, I'll give you that. But I won't be surrendering. Instead, how about I just shoot you between the eyes right now and be done with this idiocy?"

"You won't do that," said Quinn, shaking his head. "Because you know that if I'm telling the truth, killing me is the same as killing yourself. And if I'm lying, you piss off your employer and lose a big payday."

"I'm sure as hell not going to surrender to you."

"Yes you are. Because if you do, I promise you'll survive. I'll escape, yes, but I'll leave you poison-free, unharmed, and alive. And you've studied my background. You know I'm a man of my word. I have my . . . issues . . . with Matthew Davinroy, but you know if I tell you I'll leave you unmolested, you can believe it."

The mercenary remained silent for an extended period as he wrestled with conflicting thoughts. "You've played this brilliantly, Agent Quinn," he said finally. "But the book on you says you're as creative as they come. Few men could manufacture an elaborate bluff like this on the fly, and make it seem so compelling. But *you* could. You tried to *shoot* Davinroy, plain and simple. So I choose to ignore your little gambit and to continue with my original plan, as though this never happened."

Quinn cursed inwardly. He couldn't have sold his bluff any harder. The cyanide tablet he had dropped into Davinroy's drink had been coated with a substance that ensured no trace amounts of the poison would be left on his fingers or nails, a substance that would only dissolve and release its payload when it came into contact with large amounts of liquid. He would never have been sloppy enough to let the poison contact his skin. And there were no antidotes to this cyanide, secret or otherwise. But he really thought the merc would buy it.

Quinn did have one card left to play, however. "Your employer seems to know everything," he said. "So check with him. If he vouches for what I'm telling you, maybe you'll see reason. You know," he added with an insincere smile, "before your heart stops."

"Is that supposed to scare me?"

"Absolutely," said Quinn. He nodded at the merc's phone. "Go ahead. Check it out. The life you save just might be your own."

The merc frowned and began composing a text message to his employer, being sure not to reveal the quagmire he had gotten himself into. *You said Quinn would be rational*, he typed. *But he's ranting about trying to poison Davinroy, when it's clear he tried to shoot him. If he's delusional, I need to know it. Any intel to support this poison claim?*

"Okay, Agent Quinn," said the merc after hitting the send button. "We'll play it your way. Why not? We'll know any minute."

"I *already* know," snapped Quinn, with far more confidence than he felt.

While Cris Coffey had discovered by now that he had tried to poison the president, he was sure Coffey would limit this information to a handful of people. The chances that this mystery employer would be in the know were so close to zero as to be meaningless. On the other hand, the chances that he would know exactly where to find Quinn were pretty small also. If he did somehow know about the poisoning, this would be more than a little scary.

The merc's phone chimed, indicating he had received a reply to his text, the burst of sound such a stark contrast to the deep silence that had preceded it that it seemed to fill the entire small enclosure. Quinn's captor looked down. *I can confirm Quinn tried to poison Davinroy before any guns came out,* read the text. *He used a highly potent version of cyanide. On another topic, I may arrive as early as tomorrow. I'll keep you posted.*

Quinn didn't need to be told that the man's employer had confirmed his poisoning claim. Even in the dim light Quinn could see the mercenary whiten as he read the message. He looked as though he might vomit, and his gaze immediately returned to the scratches on his arm once again, almost against his will.

Quinn felt a surge of relief. He didn't have time to dwell on what this accurate intel implied about the reach of his hidden adversary, but he would consider it at length the first chance he had.

"Seems you weren't bluffing after all," said the man. He paused for a moment in thought. "But I won't be surrendering," he added with a sudden dark intensity, his jaw tightening in resolve. "Instead, *you're* going to tell me how to make the antidote. If not, I'll take out your left kneecap. Then your right. Then I'll use my knife to chop off your fingers, one at a time. You get the idea."

Quinn moved his left leg closer to his captor, and gestured toward his kneecap with his head. "Fire away," he said calmly. "Just know that if you harm me in any way, there's no coming back. You start down that path and I promise you, we both die. No amount of torture will get you that antidote. But if you surrender, we both live. It's as simple as that."

The two men locked eyes in a staring contest that seemed to last for ages, but in the end, the mercenary folded, as Quinn knew he ultimately would. A few minutes later the tables had been turned. The mercenary cut the zip-ties that were binding Quinn and surrendered his phone and weapons.

When this transfer was completed, Quinn blew out a deep breath. "We'd better get moving," he said, receiving no argument on this point.

He followed the mercenary to his car, a sleek 2022 Tesla, which explained why Quinn hadn't heard it. Battery-powered cars were far more stealthy than their gasoline exploding brethren, and the two mercs had left the car and walked the last thirty yards to the shed on foot.

Quinn knew the men who had come for him were experienced and professional. They would be well prepared, most likely harboring a veritable arsenal in the trunk of the Tesla.

"Before we get you . . . detoxified," said Quinn, "I need you to fetch a tranq gun from your goodie bag."

The merc wasted no time. He popped the car's trunk and rummaged through a large gray rucksack, stuffed to the gills with weapons and supplies, finding a tranquilizer gun almost immediately. He tossed it to Quinn. "Let's get moving already," he said, glancing anxiously at his arm.

Quinn pocketed the tranquilizer gun and extended the lethal one his prisoner had given him. "About that," he began. "The truth is, we can stay right here. You were right. I *was* bluffing."

The man screamed a curse at Quinn while his face turned a beet red.

"You aren't looking on the bright side," said Quinn. "You're perfectly fine. No danger of not getting an antidote in time. Now, I did promise to leave you alive and unharmed," he added. "And I will leave you alive. The *unharmed* part, however, will depend on how much you cooperate."

The man glared at him but said nothing

"Who do you work for?" demanded Quinn

The man studied the gun pointed at him and then stared once again into Quinn's eyes, taking his measure. He must have decided that Quinn wasn't bluffing this time, because his bitter expression was replaced by one of resignation. "I don't know," he replied. "I've never met him, and I know nothing about him. He contacted us, wired good faith money into our accounts, and we began working for him. About a month ago."

"Come on. You can do better than that."

"You can threaten me, or torture me, but I can't tell you what I don't know. You really think a guy this good, this connected, is going to tell me who he is?"

Quinn decided that the man made an excellent point.

"We talk over the phone and text each other," continued the mercenary, "but that's it. Thirty minutes before he arrived he was going to have us tie you down and move out. Get started on our next assignment. So he could arrive unseen by us. No one gets to know who he is."

"Except me," said Quinn.

"Right."

"Which means he had no intention of leaving me alive after he got whatever it is he wanted."

"Probably not," acknowledged the mercenary.

Quinn reached into his pocket with his left hand and removed the phone he had taken from his new prisoner. It was a custom model, sure to be completely untraceable. "Is he in here?"

"Yes. Under the name 302. That's what he told us to call him."

"And you have no idea what this is about?"

"None at all. Find you, hold you. That's all."

For some reason, Quinn believed him. "What's he sound like?" he asked.

"His voice is average. Not deep or high-pitched. His English is good, but he has a Russian accent."

Now *this* was a valuable piece of intel. Assuming it was true. Around the turn of the century, Russia had become largely innocuous, but many years later Vladimir Putin had thrust Russia back onto the world stage with a vengeance. He and other Russian leaders had been making moves to help the country fully regain its former glory ever since. This was likely a very important piece to a puzzle Quinn was unable to even begin to solve.

Quinn was about to end the interview when one last question occurred to him. "You mentioned your boss wanted you to move on to your next assignment just before he arrived here," he said. "What next assignment?"

The merc hesitated.

"Are you really going to hold out now?" said Quinn. "Answer me on this and we're done. You get out of this without a scratch." He glanced at the man's arm and couldn't help but smile. "Well, without *another* scratch," he amended.

The man sighed heavily. "Okay. Why not?" he said. "When you go through my phone you'll find it anyway. We were told to take out a woman in the Boston area. Rachel Howard."

"Who is she?"

"Don't know. Haven't begun planning. Her photo and bio are on my phone. And instructions from 302. All I know is that he wants her to stop being alive."

Quinn was satisfied with this answer. "Thank you," he said, removing the dart gun from his left pocket. Without saying another word he shot the mercenary in the leg, and watched as he crumpled to the dirt, unconscious.

18

Quinn stood over the unconscious mercenary's head and pulled him by his armpits toward the back of the Tesla. He would hide him in the trunk so he'd be out of sight of his partner, whom Quinn would ambush and put into dreamland as well when he returned from his mission.

As Quinn crossed a border between brown dirt and green grass he noticed a tiny shimmer on the man's shoulder, which happened to be just a foot away from Quinn's face as he dragged the man's body. He leaned closer, but the shimmer disappeared. He was about to write it off as a figment of his imagination when some sixth sense of his insisted that he not. His intuition had served him well, and he had learned not to ignore it.

He studied the mercenary's right shoulder from several angles, and when he hit one that showed the shoulder against a multicolored background, the image of a housefly came vaguely into focus.

What in the world? thought Quinn. A fly that could blend in with its surroundings? What, a fly with chameleon DNA mixed in?

But even as he thought this the fly suddenly became visible from all angles, as though it knew he was suspicious of it and had decided to appear more ordinary.

Quinn was left with only one conclusion: it must be mechanical. But as he studied it further, it began to rub its tiny legs together, and even though it was missing a wing, he realized that no forgery could possibly be this perfect. And yet, as absurd, as ridiculous a supposition as this was, he was convinced he was right.

It must be the ultimate Micro Air Vehicle, abbreviated as MAV. Drones of all kinds now filled the skies, recreational and otherwise, and the military variety had gotten smaller and smaller over many years. But as far as he knew, no one had come close to creating a perfect, working mechanical fly.

Until now, perhaps.

Which would explain so much. What advantages would someone gain if they could become a fly on the wall—literally?

Intelligence gathering would be revolutionized. The MAV that Quinn was staring at now could be camouflaged, made almost invisible. And if someone did happen to see it from just the right angle, they would only be seeing a harmless housefly, easy to dismiss.

This fly must be beaming Quinn's location to an interested party, or even video and audio. He guessed it had begun its mission at Garza's mansion, at the fundraiser. Why not? Spying on the president perhaps? When Quinn had made his move against Davinroy, its operator had sent it on a new mission: stick to Quinn. Like glue.

Or like a fly.

It could have been clinging to his back while he nearly broke the sound barrier in Garza's Maserati, saving battery power and wear and tear on its wings. The Russian—302—must have sent it. That's how he knew where to find Quinn, and even the best time and way for his hired guns to approach him. And also how he knew Quinn had tried to use poison on the president. He must have sent another drone to be a fly on Cris Coffey's wall.

The MAV could have become damaged when he had dived into the mercenary and they had grappled in the shack, which might explain how it had ended up on the merc's shoulder. Or else its operator had decided to move it there for a better vantage point, and it had later become damaged all the same.

Which explained why it wasn't trying to fly away now.

What the hell had he gotten himself into? And if this device *had* been perfected by the Russians, the US could be in a world of hurt. This had suddenly become bigger than Matthew Davinroy. Quinn may have tried to eliminate the president, but he was still a patriot. He still loved his country, despite the monster currently at its helm.

So his mission parameters had expanded. He now had two impossible missions. Kill the president. And find the Russian who was calling himself 302.

19

Quinn lowered the mercenary to the ground, keeping his eyes locked on the housefly that wasn't a housefly. When it had possessed both of its wings, he wondered if it had been as agile as a real fly.

A fly's range of vision and reflexes were too great for most people to have any chance of catching one. Bring a hand down from any position above the fly, with almost any speed, and it would deftly escape the trap racing toward it.

But he had learned as a boy how to catch one. Every time. How to kill one with his hands. Every time.

First, wait until the fly had landed on a roughly level surface. Once this happened, killing it was as simple as carefully planting both hands on either side of it, knife-edged on the surface, with palms facing each other. Center the fly between the hands and then slide them together as quickly as possible, ending in a clap. A fly would always try to escape upward, but it could only make it halfway up the giant wall of hands closing in on it before being smashed in between.

Catching one worked the same way. Plant one hand to the side of the fly and slide it toward the target as fast as possible, closing the hand the moment it was reached. Quinn had done this countless times as a boy, a feat that never failed to impress other kids.

Unfortunately, the drone's position on the merc's shoulder didn't give Quinn enough runway for this maneuver. Even so, given the damage the fly had suffered, he had high hopes that a less strategically sound grab would prove doable.

Quinn launched his right hand at the fly like his life depended on it. The tiny MAV made an attempt to launch itself into the air, even with a single wing, but Quinn was able to snatch it up, keeping his hand in a tight fist so it couldn't escape.

At least for the moment. He didn't want to hold it for long, in case it had some tricks up its sleeve, like an ability to bore through soft flesh.

Quinn popped the trunk of the Tesla and emptied his pockets as quickly as he could. There must be something in the car or his pockets he could use to cage the drone. He considered pressing it into the magazine of a gun, like it was a round. Might work, but it wasn't ideal.

His eyes lit up like fireworks when he spied a tiny canister attached to the Tesla's key fob. It was a steel LED flashlight, bright blue, the size of a woman's pinky. It was *perfect.* He managed to unscrew it with one hand and then dumped out the tiny battery inside.

As a kid he had learned that shaking his fist for several seconds, hard, would stun the fly inside, so he could let it go or transfer it elsewhere, and it would act like a drunken sailor. He couldn't make an artificial fly dizzy, but he was willing to bet that he could temporarily disorient any motion sensors inside.

He shook his right fist vigorously for almost fifteen seconds and then opened his hand, quickly funneling the fly into the tiny steel container. *Success.* He hastily screwed the lid closed and held the tiny blue canister up to his face.

The individual technologies inside this makeshift prison alone must be worth billions. But the exact combination of these technologies that had resulted in a fly drone of this sophistication would fetch a price that was truly staggering.

Quinn thought for a few moments and then dialed the phone he had taken, audio only. "Hello, Cris," he said when the phone was answered. "We need to talk."

"Kevin?" said Cris Coffey in disbelief. "Is that you?"

"Is your line secure?"

"Of course," replied Coffey.

Quinn could hear any number of people mulling about in the background, but this noise was rapidly diminishing as his former boss was no doubt rushing away from them, seeking privacy and quiet so he wouldn't miss a single word. Quinn knew he had Coffey's full attention.

"You can try to trace this call," said Quinn, "but trust me, you'll be wasting your time."

"Why did you call, Kevin?"

"What do you know about micro drones? MAVs? Specifically, the quest to make one that could pass for a housefly? One so perfect, so real, it could fool *other* flies?"

"What's this got to do with anything?"

"Answer me, Cris. How well-informed are you about this tech?"

"Very," said Coffey. "You know I spent a long time in Black Ops. A fly-drone was the holy grail. But we're a decade away. It's like AI, we keep thinking we can do it, and it keeps being a harder problem than we realize."

"Why is that?" asked Quinn.

He knew Coffey would keep talking no matter what the subject. He wouldn't take Quinn's word that the call was untraceable. And even if it was, the longer Coffey could keep him on the line the more chance he might learn something valuable, or talk him in.

"Well," began Coffey, "you could control the broad movements and behaviors of such a fly from a remote location. Theoretically. But to be truly effective, it would need to be able to act autonomously, when cut off from an operator. First, there is an operator time lag, even at the speed of light, which creates more difficulty than you might imagine. And you can't avoid blockages or interruptions to a signal. So you'd want to program in a destination and let the drone do its thing. So the operator can be passive for the most part, and obtain input from multiple flies."

"Makes sense," said Quinn. "Go on."

"Currently, even operator-dependent flies pose insurmountable challenges. But autonomous ones are out of the question. Biological systems are much more efficient than mechanical in many ways. Think about what a fly can do, with a brain the size of a pinhead. It can process enough visual information to choke a supercomputer, and it can take evasive action. It can avoid obstacles and predators.

It can find and metabolize food, allowing it to cover great distances with no need for a battery or external power source. You get the idea. As astonishing as our chips are now, constructing one with the enormous computing power needed, but small enough to fit into a fly, can't be done.

"And don't get me started on the battery power needed, the mechanical challenges, and so on. To get it to move with the agility and evasiveness of a real fly would be an extraordinary achievement, but even real flies succumb to predators, so you'd want to do even better. A perfect fly drone would seem to the uninformed to be much easier to perfect than many of the miracles science has managed already, but it's just the opposite."

"So you're telling me the US doesn't have this technology working?"

"Not a chance. I'm not sure of many things, but I am sure of this."

The certainty in Coffey's voice and manner was enough to convince Quinn that this was the truth, and it matched the more limited intel he had heard through the grapevine. "Then we've got a big problem, Cris."

"What are you talking about?"

"Long story short, while running from you, I was captured by two mercs. Ex-military. The man who hired them wanted to see me. I have no idea why. I'm not sure about this, but I have reason to believe he's a Russian."

"A Russian?" repeated Coffey skeptically.

"I know. None of it makes sense. But something big is going on. I have no idea how I play into it, but I do. And it gets even stranger. I managed to escape. But I've since learned how they were able to find me. Whoever is behind this has perfected a micro drone. A perfect copy of a housefly. The one you say is impossible."

"Kevin, I . . ."

"I know you don't believe me. I don't blame you. But if you had this fly in your hands, could you get it analyzed by someone you trust? Through back channels? I'd need you to keep this completely off the radar. Any knowledge of it kept between you and this one other person. We have no idea who knows what, even in our own government, so you'd have to make this the ultimate secret."

Coffey sighed loudly. "I could have it analyzed as you ask, yes. But I'm sure you're mistaken about what you think you've found."

"I hope I am. But I have the fly, and I'm going to mail it to you. Because as much as I want Davinroy dead, I still love my country. And this is important. So prove me wrong about this drone. Or prove me right, and then take it from there."

"Sure, Kevin. Send me the fly. I'll take a look."

"Don't patronize me!" screamed Quinn. "I know you and I know your voice. You're just humoring me. Like I'm a mental patient. Promise me you'll at least check it out, even if you're sure I'm wrong. Promise me! I know you're a man of your word, Cris."

"I will," said Coffey. "I swear it."

"Good," said Quinn, satisfied. "I'll send it."

He planned to find a courier service in the area so his ex-boss could get the canister in hours rather than days, but he couldn't tell him this, or Coffey would have every courier service in the region monitored.

"Whatever you think of me now," added Quinn, "I'm still one of the good guys. I have reason to want Davinroy dead, but I'm still loyal to my country, and even to you." He paused. "And you have to admit, this isn't exactly an ideal time for me to be calling and mailing you packages. I'll contact you later so you can let me know what you learn."

"Kevin, why don't you come in? Let's talk this over in person. You can be involved in the MAV study yourself."

The tone in Coffey's voice made Quinn's blood begin to boil. He still thought Quinn was crazy.

Quinn took a deep breath and forced himself to calm down. How could he blame his former boss for thinking this of him? Of course he did. Coffey thought he was mad when he had tried to take out the president, and this fly business only added fuel to that fire.

"Cris, I respect you more than any person I've ever worked with. Really. And I want nothing more than for us to be on the same side again. So promise me one last thing. Promise me you'll investigate Davinroy. He has a system of tunnels under a number of rooms at the Catskill Mountain retreat. Find them. Find evidence. Davinroy is a monster. The tunnel system isn't a smoking gun, but it's a start. You have to admit, if you find these secret tunnels, my story is starting to look at least a little more credible."

There was no response.

"Humor me, Cris," implored Quinn. "What I told you about Nicole is true. Look into it. Promise me you will."

Coffey hesitated. "Kevin, I don't know the right way to proceed here. I don't know how fragile you are. But I am a man of my word, and I can't make that promise."

"*Why not?*" thundered Quinn. "Davinroy is good, I get that! Persuasive! I know it seems far-fetched that the president is the monster I paint him to be. But you've known me for *years*! How can you be so absolutely certain that my accusations aren't true? How are you so convinced that I've lost my mind?"

Coffey let out a long sigh. "Kevin," he said, "I am truly sorry. You are a very good man. But I know a hundred percent that Davinroy didn't torture and kill your wife."

"How can you be so goddamned sure!" screamed Quinn.

There was a long pause. "Because you don't *have* a wife," replied Coffey grimly. "You never did."

The world spun around Quinn's head like he was on a rocket-propelled merry-go-round. He was suddenly weak and light-headed. "What?" he whispered into the phone in horror. "*What are you talking about?* You *know* I had a wife. Nicole! And a daughter on the way."

"I'm sorry, Kevin. You never married. There is no Nicole. And you weren't even *at* Davinroy's retreat this year. You were invited to be a guest instructor that week for the Navy SEALS in Coronado,

California. Google yourself and you'll learn I'm right. And then come in and get some help," pleaded Coffey.

But Quinn didn't reply. The phone slipped from his fingers and he fell to his knees.

His world continued to spin around him at a furious pace, and he fought back vomit.

PART 2
Omniscient

Omniscient: (adjective): possessed of universal or complete knowledge

—MerriamWebster.com

"Yet misattributions in remembering are surprisingly common. Sometimes we remember events that never happened, misattributing vivid images that spring to mind to memories of past events that did not occur. At other times we mistakenly take credit for a thought, when in reality we are recalling it—without awareness—from something we read or heard. Misattribution can alter our lives in strange and unexpected ways."

—Professor Daniel L. Schacter, Head of the Schacter Memory Lab at Harvard University, and former chairman of the Harvard Psychology Department

"Neuroscientists have taken advantage of these clues to explore the strong links between imagination and memory, to demonstrate how social factors influence our recollections, and to show how memory may actually have evolved to predict the future rather than keep track of the past. There is arguably little evolutionary advantage to being able to recall the past in vivid detail; it is much more useful to be able to use past experience to predict what comes next."

— Charles Fernyhough, *Time* Magazine, March 20, 2013

"Most of what we do and think and feel is not under our conscious control. The vast jungles of neurons operate their own programs. The conscious you—the I that flickers to life when you wake up in the morning—is the smallest bit of what's transpiring in your brain. Although we are dependent on the functioning of the brain for our inner lives, it runs its own show. Most of its operations are above the security clearance of the conscious mind. The I simply has no right of entry. Your consciousness is like a tiny stowaway on a transatlantic steamship, taking credit for the journey without acknowledging the massive engineering underfoot.

"Your most fundamental drives are stitched into the fabric of your neural circuitry, and they are inaccessible to you. You find certain things more attractive than others, and you don't know why. Like your enteric nervous system and your sense of attraction, almost the entirety of your inner universe is foreign to you. The ideas that strike you, your thoughts during a daydream, the bizarre content of your nightdreams—all of these are served up to you from unseen intracranial caverns."

—David Eagleman, *Incognito*

20

Kevin Quinn loaded the merc's body into the trunk of the Tesla in a daze. He then managed to stumble back to the shack with the large rucksack that contained the mercs' cache of weaponry and supplies.

He entered the structure and laid on his back on the deteriorating gray floorboards in one dark corner, struggling for some semblance of equilibrium. He closed his eyes, his mind still reeling, struck by how fitting it was to be in a dark, rotting structure contemplating his own mind, one that had suddenly taken on these same characteristics.

If the second mercenary arrived back from his mission a few hours early, Quinn would be toast, but he couldn't bring himself to care.

He had Googled himself on the merc's phone as Coffey had suggested and verified what his former boss had said: he *was* listed as having been a guest instructor for the SEALS in Coronado during the week of Davinroy's retreat. It was always possible the Web entries for this had been doctored, but why?

If Coffey had been right about this, could the rest of his claims be true as well? Quinn was terrified by what an examination of his past might reveal. Even the thought of exploring this further sent a shiver down his spine.

But such an examination could not be avoided, no matter how scared he was. He took a deep breath, closed his eyes even tighter, and thought back to his first date with Nicole, their first kiss. The first time they had made love.

His breath caught in his throat as his worst fears were immediately realized: he was drawing an absolute blank. He had a memory of what an extraordinary woman she had been, and how very much he had loved her. But in the abstract. There were no *specific* memories to support these overarching ones.

Which was impossible. Yes, many men weren't good at remembering anniversaries and birthdays, or what their spouse was wearing on their first date, but there wasn't a one who didn't remember his first date with his future wife, or their first kiss.

And what about Hailey? He thought back to the pregnancy. Nothing.

He tried to recall how they had decided on the name *Hailey*. Again, nothing.

He had absolutely no recollection of her conception. Of Nicole's pregnancy. *Nothing*.

So everything Coffey had claimed was true. He had never married. There was no Nicole, no Hailey. And no torture and murder, even though the memory of both continued to be stubbornly persistent, as much a part of him as his arm. He had been driven so single-mindedly to revenge that, if not for Coffey, would he ever have realized that the existence of his wife and daughter didn't hold up to a more comprehensive scrutiny?

Were *any* of his memories accurate?

Nothing could be as disorienting, as *devastating*, as learning that the most powerful, life-changing memories you've ever had were unreal, imaginary. If you couldn't trust a memory this profound, this visceral, what could you trust?

He had been driven to desperation. He had tried to kill an innocent man!

This new perspective explained so much. How the president had managed to drug him so easily. How tunnel entrances could be hidden inside closets for decades without a single guest, a single rowdy kid, having discovered one.

This explained why his recollections were so spotty. He could remember Davinroy's horrific words with almost photographic detail, every one of them scorched into his mind. But *images* were hazy, undefined. He couldn't recall the hidden structure in the Catskills he had stumbled upon, or how he had managed to gain entry. And how could he have been inside long enough to see the president delivering killing blows to his wife without moving to stop him much sooner?

And while the president could be many things, duplicitous, narcissistic, self-serving, and wrong-headed, it had always seemed surreal to Quinn that he had transformed into such a caricature of a psychopathic villain. The more he considered what he thought had happened, the more flaws he found in the logic of the situation.

This also explained why no one had given him the benefit of the doubt. Because he didn't deserve it.

So how had this happened? It could be that the memory erasure drug he remembered receiving was real, but delivered by someone else in a different setting. Perhaps when he had thrown off the effects his wires had gotten crossed, somehow converting a nightmare starring an imaginary wife into an indelible memory.

Or he could be stark, raving, mad? How would he know otherwise? In fact, how could he know *anything*? His entire sense of self was shaken to his very core. Was his name really Kevin Quinn? Impossible to know.

He believed he was sane and that his memories of everything but the torture and murder were accurate. But there was no way to be certain. Sleepers believed their dreams were real until they awoke. Schizophrenics had absolute belief in their delusions.

Quinn could well be psychotic, imagining that he was in a shack, imagining a fly drone, imagining his recent conversation with Coffey. He could be a late-stage Alzheimer's patient, whose brain had temporarily come to life to create random memories. His time on the run and on this mountain seemed quite extensive, but experiments had shown dreams could impart the illusion of duration, even when they were seconds long. The mind played tricks on itself.

It was possible Quinn had come into existence that very instant, but with a full set of memories. He couldn't know otherwise. Not for certain. This was a far-out conjecture made by philosophers and re-explored by a stoner friend of his who was higher than Mt. Everest at the time.

It was also possible that Quinn was the only thing in existence, that everything else was just an illusion. Again, this conjecture, no matter how ridiculous it seemed, could not be disproved.

Quinn might think there were billions of other beings on Earth and that he had interacted with many thousands, but what if this was all just his own overactive imagination? What if he was a god, the only being in existence, and had constructed the entire universe in his own mind to alleviate boredom?

Rene Descartes had famously concluded that it was impossible to know for certain if the input coming in through his senses, or anything he *thought* he knew, was real. It could all be an illusion, and he would have no way of knowing it. He then took this question one step further: could he even be certain that *he* existed?

Descartes realized that the answer to this question was *yes*. The act of pondering if he existed or not, *required* him to exist. This was, in fact, the *only* thing he could be certain of.

Cogito ergo sum, he had famously written. *I think, therefore I am.* Or more accurately, *I am thinking, therefore I must exist.*

Quinn shook his head to clear it. This thought process was getting him nowhere. His confidence about the nature of his reality had been shattered to its core, but he had to find a piece of wreckage and cling to it while the sea of confusion raged around him.

He removed the small blue canister now containing a fly drone from his pocket. It could well be yet another figment of his imagination. But even so, he decided he had to go forward under the assumption that it truly existed. That the incident with Davinroy at the retreat had not been real, but everything he had experienced since was. To believe anything else would quickly lead to paralysis and madness.

It was time to quit reeling from these profound revelations and get back to the business of living, of surviving.

He rose from the floor and moved to an illuminated section of the room. He took a careful inventory of the contents of the gray rucksack he had taken from the trunk of the Tesla. It contained everything his heart could possibly desire, except for his key fob cloner, which he would retrieve as soon as he put the other mercenary down.

He ignored all doubts about his grip on reality and thought about next moves for several minutes, replaying everything that had happened in his mind. First, he decided, he had a duty to warn the woman who was to be the next victim of the unseen puppet master. He removed the phone he had taken from his captor and searched for the bio of Rachel Howard. How did she play in?

"Who are you, Ms. Howard?" he mumbled to himself, but a moment later he found her bio and added, "or should I say, *Professor* Howard."

He was stunned as he finished reading her bio. Among other things, Rachel Howard was considered one of the world's foremost experts on the neurobiology of human memory. Incredible. This couldn't just be a coincidence. An expert in memory, just when he could use one of these the most.

He had planned to contact her, probably in person, and tell her what he knew, make sure she was as protected as possible. But now his interest in meeting her was considerably more urgent.

He found the Russian's instructions to the two men, which were quite simple, and supported what his prisoner had told him. Their orders were to go to Cambridge and kill Professor Rachel Howard, esteemed chair of Harvard's neuroscience department, as soon as their boss was about to arrive to retrieve Quinn. They were also told they didn't need to worry about making it look like an accident. Finally, 302 had made it clear that he didn't have her under surveillance. Since she made no effort to keep her whereabouts secret, and in fact published her daily schedule *online,* he was confident they could find her on their own.

Quinn decided this must mean that neither standard surveillance measures *nor* fly drones were in play. This was a relief. The rucksack had contained equipment designed to detect standard bugs and tracking devices, but his instincts told him the fly technology would be invisible to such equipment. But these fly drones would be expensive and likely a precious resource. Using one to surveil the president and then deploying it to stick to Quinn—literally—was one thing. Using one to surveil a sitting duck like Rachel Howard was another.

Quinn had listened to the car radio during his drive here the night before. Since the story of his attack on the president hadn't broken,

Davinroy must have decided to bury it so he could tidy things up. Quinn suspected this would continue for another day or so, but he would know for sure the moment he turned on the radio once again.

Regardless, his strategy was now clear. He would wait here to ambush the second mercenary upon his return, hitting him with a tranquilizer dart. Then he would zip-tie them each around the trunk of a slender tree in the woods. They would survive, as promised, but that didn't mean he had to make it easy on them.

After this he would don his trusty baseball cap, make a quick stop at a retail store to shore up his disguise, and have a tiny steel canister couriered to Cris Coffey. Finally, he would pay his respects to a certain neuroscience expert at Harvard University. A woman with an impeccable reputation who had somehow managed to show up at the top of a mercenary's hit list.

21

ABC News
Up-to-the-Minute Report
Online Coverage of Breaking News From Around the World
Monday, June 2

Chicago, Illinois: The storied Hamza mosque was burned to the ground late this morning in what authorities believe to be a terrorist attack, killing all of those inside. The current number of fatalities in the attack is unknown, but authorities believe it could be over two hundred, including the mosque's Imam, Azim Jafari, an outspoken leader well known for his criticism of Islamic extremism and his calls to end violence.

While authorities have only begun their investigation, a spokesman for the Department of Homeland Security (DHS) issued a brief statement, indicating that Jafari had been meeting with Muslims from around the country who shared his vision of peace and tolerance. It is believed that one or more extremists were able to infiltrate this gathering and set off a highly combustible gas.

So far, no terrorist group has taken credit for this massacre. The DHS spokesman had no knowledge of motive, but speculation is that this was carried out by extremists to silence those in the Muslim community who were critical of a radicalized interpretation of the religion, and who had the courage to speak out against those they believed were trying to hijack an otherwise peaceful faith.

While details of the events of this morning are still emerging, it is believed that DHS was alerted to a possible terrorist attack on the mosque, and was able to have the surrounding area evacuated before the fire and explosion. A DHS team on-site was in the process of attempting to contact the leader of this small group of terrorist infiltrators, to negotiate a peaceful resolution, when the mosque mushroomed into flames.

President Davinroy could not be reached for immediate comment, but his spokesman said he would be addressing the nation shortly. He added that the president is heartbroken over this heinous act of extremism that took so many good people, including Azim Jafari, a courageous man who died defending his ideals. Although unconfirmed, there have been rumors that the president will award Jafari a posthumous medal for his leadership and contributions to peace.

Azim Jafari grew up in San Diego, California, having . . .

22

Once Rachel Howard's graduate class had concluded, ten minutes after its scheduled end, she had spent the entire day working with Jason Balazs, one of the top professors in Harvard's mathematics department. She had been collaborating with him for weeks to refine an algorithm that could make sense of billions of patterns of neuronal connections in the brain, which explained why she was so burnt out and why her brain seemed to hurt, even though she knew better than anyone that there were no pain receptors in this all-important organ.

She had an excellent grasp of advanced mathematics, but Balazs was so beyond her she had to strain to her limits to understand even the rudiments of the mathematical models he was able to develop.

And she was starving. It wasn't quite six thirty at night, but while the muscles burned the highest quantity of all-purpose fuel, nothing burned through glucose more prodigiously than the three-pound dynamo between her ears, which had been running in fifth gear since late that morning.

She had ordered takeout from her favorite Thai restaurant, Siam Nara, which was only minutes away from her small colonial home in Waltham, Massachusetts.

Waltham was about seven miles west of Harvard's main campus, a distance that routinely took her between twenty-five and thirty minutes to cover. She didn't really mind the commute, and was thankful she was one of only a few people to rate a parking space right outside the neuroscience building that housed her office and labs.

Her home in Waltham was small, but after her divorce four years earlier from Ron Williams they had sold the Cambridge residence, and she was a woman of simple needs. The homes surrounding Cambridge had become ever more pricey over the years, and she couldn't justify buying a new one on a single salary.

She would have liked to blame her husband for their marital difficulties, if it weren't for the stubborn fact that it was all her fault. The truth was that she was too involved with her work—far more so than he was. Neuroscience was all-consuming to her, and she would rather be uncovering the secrets of this realm than going to movies or parties, or doing any of the myriad other activities that couples did together.

When she had decided she didn't want to take time out for motherhood, ignoring instincts screaming for her to reproduce, this was the straw that broke the marriage's back. Ron had wanted badly to be a father, and she knew he would be remarkable in this role.

He had been a good man, and she had been a good woman, but this didn't always mean things were destined to work out. She had been twenty-nine at the time, dazzling the neuroscience world with work heralded by all as brilliant and paradigm-shifting, first as a post-doc and then for two years as an associate professor.

She didn't divorce her husband because she had grown to hate him, but because she still loved him very much. Ron had been twenty-eight, and severing their marriage when she did was the most merciful thing she could do, giving him plenty of time to find and marry a partner who wanted kids as much as he did.

Two years earlier, he had done just this. At the age of thirty he had married a twenty-six year old, and she was currently pregnant with their second child. Rachel couldn't be happier for him.

Human beings were inscrutable things, and far less in conscious control of their decisions and behavior than anyone realized. Freud observed that many of his patients had no conscious knowledge of why they behaved the way they did, leading him to compare consciousness to the tip of an iceberg, with many of the true drivers of a person's thoughts and behaviors lurking below, hidden from even their own view.

And Freud, prophetic as he was, was only scratching the surface of the profound reality of this analogy. Rachel had studied neuroscience far too long and hard to spend unnecessary energy beating up on herself or regretting the course her life had taken. Human beings behaved the way they behaved, decided the way they decided, driven by an amalgam of genes and impulses and evolution and instincts and drives and mysterious unconscious controllers that fooled the conscience into believing it was in charge.

But Rachel Howard-Williams—now just Rachel Howard—knew better. The illusion of free will was flawless, but her species had far less of it than any would ever be able to truly accept.

Despite this unfortunate course correction in her life, Rachel had a cheerful disposition by nature and had decided she would likely remain single for the rest of her life, although she would date when she could. After all, she knew better than anyone the psychological importance of companionship, social bonds, touch, and sexual intimacy.

Rachel pulled into her favorite Thai restaurant and parked her car, a black Acura that was a hybrid between an undersized SUV and an oversized sedan. She was a regular at Siam Nara and was greeted warmly by several of the staff when she entered, which she decided either represented a great extension of her social web, or was pathetic and depressing, depending on the day she was having.

A few minutes later she left with her prize, crab rangoon and pad thai, which gave off a warmth and aroma that easily penetrated its paper prison, ratcheting up her hunger even further. She drove a few blocks before stopping at a red light, lost in thought, the radio on to provide background noise.

There was a faint thumping sound from the back of the SUV, behind the second row of beige leather seats. In a sedan, this is where the trunk would have been, but in her sedan-SUV hybrid it was a flat platform that served the same purpose, enclosed by a sleek hatchback.

She listened for a few seconds. There it was again, barely loud enough to hear. It almost sounded like someone was gently punching the soft leather back of one of the seats. She turned off the radio, intrigued and alert, and studied the back of the car in her rearview mirror. What car malfunction could possibly make this sound?

As she watched, a man's head rose above the second row of seats, the rest of his body still concealed behind them. Rachel gasped and jumped so forcefully that her seatbelt automatically tightened up against her, pinning her in place, before relaxing once again.

But her heart didn't relax. After almost bursting through her chest it was still pumping furiously at more than twice its normal rate, and Rachel found that she could no longer breathe.

This intruder in her car was so out of her realm of experience she couldn't have been more terrified and disoriented had a school of piranha fallen from the sky.

She had no idea how this man had gotten inside. And she had no idea what he wanted.

But she had little doubt that her life was now in serious danger.

23

Rachel wanted to spin around to confront the intruder but realized she was paralyzed. Instead, she could only study the man in her rearview mirror.

She was certain she had never seen him before. Only part of his head appeared above the row of seats, but from what she could see he was clean-cut and looked professional, although he was wearing a black baseball hat that seemed out of place somehow, as if he was trying too hard to look casual. A pair of too-large sunglasses were folded up and tucked into his breast pocket.

The man studied her image in the mirror in return and nodded, wearing an apologetic expression, perhaps trying to come across as unthreatening.

The intruder was handsome and controlled, and his eyes showed an alertness and intelligence, which in her view was preferred to wild eyes and a jumpy demeanor. Her instincts said he wasn't insane. A ruthless psychopath, possibly, but not crazy.

How could this man be in her car? She was certain she had locked up when she had parked at Siam Nara. She hit a button to unlock her doors so she would have the option of flight, but the locks clicked closed once again a moment later. This trespasser must somehow have a remote to her car. How could that be?

"I'm not going to hurt you, Professor," said the man, attempting to make his voice calm and reassuring. "Please don't run. I've learned that you're in danger, and I'm here to help."

Rachel tried to decide if she believed him, finding it hard to think with her heart continuing to pound away in her ears. She was still terrified, but the way her visitor had proceeded did give her reason to hope he was sincere in not wishing her harm.

Most importantly, he hadn't pulled a gun on her. He had also tried to lessen the shock his sudden appearance would cause her. By thumping on the back of the seat to get her attention first, he had ensured she was braced as much as possible before he revealed himself, rather than jumping up like a jack-in-the-box with no warning, which would have caused her to scream loudly enough to shatter glass and would have probably turned her hair white.

He had also waited until she was stopped at a light, so no matter how much his Houdini act had freaked her out there was no risk of an accident. This was the act of a sane and rational mind, supporting her initial impression. Hopefully.

"How did you get into my car?" she demanded. "Did you steal the backup remote from my house?"

"No, I used an electronic device that cloned your key fob," the man replied. He nodded toward the road ahead. "The light has turned green, Professor. Please drive. I'll answer all of your questions, I promise you."

Rachel pulled gingerly forward and began to pick up speed.

"Thank you," said the stranger earnestly.

Rachel kept her eyes on the road and took the next right turn, away from her house and toward the nearest police station, about three miles away, which was now her destination.

"My name is Kevin," continued the intruder. "Kevin Quinn. And I really am here to help. I need you to believe me. I realize my . . . approach makes me look like a bad guy. But I'm a highly trained American . . . operative, and your life is in jeopardy."

"An operative? You have to be kidding me. What is *that* supposed to mean? Like a spy?"

"Something like that."

"This is crazy! You do know I'm a harmless egghead, right? Not Bond, not Bourne—harmless egghead."

"Take a right here," said Quinn, gesturing at a wooden sign that read *St. Peter's Episcopal Church* and a parking lot that was empty. "Pull behind the building," he instructed, "and kill the ignition."

Rachel did as he asked.

"I'm going to join you in the front seat," said Quinn. "Not that riding around while kneeling in the back of your SUV isn't totally *normal*," he added wryly, "but being in the passenger's seat might raise fewer eyebrows. Not to mention making conversation easier."

The man continued to seem likable, but Rachel knew it could all be an act.

"While I'm popping the hatch, please don't try to run," he added. "I'm very fast, and I'd be forced to catch you—for your own good."

Rachel thought about flight, but decided she wouldn't have much of a chance.

Quinn proceeded to join her in the front seat, carrying a large gray rucksack that he placed on the floor before him, leaving barely enough room for his feet.

"That's better," he said once he had belted in beside her, placing the bag of Thai food on his lap.

She studied him further, and her instincts told her that she wasn't in danger. She had no idea if anything he said was true, but she sensed he really didn't wish her ill. And she knew better than anyone that her instincts had a better chance of being accurate than her rational mind.

He lifted the bag of food and extended it toward her. "Go ahead and eat before it gets cold. I'm sure you're hungry."

"I'll wait," said Rachel.

"Why? I've already eaten, and you obviously haven't. I really didn't mean to interrupt your meal." He grinned. "Well, other than popping out right after you bought it, and insisting that you not go home where you were planning to eat it. Other than that."

Rachel almost found herself smiling, but managed to maintain a stern expression. She decided not to argue further. And she *was* starving.

"Are you a neuroscientist?" she asked after she had swallowed her first bite.

"Not even close."

Wow, she had been in the lab too long. Had she really taken this intruder's insistence that she eat her dinner as a sign he was familiar with the Danziger study? She was truly losing it.

Years earlier, Shai Danziger had analyzed the rulings on thousands of prisoners coming before parole boards, looking at which of them were granted parole and which of them were not. After accounting for all other factors she had found that it wasn't age, looks, race, or nature of the crime that was the best predictor of whether a prisoner would be granted parole. It was the time of day of the hearing. If the hearing was just before lunch, when the board members were hungry, prisoners had only a twenty percent chance of a favorable outcome. If the hearing was just *after* lunch, on the other hand, this rose dramatically, to *sixty-five* percent.

The judges were certain their states of hunger or satiety had nothing to do with their purely rational, fact-based decisions, but the data showed otherwise. It showed that this hidden influence was profound. Yet another example of the consciousness being the last to know.

Rachel couldn't believe she had overanalyzed things to this degree. Of course this intruder wasn't aware of the Danziger study. He still might be trying to manipulate her, since everyone knew that people were grumpier and less cooperative when they were starving, but it was more likely he was just trying to be nice.

The man who claimed his name was Kevin Quinn listened to the news on the car radio while Rachel wolfed down her food, and seemed to be encouraged by what he heard. She was grateful he hadn't attempted to make small talk while she ate, which would have made the meal even more awkward.

She finished quickly, already feeling better.

"Do you prefer to be called *Dr.* Howard, or *Professor* Howard?" asked Quinn while she was putting the last of the empty food containers back into the paper bag.

"Just Rachel is fine," she replied, not sure why she always insisted on maintaining informality, regardless of the circumstances. Perhaps in her formative years she had seen doctors and professors as old, stodgy blowhards, or as intimidating elders.

Quinn was also surprised that she had offered up her first name. "Okay . . . Rachel, please begin driving again," he instructed. "Randomly." He shot her a sheepish smile. "Which means don't continue on toward the police station."

She sighed. So much for that idea. "What made you think I was headed there?"

"I mapped out its location before I hid in your car. You were headed that way. I don't blame you. It's a smart move." He made an apologetic face. "I'm really sorry," he said, "but I'm going to have to ask you to toss your phone out of the window."

"You can't be serious?" she pleaded. "Please tell me this is some kind of bad joke."

Quinn winced. "All of your photos and data are in the cloud," he said. "And I'll give you money for a new phone. When this is over, you can just get a replacement and download your data—you won't miss a beat."

"But why?"

"I have a device that can check for bugs within a fifty-yard radius. Your car is clean. But you can be tracked through your phone, so we need to eliminate this as a possibility. While we're driving, I'll be checking for a tail also."

Rachel sensed that no amount of argument would dissuade him from this course of action. Without another word she locked her phone and handed it to him unhappily.

"Thank you," he said as he sent the phone flying. "And I really will pay for a replacement."

"Are you going to tell me what this is all about?" said Rachel as she pulled out onto the street. "You've said my life is in jeopardy. From whom? And why?"

"I was hoping you could tell *me*."

"Tell *you?*" said Rachel in disbelief. "I have absolutely no idea."

Quinn studied her, as though trying to weigh her sincerity.

"Look, if you don't know what this is about," said Rachel, "then why are you here? What makes you think I'm in danger in the first place?"

"I discovered that you're at the top of a hit list. A list made by a very dangerous man."

This Quinn may have looked normal and seemed likable, but even an inmate in an asylum could come up with a better answer than that. "And you have no idea who this man is, or why he wants me dead?"

"None."

"Whatever you think you've discovered, it must be some kind of mistake."

"No mistake. I learned about you after two mercenaries abducted me. I was slated to eventually be killed myself, but I managed to turn the tables. Turns out your bio was on their phones, and you were their next target. Ordered by the man who hired them, a Russian. So this threat couldn't be more credible."

Rachel barely avoided rolling her eyes, but Quinn picked up on subtle body language clues, nonetheless, or perhaps even he knew that his story was preposterous.

"I know how this sounds," he said. "I'd have trouble believing it myself if I were in your shoes. But this is what happened." He sighed, and there was something uncertain about his expression, despite these words, that made Rachel wonder if he didn't doubt his own sanity, at least a little.

"Why did they abduct you?" she said. "Under what circumstances? Who are you, really, and what is your background? You have to give me *something* to go on."

The intruder looked even more troubled. He paused in thought for several long seconds. "I'll tell you everything you need to know. But before I'm completely honest with you, I want to have more of a dialog. I need you to get comfortable that I don't mean to hurt you. Because what I will tell you is a little . . . tricky. Complex. So let's begin by learning more about you. First, are you telling me that you don't even have a wild, far-fetched idea as to why someone might want to kill you?"

"Not a single one," she said emphatically. She thought about this a little longer and shook her head. "I'm even nice to marketers who call me during dinner to sell me aluminum siding."

Quinn laughed. "Any chance you work on a secret government team? Or consult for a Black Ops lab somewhere?"

"None," said Rachel as she steered the Acura into the left lane. "I'm just a harmless neuroscientist."

"Okay, let's start there. What is that? What do neuroscientists do? Humor me. I have more than just academic interest. Something you tell me might help me understand why you're being targeted. After that, I have some questions about memory. But first, tell me about neuroscience."

She couldn't see how a quick survey of her field would help him determine why someone had it in for her, but she was prepared to humor him for at least a little longer.

"You sure about this?" she asked. "Sure I won't just be boring you?"

"I'm willing to take that chance," said Quinn with a smile. "And between you and me, I could use a little boredom right now." He raised his eyebrows. "And how often will I have the chance to discuss a field with the scientist who is widely regarded as the best the field has ever seen?"

"Well, if you keep breaking into their cars and forcing them to drive around," replied Rachel Howard, smiling for the first time since Quinn had revealed himself, "I'd say your chances were pretty good."

24

Dmitri Kovonov expertly landed the white helicopter in a clearing at the edge of a small mountain summit that mankind had forgotten. Kevin Quinn had chosen well, he thought to himself.

He checked coordinates on his phone and exited the craft, a 2018 Robinson Turbine he had purchased just a week earlier when he had first arrived in the States. He walked at a leisurely pace toward the shack he could just make out in the distance, and then beyond, to the woods.

Kovonov missed being alone, and relished the opportunity this stay in the United States was affording him. At his base of operations in an industrial park in Switzerland—hiding in plain sight—he was now surrounded by soldiers and scientists he had collected to his cause, many who worshiped him like a god.

While there was comfort in being the queen bee at the center of the hive, forcing anyone after his scalp to fight through a gauntlet of warrior drones who would gladly sacrifice their lives to protect him, traveling with a hive throughout the US wasn't exactly the best way to avoid attracting attention. And if he did decide he wanted one or more followers to join him on one of his errands in the States, he could always have them meet him at any location he chose.

But there was a greater efficiency in traveling alone, not to mention that it took less mental energy not to have to interact with anyone else for long stretches of time, even if only to bark orders at them.

Even with none of his team with him at the moment, his reach remained formidable. He had established a network of mercenaries to work for him in the States, which gave him all the resources he might need.

And while being alone was inarguably less safe for him, he wasn't worried. He could handle himself. Besides, he was at least three steps ahead of anyone left who still opposed him, and these misguided souls would either join him or be nullified as a threat soon enough. He was forced to prioritize carefully and just hadn't gotten around to converting or eliminating all of his enemies just yet.

He was only one person, extraordinary though he might be, and there was only so much even *he* could accomplish in a given period of time. But it would all get done. One didn't dramatically change the world in a single day, although with his unprecedented talents and capabilities the day of reckoning would arrive faster than anyone would dare conceive.

Even as a scrawny nine-year-old boy growing up in the mean streets of Moscow he had known he was destined for greatness, destined to change the world. But even his prodigious genius, his unparalleled imagination, was unable to conceive of just how profound this change would be.

Now, thirty years later, he had grown into a tall, ruggedly handsome visionary with a classically Slavic appearance: gray eyes, thin lips and eyebrows, and straight, ash brown hair. And he possessed charisma and genius to spare.

He had already ensured his place in history. He would go down as a man having a greater impact on civilization than Socrates, DaVinci, Newton, or Einstein. But if he was successful in reaching his ambitious goals going forward, he would soar even higher, accomplish even more. For many years, despite his historic achievements, he had been held back from reaching his full potential. By fear. By misguided empathy.

But no longer.

He had been soft and pathetic. But he had recently shed these traits as completely as a snake shed its skin. To borrow a phrase from Christendom, he had been blind, but now he could see. Everything. With incredible clarity.

He had had fantasies about what needed to be done, but he had always held back. He had been a coward. Afraid to make the hard choices, caged by a counterproductive set of ethics sewn into his psyche.

But now he understood. The ends really did justify the means, no matter how devastating the means might be. Only the weak and unworthy allowed themselves to be squeamish when the future of humanity was at stake.

He entered the thick woods and admired the beauty he found there. The air was cool and fresh and he could hear the rustle of several small animals rushing off through the undergrowth to get out of his way.

Always a good idea.

His immersion in the natural world was short-lived as he came to his destination almost immediately. His two hired guns were each hugging a tree, literally, five feet from each other, their wrists tied together with plastic zip-ties and their mouths duct-taped shut. No doubt the very same duct tape and zip-ties these men had brought with them, judging from the empty trunk of the abandoned Tesla he had passed on his way here.

He had vetted these men himself, and both had come highly recommended. But with their faces staring at a tree trunk and their arms forming a circle around it, they looked like circus clowns.

"Hello, Captain Ridley," said Kovonov with a sneer to the taller of the two mercenaries, the man he had put in charge.

The Russian ripped the tape from Ridley's mouth, not bothering to warn him to tighten and curl his lips, although he noted absently that Ridley's lips were not torn and bleeding, so he must have remembered to do so. "You want to tell me what happened here?"

Ridley turned his head to eye the newcomer, having to press his right cheek into the tree trunk to do so. "I'll save my report for 302."

Kovonov shook his head in disgust. "I am 302, you idiot!"

Ridley swallowed hard, and his pony-tailed partner, RJ, still silenced by duct tape, suddenly looked a bit pallid. Relief at the arrival of a rescuer had turned to abject fear.

"You knew something was wrong when we failed to check in as scheduled," said Ridley. "But how did you know where we were in the woods? And how did you know Quinn hadn't staged an ambush?"

"I tracked your phones," replied Kovonov simply.

Once Quinn had been captured he had stopped monitoring his fly drone, and had put it into an autonomous, low-energy mode. He was too busy for constant control and monitoring, and had assumed the situation was well in hand, had assumed he would retrieve it when he arrived. And now he wasn't receiving a signal from it at all.

When he had tracked Ridley's phone he found it was over a hundred miles away and on the move, while RJ's phone had remained here near the hand off coordinates, motionless. It didn't take a detective to know that Quinn had slipped the noose and taken Ridley's phone. When RJ hadn't answered Kovonov's attempted call, he had further assumed his two hired hands were both dead.

But he had been wrong. Quinn had been too soft to make what he surely must have known was the right move. When being hunted, a scorched earth approach was the only way. You didn't send a player to the penalty box. You destroyed him utterly.

Quinn was a fool.

"You tracked our phones?" repeated Ridley in disbelief.

"Am I going to have to say everything twice?"

"But that isn't possible. These phones are absolutely untraceable."

"I'm sure they are. To everyone but me."

Anger flashed across Ridley's face for just a moment.

"Unhappy that I didn't tell you I could track you?" asked Kovonov. "Feeling violated?"

"Not at all," lied Ridley.

"Good thing I could, right? Otherwise you idiots would rot out here. And I'd have lost Quinn. As it is, he'll be as surprised that I can track your phone as you were."

Kovonov paused, and the icy smile he had been wearing vanished. He shook his head in disgust. "So tell me how he managed to escape."

Ridley did so without interruption. Kovonov couldn't help but be impressed. Bound hand and foot, outgunned, Quinn had escaped using his fingernails and a bluff. What guile and resourcefulness. These were traits the man was known for, but his failure to kill Davinroy and his refusal to kill the two mercs was *pathetic*. A reminder of how detestable the man really was.

"Look," pleaded Ridley when he had finished his report, "tell us where Quinn is and we'll make this right. No charge. We'll throw in the next job free of charge as well," he added, his voice as strained as if his life were on the line, which he somehow sensed it was.

Ridley's partner was unable to speak but nodded his head vigorously up and down in agreement.

"That's a very gracious offer," said Kovonov tiredly, "but I'm afraid I'll have to pass. It's like telling a restaurant you hate their food, and then having them offer your next meal free to make up for it. If you aren't satisfied with the food, more of it for free doesn't help. Surely you can appreciate my perspective."

He calmly removed an H&K 9mm handgun from a holster while Ridley pressed his cheek even harder into the bark of the tree to extend his field of vision.

"Don't do this," whispered Ridley. "We're pros. We screwed up this time, but it won't happen again."

"I know it won't," said Kovonov calmly, pulling the trigger four times, drilling two holes in each of the mercenaries' heads, carefully choosing angles to spare any damage to the trees, which had done nothing wrong.

"You don't deserve to be alive," he mumbled to the now deceased men as blood began running down their bodies and to the forest floor. "Quinn should have killed you before I arrived."

He wet his finger with each man's blood in turn and used it as a stylus, writing a large red F on each man's cheek. F for failure. F for fuck-up.

The Secret Service agent had indeed chosen his hideout well, and Kovonov wondered how many months or years it might be until the remains of these men were discovered, by that time nothing but polished white skeletons, picked clean by nature.

Given Quinn's current location, the man must be paying a visit to Rachel Howard. It was the only conclusion possible. He hadn't even bothered to ask Ridley if Quinn had learned she was their next target, as the answer was obvious.

Kovonov tilted his head in thought. Should he rethink his strategy? Should he now try to take them *both* alive?

Was *using* Rachel Howard a better choice than killing her?

After all, her mind was a treasure. Not just for what she knew, but what she had forgotten—for her rich experience. She was a proven genius whose creativity was boundless. Putting a saddle on this thoroughbred was tempting, no doubt about it. And she was attractive enough to screw, which was always a plus in his book—not that he didn't already have access to all the sex he could ever want.

But once again, his intuition warned him this would be a mistake. Better to just put her down, take her off the board. He continued to have a strong sense that Rachel Howard would prove difficult to tame, and alive she posed a danger to him like no other. Why take any chances?

He would need to scramble two other hired hands for the job, but he had resources to spare. With Quinn in the picture, his new team would need to proceed with caution, with a healthy respect for Quinn's capabilities.

But given the element of surprise this shouldn't be a problem.

Quinn's escape had been a setback, but a minor one in the scheme of things. The truth was that he didn't really *need* to acquire Quinn. Killing Rachel Howard was the more important task, and even this was just a precaution. Even if she were never touched, his plan would almost certainly succeed.

But he did hate loose ends, and why allow even the possibility of a fly in the ointment? He could continue pursuing his plan without interruption, while others focused on these minor inconveniences.

Kovonov thought for a moment longer, selected a contact from his phone, and brought the device to his ear. One quick call and he could get his ship precisely back on course.

25

Rachel was proud of her ability to summarize and simplify her field, but she wondered how fast the intruder was on the uptake. And she would just be scratching the surface, no matter what she did.

Einstein had famously said, "If you can't explain it simply, you don't understand it well enough." On the other hand, Einstein had never suggested that the explanation of millions of pages of research produced over more than a century could be done through a brief discussion in a moving car.

"Neuroscience is the study of the structure and function of the nervous system and brain," began the chair of Harvard's neuroscience department as she drove randomly through the streets of Waltham, Massachusetts. "At least that's the dictionary definition. But this doesn't do it justice. It's really about understanding what makes us tick. What drives human beings? What drives behavior? How much of our decision-making is based on emotion, and how much on reason? Can we cure neurologic disease? Improve upon the human condition? And what improvements *should* we make, provided that we're able?"

Rachel paused to let these questions sink in. "And even more fundamentally," she continued, "do we have a soul? Is consciousness divine, special, miraculous? Or is consciousness something we might someday replicate in every respect with the right bits of matter arranged in just the right way?"

Quinn raised his eyebrows. "What do *you* think?" he asked with genuine interest. "*Do* we have a soul?"

"I'm not sure. On the face of it, it seems clear that we don't. That everything we are emerges from the physical properties of the brain. Not that I'm suggesting this rules out the existence of a soul entirely, mind you, just that it makes this a more difficult position to take.

But what *is* absolutely clear is that damage to different regions of the brain can cause dramatic and insanely specific changes to your personality, behavior, abilities, and desires. Can change *who* you are."

"But not *everything* is changeable, right?"

"Just about," said Rachel. "There are changes that can impact whether you are aggressive or pacifistic, outgoing or introverted. Changes that can cause a disregard for social norms, impulsive behavior, hypersexuality, and increases in risky behavior. Changes in your level of spirituality, or even the ability to name animals or hear music."

"That does seem pretty comprehensive," said Quinn.

"And we're all aware of how dramatically our personalities and perceptions can be altered by drugs and alcohol. And not just LSD and other banned substances. Think of all the prescription drugs that change our personalities and behaviors. Drugs used to treat psychosis, anxiety, depression, hyperactivity and other conditions. All can change the *you* that your friends have come to know and love."

The light turned green and Rachel inched forward before making a right turn. Given it was early evening on a Monday night, the streets were as sparsely traveled as she would have expected.

She glanced at her passenger, and then chastised herself for even momentarily thinking of him as a passenger rather than what he was: a dangerous intruder. Even so, the man did appear to be genuinely fascinated and eager to learn more.

"Let me give you a concrete example," she continued. "It involves a boring guy named Charles Whitman. Bank Teller and former Eagle Scout. By all accounts he was a model citizen. But in 1966, this former Eagle Scout climbed to the top of the University of Texas Tower in Austin and opened fire. Before he was shot by police, he had killed thirteen people and wounded thirty-three."

She paused. "Not what one would expect from his background, is it? Authorities found a suicide note in his home. In it, Whitman said he had recently been having irrational and unusual thoughts. He requested that an autopsy be performed on him to see if something had changed in his brain."

"Let me guess. It had."

"Turns out he had a tumor pressing against a region of the brain called the amygdala. This is an almond-shaped set of neurons involved in emotional regulation, especially fear and aggression."

Quinn nodded in understanding, but she wondered if he was truly grasping both points she was trying to make. Not only that a change to the physical brain could instantly transform a man from good to what was traditionally called evil, but that the conscious mind was severely influenced by, and seemingly powerless to stop, a region of the brain whose motivations were hidden from it.

"I'll give you a second example," continued Rachel. "In the early 2000s, a forty-year-old Virginia teacher suddenly became obsessed with child pornography, and even tried to molest his eight-year-old stepdaughter. Until this point he had been strictly interested in adult females."

"Another tumor?" guessed Quinn uncertainly.

"Very good. That's right. This time in his orbitofrontal cortex. When the neurosurgeons removed it, the man's sexual appetite returned to normal." She raised her eyebrows. "But six months later, the pedophilic behavior returned."

Quinn tilted his head in thought. "Had the tumor grown back?" he asked.

Rachel was impressed despite herself. She had told this story many times, and few had jumped to this conclusion, however obvious it was in retrospect. "Yes. Exactly. They excised it once again, and once again his interest in young girls disappeared."

"*Jesus*," said Quinn. "That is so creepy. So specific a change in behavior."

"Exactly."

"Wow. I'd have to think about what these cases imply a lot harder, but they do seem to make your point. Like you said, if we do have free will, if we do have a soul, at the very least it can be subverted pretty easily by physical changes to our brains."

"Pretty sobering, isn't it? And we think we're in control when much of the time we're not. Unconscious subroutines, seared into our brains, are calling a lot of the shots, and then we're expert at taking credit after the fact."

"But you said you couldn't rule out a soul. Given what you've just told me, why can't you? You've demonstrated that the *you* inside is totally dependent on the physical state of your brain. So how can consciousness be divine, or miraculous? Seems like consciousness, and the soul if you'd like, could be recreated by using wires and switches to duplicate the exact functionality of the human brain."

"Well said," she replied, impressed with his grasp of the material. If he ever got tired of abducting women, he should really consider a career in neuroscience. "I can't rule out divine consciousness because while scientists think they're zeroing in on what makes us tick, there are those who argue there is far more to the system than meets the eye. Let me give you an example involving a transistor radio."

"Do they even make those anymore?" said Quinn.

Rachel smiled. "No, but it's still a good example."

She organized her thoughts. "Imagine you're a Kalahari Bushman who finds a radio," she began. "As you're messing around with it, sound suddenly emerges from inside. Voices, music, intelligent conversation, all streaming from this mysterious little box. If you're a Bushman scientist, you'd open the box and begin to study the insides. You might find that if you pull a wire from its contact the voices stop, or maybe they get softer. You put it back and the voices return to normal. Soon you'd discover what *we've* discovered about the brain, that a huge number of changes to the wiring will have a major impact on what comes out of the other end."

"I'm with you so far," said Quinn.

"Good. So what if someone asked you *how* these bright plastic wires are able to produce music and voices? You wouldn't know, but you'd be confident you were getting close to understanding."

Rachel shook her head vigorously. "But you *aren't*. Nowhere near. Because you can't possibly imagine that what you're hearing has nothing to do with the wires, nothing to do even with the radio. You'd never even dream that this content is generated by a transmission tower hundreds of miles away beaming out powerful radio waves. If someone suggested this was the case, you'd be sure they were insane. 'It's all about these invisible waves,' they would tell you. 'You can't see, taste, or feel them, but they're racing through your body even now, fast enough to circle the globe seven times in a single second. And these *invisible waves* are carrying the voices and music, *not* the wires.'"

"When you say it that way," said Quinn, "I'm not even sure that *I* believe it."

"Exactly. And the Bushman scientist lives in a world with no technology whatsoever. He'd never be able to guess this truth in a thousand lifetimes. He would never believe that while the radio's wires need to be configured just right to pick up the voices, the content of the voices has absolutely nothing to do with the configuration of the wires."

"Now *that* is a fascinating analogy," said Quinn.

"The moral of the story, of course, is that while many of us believe that consciousness, the soul, and everything else resides in our neuronal wiring, there could well be far more to it than we're even capable of imagining."

She let Quinn digest this for a moment and then said, "But I brought up the soul just as an interesting side discussion. To really give you a sense of what neuroscience has learned, I should start at the beginning."

"By all means," said Quinn.

"Let's compare human beings and animals. Animals are born pretty much complete and ready to go, with instincts and behavior already wired up in their brains. A baby zebra can run less than an hour after birth. Many animal species don't tend to their young at all, they're born with all the physical skills and behaviors they need to survive."

Rachel paused. "In contrast, human infants are as helpless as it's possible to be. We're born with our brains largely unfinished. Which isn't to say we aren't prewired to some extent."

"How so?"

"Within minutes of birth a baby knows to seek out a face. We're prewired for language acquisition, math, fear of heights, suckling, and so on. But instead of wiring up in the womb, babies mostly wire up through exposure to their environment. Which makes us flexible, versatile, able to readily learn new tricks. Instead of being hardwired, we're more like live-wired. Millions of new synapses form in an infant's brain every second."

"Not sure I totally get how the environment impacts this wiring," said Quinn.

"Well, an easy example is language. If you're born in Japan, your brain gets wired up to understand Japanese. In America, to understand English. You become better able to hear the sounds of your language, and less able to hear the sounds of other languages. Through time, a baby raised in Japan will no longer be able to hear the difference between the sounds of R and L, since these sounds aren't distinct in the Japanese language."

"I thought they just couldn't get their mouths to form these sounds."

"That too. But they aren't even wired to *hear* them. Just like those who are red-green colorblind can't detect any difference between these two colors."

Rachel stopped at a red light and turned to face the man sitting beside her. "But the point I'm trying to make is that we're born unfinished, to maximize versatility. You can't teach an animal to excel at tennis, play chess, do the backstroke, play a piano, touch type, or solve a Rubik's cube. For each of these skills, the human brain creates unconscious subroutines. Burns the proper circuits into our brains. When you have to do an activity consciously, you are slow and inefficient. Unconscious subroutines programmed in are just the opposite, fast and efficient. But in many cases, learned activities that become part of your unconscious wiring can no longer be accessed by your conscious mind."

She studied Quinn's face for just a moment longer before turning her attention back to the road. "You just spoke of the process you use to make sounds in a language. If you were to try to consciously move your lips and tongue to form each sound you make when you speak a sentence, you'd find you couldn't do it. Thankfully, the proper subroutines are burned into your brain, freeing you up to concentrate on what you're saying. But go ahead. Without moving your lips or tongue, try to visualize the ballet of movements your mouth would need to make to say the word, *oblique*. Or *petulant*. Or any other word for that matter."

"No need," said Quinn. "If you say I can't do it, I believe you."

"Conscious meddling with our unconscious subroutines actually makes things worse, not better. When you're really great at a sport, for example, you perform better if you don't consciously think about what you're doing."

Quinn nodded. "Fascinating. When a basketball player can't miss a shot, or a tennis player is hitting every line, the athlete is often said to be playing *unconscious*. I always thought this was just a figure of speech."

Rachel smiled. "Not so much," she said. "So our efficient systems let our inefficient consciousness believe it's always in control," she continued, "when the reverse is more often the case. The unconscious controls our bodies and the random thoughts we have, and far more of our lives than we'd ever imagine. I've studied the mind for many years and I still can't truly believe how little the conscious *me* controls my thoughts and actions. That's the genius of the unconscious. It helps us survive, secretly running much of the show, but graciously letting us take most of the credit. Take taste in women, for example. Some men are hopelessly attracted to tall blondes. Some to women who are overweight. Some to big rear ends, some to small. And some are even attracted to one-legged aborigines, for all I know."

Quinn laughed. "Wouldn't surprise me at all."

"Most would agree that we don't choose who we are attracted to. This is somehow decided by brain circuitry that we can't access. We don't consciously decide we're going to have the hots for one-legged aborigines."

Rachel was intent on keeping the discussion G-rated, but an even more interesting example was the catalog of what certain people liked in bed, an assortment of sexual preferences across the species that was exceedingly varied and sometimes disturbing. This made the point also—people often had no idea why they liked what they liked, why their bodies responded to what they responded to—but she had decided that discussing unusual sexual preferences with a stranger who had accosted her was a very bad idea.

"In 1965 a guy named Hess did an experiment," she continued. "He showed men various photos of women. But in half of the photos, he artificially dilated their eyes, which is a biological sign of sexual arousal. The men ranked women whose eyes were dilated as being more attractive than these same women when their eyes were not. When asked why, not one noticed this difference in the eyes, minor as it was. At least not consciously. When asked specifically if their ratings were due to levels of dilation, the men shrugged this off as being ridiculous. They weren't even aware that this was a sign of female arousal. Their unconscious not only detected this difference, but managed to get their conscious to respond to it. None had any idea that genetic programming stitched into their brains from the earliest days of evolution was secretly dictating this response."

"Doesn't this imply that intuition is a real thing, then?" asked Quinn. "My instincts, my intuition, have saved my life on more than one occasion. But I was always under the impression that scientists thought this was a load of garbage."

"Just the opposite. Your unconscious systems can be brilliant, far smarter and more observant than you are. Like directing your mouth to form words, your unconscious understands body language better than you do, for example. And it picks up on patterns faster than you do. There are endless examples from real life and the lab."

"This explains a lot," said Quinn. "So I might not be all that talented, but I'm lucky enough to have some gifted subroutines helping me out behind the curtain."

"Give your conscious some credit. You're smart enough to trust these subroutines. They aren't always right, of course, but more often than you would be. When you first appeared, I had to decide what to do. I could run, scream for help, be defiant, cooperate, and so on.

And yes, I consciously thought through the logic of the different actions. But what were my data points? Feelings? Intuition? My hidden mental wiring tried to read your body language, estimate risks based on limited information. If you asked me why I decided to cooperate, what could I tell you? Could I lay out an algebraic equation? No, my inner self weighed all of the options and came to a decision, which I immediately took credit for."

"You made the right one, Professor," said Quinn. "I promise you."

Rachel sighed. That remained to be seen.

She noticed that Quinn was scanning her mirrors whenever there was the slightest break in the conversation, studying the cars behind them.

"All of this is not to say that the conscious mind still doesn't have a huge role," she continued. "For one, it's there to handle surprises, the unexpected. Right now, my consciousness is absorbed in our conversation. So I'm driving on autopilot, using subroutines etched into my unconscious. But if a kid suddenly runs into the road in front of me, my conscious mind will immediately take over, ignoring you completely." She paused. "And, of course, it sets goals and makes decisions."

"But you're saying that even these goals and decisions are heavily influenced by the unconscious. Which we can't reach or influence."

"Yes," said Rachel, unable to keep a smile from creeping across her face. Quinn made an excellent student. "Think of your conscious as the mayor of a major city. An immense amount of activity and politicking go on in the city, and you can't possibly be aware of the vast majority of it. The city mostly runs itself, although as mayor, you take credit when things go smoothly and get blamed when they fall apart—although many times you have nothing to do with either outcome. Your unconscious subsystems are what have been called a team of rivals, each lobbying you in a different direction whenever you have to make a decision, winner take all. But again, even when they drive you to a behavior for reasons unknown to you, your conscious self will make up a story to rationalize this behavior and take full credit for it."

"What role do our emotions play in all of this?" asked Quinn.

"They're important drivers of behavior also, with fear and love being obvious examples, causing us to drop everything and attend to whatever caused these emotions. But there are people with damage to their prefrontal cortex such that their emotions can no longer influence their behavior. When this happens, the simplest decisions become difficult or impossible for them. What to make for dinner? Which movie to see? Some days they never leave the couch, almost entirely paralyzed, unable to decide on anything. They feel overwhelmed by information they can't seem to prioritize. They often can't make themselves care about one decision over another. So emotions are a weighting system for our choices. To make a decision, we have to value one choice over another."

"You really are doing an amazing job of this," said Quinn. "Even under duress, your knowledge and passion really shine through."

"Thank you."

"I'd like to take a pause right now, though," said Quinn. "Please drive home. I'm convinced no one is following us, which is good. So now I'd like to check out your house, and make sure it's safe. But I need to focus all of my attention on watching for possible tails until we arrive."

"Sure," said Rachel, pulling into the left lane so she could take the next U-turn. Since she had been traveling in random circles, they were only five or ten minutes from their destination.

They drove in silence while Quinn's eyes bored holes in the Acura's mirrors. When they neared her house, he had her complete several concentric circles around the neighborhood before declaring that the coast was clear.

"Outstanding," he said. "No tail and no stake out. I expected you to be safe and unwatched for another day or so, but under the circumstances I wanted to be extra cautious."

Rachel pulled the car into the driveway and turned off the engine.

"I'd like to pick up where we left off," said Quinn. "And I promise you, I will explain everything. Soon." He paused. "But one last precaution. When we get inside, stay with me and don't say anything."

He nodded at the rucksack by his feet. "I just want to do a quick scan. My understanding is that your house isn't bugged, but better safe than sorry."

Rachel nodded, but couldn't help frowning. Because the truth was, this further display of paranoia was alarming. The more cautious Quinn was, the more likely he was delusional and dangerous, and the *less* safe she felt.

"Sure," she said, swallowing hard. "You can never be too careful."

26

Quinn shoved his doctored hat and oversized sunglasses into a side pocket of the rucksack and entered Rachel Howard's small home with the owner leading the way. Her research might be leading edge, but the house was many decades old and the furnishings and decor were anything but modern. On the other hand, they were tasteful and attractive. He knew the joke in real estate was that a home was never *cramped* and *old*, it was *cozy* and *quaint*, but in the case of Rachel's home these more complimentary adjectives were accurate.

Quinn's plan had been to build rapport with the professor, and he knew that this was exactly what was happening. She had turned out to be extraordinary, and not in the ways he had expected. Of course she was brilliant, but he hadn't counted on her charm, her approachability. He had no idea that he would find her personality appealing, that she could make neuroscience so damned fascinating.

He still needed to keep her calm, to win her trust, knowing that even then it would take a miracle for her to believe him when he finally told her his story. He imagined the conversation they would soon have. *Here is why you should believe me when I tell you you're on a hit list*, he would say. *Turns out I'm a Secret Service agent being hunted for trying to kill the president. But I did have a good reason. You see, he tortured and killed a wife I never had. In front of me. While we were both at a retreat I never attended.*

Nothing alarming in that story.

He had been procrastinating, but he knew he needed to share his side of the story with her soon, before it hit the media. Once they set the narrative, she was even less likely to believe what he told her.

Before admitting to having false memories, Quinn intended to discuss the subject of memory in general with a woman who was a world leading expert on this subject. Learn how often something like this might happen. What could cause it. Was it always a sign of insanity, or did this kind of memory malfunction sometimes occur in the sane?

He removed the small electronic surveillance detection device from where he had left it on top of the weapons and other equipment in the mercenaries' bag and casually switched it on.

Quinn's body visibly stiffened, transforming from relaxed to tense in an instant. His eyes widened as he stared at the device in his right hand.

"What's wrong?" said Rachel anxiously.

He brought a finger briskly to his lips, reminding her she was supposed to remain silent until he was finished. *Three bugs detected*, he mouthed.

Quinn's mind raced. How could this be? He had seen the Russian's instructions himself, and no bugs should have been present. Had the mercs escaped already, or had 302 decided to change gears and send in someone else while they had been babysitting him on the mountain?

And even if he had decided to accelerate the timetable, why the need for bugs? They wanted her dead, not a recording of her singing in the shower.

Regardless of the answer to these questions, they were in trouble. He had been seen with the professor the moment they had entered, which meant a clock was ticking. They could have a day before alarms were sounded and the walls closed in, or hostiles could be converging on her home in minutes. It all depended on who was at the other end of the bugs, and how closely they were being monitored.

He considered having Rachel watch the outside for possible unwanted visitors while he removed the bugs, but decided against it. If he let her that far out of his sight, she'd be a fool not to run at this point, and she was anything but a fool.

He motioned for her to follow him while he located the first bug, which jutted out just a few millimeters from a spindle on the stairs that faced the front door. It had been painted white to match the wood and cemented nearly flush with it, making it almost impossible for a casual observer to detect. Quinn carved it free with a combat knife while Rachel looked on in dismay. He pried the tiny device open with the tip of the knife and then used the edge to sever three wires that were the diameter of angel hair pasta.

Quinn handed the disabled device to Rachel so she could see for herself that it was tiny, sophisticated, and camouflaged. He took satisfaction from the play of emotions that ran across her face, and a mind that was factoring in this new data at a furious pace. She had humored him, but had never taken his warnings seriously. For the first time she was beginning to appreciate that he might not be the most dangerous threat she faced, after all.

Ironically, these bugs and what they represented could be a godsend. Not only did their presence here imply that Quinn really did still have a grip on reality—if one didn't count his imaginary wife—it gave him much-needed credibility with Rachel.

"Audio and video," he half-mouthed, half-whispered, placing his face inches from her ear. "Military grade," he finished, motioning her to follow him.

During the next several minutes he found and disabled the remaining devices planted on the premises.

"Okay, we can talk now," he announced when he had killed the last bug. He shook his head. "I have to say, I'm at a loss to explain this."

"You did say someone was after me, right?"

"Yes. But you weren't supposed to be under surveillance. Why bother? You advertise your whereabouts and you're as easy a target as it gets."

Rachel swallowed hard. "Thanks," she muttered.

Quinn winced. Nothing like reminding a woman who suddenly discovers her life really is on the line that she's a sitting duck.

"What now?" asked Rachel.

"We need to get the hell out of here. But I need to think for a few seconds."

The room fell silent. A moment later something within Quinn caused the hairs to rise on the back of his neck. Had he heard something? He didn't think so, but he wasn't about to ignore attempts by his unconscious to contact headquarters.

He rushed to the wide, rectangular front window in the family room, which was completely obscured by a pleated teal curtain. He pulled an edge of the curtain away and peered out. Sure enough, a car was slowly approaching from the north.

Rachel had taken his lead and was peering through the window on the other side when the car turned into her driveway and parked beside the Acura. While darkness had fallen, there was sufficient light inside the car for Quinn to see it contained only the driver, a handsome, athletic-looking man with black hair and a dark complexion.

Rachel's eyes widened. "I know this guy," she whispered in astonishment. "Just met him this morning in my class. He's an Israeli grad student named Eyal Regev. Very talented guy."

Her initial relief that the driver had turned out to be a student and not an assassin was short-lived as her expression turned grim. "What are the chances this is just a coincidence?"

"Slim to none," replied Quinn ominously as a gun appeared in his hand, almost as if by magic. "And that might be optimistic."

27

Quinn made sure the opening in the curtain they were peering through was even less conspicuous than before. "Any reason for a student to track you down at home?" he asked hurriedly as the man exited the car and shut the door loudly.

"No," said Rachel. "But he doesn't have a gun or anything," she noted hopefully as he walked casually toward the door.

They both pulled their heads back from the living room window as Regev rapped loudly on the front door, which was in the next room over. Quinn caught Rachel's eye and shook his head, letting her know not to answer.

Quinn couldn't imagine that this man's appearance minutes after they had arrived and disabled the bugs could be random, despite the visit coming even sooner than he had expected. He had to assume Regev was working for 302. But if he was here to kill Rachel, why such a noisy approach? Why announce his presence?

If Quinn wasn't with her, hadn't warned her, this would have worked. She'd be unclear why a student was visiting her at home, but she'd invite him in, and he could dispatch her at his leisure. He'd leave no witnesses and attract no undue attention.

But surely Regev must know the video and audio feed had been disrupted, and had viewed the footage to see who was responsible. Surely he now knew that a competent player was on the scene, and Rachel would never fall for his obvious ruse.

Regev rapped sharply and repeatedly on the door a second time, underscoring his clumsy approach. For the Israeli to be proceeding this way he had to be a rank amateur.

Or a true professional, thought Quinn in alarm.

Regev was a *decoy*, he realized. He was being loud on purpose to distract them from the real danger. Quinn could see it in his mind's eye, a second man breaking in through the back door, masking the noise by timing it to his partner's raps on the door.

Quinn tackled Rachel and drove her to the carpeting even before the logic of this realization had fully played out. She gasped in shock as he rolled off her body and came up firing, piercing the chest of the man who was just then entering the room from the back end, a moment before the intruder could squeeze off his own shot.

The instant Regev heard gunfire he dropped the innocent visitor act and shot at the door lock. Quinn jumped to his feet and ran into the next room, to the front door, staying out of the line of fire and waiting for Regev to burst through.

Only this never happened. The shots at the door were another decoy. Regev had doubled back to the front window. He shattered the glass with a single bullet and dived through into the teal curtain. He extricated himself from the fabric in record time and began to raise a gun while Quinn rushed back into the living room.

Rachel was between Quinn and the assassin, but Quinn was forced to risk a shot to have any chance of saving her life. The shot streaked by the Harvard professor, missing her by less than an inch, and hit Regev in the chest, leaving a red bloom on his shirt. The force of the shot slammed the Israeli's head into the hard window frame. Small shards of glass cut his head and face as he tumbled backwards out of the window and fell several feet onto a bed of tulips.

Despite the darkness outside, Quinn was able to verify that the man wasn't moving. He raced to the back of the house with his gun at the ready. It appeared that the strike force had consisted of only two men, whom Quinn had taken out, but it paid to be sure. He made his way quickly but cautiously through the rest of the house and minutes later was satisfied that they were clear, at least for now.

Rachel Howard was stunned. Tears streamed down her face as she stared in horror at the dead body in her living room, the first man Quinn had shot. Gorge rose in her throat but she was paralyzed and unable to look away.

"Come on!" shouted Quinn, knowing he had to snap her out of it. "We have to go! Now!"

Rachel finally turned away from the corpse and life began to return to her eyes. "Where?" she mumbled weakly.

"I don't know. But your neighbor must have heard the shots and is calling the cops, so we can't stay."

Rachel shook her head, still more zombie than human. "She's not home," she whispered. "On vacation. I'm putting out food for her cat until Monday."

They still had to move, pronto, but Quinn knew this was the exact break they needed. He had been having nothing but bad luck lately, so maybe it was about time for the universe to balance the scales. "I assume you believe me now that someone wants you dead?"

Rachel looked ill but managed to nod.

"Do you trust that I'm here to help you?"

She glanced back and forth between Quinn and the body on her carpet. "Yes."

"Then do exactly what I tell you. Go to your neighbor's house and sit tight. Don't do anything to advertise your presence. Don't make any calls, don't do *anything*. When the cops come pounding on the door, looking for witnesses, don't answer."

"You aren't going to stay with me?"

"I need to lead the search away from here," he replied. "I'll take your car somewhere else and work my way back to your neighbor's house some other way. Give me an hour or so. When you hear me knock, let me in. I'll knock three times. Then one time. Then four times. That'll be me."

"You chose *Pi* as your secret code?" she said. "Really?"

Quinn smiled. "Well, not *all* of it," he replied in amusement. "Just the first three digits. Since you're a scientist, I thought you'd like that."

Rachel nodded and blew out a long breath. "Hurry back," she said grimly.

28

Quinn drove as calmly as he could away from Rachel's house, removing the black baseball hat from the rucksack beside him and placing it on his head. He parked six blocks from the Waltham train station. He didn't know if this ruse would work again, assuming it had worked when he had tried it in Trenton, but it was worth a shot.

He had a cab pick him up a mile from the station and drop him off several blocks away from the Thai restaurant at which he had intercepted Rachel. The stolen Ford Fusion was still in the lot. He drove to Rachel's neighborhood and parked four blocks from her house, making his way toward it cautiously on foot, invisible in the darkness, carrying the heavy gray rucksack with him.

Homes appeared only sporadically, the acres of distance between them the principal advantage of buying in a part of town that time had forgotten rather than buying a more modern tract home, larger but wedged together with others in tight bunches.

He had expected to see three or four police cars in front of Rachel's home, blue and red lights carving up the night, but there were none. Her residence abutted a wooded hill on one side, leaving her only a single neighbor forty yards away, but he thought it likely the sound would have carried to at least a few other houses in the distance.

Just then he realized Regev's car was no longer in the driveway.

What in the world?

He returned to her home as stealthily as he could and investigated.

The bodies were both gone.

Someone must have been waiting for confirmation of the kill. When it wasn't received, they had managed to clean up after themselves *already*. Quinn swallowed hard. What was he up against here?

The good news was that whoever had retrieved the bodies had left, having no idea that their target was only forty yards away. As scary as their competence was, this was at least reassuring.

He made his way to the neighbor's house and rapped out 3-1-4 on the door. Rachel was relieved to see him, and handed him a hot mug of cocoa she had prepared for his return before leading him into the basement. The glazed look in her eyes had disappeared and she seemed to have recovered.

The neighbor, a retired schoolteacher named Debbie Steele, had done a beautiful job converting the basement into a much larger family room. The entire floor was covered in thick-pile beige carpeting and a steel basement pole had been painted a pleasant white. Two identical blue couches faced one another, each made of a comfortable fabric, and each with a skirt that hung down from the bottom of the couch to the floor to give it a more cozy look. Four throw pillows, two pink and two light blue, adorned each couch, with short oak tables positioned at the ends of each. A holographic television was set within a bookshelf that harbored photographs in wrought iron frames along with various knickknacks.

Quinn and Rachel settled in on opposite couches, facing each other, while Quinn described how someone had cleaned up after themselves at her house.

"So what else do you know about this Israeli?" he asked. "This Emil Regev?"

"*Eyal*," she corrected. "*Eyal* Regev. There's not much to tell. He showed up in my graduate class this morning. A transfer from Johns Hopkins. Speaks great English." Rachel paused for a moment and her face fell. "Well, I guess I should use the past tense. He *spoke* great English."

Quinn watched as she visibly struggled to suppress the visceral memories of the gun battle and deaths and remain dispassionate.

"He was tall and well built," she continued finally, composed and relatively upbeat once again. "And permanently tanned. Very bright and thoughtful."

"And an imposter. Not to mention a killer."

Debbie Steele's cat, a beautiful white Turkish Angora named Duke, had settled in next to Rachel Howard and seemed to be as engaged in the conversation as she was.

"He stayed for a few minutes after class to chat. The first two lectures in this course are big picture discussions. We don't really drill down to the neuronal or molecular level, nor talk about specifics in the field. But when we spoke after class, he seemed knowledgeable. Training a guy like that to fool someone like me for even a few minutes is impressive."

"Anything else you can remember about him?"

"Not much. Just that I really liked him. He had a lot of positive qualities. He had this air of confidence, a great intellect, and a great sense of humor. He only had one tiny flaw as far as I can tell."

"What's that?"

"He tried to kill me!" she said emphatically, but with a smile to indicate she had set Quinn up for this. "This is the sort of thing that can make you reevaluate your opinion of someone."

Quinn laughed. "No doubt," he said. "Even if you're the forgiving type."

Rachel held her smile for a moment longer before it faded. "Okay," she said, "now that I'm finding you more believable, why don't you tell me who you are. And how you came to be in my car."

Quinn sighed. "I'll tell you everything. Soon. But before I do, as I said before, I want you to give me an overview on the subject of memory. Like you did with neuroscience in general."

"Did anything I've already told you help you understand why people might be after me?"

Quinn shook his head. "I'm afraid not."

"This exercise won't either."

He understood her frustration. But he needed this to get a sense of how his story would come across to her and for his own edification, so he felt this was the best way to proceed. Listening to his instincts again, as Rachel herself had recommended. "Maybe so, but I like to be thorough."

"Can't you be thorough after you've told me more about what's going on?"

"I promise, we can make this quick." He flashed his most disarming smile. "All I want to know is everything that has ever been learned about human memory. Ever. In ten or fifteen minutes."

"Oh well, in that case . . . I thought you would be asking for something difficult."

Quinn laughed.

"Okay, let's get this over with," said Rachel, taking a sip of hot cocoa from the mug in her hand. "This will be very big picture. I won't get into the molecular mechanisms of memory, or where they are laid down in the brain. I won't tell you all the theories of memory at the chemical and neuronal level. Too complicated and involved for our quick overview."

"Whatever you think makes sense."

"The most important concept to know is that our minds don't reflect reality. There really is no objective reality but what our minds make of the data coming in through our senses. Different wavelengths and configurations of light hit our eyes, and our minds imbue meaning and reality. It's just light, but if it's reflected from a naked supermodel, it might provoke lust, or from a mass of writhing maggots, disgust. But these are simply our interpretations, driven by wiring and evolution."

Quinn nodded.

"For example," she continued, "we find oranges delicious and feces disgusting. But why? Do you think this is just random?"

"I'm going to say, um . . . no," said Quinn.

"Way to be decisive," said Rachel in amusement. "Oranges contain energy we need, so our bodies and brains evolved to respond positively to them. Fecal matter carries disease, so our brains cause us to be disgusted by the light waves and odor molecules that emanate from it. But the odor molecules that hit our olfactory receptors aren't repugnant. They aren't anything. Our brains are just wired to respond to them with revulsion. This property is in our minds, not the molecules themselves. Baby koalas eat their mother's feces to obtain bacteria they need to detoxify eucalyptus leaves. To them, fecal matter smells and tastes as good as an orange does to you."

Quinn's face curled up into a picture of disgust, a further demonstration of the point she was making.

"So the *reality* of our world is dictated by our minds," she continued. "And this applies to our most heartfelt beliefs about ethics, politics, society—everything. But back to our sensory input. Even if we pretend there really is an objective reality to this information, our brains don't present this objective reality to us anyway, feeding us a highly edited version instead. Your brain tells you the best story it can come up with, so you can navigate the environment and stay alive long enough to reproduce, creating additional brains that operate in this same way."

"Can I assume you'll provide an example or two?"

"Sure," said Rachel, rolling her eyes, "an overview of everything known about human memory in ten minutes, with examples."

She paused and gathered her thoughts. "You may know that everything you see comes into your retina, and thus your brain, upside down, backwards, and two-dimensional. With a sizable blind spot in the center. But you don't see things this way. Your brain adjusts it for you. It performs the treacherous math needed to put everything right-side up, and takes a best guess as to what's in the blind spot, filling it in for you."

She raised her eyebrows. "But here is something truly remarkable. Suppose I give you a pair of glasses that flip the world you're seeing now upside down. During the first few days of wearing them, you'd be helpless. But if you kept wearing them, within a few weeks your brain would lay down new pathways, re-map your input spatially, and flip the world right-side up for you again. You'd be back in business."

Quinn's mouth fell open. "Someone actually did this?" he said. "Wore upside-down glasses for a few weeks?"

Rachel grinned. "Multiple someones. And if you then took the glasses *off*, the world would look upside down to you again. Until you adjusted back."

"I'll be damned."

"Your brain takes all kinds of liberties with visual information, processing it for maximum usefulness. Which explains why there are so many optical illusions. Set things up just right, so the mental gymnastics your mind uses to display the world without a blind spot and in three dimensions work against you, and you can be easily fooled."

Rachel paused. "The key point, which I've made several times now, is that your brain isn't about reality as much as it's about presenting you with the best possible narrative to explain the inputs coming in. Memory is the same way. It helps us avoid danger and recall the location of a watering hole. But it's an approximation of reality, and often not a very good one. People think memory works like a video recording. This couldn't be further from the truth. Our memory isn't nearly as reliable as we think."

"Is there a difference between *reliable* and *good?*"

Rachel nodded in approval. "I can't believe you picked up on that. Yes, I used the word reliable for a reason. To me, saying our memory *isn't very good* just means that we remember things poorly. But forgetting isn't the biggest problem we have. When you fail to remember, at least you *know* your memory is letting you down. I forgot the quadratic equation, or where I put my car keys. You *know* you forgot. But it's worse when we remember things incorrectly. When we're certain we remember, but we're dead wrong."

Quinn was more intrigued than ever. Perhaps what he experienced wasn't as impossible as he thought. "How often is this the case?"

"More often than you'd think. A video record always stays the same. But with memory, subsequent events color our recollections. I'm at a café talking with a friend about my home when I witness a car crash. Two years later my wires can easily become crossed. Even though I was at a café, my mind was focused on my home, and I can conflate the two. Now I remember having seen the crash while looking out from my living room window."

Rachel finished the cocoa, now lukewarm, and set the mug down on an end table beside her. "Shockingly," she continued, "our recollections can be unreliable even for events that are singular, traumatic, powerful. Events you would bet your life you couldn't possibly forget. In January of 1986, the Space Shuttle *Challenger* exploded, killing everyone inside. It was a news story that had a huge impact on the national psyche. The day after it happened, two researchers at Emory University handed out a questionnaire about the event to over a hundred students in their psychology 101 class. Where were the students when they heard the tragic news? Who were they with? What were they doing? That sort of thing.

"Two and a half years later they found these same students and had them fill out the questionnaire a second time. When the researchers compared the responses to those given previously, they were astonished. The differences in the two accounts were often like night and day.

"When questioned the day after the event, one student explained she had been in her dorm watching TV with her roommate when she heard the news. She was so upset, she told a few others and then called her parents. Less than three years later, she remembered it much differently. She first learned the news in a religion class when she heard other students talk about the explosion. She then went to her dorm, watched TV alone, and didn't call anyone."

Quinn shook his head skeptically. "Sure, there are always exceptions. But I'm sure most students remembered things accurately."

"You would think so," said Rachel with a smile. "But you'd be wrong. When the researchers rated the accuracy of the students' recollections, with respect to where they were and what they were doing, the average score was less than fifty percent. A quarter of the students scored *zero*. But here is the most amazing, maybe *frightening* thing: they were all exceedingly confident they still remembered the aftermath of the tragedy perfectly. Their memories were crisp, detailed . . . and absolutely wrong. Turns out there isn't much of a relationship between confidence in a memory and the *accuracy* of this memory."

"I see why you chose to use the word *unreliable*."

"Exactly," said Rachel. "Even after I read this study, I refused to believe it. Maybe for the space shuttle disaster, but what about something like 9/11? Surely every adult in the country remembered how they heard about this event, as it was seared into our collective consciousness. So much so that the words *9/11* are all that are required to call it back to mind. In my own case, I was just starting high school at the time, and I was at a sleepover with my two closest friends. We woke up and were having breakfast when we all heard the news."

Rachel paused. "So after reading the space shuttle study, I called each of these old friends in turn to prove to myself that its conclusions were ridiculous." She frowned and shook her head. "Only I confirmed the opposite. I asked each friend how they had learned of 9/11, expecting them to chide me for even asking, since we had been together at the time. My friend Kim did remember being with me and Julia at a sleepover when it happened, but remembered not hearing about it until long after breakfast. But my friend Julia remembered hearing about it on the car radio while her mom took her to the store to buy a new coat."

"Holy hell," said Quinn in amazement. He'd had no idea memory was this fallible.

Perhaps Rachel Howard could explain what he had experienced after all. He would need to ponder the implications of what she was saying at length. Not only for what it suggested about his current situation, but life in general. Husbands and wives legitimately remembering two very different versions of what happened during a past argument.

It was alarming that people could be so certain of memories that were so inaccurate. If this knowledge became more widespread it could shake the foundation of what everyone thought was true of their past.

But this reflection would have to wait. He decided it was finally time to come clean. "Thanks for this overview," he said. "It's been very helpful. But that's enough for now. I'm ready to tell you what you want to know."

His memory of the assault that never happened seemed so real to him, even now, that it still made his blood boil. At the same time it was embarrassing, and what it said about his sanity was deeply disturbing. He would have given anything not to have to revisit it, *ever*.

But he didn't have that luxury. He would just try to get it out as quickly, accurately, and efficiently as he could. "I'd like to ask you to hold your questions until I'm finished. And try to keep an open mind."

And then, blowing out a deep breath, he added. "Because you're going to need one."

29

Quinn proceeded to tell his story to perhaps the most accomplished neuroscientist in the world. All of it. Of the torture and murder. His attempt on the president's life. The subsequent chase. The two mercenaries at the shack, and finally, his call with Coffey, learning that none of the memories that had launched him on this odyssey were true.

Rachel Howard listened without interruption, her expression grim.

"So do you believe me?" asked Quinn when he was finished. Rachel had learned he was telling the truth about the threat to her life. But that didn't mean he was telling the truth about this.

"I don't know," she replied. "Can you prove that you're a Secret Service agent?"

"No. And after last night, I'm *not* one anymore. I'm not sure of all the fireable offenses an agent might commit, but I'm guessing that trying to kill the president is one of them."

A quick smile played across Rachel's face. "I caught some news online this afternoon," she said. "Big headlines about an explosion at a mosque in Chicago. But not a word about any assassination attempt on the president."

"You say the brain takes in information and then creates a narrative to feed back to us. Well, politicians put the brain to shame when it comes to massaging reality. News is often delayed by those in power, and distorted beyond recognition. I'm sure Davinroy has his reasons for wanting to bottle it up for a while. But it will come out. Soon."

Rachel chewed on her lower lip. "You just saved my life and proved at least some of your claims are credible. So just for the sake of further discussion, I'm going to say that I do believe you."

She raised her eyebrows. "But I should also point out that I'm, ah . . . *open-minded* to the possibility that you've lied about this."

"Fair enough," said Quinn. "So assuming everything I said is true, does this make me crazy? This is different from misremembering where I was when I heard about 9/11. This is remembering 9/11, and then learning later that it never happened, that the Twin Towers are still standing."

"You could be delusional, yes," replied Rachel. "But your behavior in every other way seems rational." A troubled look came over her face and she lowered her eyes. "I just hope like hell that you are crazy," she whispered.

"Why would you say that?"

"Because the alternative is much worse. If you *are* totally rational, then these might be *implanted* memories. And much more sophisticated than the run-of-the-mill kind."

"What run-of-the-mill kind?" said Quinn.

"As we've discussed, if something bubbles up from the unconscious, our minds seize on it and construct a reality, a mythology, to explain it and pretend we're running the show. There are patients whose brains are split, whose left and right hemispheres can't communicate with each other. With these patients there are ways to give instructions to the unconscious without the conscious knowing this was done. Say you instruct a patient who doesn't cook to walk to the kitchen and turn on the oven. His conscious mind doesn't know you gave this instruction. But if you ask him why he did this, he won't confess he has no idea. He'll fabricate a story, a logic, sometimes laughably elaborate, to explain it. 'I turned on the oven to make sure it still worked—in case I decide to sell the house.'"

Rachel paused briefly to stroke the cat who had moved closer to her while she spoke. Duke issued a satisfied purr and settled in even closer.

"Same thing with dreams. Your brain takes wisps of stray electrical impulses and immediately constructs an elaborate story around them. Psychotics have delusions, hallucinations, their minds constructing false visual and auditory images they can't distinguish from reality."

"So how does this connect to implanted memories?"

"Our past is nothing more than a reconstruction, sometimes so exaggerated or inaccurate it borders on fantasy. Our minds are inventive. You read a description about a place and this later becomes a false memory of actually having been there."

She frowned. "More worrisome, our memories are susceptible to manipulation. The first researcher to show this unambiguously was a woman named Elizabeth Loftus. She recruited subjects and contacted their families to get three stories about their past. Then she added a fourth story that was entirely made up, about the time they were lost in a mall as a child. She presented each of these stories to the participants. Turns out, many of them remembered the fourth story happening, along with the other three. Not only that, but when she had them back later for subsequent interviews, they began to remember ever more detail about the experience—an experience that *never really happened*. They now remember who found them. How their mom hugged them and cried when they were finally reunited. And so on. So it's not only possible to implant false memories, but once this has been done, the mind will *embellish* them."

"Fantasy becomes reality," said Quinn.

"Yes. And don't get me started on so-called *recovered memory* therapy. Sometimes memories of childhood abuse drudged up by therapists are accurate, but they're usually not. Like getting lost in the mall. Your memories are wide open to suggestion and manipulation. There was something called the 'satanic panic' decades ago, when dozens of children made allegations of satanic abuse. It was later proven to be a collective delusion."

"But you don't think this kind of manipulation would explain what happened in my case?"

"No. Your recollection of what was said during your fantasy encounter with the president is too precise. You seem to have an almost photographic recall of it. I think this was done using sophisticated techniques, well beyond even my capabilities."

"What do you mean, *your* capabilities? Are you saying you're working on the implantation of false memories?"

"No. But this is the dark side of what I am working on."

Rachel explained Matrix Learning briefly, and how her goal was to achieve techniques that would allow her to implant vast knowledge into minds with the ease of loading a software program into a computer.

"If you can implant knowledge," she said, "you can implant false memories. Two sides of the same coin. And it sounds as though whoever did this tied these false memories to the highly charged, emotional regions of your brain, like the amygdala. They counted on the fact that whenever you tried to think about your wife, your rage would keep you from exploring other memories of your life with her—memories you'd be unable to find."

Quinn felt a wave of nausea sweep through him. What could be more insidious than this, more of a violation of his being?

"You *are* your memory," said the professor, looking more than a little distraught. "It's as simple as that. The implantation of false memories is the ultimate manipulation, far more troubling even than the lack of memory, than amnesia. If a man approaches and you don't remember he's a hired killer, at least you'll be somewhat on your guard—simply because he's a stranger. But if the same killer approaches, and you *falsely* remember him as being a close friend, someone who once saved your life, your guard is completely down."

"Or if you remember the President of the United States savagely killing your pregnant wife."

Rachel shuddered. "They turned you into a weapon," she said. "One pointed at the president. And if someone out there has not only perfected these techniques, but isn't hesitating to use them in the most despicable way possible, this would be . . ."

She shook her head in frustration, unable to find words powerful enough to express her anxiety over this possibility. "Well, let's just say we'd have a really bad situation on our hands."

"In a world where this can be done, how can you ever know what to trust?"

"Partly by searching your memories for texture. Like with your wife. If you can't remember the most fundamental things about her, you know you've been tampered with. And I have been working on more sophisticated and foolproof solutions."

"I'm confused," said Quinn. "I thought you said you were five to ten years away from this Matrix Learning."

"This is true. But the possible misuses of this technology once it's been perfected are obvious. So I'm working on preventing this misuse at the same time I'm working on solving the problem in the first place."

"Really?" said Quinn, intrigued.

"I wish you'd been in my class this morning. We discussed this at length. Those of us developing breakthrough technology have a responsibility to predict how the bad actors of the world will bastardize it, and develop preventative measures. I discussed Matrix Learning with my class and some of the dangers. Interestingly enough, the malicious implantation of false memories was a danger we didn't get to. But my class realized that even for positive applications of the technology, it will be critical to develop a diagnostic that tells you when your mind has been tampered with. Or something that can actively prevent any tampering being done in the first place." She tilted her head. "Interestingly enough, this last point was raised by Eyal Regev."

Quinn paused in thought for several seconds. "So maybe that's what this is all about. Maybe whoever perfected the false memory implantation technique doesn't want someone like you developing a way to detect it. Or prevent it."

"That's the first explanation that makes *any* sense," said Rachel. "But I know everyone in the field. They don't necessarily publish all of their findings, but everything I know tells me I'm years ahead of anyone else in this area. Yet whoever did this is years ahead of me. It's almost impossible to believe."

"If I truly am sane, then isn't this conclusion inescapable?"

Rachel forced a weak smile. "Like I said, I'm hoping it turns out that you're as mad as a hatter."

"Given everything we've discussed," responded Quinn with a deep frown, "I'm suddenly hoping the same thing."

30

The conversation between an ex-Secret Service agent and a future Nobel laureate continued for several hours. When it concluded, Rachel used Quinn's phone to leave a message at her lab, indicating that she had fallen ill and wouldn't be in until further notice, and then they retired to separate rooms for the night.

They both slept like the dead and arose refreshed. After a shower and an orange juice and omelet breakfast, Quinn felt like himself for the first time in ages. Could it really only be Tuesday morning? Could his attack on Davinroy really have taken place a mere thirty-six hours before?

He felt as though he had lived a lifetime in these few hours. And now that he knew his memory of Nicole's death, and life, were fabricated, the rage and hate that had been consuming him had finally relented, and he felt at peace, despite his unenviable circumstances. He still felt a residual sense of loss, but not much of one. He guessed this was because he wasn't in love. Had never been. While the implanted memory of Nicole having been the love of his life was still present, this was now hollow, not even close to the *real* emotion, which he had never actually felt.

Rachel had turned on the television after breakfast and they had both been barraged by Quinn's story, which had finally burst onto the scene like an ocean of water through a shattered dam.

Quinn was thankful he had told his version to Rachel when he had.

The coverage was wall to wall, and there was nowhere other than a monastery to get away from it. Two nights earlier, at a fundraiser at the Princeton home of David Garza, Secret Service Special Agent Kevin Quinn had attempted to kill the President of the United States. Luckily, he had failed, but he had also managed to escape. Authorities had delayed putting this out in the media until they could be assured there were no accomplices and the president and public were as safe as possible from this deranged lunatic.

And deranged he was. Interviews with witnesses indicated this Quinn had ranted about the president torturing and killing his pregnant wife, even though it was well known that the man had never married. Psychiatrists were interviewed on every channel, expressing their opinion about psychosis and the dangers that this man posed.

"I'll be damned," said Rachel after having watched the coverage for ten minutes. "How could I have ever doubted you? Maybe I was just jaded. You know," she added with an impish grin, " if I had a nickel for every time I've been accosted by a man who says my life's in danger, and that he tried to kill the president . . ."

Quinn laughed. "Yeah. It's a tale as old as time," he deadpanned back.

While Rachel was transfixed by the television coverage, Quinn made a call with the untraceable phone he had acquired. Coffey answered on the first ring, but asked Quinn to call him back in ten minutes so he could move to a more private location.

"Jesus, Kevin!" began Coffey when they had reconnected, the phone projecting a life-sized 3-D image of his face at Quinn's eye level. Quinn kept his end audio-only so as not to give Coffey any clues to his whereabouts. "I got the present you couriered over. I had a top scientist I trust in one of our nearby Black labs take a look at it. A PhD computer specialist named Justin Beam. I was sure you were delusional about this. I only checked it out because I'd given you my word."

The stunned expression on Coffey's face told Quinn everything he needed to know.

"Dr. Beam confirmed what I told you, didn't he?"

"He did," said Coffey, shaking his head like he had just verified that Elvis was still alive but couldn't get himself to fully believe it. "Justin studied it under an electron microscope and ran some tests. He identified computer circuits, but smaller than he's ever seen, and with a much different architecture. Crazy advanced shit. He's certain that there was too much damage for us to activate it, or reverse engineer it. The eyes are tiny cameras—also crazy advanced—that were still working."

"Let me guess," said Quinn. "This Justin Beam is in charge of *our* fly drone program, isn't he?"

Coffey took a deep breath and nodded. "He was blown away. I told you this was impossible. He would have told you the same thing. At least he would have *yesterday*."

"I've had some revelations myself since our last call," said Quinn. "I did what you said, Cris. I Googled myself. You were right, of course. I wasn't even at Davinroy's resort this year. Which shook me up, more than I think you can possibly imagine."

Quinn went on to explain how he was unable to remember anything about his wife.

"I can't say how," he continued, deciding not to tell Coffey about Rachel Howard just yet, "but I've come to believe my memory has been tampered with. The memories of Davinroy's assault were implanted, using sophisticated techniques. And in such a way as to drive me mad with rage whenever I considered them. I was nothing more than a tool."

Quinn recounted the history of Charles Whitman and his tumor-motivated shooting spree. "So think of it this way," he said when he had finished. "It's like I had a brain tumor that caused me to try to kill Davinroy. But now this tumor has been removed, and I'm back to being myself again."

Coffey nodded but didn't reply, and Quinn suspected he wasn't fully convinced.

"Look, Cris, this fly drone is real! Much more is happening here than meets the eye. I know the idea of memory tampering is far-fetched. I know it seems impossible. But didn't you just say the same thing about the technology I sent you?"

There was a long pause. "Okay, I'm with you," said Coffey finally, and this time Quinn sensed he had come to a final, definitive position. "You're absolutely right. Things aren't what they seem. And I do know you, Kevin. You passed your recent psych evaluation with flying colors. Your attack on Davinroy never made sense. And during our recent interactions you've never come across as anything but fully rational. And the fly drone *is* extraordinary. So I'm onboard. I believe you're innocent."

"Thank you."

Coffey's face fell. "This being said, the hole you're in is getting deeper. I'm not sure if you're able to get media wherever you are, but the story broke this morning."

"I'm aware."

"The timing of this wasn't my idea, it was Davinroy's. After Justin got back to me last night that the drone was real, I tried to convince the president to continue to keep this buried, sit on the witnesses and media. But since you insisted I not tell him about the drone or our interaction, it was hopeless. Unfortunately, now that your identity is known by every adult in America, you're well and truly screwed. Even worse than before."

"Trying to cheer me up?" said Quinn dryly.

"Of course," replied Coffey in amusement. "That's what I do. Plus making sure you aren't bored."

"Very thoughtful of you. How's the manhunt going? Making any progress finding me?"

"Yes. Just this morning we finally got a break."

"Sorry to hear that," said Quinn.

"Hey, you were the one who asked," said Coffey with a smile. "Seems a guy returned from a short business trip to find his Ford Fusion had been stolen. From a parking lot in Trenton near the train station. He left Sunday night, at about the same time *you* were reported to have been in the area. We guessed it likely you'd steal a car so we had our ear to the ground. Paid special attention to any stolen car reports within five hundred miles of Princeton. Taking one that wouldn't be reported for days would be inspired, so I thought of you immediately." He raised his eyebrows. "Well done."

"Thanks," said Quinn. "You too. But this could be a problem for me. I don't want the manhunt getting too close just yet."

"I understand. I'll take responsibility for finding this car myself. I'll send the team in the wrong direction until we can figure something else out."

There was a chance Coffey was still trying to capture him, and this was a ruse intended to keep him from looking over his shoulder, but Quinn had too much to worry about to consider this further. There came a point where you had to trust something, and he chose to trust that Coffey was now on his side.

"Cris," he began, almost at a loss for words, "I can't thank you enough. And I won't let you down. We're just scratching the surface, but something very big is brewing. I promise you I'm going to find out what it is."

"Amen to that. We'll find out together."

"In the meanwhile, if you find yourself remembering something that's emotionally charged and seems crazy, think twice about trusting it."

"You mean like everything that's happened in the past few days?"

Quinn grimaced. "It does mess with your head. My definition of the ultimate nightmare is living in a world where you can never be sure of what you *think* you know. If something unlikely does emerge as a potent memory—you know, something *else* unlikely—just be sure to take the time to explore it carefully. Search for texture. For depth. If you can't find other memories that should connect with it, the memory is bogus."

"Roger that," said Coffey uneasily.

31

Quinn and Rachel retired into the basement of their borrowed home once again, and Quinn recounted his conversation with Coffey, telling her about the fly drone he had discovered. As long as the life of this innocent woman was on the line, he wasn't about to play games. She deserved to have all information available, even if classified. Besides, with a mind like hers, perhaps she could solve this puzzle where he couldn't.

"So what now?" she asked when he had finished. "I'm guessing you don't think it's safe just yet to go back to my life."

"I wish I could tell you otherwise," said Quinn. He was about to continue when the cat issued a screech from upstairs like nothing Quinn had ever heard. It was aggressive, and violent, and the most threatening sound that could possibly come out of a domestic feline.

Quinn motioned for silence at the same time as his eyes darted around the room. He had little doubt they had at least one visitor, and probably two or more. And while the cat had warned Quinn, the intruders would know that he was now on alert and act accordingly. Which meant whoever had entered the house wouldn't open the door to the basement and make themselves sitting ducks.

Quinn had to act quickly. They had broken in soundlessly, despite dead-bolted doors, so they were pros. If not for the cat's warning he and Rachel would have been easy prey. But the intruders couldn't be sure their targets were in the basement, and there would be too many windows for them to be able to cover all possible exits.

Quinn looked up at the sole basement window, set into the outside yard within a large steel window well with a gravel floor, and assessed his chances. If this were *his* op, he would plant a man with a gun pointing at the closed basement door and send others on his team to clear the rest of the house, room by room.

He had to assume that any attempt to open the door to the upstairs would be met with a barrage of gunfire. Climbing into the window well and then the yard beyond, on the other hand, was at least a fifty-fifty proposition, maybe better. But he wasn't about to risk Rachel's life on these odds along with his own. He needed a place for her to hide, and there were precious few options.

He lowered himself to the carpeting and lifted the heavy fabric skirt at the bottom of one blue couch. There was about an eight-inch gap between the bottom of the couch's wood frame and the floor. Rachel Howard was slim, but he wondered if she was slim *enough*.

"Hide under here," he whispered, urgency in his voice.

"I'll never fit," she whispered back. "And it's the first place they'll look."

Hiding under a couch might seem obvious and cliché, but Quinn had a feeling it would not be searched. Like a hidden compartment in a magician's box, it seemed too tight a space for a grown man to consider as a possible hiding place. And once she was under, Quinn would re-straighten the fabric skirt, which was so thick it almost appeared rigid and unmovable. This was also their only option.

"You'll fit," he whispered, hoping this was true. "Trust me! It'll work," he added with far more confidence than he felt. "Now!" he insisted. "Hurry!"

Rachel flattened herself against the carpet and slid underneath the couch. The wooden frame compressed her back like a girdle, but she was just able to force herself under. Quinn hastily straightened the fabric skirt, jumped to his feet, and repositioned one of the oak end tables. He stood on top of it and slid open the window above him, popping out the screen. He then pulled himself up and through as quietly as he could.

But he only made it halfway.

As he was pulling himself through he was hit with a blast of electricity, the type he falsely remembered Davinroy having delivered. He fell back to the carpeted basement floor like a brick, gouging his right leg on the edge of the end table on his way down, drawing blood.

The man who had stunned him propelled himself through the open window and onto the floor with the ease and grace of a gymnast. He stood over the bleeding, still-paralyzed figure of Kevin Quinn with a smug expression on his face.

"My partner's clearing the house," he said calmly. "But I knew if you were in the basement you'd never come through the door. So I made sure to cover your only other exit." He shrugged. "It's what I would have done in your position."

While Quinn was still incapacitated the man pulled him a few feet to the white steel pole that ran floor to ceiling and linked his wrists together around it with a plastic zip-tie.

He then contacted his sole partner, who was soon descending the stairs to join him. Duke the cat cautiously and silently flowed down the steps also, well behind the incoming killer, alert and ready for action. Quinn shot an imperceptible nod at the small feline in appreciation for his warning, which had at least given Quinn the chance to hide Rachel.

The newcomer had a prominent scar on the left side of his neck. "Where's the girl?" he demanded the moment he stepped off the stairs, and Quinn found himself wishing whoever was responsible for the scar had managed to finish the job.

"Not here," said Quinn, having recovered from the effects of the stun gun. "I stayed as bait. To draw out any hostiles."

"Looks like you succeeded," said Scar with a smile of superiority. "A little *too* well. You didn't think these hostiles would end up on top, did you?"

He gestured to his partner, the gymnast. "Make sure she's not here."

The man who had stunned Quinn walked around the room and looked for a hidden door or possible hiding place, returning to his original position moments later. He caught his partner's eye. "How confident was our employer that she was with him?"

"Very. But he wasn't *certain*. We'll worry more about her in a second. First, I need you to search this guy carefully. From what I was told, you're looking for some miniaturized tech. It's supposed to look like a fly, although it's damaged, so who knows. Our employer thinks he might have it on him."

The gymnast squinted at Quinn. "You want to make this easy," he said, "and just give it to me?"

"I have no idea what you're talking about. Tell your Russian employer that he's lost his mind."

The man laughed. "For what he's paying us, he can send us on as many snipe hunts as he wants."

He searched Quinn for a full five minutes—thoroughly—before finally giving up.

"So I assume the Russian still wants me alive?" said Quinn when the search was abandoned.

"Barely," said Scar. "Having you alive is a nice-to-have, but not a need-to-have. He told us to kill you if there was any chance you'd get away. And to feel free to waste you the moment you became a burden. I'd remember that if I were you."

"How did you find me?" said Quinn, lowering himself to a seated position on the carpet, his linked arms sliding down to the bottom of the pole and his right leg still bleeding.

"Apparently the stealth phones used by my predecessors weren't as untraceable as they thought," said Scar. He pointed a semi-automatic pistol at Quinn's chest. "Now tell me where the girl is!"

"I have no idea," replied Quinn. "I warned her the Russian was after her. After that I convinced her it would be best for us to split up. I told her to go into hiding, but purposely made sure I didn't know where she was going." He delivered a fake smile. "You can't tell what you don't know, right?"

"I don't believe you," said Scar simply.

"I don't give a shit what you believe."

Scar shook his head, almost in pity. Without warning he kicked Quinn viciously in the leg, in the center of his wound, which sent waves of searing pain throughout his body. Quinn groaned in agony.

"Where is she!" demanded Scar.

"I don't know!" spat Quinn through clenched teeth. "If I knew, I'd tell you."

Scar bent down and pressed the barrel of his gun into his prisoner's forehead. "Did I mention our employer said you were expendable? Last chance to tell me the truth."

Quinn closed his eyes. "Do what you have to do," he said. "I can't tell you what I don't know."

The man paused for several agonizingly long seconds and finally removed the barrel from Quinn's forehead and backed away. "My partner and I are going to go upstairs and have a talk," he said, and then with a cruel smile added, "wait here."

They had just reached the stairs when Duke made his presence known once again. He issued a tentative meow and began to push his way through the fabric skirt at the bottom of one couch.

"What do you two *assholes* need to talk about?" barked Quinn suddenly, but his desperate attempt to create a distraction was too late. Both men had already turned to observe Duke.

Shit! mouthed Quinn. He had been so close. Live by the cat, die by the cat.

Both men moved quickly. Scar pointed his weapon where the cat had sought ingress under the sofa while his partner crouched down by its edge and used his considerable strength to topple it over backwards.

Lying flat on her stomach, but no longer pinned to the carpet, Rachel Howard was as exposed as a cockroach under a sudden spotlight. She rolled onto her back and then to a seated position, taking exaggerated breaths now that the weight had been lifted from her struggling lungs.

Scar followed her with his weapon. "I'm really sorry about this," he said with a shrug, preparing to fire.

"Then don't do it," she pleaded, tears beginning to well up in her eyes.

"Nothing personal," he said, his expression not showing a hint of pity or mercy. "But there's a lot of money involved."

Rachel squeezed her eyes shut and braced for oblivion.

Quinn had risen from the floor and was trying frantically to defy physics and disengage himself from the steel pole, but his attempts were useless. As Scar pointed his gun at Rachel's forehead, Quinn closed his eyes as well, unwilling to bear witness to the brutal murder of an innocent woman.

The near-deafening sound of two gunshots exploded into the air and Quinn screamed out in anguish, knowing that all of his skills, all of his experience, had failed to save the brilliant woman he had come to like and respect so very much.

32

Even before Quinn's scream ended he knew his assessment of the situation was flawed. Two gunshots had been fired, yes, but Scar had not been responsible. Instead they had originated from the window well, angling down precisely through the still-open window and taking out both mercs, leaving Quinn and Rachel unscathed.

The man responsible poured himself through the window and jumped to the basement carpet, landing softly, while the cat bounded silently up the stairs and through the open door, deciding he had seen more than enough human aggression for one day.

Scar had fallen across Rachel and she was almost hysterical as the man's blood began soaking into her shirt. The newcomer removed the merc's body and knelt down beside her and repeated, "It's okay," over and over again in his most soothing voice. "It's okay. It's okay. It's okay." Hypnotically.

Quinn's mouth fell open as recognition finally wormed its way through a disbelieving skull. It was the Israeli. Eyal Regev.

Impossible. He was dead.

And if he wasn't dead, as Quinn's senses now seemed to suggest was the case, what was he doing here? Eliminating competitors so he could hog the reward?

"Eyal?" whispered Rachel, coming out of her shock, but immediately tensing once again as she remembered the night before.

Regev looked relieved that she had found her bearings. "It's okay," he repeated one last time. "You're safe. No one is going to hurt you. I promise."

"How are you alive?"

Still lashed to a steel pole, Quinn had never felt so helpless. The best he could do was remain quiet and see how the conversation developed, which was maddening.

"I was wearing an advanced bulletproof . . . well, not vest," replied Regev. "Call it an undershirt. Much lighter and stronger than the current gold standard."

"But I saw the blood," said Rachel.

"You were supposed to. They're engineered to produce a blood-like fluid when hit. Even with a vest, a bullet will put you on your ass. While you're down, the last thing you want is for the shooter to realize you're wearing body armor. His next shot will be between your eyes."

Regev stood and backed away, so he now had both Quinn and the professor in his field of vision. "Special Agent Quinn," he said, studying him carefully for the first time. "Nice to see you again. I have to say, I like you better strapped to a pole."

"I like you better with a bullet in your chest," said Quinn. "On the other hand, given what just happened, I may have to rethink that." He nodded at the Israeli. "You look good for a dead man. My compliments to your tailor."

Regev laughed. "The tech truly is amazing. They're having to develop new physics to account for how well it's able to spread out and nullify the force of a bullet. And just so you know, after a few patents, we are planning to share it."

"We?" said Quinn intently. "Are you going to tell us who you work for? Who you really are?"

"My name really is Eyal Regev," replied the Israeli. "And I suppose I don't have much choice but to come clean at this point." He sighed. "I'm with Israeli Intelligence. The Mossad."

"The Mossad?" repeated Rachel with a look of confusion. "Why in the world would the *Mossad* want me dead?"

Eyal laughed. "Dead is the last thing we want you," he said.

He reholstered his weapon and rubbed his chin in thought. "We both were operating under some poor assumptions last night, I'm afraid. I wasn't trying to kill you. I was trying to save you from *him*," he explained, nodding toward Quinn.

"*He* wasn't trying to kill me, either," said Rachel.

Regev nodded in amusement. "Yeah, I get that now. I did say we were *both* misguided. Good thing I didn't kill him last night when I had the chance."

"When did you have the chance?" snapped Quinn, his pride refusing to allow him to take the Israeli's contention lying down.

"When you shot me. I had you in my sights first, but I couldn't risk hitting Rachel."

Quinn thought back to the positioning of the relevant parties the night before and realized this might be true. Either way, there was no point in discussing it further. "Tell us about last night, then," he said. "How do you figure in?"

"We were running surveillance on the professor's house and phone," began Regev, "and—"

"Shit!" interrupted Rachel in outrage. "My phone was bugged too?"

"Not bugged," said Regev. "Just tracked. But still, I am truly sorry about the invasion of privacy," he added, looking genuinely contrite.

The Israeli faced the Secret Service agent once again. "When her phone remained stationary at a church parking lot," he said, "the AI we have monitoring things alerted me. So I began paying close personal attention. I was watching when you entered her house. When you immediately found and disabled my bugs, I knew you were a player."

"And not her favorite uncle coming for a visit?"

"Exactly. I ran you through Mossad's facial recognition software, which is top drawer."

Quinn didn't doubt this for a moment. The Mossad had maintained an unsurpassed reputation for innovation for decades, and he wouldn't be surprised if their facial recognition systems were as good as their bulletproof vests.

"Turns out I got a match to a special agent the Mossad had learned through the grapevine had tried to assassinate Matthew Davinroy the night before. A raving mad lunatic, foaming at the mouth about a pregnant wife he didn't have. I know you've been busy, but the story broke in the media this morning."

"Thanks," said Quinn dryly. "I'll be sure to check it out."

"I wasn't sure what you wanted with Rachel Howard, but I didn't care. You're clearly dangerous and unstable. I wasn't willing to take any chances. You hadn't killed her yet, but I wasn't going to wait for that to change. The Mossad is spread a little thin so I'm working with a gun for hire, in a house that, not coincidentally, is less than five minutes from here. The moment I learned who you were, Agent Quinn, I set an attack in motion."

Regev paused and assessed the man before him. "I have to say you were very impressive. I still can't believe that we failed."

"So your partner is alive also?"

Regev's face fell. "No. These vests are in short supply, and meant to be kept secret, so he didn't have one. I'm afraid he really is dead. My fall through the window knocked me out for a short while. When I came to you were gone. I gathered up my fallen . . . employee, cleaned up a bit, and left."

"I'm sorry about your man," said Quinn. "But he *was* trying to kill me."

Regev shrugged. "It's unfortunate, but he did know the risks."

"How did you find us here?" said Rachel.

"I had no idea where you went after last night. But while I was trying to pick up your trail I decided to set up video surveillance of the outside of your house and vicinity. When I noticed your two visitors staking out your neighbor's house, I put two and two together and got here as soon as I could."

Quinn's eye narrowed. "How long did you have them in your sights?" he asked.

"Almost from the moment you were hit with the stun gun."

"So what took you so long to act?" demanded Quinn.

"You obviously haven't been paying attention," said Regev. "*Rachel* is my priority. You aren't. And she wasn't in play for some time. So I thought I'd listen for as long as I could to gather intelligence. You know," he added, gesturing toward himself, "*Mossad* agent."

"Learn anything valuable?"

"Very. First, a clear confirmation that you weren't trying to kill her. The opposite, in fact. You were willing to die to protect her. That's why you're still alive."

"And second?" said Quinn.

Regev hesitated. "Maybe we'll save that for later. Or maybe not. Depending."

"Depending on what?"

"Depending on how you factor into things, Special Agent Quinn. Why don't you tell me how you came to be interested in the professor."

"You first," said Quinn. "Why were you and the Mossad monitoring her?"

"No, *you* first," said Regev firmly, making a show of raising his gun once again. "I insist."

Quinn sighed. "You're going to find what I tell you impossible to believe."

"Try me."

"The media accounts of what happened are true," said Quinn. "I really did try to kill the president and I really did make the accusations you've heard about. But I've since learned my memories of what happened, what set me off, were false. Implanted. I came to realize my mind was tampered with."

Quinn expected Regev to be rolling his eyes, but instead he was nodding. "Yeah. We guessed as much."

"What?" said Quinn, and Rachel looked just as shocked as he did.

"I'll tell you all about it. But please finish your story."

Quinn wanted badly to press the Israeli, learn what he meant by his last statement, but he knew this wouldn't get him anywhere. Regev was in control and would decide if, and when, he provided further information.

"Not much else to tell," said Quinn. "I was abducted by two mercenaries."

"Were they working for the Russian I heard you talk about?"

"Yes. I got the drop on them and learned this Russian wanted Rachel dead. When I realized she was an expert in memory, I thought

I could protect her and get some answers. Kill two birds with one stone. That's it." He stared hard at the Israeli. "Now it's your turn."

"Not just yet," said Regev. "Tell me about this fly drone these men were looking for."

"Fly drone? Is that a drone that flies?"

"Very clever. So you found one. A damaged one. What did you do with it?"

"Scar spoke about tech that resembled a fly. He never said anything about a drone. So why would you draw that conclusion?"

"Scar?" said Regev.

"The merc about to shoot Rachel," explained Quinn. "That's how I thought of him." He gestured with his head toward the man's body on the ground, and to the scar on his neck that was still visible. "So are you going to answer my question? Where did you get the idea he was talking about a drone?"

"What else could it be?" replied Regev. "Every intelligence agent in the world knows that a flawless fly drone is the holy grail." He paused. "So where did you hide it?"

"I didn't hide it. I don't even know what you're talking about. But even if I did, why would I tell you? You're a foreign spy working on American soil, illegally surveiling a prominent scientist. You haven't said word one about your reason for this, or your intentions. And while you saved Rachel's life, you've been pointing a gun at me and haven't cut me loose from this pole."

Regev smiled broadly. "Well, you *are* the most wanted man in the country," he pointed out in amusement. "I'm pretty sure I could get arrested for letting you go."

"I'm not laughing."

Regev sighed. "Okay. You make some good points. I suppose I could give you better reasons to trust me." He removed a phone from his pocket. "So let's take a pause while I check in with headquarters. The decision to bring you up to speed is above my pay grade."

Seconds later Regev was speaking Hebrew into the phone at a furious pace, rightly convinced that neither listener could decipher more than one or two words, at best. Unsurprisingly, the call was audio only.

After ten minutes, Regev returned the phone to his pocket.

He faced Quinn and nodded. "Okay, Special Agent. I have a green light to trust you with some sensitive information. This being the case, it's time to become civilized again. I'll cut you loose and the three of us can adjourn to a safer, more comfortable place."

"Somewhere that isn't knee-deep in dead bodies might be nice," said Rachel.

"Where do you have in mind?" said Quinn.

"I told you I bought a place five minutes from here. I've introduced some security upgrades. Basically, I've turned it into a fortress. Trust me, no one will find us there."

"Good. I've got a rucksack with weapons and supplies I'll want to bring. Including the equipment that identified your bugs. But I assume you'll want to scan us and the bag for possible electronic surveillance anyway—just in case."

"*Baytach*," said Regev in Hebrew. "Of course," he amended. The Israeli rolled his eyes. "But do us all a favor, leave the phone you took from your mercenary friend here, okay?"

"Yeah, thanks for the tip."

"Don't mention it," replied Regev. Then, with a grin spreading across his face, he added, "And let's leave the cat behind as well. I think he may be working for the other side."

33

Since the Mossad agent was using his newly acquired home as a military outpost, it was exactly what Quinn had expected. Barren. Undecorated and unlived in. But with enough televisions, computers, monitors, weapons, and electronics to supply a Walmart. He had one black leather couch facing the biggest of the monitors and a chair pushed under a large glass desk.

Regev gave Quinn an aerosol can that he explained contained an experimental wound sealant. The can was small enough to easily be included with other gear taken into battle, but contained all the sealant any solider might need, kept under considerable pressure. It didn't act immediately, and it didn't staunch the flow of blood entirely, but in conjunction with bandages it was proving to be an excellent stopgap measure that had already saved Israeli lives.

Quinn used his host's sink to clean his wound, and while he ordinarily would have required five or ten stitches, Regev assured him that the sealant and bandages would obviate this need.

Once this was complete, Quinn sat next to Rachel on the Israeli's couch, ready to pick up the discussion where they had left off. Regev sat in the desk chair facing them.

"Over the past few months," began the Israeli, "two of our agents, Mossad agents, have been compromised. It took a while for us to discover what was going on, and even longer to convince ourselves of the truth, but their memories had been tampered with. For malicious ends."

"Which is exactly what happened to Kevin," noted Rachel unnecessarily.

"That's right. And I don't need to tell either of you how alarming this is. What a game changer it represents."

"What memories were implanted in your agents?" asked Quinn. "And to what end?"

Regev frowned. "You know I can't answer that. We may have forged something of an alliance . . . Kevin . . . and I am reading you in here, but you know I have to keep the classified information I tell you to a minimum."

"Fair enough," said Quinn. "But I take it this is why you guessed what had happened to me?"

"Yes. We know Secret Service agents get frequent psych evaluations, so we felt this was the most likely explanation, especially since you sought out Professor Howard."

"And yet you still tried to kill me."

"Our plan was to incapacitate you if possible. But if we had to kill you to protect Rachel, we were willing, yes. Because we couldn't know for certain we were right. And we couldn't know what other memories had been implanted. Maybe you had false memories of Rachel slitting your sister's throat two days earlier, and were planning to torture and kill her in revenge."

He raised his eyebrows. "It isn't like you haven't shown a willingness to kill in the name of getting even."

Quinn frowned but had to concede the Israeli made a valid point.

"We investigated what happened to our agents but got nowhere," continued the Israeli. "No idea who or why. According to our research such a capability was five or ten years beyond the current state of the art, at minimum. We only identified a single scientist who had the slightest chance of making such a breakthrough."

"Let me guess," said Quinn. "She's sitting right next to me."

"Good guess."

"So you came here to make sure she wasn't responsible?"

"Yes. That was one reason." He turned to face Rachel. "I'm afraid we were quite thorough. We had to be. We hacked your computer, read your e-mails and texts, and surveiled you. As I've said, I'm truly sorry about this."

"So don't keep me in suspense," said Rachel dryly. "Did I turn out to be the bad guy?"

"Of course not. We didn't think you were, but we had to rule this out."

"Then why are you still here?" said Quinn.

"Because this was only one of the reasons I came. We didn't really think she was behind what happened to our agents. But if she wasn't, we wanted to enlist her help."

"To find out who *is* behind it?" asked Rachel.

"Yes, but even more importantly, to develop countermeasures. We know you're big on these. Big on finding ways to counteract the uses bad actors might make of scientific advances."

"So you had a bug in my classroom also?" said Rachel.

"Your views are well known. And I was at your last lecture in person, remember? I heard every word you said." A guilty look crossed his face. "But yes, your classroom was bugged. My boss wanted to listen in. We were both very impressed."

"Why pretend to be a grad student? And how did you even manage that?"

"To answer your second question, it wasn't easy. I took a crash course in neuroscience over two weeks while the Mossad doctored records, pulled strings, and called in favors to get me into your class."

"As a transfer from Johns Hopkins?"

Regev nodded.

"Hard to imagine you could really pull that off," said Rachel.

"The results speak for themselves. I was registered in your class, as you know. The Mossad is very good at what it does."

Quinn nodded at Rachel beside him. "This is true," he acknowledged. "This probably wasn't even that much of a challenge for them in the scheme of things."

"So that's the *how*," said Rachel. "What about the *why*?"

"My job was to clear you of any suspicion and then recruit you to help us. Which would entail giving you highly classified, sensitive information. And also asking you to work with a foreign government. Not an easy ask."

Regev paused. "So we wanted to get to know you. Establish a rapport. Gain your trust. But also understand you the best we could.

The better we could understand your drives, your motivations, your loyalties, your ethics, your—"

"The better you could manipulate me," interrupted Rachel.

"That's one way to put it. I was going to say, the better we could make our case. I don't think you appreciate just how much we'd be asking. Working in secret with a foreign intelligence agency could be construed as treason."

"Why not share this with the US government?" said Quinn. "Get the help of CIA or DHS to recruit Rachel?"

"Given what's happened with you, that *is* the new plan. But only because this problem seems to have spread to your shores. Before this we thought it was confined to Israel. So your government would have been less inclined to join our efforts. And what would we tell them? How would we make a convincing case that this was really happening? Not easy to wrap your head around, especially given that your experts would conclude what our experts concluded: this can't be done. Not given the state of current knowledge and technology."

"You're right," said Rachel. "They wouldn't have believed you."

"And even if we were able to convince them," continued the Israeli, "we'd be shooting ourselves in the foot. How could they trust us if the memories of our agents could be tampered with for malicious purposes? Our agents serve on a number of teams with US counterparts, joint initiatives. And we provide considerable intel to you. Trust is hard enough to come by in the intelligence community when agents *can't* be tampered with. How disruptive do you think *this* disclosure would be?"

"So you chose to keep it in-house," said Quinn. "But now that's changed. Now it's become our problem too."

"Yes. So even now, the head of Mossad and the Prime Minister of Israel are setting up a vid-meet for later today. A very high-level vid-meet. To start a discussion between our two governments. Turns out you've become a very important man to us, Kevin."

"Because I'm living proof of what you're claiming?"

"Yes. I was slow to appreciate just how important you are. Not only in convincing your government that this tampering is real, and that it represents a potentially devastating threat, but in convincing Rachel of the same. My superior just chewed me out for my lack of foresight, and for taking any chances with your life."

Quinn shook his head in wonder. "So what are you saying, Eyal? That I've become as important to the Mossad as Rachel is?"

"Not even close," said Regev with a good-natured smile. "You're very important, no question. But not *Rachel Howard* important."

He paused and stared intently at the professor. "So what about it? Before this vid-meet happens, I'd like to know your thoughts. If your government is amenable, are you in? Will you help us?"

Rachel considered. "I won't commit to anything now, but almost certainly yes."

The Israeli closed his eyes and blew out a heavy sigh of relief. "Thank God," he mumbled.

"Everything you've said makes a twisted sense to me," said Quinn. "At least given this bizarre reality we find ourselves in. But it seems to me the Russian must be the scientist behind this capability. Why else would he try to capture me? Or want Rachel dead? He has to be key."

"Oh, he's key all right," said Regev. "Your logic is sound. But there's a different player behind the memory tampering. The Russian didn't develop the technique. Because he knows absolutely nothing about neuroscience."

Quinn's eyes widened. "Does that mean you know who he *is*?" he said.

"Yes. This is more intel we plan to share during our upcoming vid-meet. But before this happens, you and I need to be honest with each other. I'll tell you what I know about fly drones, for example, and you tell me just what it is you did with the one you discovered."

"Are you willing to go first this time?" asked Quinn.

"I wouldn't have it any other way."

34

Dr. Carmilla Acosta paced in front of the hotel room door like a giddy schoolgirl, dressed in a revealing black lace-and-mesh teddy. After ten minutes of this, fearing she might wear a hole in the carpet and ready to jump out of both the teddy and her skin from anticipation, she sat on the edge of the hotel's king-sized bed and tried to calm herself.

And failed miserably.

All she could do was fantasize about what would soon occur on what she thought of as a cushiony playground. Dmitri's vise-like arms wrapping around her, pushing her down, first nibbling at her lips unhurriedly, and then slipping his tongue inside her mouth, at first gently and then with growing urgency.

It would take all of her willpower not to hurry him, to let him control the pace when all she wanted to do was feel him inside her mouth, inside her body.

She knew she was in love with him, romantic love, at a point in her life when she had been certain she would never feel this emotion again. At one time her marriage had been relatively fulfilling, but the passion had died half a decade earlier and the marriage would soon follow.

Perhaps it had been a combination of things. Of catching her husband in the act with another woman, almost two years previously, feeling unwanted and betrayed, and eager to return the favor. Of the appearance of Dmitri Kovonov a few months later, a man of dazzling strength and self-assurance who wanted her with an unrelenting passion that she had never experienced, a hurricane who would not be denied.

He was a handsome knight from a storybook. Charming, but mysterious. Powerful and hard, yet gentle. Brilliant and uncompromising.

Carmilla was thirty-three years old and had come far since she had left her native Argentina as a girl for the land of opportunity. Stanford undergraduate, Yale to earn her PhD, and for many years now a full professor of molecular biology at Princeton, a school whose reputation in this field was impeccable.

Yes, her marriage was failing. Her husband hadn't known she had witnessed his infidelity and she had yet to confront him, or tell him about Dmitri, but she would very soon. She would trade him in for someone she cared for a hundred times more, a man who made her feel alive, electric, each and every instant he was with her.

She would have Dmitri and then a few years down the road, a Nobel Prize. She had leveraged several inspired insights to perfect a high-speed automated DNA synthesis procedure, and the paper she had written describing the process would be published in only five weeks, revolutionizing the field. CRISPR technology had shaken the biotechnology world less than a decade before, allowing for unprecedented, pinpoint control of the editing of genes. And the scientists involved had all received their expected Nobel Prize right on schedule two years earlier.

But what she had done went far beyond CRISPR, far beyond mere editing. In a day her system could churn out strands of DNA of virtually any length to exact specifications. Enter into a computer the equivalent of a thousand pages of nothing but As and Ts and Gs and Cs and the synthesizer would make a batch of DNA of this precise sequence, without a single letter out of place. It was the difference between editing a gene or building it from scratch.

Dmitri was one of the few people outside of her lab to know what she had accomplished. She had told him about it as a gift to him. A surprise. She had gone on to explain how she might use this technology to perfect a designer virus with very special capabilities, one that might save his sister's life.

He had wept when she had told him of it. She had never loved him more than at that moment.

Finally, there was a light tap at the door. He had arrived!

Carmilla threw open the door and embraced the man of her dreams. As usual, he showed far more control than she ever could, extricating himself after less than a minute, much sooner than she could have managed. She pulled him inside the room and closed the door, breathing deeply of his aftershave, which had notes of ginger and leather and which had become like catnip to her.

"I've missed you so much, Dmitri," she whispered.

Kovonov made a show of looking her up and down approvingly. "I've missed you also," he said. He raised his eyebrows. "I hope you didn't start without me."

Carmilla laughed. "Since I was thinking of *you*, it took all the self-control I have—but I managed it."

"You have the virus?" he said eagerly.

She couldn't hide her disappointment. He seemed more excited about the completion of the virus than he did about seeing her.

On the other hand, she knew she was being selfish. His sister's life was on the line, so of course he was eager. And his joy at this project coming to an end reflected well on her, after all. She had proposed it. And he knew that she was the only one on Earth capable of making it happen. Not just because she could build a virus from scratch, copying the principal survival and infectious machinery from a virus that nature had forged and adding in whatever she chose, but because she was one of only a few who had the genius to know *what* to add in to accomplish her goals.

"I have it with me," she said. "I think you'll be very pleased."

"Give it to me now."

Carmilla shook her head. "That can wait," she replied.

She sat on the edge of the bed once again, the same place she had sat when she had fantasized about being taken by this bear of a man. "The virus is my gift to you. But before you take it," she said suggestively, reaching out to undo his belt buckle, "I need a gift in return."

Kovonov grinned lecherously. "You drive a hard bargain, Carmilla," he said.

He sat beside her and gently lowered her onto the bed. He brushed his lips against hers and placed his left hand between her legs. "But if that's the way it has to be," he added, rubbing his hand slowly up and down against the flimsy material of the teddy, "well, I guess I'm prepared to make that sacrifice."

35

Rachel Howard had a near mythical capacity for assimilating new information and adjusting to new situations, but even she was reaching her limit. One minute she was picking up Thai food for dinner and the next she was catapulted on a fantastic series of events that seemed never-ending.

Learning that her home was bugged and fending off an attack there. Hiding under her neighbor's couch. And worst of all, being an instant away from death, certain she had taken her last breath. And for the first time in her life she had seen men die—be killed—right in front of her.

More than in front of her—one had died *on* her.

So much for her relationship with Debbie Steele. After leaving two dead bodies in her neighbor's home—which wouldn't exactly do wonders for resale value—Rachel had to believe her days of being trusted to feed the cat were over.

And now she found herself under the protection of both a Secret Service agent and an Israeli spy, and had learned that someone out there had leapfrogged her research and was using these discoveries, not in service to mankind, but to its detriment.

Surprisingly, she was drawn to both men more than she wanted to admit, even to herself. As she knew and had preached, you liked who you liked, with very little conscious control. They were both decisive and talented. Both direct and down to earth. No putting on airs. And while she was sure they were both accomplished liars, she was convinced their lies were never told for the purposes of political jockeying or to backstab a colleague. Neither man was an academic, but both were very sharp. She was astonished at how quickly the Israeli had managed to learn enough neuroscience to fool her, even for a short period.

Perhaps these men appealed to a latent bad-boy-seeking gene she didn't know she had. Perhaps she had been in academia too long. In a politically correct university culture packed with too many spoiled rich kids complaining of micro-aggressions, parsing every word and statement for any hint it might give offense, no matter how convoluted the logic behind it, desperately needing to separate the world into victimizers and victims. People with so much time on their hands, and so few actual struggles, that the brush of a metaphoric butterfly wing would send them howling in outrage.

Kevin Quinn and Eyal Regev lived in a world with *macro*-aggressions. They were too busy dodging bullets and protecting their countries to worry that an innocently delivered word might be misunderstood, or become crusaders for safe spaces in which reality was never allowed to intrude. In their world, those who lost didn't get a trophy for participation, because the losers might not be alive to receive one.

Both men were now silent, mentally preparing for the vid-meet that was scheduled for three p.m. sharp, less than five minutes away. Rachel realized she had been in this alternate reality, this impossible reality, for almost exactly twenty-four hours.

When Eyal had said the meeting would be high-level, she had no idea how much of an understatement this would be. Both of her male companions had confirmed the guest list for the upcoming meeting, which she still refused to believe. Not until it really happened.

She was actually going to be in a meeting with Matthew Davinroy, virtual though it might be. The President of the United States. The hit parade of absurdities was about to continue.

In addition to the president, attendees on the Israeli side would be the Prime Minister, Ori Kish; the head of Mossad, Avi Wortzman; his Deputy Director, Yaron Hurwitz; and, of course, Eyal Regev. On the American side there would be Secretary of DHS Greg Henry and his second-in-command, Matthew O'Malley, along with Special Agents Cris Coffey and Kevin Quinn.

And a Harvard neuroscientist who might well be dreaming it all.

It turned out that her host had a special room for vid-meets that was highly secure. She and her two companions took their places at the small table in the room and waited for the meeting to begin. Their wait was very short-lived, as holographic software from a set of cameras built into the walls turned their tiny square table into an imposing oval specimen, and began populating the virtual conference table with participants, looking for all the world as though they were really in the Israeli's home. The projections of the participants, from multiple locations, was done even more seamlessly than usual, and each had an identity and location tag floating nearby.

As the chair of Harvard's neuroscience department, Rachel was used to being the most senior and influential person at a conference table. At this particular meeting—not so much.

The tags floating near the Israeli attendees indicated they were all together at Beit Aghion in Jerusalem, the Israeli equivalent of the White House. And they all looked weary, not surprising since six o'clock on a Tuesday evening in Washington was one o'clock on Wednesday morning for them.

As the most powerful human on the planet, Rachel had expected Matthew Davinroy to begin, but since Ori Kish had asked for this gathering the duty fell to him.

"Mr. President," he said. "Thanks to you and your team for meeting with us on such short notice."

"You made it quite clear how important you felt this was," said the president bluntly, looking slightly annoyed. Not exactly *you're welcome*. The relationship between Davinroy and Kish was rumored to be ice-cold.

"I'm confident you'll agree that it is," said Kish.

"I've been briefed on all relevant background," said Davinroy, "and the information you supplied us. Apparently, there are some troubling events involving miniaturized drones and advanced neuroscience that have arisen. And some further disclosures that you'd like to make."

"Before we begin," said Greg Henry, "I did want to thank Avi for the heads-up on Azim Jafari and the Hamza Mosque."

"Yes, of course," seconded Davinroy insincerely. "Much appreciated."

"Glad we could help," said Wortzman, trying to be diplomatic while his boss, the prime minster, couldn't quite manage to keep all the hostility he felt toward the president from his face. "We're relieved that his plan was averted, and grieve with you over the loss of innocent life in the mosque."

"Thank you," said the president. He turned his focus to the man sitting beside Rachel at the virtual table and his expression darkened. "Special Agent Quinn. I must admit, you're the last person I expected to be conferencing with today. Or any day."

"Mr. President," said Quinn, "I don't have words enough to apologize properly. As you've been briefed, I wasn't myself. I was manipulated. I hope that one day you'll be able to forgive me."

The president glared at Quinn for several long seconds but didn't acknowledge his apology. He shifted his gaze to Rachel. "You must be Professor Howard," he said. "I'm told your presence is important. So thanks for attending."

Rachel was frozen for just a moment, unable to believe the man she had seen so often addressing the nation was now addressing her. For once she decided not to ask the participants at this meeting to call her by her first name. She already felt small enough.

"Thank you, sir," she replied, hearing these words as if they were spoken by someone else.

"Professor Howard," said the Secretary of Homeland Security, "Greg Henry here. I should tell you that during the past several hours we've had swarms of people picking through your background in a bit of a frenzy. As of ten minutes ago, you've been granted our nation's highest security clearance. We'll give you a more formal rundown of what that entails another day, but I thought you should know. Every word said in this meeting is confidential. Do you understand?"

Rachel nodded woodenly. "Of course."

"Can I assume you've implemented the jamming protocol we sent you at each of your locations?" said Avi Wortzman.

"We have," said Henry.

"Good," replied the head of Mossad. "This will ensure any possible listening devices get nothing but static."

"Are we ready to begin?" said Davinroy, making no attempt to hide his impatience.

"We are," said the Israeli prime minister. "This will not be an altogether comfortable meeting for us, I can assure you. But it's time to bring our great friend and ally up to speed on some . . . issues we've been encountering. Despite having to air more dirty laundry than we'd like."

For the first time, Rachel detected a glimmer of enthusiasm from the president, who hadn't realized the coming disclosure might be humiliating to Kish, and was relishing the prospect.

"This being said," continued Kish, "let me give the floor to Avi Wortzman."

"Thank you," said the Mossad leader. "Everyone here is now aware that yesterday, Special Agent Quinn discovered a working fly drone and sent it to Special Agent Coffey for analysis. I understand that the result of this analysis showed that this drone is very advanced, beyond any known technology."

Rachel was transfixed, even though she knew what was coming, since Eyal Regev had come clean with her and Kevin that morning. Kevin had taken time to carefully explain to her the full significance of what had been disclosed.

Every major country in the world had been working furiously on drone tech for many decades. She already knew that drones, civilian and military alike, had become as plentiful as the stars in the heavens—who didn't?—but she hadn't known that the ultimate military and intelligence goal was to perfect a drone that could perfectly mimic a tiny insect. If a technology that was impervious to state-of-the art bug detection could be perfected also, such a drone would be the perfect spy device. A bug that was actually a bug.

Small. Mobile. Self-installing. Undetectable.

The phrase, *I'd like to be a fly on the wall* had come into common usage for a reason. A housefly was the ultimate spy. Which is why Kevin's discovery had created such interest, and such angst. In one's own hands such a device was a godsend. In the hands of one's enemies an unmitigated disaster, a cause for serious alarm, perhaps panic.

Even Cris Coffey didn't know where Avi Wortzman was heading. Kevin had contacted his old boss at eleven that morning and asked him to tell the secretary of Homeland and the president about the fly drone, and Dr. Beam's analysis, despite having insisted that he not do so only the day before. Quinn had explained he needed to get Davinroy's attention so he would accept a meeting request from the Israelis that would shed light on this.

Coffey had been stunned. How in the world had the nation's most hunted man managed to suddenly get into bed with the Israelis?

Quinn had assured him all would become clear during the meeting, and had ended the conversation. Now, less than seven hours later, Coffey was about to get his answers.

"Your understanding is a little off," said Greg Henry, ever cautious with information. "We believe the drone *may* represent a leap forward. But it isn't yet clear. It came to us damaged. So we really couldn't put it through any paces and verify its effectiveness. But why don't you tell *us* how well it performs. When Prime Minister Kish asked for this meeting, he said you know who's behind it."

"More like which country," said Wortzman. He opened his mouth to speak, but hesitated.

"What are you waiting for?" spat Davinroy, "a drum-roll? Which country is it?"

Wortzman grimaced uncomfortably. "Ours," he said simply. "*We're* behind it. Israel. After putting our best minds on the problem for decades we got a few lucky breaks and perfected the drones. They can fly great distances, blend in with surroundings, and plant themselves in cars and offices. They've been in deployment for the last four years."

"Four years!" thundered Davinroy. "You've used these things for *four years* and kept us entirely out of the loop?"

Ori Kish blew out a long breath. "Yes. Both our countries support numerous Black projects. With all due respect, Mr. President, are you telling me you don't have advanced tech you haven't shared with your allies?"

"That means nothing!" barked Davinroy. "The difference is that *we're* the superpower here. The mother ship. And we provide you with substantial support. Financially, militarily, and at bodies like the UN."

"And we've given you substantial intelligence in exchange!" retorted Kish, not backing down an iota. "Even before this drone was perfected. We're your only true friend in the most deadly region in the world, where scores of countries think of America as the Great Satan and want to destroy it as much as they want to destroy Israel. I know you're aware that we've upped the intel we provide to you considerably in the past four years. What you don't know is that we've given you even more anonymously. I won't disclose specifics, but intel from our fly drone program enabled us to stop Kim Jong-un from nuking six of your cities a few years back, including Washington DC. We had him bugged for years. Believe me, that was one crazy bastard, but he managed to sneak the nukes in and bury them in these cities. This wasn't just an idle threat. He couldn't *wait* to carry it out. If we hadn't stepped up, President Davinroy, neither Washington nor *you* would be here right now. I know for a fact that he planned to be sure you were at the White House when he set his devices off."

Davinroy looked stunned by this earth-shattering revelation. Rachel could tell he wasn't just horrified that North Korea had come close to destroying six major cities, without America having a clue, but more so that he and tens of millions of American citizens might owe their lives to Israel and Ori Kish. It clearly grated on him.

"If you had shared this program with us like you *should* have," said the president, now recovered from his shock, "we wouldn't need your rescuing."

"Again, with all due respect," said Kish, "you wouldn't have shared it either if you were in our shoes. We're a tiny country. We aren't surrounded by Mexico and Canada. We're surrounded by militant enemy states that have vowed to destroy us. This drone technology gave us an enormous advantage. It did more than ensure we got the intel to prevent Kim Jong-un from nuking *you*. It allowed us to stop Iran from nuking *us*, and at the eleventh hour. If this tech had leaked, Israel wouldn't still be standing today. Others would have learned how to detect these drones. They would still be valuable, but those at the upper echelons of power would protect themselves from this surveillance."

"What are you saying, that we would have leaked it?" said Davinroy.

"Not *intentionally*," said the prime minister. "And not for certain. But bringing you into the tent would have increased the risk of a leak dramatically. We can keep a secret because our existence *depends* on it. But you are forty times our size, in population and bureaucracy. *Our* necks are in the noose, not yours, and you can't say your record when it comes to keeping secrets is spotless. China has hacked you repeatedly. Look at the damage done by Edward Snowden, and there are many other examples. I'm not being critical, but two people have a better chance than a thousand of keeping a secret. And you're the thousand."

Heated expressions appeared on multiple faces around the table. The president glared at his counterpart but didn't respond further.

"So why tell us about these drones now?" said Henry. "Because Agent Quinn found a disabled one? You didn't want us to panic? Wanted to make sure we knew it was friendly fire?"

Wortzman gritted his teeth. "I wish this were the case," he said. "But I'm afraid it's *much* worse than that."

36

Just when Rachel had thought the tension among the conference participants could not be greater, it promptly grew. Now there was anxiety mixed in with the anger. Both men *actually* in the room with her, rather than *virtually*, had remained silent and had kept their faces largely impassive. When emotions ran high and there were titans present, it was best to try to blend into the walls rather than speaking up and risk drawing fire.

Avi Wortzman pressed a button on a computer pad in front of him and the vid-meet software projected a holographic image of a middle-aged man above the center of the virtual table. Clean-cut, relatively handsome, with gray eyes and brown hair.

"You're looking at a man named Dmitri Kovonov," said the head of Mossad, as the man's age, weight, and other relevant physical data appeared beside his image. "He's a Russian Jew. He emigrated from Moscow to Tel Aviv with his family at the age of fourteen. Brilliant. Obtained a PhD from Technion University in Haifa at the age of nineteen. I'll have his full dossier sent to all of you after this meeting. But what is relevant right now is that he was the number two scientist on the team that developed these drones."

"Who was number one?" asked Henry.

"We promise our scientific heads a certain degree of anonymity," said Wortzman, dodging the question. "But back to Kovonov. A month ago he went rogue. He killed four members of the team and destroyed the one factory that fabricates the fly drones' microelectronics. He made off with our entire supply of inventoried drones, and left us with no way to make more until we can rebuild the factory. An expensive and time-consuming undertaking."

"And you had no safeguards against something like this?" said Henry in disbelief.

"We had *plenty* of safeguards," replied Wortzman. "But he outsmarted us. We trusted him implicitly and were caught with our pants down. Around our ankles. It's a failure of epic proportions. I offered my resignation to the prime minster afterward, but he wouldn't take it."

"Do you know why Kovonov did it?" said Henry. "His endgame?"

"We aren't certain. Our best guess is that he was loyal to Mother Russia all along, possibly having renounced his Judaism. We think he bided his time until he had a clear path to make off with the drones. I know you're aware this is a breakthrough technology, a game changer. But until you've worked with it like we have, you can't fully appreciate just *how much* of a game changer."

"So Kovonov could be using these flies to monitor this very meeting," said Henry. "With Russia or someone worse behind them."

"He could be *trying*," said the head of Mossad. "But as you assured us when we began, you've implemented the jamming countermeasures we provided. Any flies in your offices are hearing nothing but static. We currently also have the ability to detect these drones, which we'll share with you immediately after the meeting. Although if he makes certain changes to the drones, we may lose this capability in the future."

"*Perfect*," said the president sarcastically.

"The bottom line," said Wortzman, "is that these drones, this technology, could now be in the hands of an expansionist Russia, with its sights on regaining its superpower status at any cost. Or if Kovonov went freelance, the situation could be even worse. He could be selling them to more dangerous players even than Russia."

"So you've been trying like hell since he left to clean up your own mess," said Henry.

"Yes. Without success."

"And now without any fly drones of your own," said Davinroy.

"We had a number in the field when the factory and inventory were destroyed," replied Wortzman, "so we still have some capability. We had one assigned to Jafari for several months based on other fly drone intel we had gathered. We were about to reassign the drone to more important work when Jafari announced his grand plan. We lucked out on the timing."

"Jafari was an American citizen," said Davinroy. "So you were spying on *our* citizens on *our* soil. And I have to believe you didn't limit these activities to suspected terrorists. Why do I have the feeling the Oval Office may have had a pest problem the last four years?"

"Unlike your NSA," replied Kish smoothly, "which has acknowledged spying on leaders of countries allied with you—including a former prime minister of Israel—*we* wouldn't do that." He shook his head as if the very idea was unthinkable. "Even if ethics would allow it, if this were somehow discovered it would forever drive a wedge between our friendship."

"Uh-huh," said Davinroy, glaring at the prime minister in disgust. "I'm not buying it. I'd say you're *full of shit* but diplomacy and decorum prevent me."

The president paused. "But let's move on. For now. I'll want to come back to this at another time."

"Of course," said Ori Kish.

"So have you made *any* progress finding Kovonov?" asked O'Malley, who along with Hurwitz, Wortzman's second-in-command, had remained silent until this point.

"Almost none," said Wortzman.

"I'm surprised," said Henry. "The Mossad's bloodhound skills are legendary."

Wortzman frowned. "Kovonov knows all of our secrets. Our methods and the identities of our agents. We don't know how much spying he did on us before he left, but we believe it was extensive. Since the fly drones were our technology we didn't monitor their possible use against us. So we have to assume Kovonov knows everything we do. The most classified Mossad data. Not just on our methods and intel, but all the data we have on our friends. On joint programs with the US. The identity of the American agents involved. Classified data on US methods."

"*Are you kidding me?*" shouted Davinroy. "And you're lecturing *us* about leaks! You've just opened up Pandora's box!"

Ori Kish's face hardened. "No question this is a spectacular failure on our part. But you've had yours as well. All governments have. We humans are fallible beings, and mistakes happen. But while you're rightly angry, please try to keep this in perspective. Yes we've created a problem. But we also saved Israel. Saved Washington and five other American cities. Even after our failure, we helped you stop Azim Jafari."

"So what do you want?" said the president. "Just to warn us? To rip off the Band-Aid of secrecy from an episode that will have severe repercussions between our two countries? Or did you bring us in to get our help with your hunt for Kovonov?"

"We would like your help, yes," replied Kish. "But before we discuss this further there is more we need to talk about."

"Right," said Davinroy. "The second order of business that you alluded to. At least it can't be as bad as the first."

Wortzman grimaced. "That remains to be seen," he said. "You've been briefed on how Agent Quinn was manipulated into trying to kill you."

"Yes. And I only believe it because I was told your side insisted something similar happened to two of your agents."

"That's right. I won't give you all of the details, but I'll paint as much of a picture as I can."

Wortzman spent several minutes sharing a sense of what had happened and how the Mossad had become convinced these agents' memories had been tampered with. He then gave the floor to Kevin Quinn, who described his own experiences in colorful detail. How these nightmarish memories, almost certainly tied into the rage centers of his brain, had begun to emerge days earlier. He described how real they had felt, bubbling up through a memory erasure drug he had thought had been forced on him by the president. His emotions and description of these events were quite compelling.

Quinn went on to detail his journey to a secluded shack and his encounter with two mercenaries there. How he had turned the tables, and how he had learned of the Russian behind it. "I know now that this man was Dmitri Kovonov," said Quinn. "At the time, of course, all I knew was that he was Russian, and that his hired hands had been told to address him as *302*."

Rachel's eyes widened. This was the first she had heard of this.

"302?" repeated Henry. He stared at the head of Mossad. "Does that have any significance?"

"None that we know of," replied Wortzman, "but you should run it yourself and see if you turn up anything in your databases."

Rachel locked her gaze on Avi Wortzman. He may have been in Jerusalem, but he was also ten feet away at the virtual conference table. "Does Kovonov have a neuroscience background?" she asked for the second time that day.

Wortzman appraised her carefully. "None at all," he replied, the same answer Eyal Regev had given.

"You're certain?"

"Yes, very certain. I know why you're asking, Professor Howard, but let's not get ahead of ourselves. We should let Agent Quinn finish his report."

Quinn picked up the story where he had left off, describing how he learned of the danger to Rachel Howard and had sought her out. He then passed the baton to Regev, who went on to describe his own activities and how he had come to cross paths with Quinn.

When he admitted he had been spying on the professor, and why, Wortzman jumped in. He was quick to point out that until Quinn had gone off the rails, they had thought the problem was confined to Israel, which explained why the US had not been told of it.

When he finished there was a lengthy silence, as the Americans digested all that had been said.

The president leaned back and locked his hands behind his head. "So you—*we*—have two major crises occurring at the same time," he said, breaking the silence. "A Russian named Kovonov ran off with your spy drones. And someone is manipulating the memories of agents. So how are these related?"

"We aren't sure," said Wortzman. "Despite the timing, we thought they were separate. Until today. We have people turning over every rock to find Kovonov. And we have Agent Regev taking the lead on our false memory investigation. Imagine our surprise when Kevin Quinn intersected with Regev and we realized these two thorns in our side were somehow connected. We were stunned to learn that Kovonov was behind Quinn's capture, and that he planned to murder Professor Howard."

"Which is why the professor asked if Kovonov had neuroscience expertise, right?" said Henry. "She was wondering if he was behind the memory implantation also, and not just the theft of your drones."

"Yes," said Wortzman. "But this isn't possible."

"I know we're all alarmed by these events," said Cris Coffey. "But I'm not sure we're alarmed *enough*. Let's not forget that whoever *is* behind this memory trick wants President Davinroy dead."

The president frowned deeply as this point hit home.

"So we're looking at two different people?" said O'Malley. "This makes no sense to me. The odds against Kovonov just magically finding someone able to screw with people's heads are astronomical."

"Not *magically* finding them," said Wortzman. "Only through considerable effort, I'm sure."

"Right," snapped Davinroy coldly. "When you can be a fly on the wall anywhere, at secret commercial, university, and government labs, you can learn about a lot of interesting projects, can't you?"

"That's undoubtedly how this came about," agreed Wortzman. "Our agents' memories had been tampered with before Kovonov left. Something he would have learned about. So he must have set his sights—or the sights of his swarm of fly drones to be more precise—on learning who was behind it."

"So he's teamed up with this other party, hasn't he?" insisted the president.

"Unclear," said the head of Mossad. "He may have. But it could also be that he hasn't even found this other party yet. His actions with respect to your Secret Service agent and Professor Howard may represent an effort to learn more, or to flush out the person responsible."

"What if *Kovonov's* memory was tampered with?" said O'Malley. "Maybe he *was* loyal. Maybe he went off the reservation after a false memory emerged about his poor treatment at the hands of the Mossad." He gestured at Avi Wortzman and raised his eyebrows. "Who knows, maybe you tortured and killed a wife of his that he doesn't have."

Wortzman shuddered. "A chilling possibility. I don't think this is the case, but I suppose we can't rule it out."

"If Agent Quinn's report is accurate," said Davinroy, "this Kovonov is in the continental United States, even as we speak. And we know what he looks like. If we use facial recognition and put our people in airports and train stations, I would think we could snare him fairly readily."

Rachel thought she detected the head of DHS reflexively rolling his eyes at what she guessed was Davinroy's naivete. She knew nothing about these matters, but it was clear even to her that if it would have been this easy, the Mossad would have captured him already.

"Can you address this, Avi?" said Henry, passing the duty of making the president look stupid to his Israeli counterpart.

"It's a great thought, Mr. President," said Wortzman, "but Kovonov is very slippery. Top agents in both of our intelligence agencies have multiple methods to defeat facial recognition technology. This won't be a problem for him. He can pilot both helicopters and planes and has the means to purchase small private aircraft. If he chooses to use commercial transportation, he has a number of ways to change his appearance, with forged documents to match."

It seemed to Rachel that Wortzman was about to say more but had stopped himself. She suspected he was going to remind the president that Kovonov also had intimate knowledge of how the US conducted manhunts, which made it easier for him to elude them, but had decided not to pick at this sensitive scab yet again.

Ori Kish cleared his throat and all eyes turned in his direction. "I think we should stop here for now. We've now disclosed what we came to disclose. So I wanted to make a proposal."

Everyone around the virtual table gave him their undivided attention.

"We're prepared to give you everything we have on the fly drone technology. Full specs. No need spending years reverse engineering any drones you find."

"And in exchange?" said Davinroy.

"First, you agree to institute extraordinary measures to keep this technology closely held and secret so we can both benefit from it as long as possible."

"Again," spat Davinroy, shaking his head, "do you really have the balls to sit there and lecture *us*?"

"Yes, I get the irony," said the Israeli Prime Minister. "We've been breached. But we have to operate under the assumption we'll take out Kovonov and return to full stealth mode."

"Go on," said the president.

"We'll be giving you at least four major breakthroughs. Nano-scale computer chips and electronics, miniaturized and advanced sensors, miniaturized and more efficient energy systems, and advances in flight mechanics. You agree to let us file patents when our governments decide—jointly—to go public with these advances, to the benefit of the Israeli economy."

Davinroy rubbed his chin in thought. "Since these were your inventions, we wouldn't have a claim anyway. Go on."

"You rush to build your own factory, so between us we'll have two. Again, we'll give you the exact specifications. Most importantly, you help us find the Russian. But we need you to agree to pull out all the stops. We want this to be a very, very, very high priority for you." Kish paused. "Have I used enough verys to get my point across?"

"Believe me," said Henry, "we understand how dangerous it is to have Kovonov on the loose."

"Good," said Ori Kish.

"Not to interrupt the prime minister," said Wortzman, "but it's vital I make it clear that if your side does find him, this is to be a *kill on sight* mission. Kovonov pulled off some real magic when he made his move against us, and he's proven more clever and dangerous than any man we've ever hunted. So there is no capture—only elimination."

Rachel found it interesting that the prime minister had outlined every other term of his proposal, but it had fallen to Wortzman to insist that Kovonov be assassinated. Wortzman's delivery of this requirement must have been planned ahead of time so Kish wouldn't have to sully himself.

"One last thing," said the prime minister, retaking the stage. "We propose placing our man Regev in charge of a joint US-Israel op aimed at stopping whoever is behind the false memory implantation. We'll get a bigger task force together, but for now we believe it's critical that Rachel Howard be part of our efforts. As we've said, that was what Regev was doing in the States. We're convinced she's our best hope of discovering how these false memories were implanted and developing detection methods and countermeasures. Provided she's willing, we're prepared to accommodate her however she would like, at whatever compensation she would like. Given her stature, I'm sure Harvard would be willing to let her go on a year sabbatical, beginning yesterday, as long as they think they'll get her back."

Rachel still couldn't fully assimilate the magnitude of this meeting, of these people, but no one could ever have convinced her that she might one day be part of a proposal made by the Prime Minister of Israel to the President of the United States. She couldn't quite get it to sink in that these powerful men were deciding her future. If she was willing.

"Is that everything?" said the president.

"Oh, sorry," said Kish. "Not quite. We'd also like you to assign Kevin Quinn to this effort. He's already in place, he has an extremely personal interest in this matter, and Agent Regev tells me he's as good as it gets."

Davinroy waited for several seconds to make sure Kish was really finished this time. "You're asking an awful lot in exchange for sharing technology we'll be able to crack on our own," he said in disgust. "And tech you should have given us anyway. Or do I need to remind you of what we give to you?"

"We've already been through this," said Kish. "I could remind you of what you get in return."

"With all due respect, Mr. President," said Wortzman, jumping in to help defray the growing tension, "we spent a decade on this fly drone tech, getting out the, ah . . . *bugs*. And there are tricks that reverse engineering won't teach you. You might crack this on your own, but it really will take years."

"Look," added Kish, "we aren't asking anything that isn't in your own best interest, that we wouldn't expect you to *want* to do in the first place. These were our problems. But you know that they're now yours as well." He paused. "And I'm sure you don't need to be reminded again, Mr. President, that whoever is behind the memory implantation seems to be gunning for *you*."

The president's demeanor remained ice-cold. "I believe we understand your proposal, Prime Minister Kish," he said. "I'm going to have my side temporarily sign off so we can discuss this privately. I'll have my answer for you when we return."

37

The massive virtual conference table collapsed once again into Eyal Regev's small square table and Rachel and her two companions were now alone with their thoughts. The call had been even more remarkable than she had expected. This time *she* had been the fly on the wall when some seriously historical discussions were taking place.

"What do you think, Kevin?" she said. "Will the president agree?"

Quinn nodded. "Absolutely," he said, not caring that Regev was privy to his analysis. "He's just pissed off at the entire situation and doesn't want to seem to be caving too easily. But don't let him fool you, he'd give Israel the state of *Texas* to get such game-changing technology. And the prime minister was right, he's only asking the US to do what it should want to be doing anyway, for its own best interests."

Rachel considered. "If the Mossad is so legendary," she said, this time directing her question at Regev, "why do you need our help with Kovonov?"

The Israeli laughed. "Are you kidding? The resources America can bring to bear on something like this are staggering. The Mossad is a miracle of efficiency and cleverness. But if we're the best bantamweight fighter who ever lived, the US is a dozen heavyweight fighters in one."

They continued discussing what they had just witnessed for about twenty minutes, when the president signaled that his party was ready to return to the meeting. When everyone reappeared around the virtual table, President Davinroy wasted no time getting to the point.

"Prime Minister," he began with a look of contempt, "I want to make it clear that I'm outraged by the actions you've taken. And I have to assume your country has spied on me and my government over many years. This is something I will not forget, and something we need to address further."

Davinroy paused for effect. "But given the position your mistakes have put us in, and in the interest of our two countries, I am forced to agree to your proposal."

Kish was clearly chomping at the bit to respond to Davinroy's barbs, but visibly stopped himself. "Good," he said, managing to keep any anger from his voice. "I think this is the wisest course of action."

"I assume you have this proposal in writing?" said Davinroy.

"We'll have a version for you and your team to consider in a few hours. It will mostly outline the broad principles of our understanding. A battle plan that will leave ample room for the heads of the various initiatives to react with maximum flexibility to changing conditions on the ground. My hope is that we can incorporate any changes you have and arrive at a finished product by the end of the week.

"In the meanwhile," continued the prime minister, "if you could begin deciding what resources you intend to apply to the Kovonov manhunt, and putting together a fly drone team, we'll have our scientists ready to fly out and smooth the technology transfer over the next several months."

"That is acceptable," said the president.

"There is one last issue we need to resolve," said Henry. "What to do about Kevin Quinn."

"Sir?" said Quinn in surprise. "In case it wasn't clear, I'm eager to be assigned to Regev's operation. As the prime minister said, I couldn't have a more personal interest."

"I'm well aware," said the head of DHS. "But that isn't the issue." He turned to face Coffey. "Cris, could you jump in here?"

Coffey frowned, and it was clear from his demeanor that he had been elected to be the bearer of bad news. "The issue," he said, "is that you're the most wanted man in America. Not only is half the law enforcement in this country actively hunting you, but your face is now widely known."

Quinn looked confused. "I had assumed you'd just call off the manhunt and clear my name," he said. "With the president's help."

"We discussed this just now," said Coffey. "And it isn't that easy. Too many people saw you try to kill the president. Too many people heard what you accused him of. So we'd have to go public with memory tampering. It's the only way you could be seen as completely innocent. Even if you turned yourself in and claimed temporary insanity, you'd be tied up in the courts and with psychiatrists for ages, with no guarantee you'd go free at the end of it."

"Okay, so we'll have to go public with what happened, like you said," replied Quinn, who suddenly had a very bad feeling about this.

Coffey shook his head. "I'm afraid we can't do that. The public will think it's bullshit unless the government convinces everyone that it's true. But do we really want to raise this specter? Do we really want people to worry that false memories can be implanted into their own minds, or the minds of others around them? Even if we forget the anxiety this will cause, the day after it's disclosed lawyers for every criminal in the country will have a new defense strategy. Their poor clients were manipulated into their crimes by heinous false memories. And at the moment, there is no way to prove they weren't."

Rachel nodded appreciatively. While the news couldn't have been worse for Kevin, Coffey was absolutely correct. Even without memory implantation, advances in neuroscience were bringing a number of legal issues to the fore. And these would only get thornier the more the inner workings of the human brain were decoded.

The legal system in the West was based on free will, on blameworthiness. If a man intentionally drove off the road to hit and kill an innocent pedestrian, he'd rot in jail. But what if he drove off the road and killed an innocent pedestrian because he was in the throes of a heart attack? What if he blacked out and lost control of the vehicle? Should he still go to jail?

Of course not. Because it wasn't his *fault*. The first driver killed on purpose. He exercised free will and made a *choice*. The second driver had no free will. It was an accident.

But what if the first driver was later found to have a tumor like that of Charles Whitman? Perhaps he didn't have as much choice as it might have seemed.

The more science discovered biological drivers behind certain actions, the more the definition of blameworthiness might change. Not that criminals shouldn't be found guilty and incarcerated in most cases. But this did introduce new and fascinating ethical and legal vistas for consideration.

Rachel could see in Quinn's face he agreed with Coffey's points. Convincing the population that their inner sanctums, and those of people they trusted, might be open to tampering would be a disaster. At least until such tampering could be detected. She had pondered these scenarios more than anyone but had failed to consider the future of her new friend in this context.

"So what do you propose to do?" said Quinn. "Feed me to the wolves?"

Coffey shifted in his seat uneasily. "There is really only one workable solution," he said. "And you're not going to like it. Although compared to the wolf thing . . ." he finished, leaving the thought hanging.

"I have to die, don't I?" said Quinn, as the solution suddenly became clear.

"I'm afraid so. And soon. It's the only way to take you completely off the grid. What do you say?"

"I'm in, of course. Everything you said is correct. I have no other choice."

"Good. I'll take responsibility for staging it. I have some Black Ops folks I've worked with previously who can help. It'll have to be a fire, naturally. We'll make sure *our* doctors are called in, so we don't have to worry about a perfect dental and skeletal match."

"Where will you find the skeleton?" asked Quinn.

"We'll figure something out," replied Coffey, and then with a grin added, "assuming they don't have them at Amazon. You know, for one-hour delivery."

Quinn couldn't help but smile.

"Here's what we'd like you to do, Kevin," said his former boss. "Sit tight where you are and check the news periodically. We'll try to make this happen very soon. When your death has been reported to every corner of the globe you're free to join Eyal Regev to find the jackass responsible for what happened to you."

"Now *that* is something I'm looking forward to," said Quinn, his expression darkening. "And when I do find him, he's going to wish like hell he'd killed me when he had the chance."

38

The inhabitants of the home Eyal Regev had set up as a headquarters in Waltham—three people who would form the nucleus of a critical joint American-Israeli operation—spent the rest of the day and evening poring over intel and getting to know each other. They had pizza delivered for lunch a few hours before the vid-meet and Chinese food delivered a few hours after.

Quinn tried not to reflect too much on the imminent death of his old life, of almost everything, and everyone, he had known. Like a participant in a witness protection program, he would be reborn, never able to go back, only forward.

The pain and disorientation he would have otherwise felt was muted by the affection he quickly developed for both of his new teammates. He couldn't remember the last time he had taken to anyone as quickly as he had to a professor who was effortlessly able to bridge the vast intellectual gulf between them.

And he and Eyal Regev developed an instant rapport, unlike any he had ever experienced. After only a few hours, Regev had become like a brother to him, although one who seemed to be just a slightly superior version of himself in every way. They had everything in common. They were of the same height and largely thought in the same way, which was remarkable given the differences in their cultures and language. But Regev seemed to be just a little sharper than Quinn, a little more knowledgeable on a broader base of topics. His sense of humor at least as good as Quinn's and maybe even better. Most impressive of all, while Quinn prided himself on his use of the language, on being articulate, Regev seemed a little better here as well, astonishing since this was his second language.

Quinn guessed Regev possessed elite skills, even for a Mossad agent, which made sense to him. When choosing an agent for a mission that was extremely important, an agent who had to pretend to be a neuroscience graduate student at Harvard, you chose the sharpest one you had.

Quinn had admired and respected his last boss, Cris Coffey, who would be one of the few people from his past life he would continue to work with. But he suspected he would soon come to admire and respect the Israeli even more.

At nine that night a package was left at Regev's doorstep, one containing a passport, California driver's license, and several credit cards, each in the name of Kevin Moore, who bore a striking resemblance to the soon-to-be deceased Kevin Quinn. At least they had let him keep his first name. Thank God for that.

At midnight they checked cable news one last time before turning in. Regev only had two beds, so Quinn took the couch while his two companions each retired to separate rooms.

They agreed to reconvene in the family room at eight the next morning. When this time arrived, they greeted each other but said little else as Regev immediately turned on his television to learn if they were free to move, or would need to remain in place a little longer.

The words *BREAKING NEWS* were splashed across the top and bottom of the seventy-inch screen in three-dimensional red letters.

"Just to repeat our top news story this morning," said a woman named Ann Keeran, a striking news anchor who could well have been a model, "the manhunt for Secret Service Special Agent Kevin Quinn ended in the wee hours of the morning, at around two o'clock Eastern time. FBI agents located Quinn, wanted in connection with an attempt on President Davinroy's life, just minutes before, on the I-75 highway in Cincinnati, Ohio. During a high-speed chase, Quinn lost control of his car in the Cincinnati suburb of Finneytown, crashing into a parked semi at over a hundred miles an hour. The car erupted into flames from the force of the collision, incinerating both it and the man inside."

Quinn felt sick to his stomach as the anchor threw the coverage to a reporter on the scene, in what had already become a media circus, with images of the remains of a collision from hell pictured behind the throng of reporters, cameramen, and officials. Broken glass, mangled steel, and the burned-out and demolished husks of a semi and sedan gave witness to Ann Keeran's reporting.

"Are you okay, Kevin?" asked Rachel.

Quinn nodded woodenly. "Yeah. It's just not every day that . . ." He shrugged. "You know."

"I do," she replied. "It's like reading your own obituary. But worse."

"I have to say that your Cris Coffey did an impressive job," noted Regev as he continued to watch the coverage.

"I owe him one," said Quinn. "I'm grateful that he didn't have me committing suicide. Having me lighting myself on fire after being found in an abandoned building would have been much easier to stage. At least he let me retain *some* dignity. And it is a relief to be out from under the manhunt."

"I'll bet," said Regev. "And just to return your compliment from yesterday," he added in amusement, "you look good for a dead man too. And *you* didn't even need a bulletproof vest."

They continued to watch in silence. After five minutes of further coverage on the scene, the reporting was thrown back to Ann Keeran. "An hour ago," she said solemnly, "the White House issued a statement, thanking the law enforcement agencies for their efforts in tracking down a dangerous fugitive, and expressing their sorrow at the way this ended. President Davinroy was quoted as saying, 'It is well known that the actions of Special Agent Quinn were brought on by a psychotic break with reality. While he did become a danger to himself and others, we should all remember his long record of serving his country with honor and distinction. While I am grateful to have this behind us, the loss of this good man is nothing short of a tragedy.'"

"Wow," said Regev, lifting the remote to switch off the television. "That was . . . thoughtful."

Quinn nodded. "It has Coffey's fingerprints all over it. My guess is that he wrote it. I just can't believe he convinced the president to release it."

"I can," said Rachel. "Davinroy's a politician, so he didn't do it to make *you* look good. He did it to make himself look good. It's a huge story, and he gets to go on record being gracious and forgiving. Irresistible to any politician worth his salt."

"I had no idea you were this cynical," said Regev with a grin. "I'm liking you more every minute."

Rachel smiled, but the magnitude and sincerity of her expression was less than Quinn might have expected. "So I guess we're free to be on our way," she said.

"My government has a plane waiting for us at Logan. Have you ever been to Israel?"

"Yes," said Rachel. "Once. At a scientific conference."

"Did you have fun?"

"Yes. I didn't have the chance to go to any of your resorts," she replied, "but I was impressed. Given the terrorism issues you hear about, I didn't expect such thriving cities, or that they'd be even more modern than ours."

"We'll make sure to get you to the resorts at some point," said Regev. "I think you'll enjoy your stay." He smiled. "It should help that you'll be given unlimited resources and treated like royalty."

Again Rachel flashed a smile, but to Quinn's eyes it seemed forced somehow.

Quinn was ready to travel, the rucksack he had taken being his sole possession. He thought about ceremonially destroying the black baseball hat he had thought would prove so important, but decided to keep it as a reminder of the adversity he had managed to overcome since this episode had begun.

Rachel wanted to return to her home to pack some belongings, but both men ruled this out immediately, and Regev promised her a fabulous shopping spree in Tel Aviv as soon as she felt up to it after landing.

When the Israeli left them temporarily to pack a bag, Rachel pressed a folded piece of paper into Quinn's hand and put a finger across her lips. *Read this in the bathroom*, she mouthed.

Quinn's eyes narrowed in confusion. Was this some kind of practical joke? Given all that had happened and his assessment of Rachel Howard's personality, he couldn't believe this was true.

Go! she mouthed adamantly as he stood there, dumbfounded.

This shook Quinn from his momentary trance and he hustled off to Regev's bathroom as she had instructed. He shut the door, unfolded the paper he had been given, and read.

Don't trust Eyal. Much of what the Israelis said during the vidmeet was a lie. We need to learn the truth, once and for all. I didn't want to share this with you earlier because Eyal was always close by. Even when we were alone for a short time I couldn't risk that we were still being watched—maybe by his AI system, maybe by him personally. But now that you've been declared dead, it's time to make our move. When you exit the bathroom, hold Eyal at gunpoint, and I'll take it from there. I can tell you like him. And while he does seem like a great guy, I'm counting on you to trust me on this.

Quinn swallowed hard. This was yet another twist he hadn't seen coming. What in the world was going on? Had Rachel lost her mind?

Maybe so, but she was brilliant, and he had no choice but to trust her, although he couldn't guess why she had become so distrusting of the Israelis for all the world.

Quinn made sure to flush the toilet and run the sink, and then returned to the living room. Regev now held a small travel bag and had rejoined Rachel.

Taking a deep mental breath, Quinn pulled a gun on the Israeli and pointed it at his head. "Drop the bag, Eyal!" he demanded. "Raise your hands!"

The startled and confused expression on Regev's face could not have been faked. "Kevin?" he said.

"Do it!" said Quinn.

Regev let go of his bag and raised his hands above his head. "Kevin, what's all this about?"

Quinn shook his head. "I have absolutely no idea," he replied.

39

A life-sized 3-D image of the face of Daniel Eisen hung across from Dmitri Kovonov, at a distance software indicated would have been a comfortable degree of separation if both men were actually together. Eisen was Kovonov's most trusted lieutenant, a man who had proven himself over and over again in the short time they had been working closely together. He was bald, short, and lithe, but had the wiry strength of a rock climber and was expert in weapons, tactics, and multiple forms of hand-to-hand combat.

"We landed at O'Hare about an hour ago," said Eisen in Hebrew, sounding understandably tired, "and we're in the hotel awaiting your instructions. I take it you had no trouble getting the virus from Dr. Acosta?"

Kovonov displayed a wolfish grin. "No. You might even say it was a *pleasure*. She's just attractive enough to arouse genuine . . . interest."

"What would you have done if not? A blue pill?"

"Yes," said Kovonov in amusement. "Along with closing my eyes and thinking of someone else."

Eisen laughed.

"I want the two of you to fly to Connecticut as soon as you can," said Kovonov, his smile vanishing. "I've found a group that should be perfect for our needs. It's called the Danbury Evangelical Fellowship. Turns out twenty members are on the first day of a week-long bible study retreat. They've helpfully put the details online. They're at an isolated campground inside something called Cockaponset State Forest."

"We'll familiarize ourselves with the group and the retreat on the plane," said Eisen.

"Good. I want you to fly into Bradley International in Hartford. I'll arrange to have a hired gun meet you there."

Eisen looked confused. "With all due respect, Dmitri, we can handle this ourselves."

"Don't be an idiot! You're better than that. Yes, you can handle the operation yourselves. But where are you planning to get supplies and weaponry, Chicago? Just put some submachine guns in a carry-on bag while you fly the friendly skies of United fucking Airlines?"

Eisen's face remained impassive, taking this reprimand in stride.

"The man who meets you—in Hartford, Connecticut," continued Kovonov, "will have weaponry, night-vision equipment, electronics—everything we'll need. After he makes the transfer he'll be out of the picture."

"Of course," said Eisen.

"After that get to Cockaponset Forest and make your way to where these Danbury evangelicals are lodging. I need a full reconnaissance of physical structures, sleeping quarters, mess hall, and the entire area. Make sure we'll be able to easily disrupt all cell and Internet coverage. Get a feel for possible routines and if any of them had military training before they were, um . . . born again. Most importantly, set up surveillance and physical obstacles so we can minimize the chances of getting unwanted company."

"We'll see to it, sir."

"Last thing, Daniel. You know the kind of impact this virus will have on the world. There will be no going back. I just want to be certain you're still with me. Still willing to make such a profound, permanent change. You aren't going to have second thoughts about this, right?"

Eisen shook his head adamantly. "I can speak for both of us here when I say that isn't going to happen. We aren't happy about certain . . . necessities, no question. But we believe in you and what you're trying to do. We're committed to your cause."

"Good," said Kovonov. "The achievement of our goals will come at a great cost. But there are no cheap solutions. And if you ask me, this is one that is long overdue."

As the call ended, Kovonov's thoughts turned back once again to Kevin Quinn and Rachel Howard. His first pair of mercenaries had failed to capture Quinn. The two mercenaries he had sent after this to capture Quinn and kill the professor had turned up dead.

Quinn must have grown some balls, after all.

Ironically, after Quinn had eluded four seasoned mercenaries, he had been killed running from his own people. Kovonov doubted Quinn had suffered as much in the deadly car crash as he would have liked, but knowing this asshole was finally dead was still immensely satisfying.

So should he send additional men after the professor? He thought for a few minutes and came to the same conclusion he had come to previously. It was time to let this one go. Just as he had underestimated Quinn, he was certainly *overestimating* the danger that Professor Howard represented.

She had no idea what was really going on. He may have studied the professor for many years, but she was totally unaware that he even existed. This was a case of respecting someone *too* much. He had become obsessed with her genius, convinced she was the only one clever enough to hurt him.

But he no longer had time to indulge this whim. He had wasted too much effort on this already. He needed to let it go.

There were far more important things that now demanded his attention.

40

At first, Eyal Regev had his hands in the air and a hurt look on his face. As though he were being betrayed by a close friend. But when Quinn admitted he didn't know why he was holding him, his expression registered nothing but alarm. "You don't know why you're doing this?" he said in disbelief. "Come on, Kevin. Does that sound rational? Consider that this may be a result of having your mind tampered with. Please. Before you do something you'll regret."

"He doesn't know what's going on," said Rachel evenly, "because he's doing this at my request."

"What?" said Regev, squinting in disbelief.

Rachel rummaged through Quinn's rucksack and removed a pair of zip-tie handcuffs. She tossed them to the Israeli. "Put these on and ratchet them tight with your mouth," she said. After all she had been through, it almost seemed normal to instruct the man who had abducted her to hold the man she had thought was her student at gunpoint.

"You do realize the President of the United States agreed to make him our boss?" said Quinn.

"He agreed to that under false pretenses," said Rachel. "Put on the cuffs!" she snapped at Regev.

The Israeli sighed deeply and did as she asked. "You don't need to hold a gun on me," he said evenly, "or have me restrained. Kevin and I would both give our lives to protect you. He's already demonstrated as much. Although I suppose that isn't entirely unexpected from a Secret Service agent. But I'd do the same. There are no words that could possibly convey your importance to Israel."

"Good," said Rachel. "Because I'm not looking for glib words, or false compliments. I'm looking for the *truth*. Or are you going to stand there and insist you've been honest? Which will only dig the hole deeper."

"Look—Rachel—we really are the good guys. That is the truth. And we really do see you being of paramount importance. Once you were in the fold, we were planning to tell you everything. We couldn't proceed effectively otherwise. You could well be the key to our future. But like I said before, we wanted to give you the chance to get to know us. And when we finally aired all of our laundry, we wanted to do it in private."

"Oh well. Guess your plans have changed."

"How can you be so certain you've been misled? I thought the take on events Kish and Wortzman provided was compelling. Where did we go wrong?"

"Kovonov. He's a neuroscientist, isn't he? I asked a second time at the vid-meet. Your boss repeated the lie you had told me, that he has zero neuroscience background. The only reason you'd deny this is because you know he's responsible for the false memories. Which makes sense given his interest in me and Kevin. I have no idea what connection Kovonov has to fly drones, but I do know a good part of your story about him is a lie."

Regev remained silent for several long seconds, deep in thought. "Okay," he admitted finally, "he's a neuroscientist. But how could you possibly know that?"

"Three numbers," said Rachel simply. "Three. Zero. Two."

Regev blinked rapidly, a blank look on his face. Rachel noted in her peripheral vision that Quinn looked just as confused.

"I'll spell it out for you," said Rachel. "There's a one-millimeter-long roundworm found in certain soils," she said. "A species called *C. elegans*. I'm guessing you've never heard of it."

Regev shook his head.

"It's been one of the most important model organisms in neuroscience research for fifty years. It's cheap to breed, can be frozen and thawed and remain alive, and it's transparent, which is very convenient. It was the first multicellular organism to have its entire genome sequenced and the first to have its connectome—its neural wiring diagram—completed as well. But the main reason it's been such a valuable research tool is the simplicity of its nervous system. The human brain has almost a hundred billion neurons. This particular roundworm is able to thrive with just a tiny bit fewer. I'll let you guess the exact number."

Regev nodded, the light of comprehension finally shining on him. "Three hundred and two," he said miserably. "Shit! That's really bad luck. Who knew?" he mused.

"Anyone who has truly studied the field," replied Rachel. "So even when Kovonov is making up a ridiculous alias for mercenaries to use, he can't help but pay homage to this important model system. When Kevin said during the vid-meet that this was what Kovonov wanted to be called, I knew. Not only is he a neuroscientist, he's a diehard *geek* of a neuroscientist."

She stared at Regev, unblinking, for several seconds. "How about it, Eyal? Do you want to finally tell me what's really going on?"

"I'll tell you everything," he said. "But not in front of Kevin. Just you and me."

"No deal. He stays. Anything you can say to me, you can say to him. As you mentioned, he was willing to die to protect me. Se we're in this together."

Regev hesitated.

"Why is this a problem?" said Rachel. "If you're on the side of the angels as you say, convince me. Convince us both. Or remain silent and alienate me forever, proving that you're lying about my importance as well."

"I need you both to agree to keep what I tell you absolutely confidential. I need your word."

Kevin shook his head. "No good, Eyal," he said. "I can't make that promise. The best I can do is this: I'll maintain confidentiality on anything you tell me that isn't in conflict with the interests of the United States."

"I'll make the same promise," said Rachel. "But that's all you're going to get. So what's it going to be? Time for you to make some decisions."

41

Regev asked to at least get more comfortable, and Quinn saw no reason not to honor this request. He had the Israeli sit in the same chair he had taken earlier, but ten feet more distant from the couch, and gave him another zip-tie to cuff his ankles. Regev used his outstretched hands, still bound, to pull it taut.

Quinn and Rachel took their previous positions next to each other on the leather couch. Given his prisoner's hands and feet were cuffed, Quinn felt comfortable resting the gun on his lap, although he still maintained his grip on it.

"It seems like only yesterday that *I* was holding the gun," said Regev wryly, "and you were bound to a pole. We really need to stop having conversations this way."

Quinn allowed the hint of a smile to cross his face. Maintaining a sense of humor in the face of adversity was a personal quality he admired.

"I guess I should begin at the beginning," said Regev. "Dmitri Kovonov did emigrate to Israel from Russia at the age of fourteen. And he was absolutely brilliant, taking to neuroscience like a fish takes to water." He nodded at Rachel. "Not as brilliant or inventive a neuroscientist as *you* are, of course, but very close."

"As I said, flattery won't help you," said Rachel.

"Not flattery," insisted Regev. "*Honesty*."

"So Kovonov was never on the fly drone team?" said Quinn.

"No. We didn't even have a fly drone team at the time. But he soon earned the right to head the secret scientific initiative that my country deemed its highest priority." He paused for effect. "What Rachel calls Matrix Learning."

Quinn's eyes widened. Matrix Learning. He remembered from his discussion with Rachel in her neighbor's house that this was the primary goal of her research. But judging from her less than surprised expression she hadn't found this revelation totally unexpected.

Eyal turned to Quinn. "Let me explain what this is," he said. "The idea is to—

"I'm familiar with the term," said Quinn, cutting him off.

"Good," said Regev, although he seemed surprised that this was the case. "We began the program as far back as 1999. Not coincidentally."

"The year *The Matrix* came out in theaters," said Rachel.

"Yes. The depiction of instant learning from the movie seized the imagination of our prime minister at the time, Ehud Barak. Not that this was the first time this idea appeared in science fiction. As far back as 1957, Isaac Asimov used this concept in a story called *Profession*."

Asimov may have been the first to come up with the idea, but Quinn doubted he had a character learn kung-fu instantly and then engage in such entertaining fights.

"The movie was like a demonstration video to the higher-ups in Israel at the time," continued Regev. "To understand just how profoundly the prospect of Matrix Learning hit us, you have to understand the Jewish people. In Jewish culture education—knowledge—is *everything*. There is a reason so many luminaries have been Jewish. Einstein, Fermi, Freud, Pauli, Feynman, Bohr, Oppenheimer, Salk. The list goes on. Jews make up one five-hundredth of the world's population. One five-hundredth. But they have earned twenty-two percent of all Nobel Prizes. Not only is education our strongest cultural imperative, we have been persecuted more than any other people throughout the ages. At a time in world history when land ownership meant everything, Jews were often prohibited from owning land. Not able to farm, to use their hands to get ahead, they had little choice but to use their brains."

Rachel nodded. "Jewish colleagues over the years have mentioned that nothing is more important in their religion than education," she said. "And I have found them to be more captivated than average at the prospect of Matrix Learning."

"Israel has always been a resource-poor country," said Regev. "We weren't blessed with oil, like our Arab neighbors, so education and innovation were always the keys to our survival. Hated, outnumbered, and outgunned. So not only did the possibility of instant education capture many imaginations, the potential this offered if perfected—to keep us many steps ahead of our enemies—was irresistible."

"Okay," said Rachel. "So your leaders saw the movie when it came out in '99 and began a secret program."

"Not just a secret program. *The* secret program. Israel's Manhattan project. No other program we've ever mounted was nearly as well manned or well funded. Progress was modest for the first decade, because our goals and ambitions were ahead of the technology, but we did make progress. Progress that would be key when the tech—computers, neuronal maps, and the like—did finally catch up."

"And Kovonov came to lead this effort," said Rachel.

"Yes. He led our best people. And we succeeded. Five years ago, under his leadership. He used trial and error, audacity, outside-the-box thinking, and hundreds of millions of dollars in funding. In the end this wasn't enough. We benefited from what we thought of as divine intervention. Kovonov made some guesses that worked out that even he characterized as blind, random luck."

Rachel nodded solemnly. "Last week I thought I was closer to perfecting Matrix Learning than anyone," she said. "After what happened to Kevin, I've had to readjust my thinking, acknowledge that someone was ahead of me. But I would never have believed *this*. I've gone from being ten miles ahead in a marathon to being an also ran. It's a difficult pill to swallow."

"I understand. We got lucky, we're the first to admit it. And we poured dozens of times more resources at it than the rest of the world combined. Quantity has a quality of its own. But there was never any question that you were the singular talent in the field. Kovonov worshiped you."

"The same Kovonov who just tried to have me killed?"

"Yes. But that came later. For years he sang your praises, telling anyone who would listen you were the only neuroscientist in the world with greater insight even than his own. He called you a visionary and a genius. He admitted to borrowing liberally from your work. He lobbied the head of Mossad and the prime minster to do whatever it took to recruit you. Repeatedly. In the end we decided not to approach you. It was too risky. Secret program. Foreign government. If only you had been lucky enough to be a Sabra," he added with a smile.

"Sabra?" said Rachel.

"What we call a native-born Israeli. Taking a name from a cactus that thrives in my country. Thorny, tenacious, and thick-skinned on the outside." Regev raised his eyebrows. "Sweet and soft on the inside."

"Well, you've definitely demonstrated the thorny and tenacious part," said Rachel with just the hint of a smile.

"So you perfected this Matrix Learning five years ago?" said Quinn. "Why didn't you go public? Then Rachel could have joined your efforts."

"This is a greater advantage than our fly drones. We wanted to milk it for all it was worth. Still do. Maintain our advantage for as long as possible. The technology is totally disruptive. Once it's unleashed the world will never be the same." Regev paused. "I only wish you could have been in the professor's recent lecture. She covered many of the ramifications at length."

"How good is the technique?" asked Rachel. "And how is it done?"

"The results are flawless. Astonishing. One minute you know nothing about a subject, ten minutes later you're an expert. Like Trinity learning to fly a helicopter, only not quite as fast. As to the how, Kovonov and his team developed a robot that injects micro-implants into eight regions of the brain, with very high accuracy. They're extremely advanced electronics shaped like tiny needles and can be punched into place in the brain like a vaccine is punched through the skin when you get a shot. The companion to this is a very complex, very expensive device that reminds me of an MRI. Same large doughnut-shaped opening at one end, in which your head is immobilized. But it's not an MRI."

"What are the principles of its operation?" asked Rachel.

"I really would tell you, but I don't know. I just know that it works. The subject has to have the implants injected first. And has to be inside the MRI-like device. But there is no physical connection between the two. You don't have a giant jack embedded into the back of your skull that you plug a cable into like in the Matrix movies. But it also isn't free-range."

"So what have you been doing with it all these years?" said Quinn.

"We've used it to flash-educate the most innovative people in Israel," replied Regev proudly. "We've established the greatest league of inventors in world history. Geniuses who have broad and deep knowledge of a field implanted and who use this to produce breakthroughs."

"What, like fly drones?" said Quinn.

"That's right. This was the first technology to come out of the program. The ultra-light bulletproof vest and the wound sealant are other examples you've witnessed. And so much more you haven't seen. Breakthroughs in electronics. Supercomputers that are desktop sized. Advanced algorithms. Improved ability to hack computers. Dramatic advances in AI, supercapacitors, lasers, solar energy, 3-D printers, genetic engineering, nanotechnology, sensors, and dozens of other areas. We believe that even a tabletop fusion reactor is just a few years away. It wasn't just the fly drones that kept us ahead, that allowed us to stop North Korea and Iran from carrying out their nuclear ambitions."

"So your military is what . . . just hoarding all of these innovations?" said Quinn accusingly.

"Most we're helping to commercialize. Some inventions we license cheaply to Israeli companies. For others, we provide seed money for the inventor to launch a new company. We've been known for innovation for some time, but if you did a statistical analysis you'd find that the number of breakthrough inventions coming out of Israeli companies has tripled during the last several years."

Rachel shook her head. "You shouldn't have been this successful," she said. "We discussed this in class. Matrix Learning won't improve native intelligence. Won't improve creativity, or inventiveness. It's just knowledge. Instead of pounding the principles of chemistry into your head for an entire semester, they're shoehorned in, in minutes."

"Which is why we only flash-educate the most creative people possible. You'd be surprised by how many highly educated people really aren't that bright—or inventive. And also how many brilliant, creative people are uneducated. Some are lazy. Some don't have the funds or access to quality education. Some come from farming or blue-collar families, where following in their parents' footsteps is all they know, all they aspire to. Some aren't able to sit still long enough to learn what they need to know. There is a worldwide high IQ society called Mensa. Some members are accomplished scientists, true, but many are truck drivers. Firefighters. Laborers."

Rachel nodded appreciatively. "I see. You recruit those with raw ability but without the patience, or money, or ambition for advanced studies. You implant a PhD equivalent in days, and then let them apply their genius."

"Exactly. We have a program to identify and recruit the most gifted people in Israel, not just using IQ scores, but other measures of inventiveness, of thinking outside the box, of bold vision. Are you familiar with Alan Turing and the group that broke the unbreakable German code in World War II?"

Rachel and Quinn both nodded. Quinn had learned of this effort while in the military. Alan Turing had successfully created a machine at a place called Bletchley Park able to break the German Enigma code, turning the tide of the war and ushering in the computer age.

"Turing also recruited people from all walks of life. Some with no experience in code breaking or mathematics. People no one would ever think of hiring based on any known criteria. The group published a thorny crossword puzzle in the Daily Telegraph and offered a prize to anyone who could solve it. No one knew the British War Office was behind it. Those who were able to solve it were summoned to be interviewed to join Turing's top-secret team, the biggest surprise of their lives."

"So you've adopted similar methods," said Quinn.

"More sophisticated and far-reaching, but the same idea. Our success at finding diamonds in the rough has been extraordinary."

"I see," said Rachel. "And then you polish up these diamonds in the rough with the greatest buffing machine in history."

"That's right. With most of them we didn't stop at one branch of knowledge, but imparted a few that were adjacent. This has played a huge role as well. The synergy produced by implanting expertise in multiple fields has been far greater than expected. There's a famous quote we took to heart: 'To be the master of any branch of knowledge, you must master those which lie next to it.'"

"Oliver Wendell Holmes," said Rachel.

Regev smiled. "I should have known you'd be familiar."

"This is all very fascinating," said Quinn. "But let's get back to Kovonov. What the hell is going on now?"

"I'm getting there," said Regev. "And trust me, this background is useful. When the first breakthroughs were made, Kovonov didn't test this on himself. The government wouldn't let him take the risk. You make gambits with your pawns and knights, not your queen."

"So you had others take the shakedown cruise," said Quinn.

Regev nodded. "After fourteen months with no discernible issues in hundreds of test subjects, and with no discernible behavioral or brain abnormalities, Kovonov insisted he be allowed to use his own invention. And he went hog wild with it," added Regev. He raised his eyebrows. "Although this may be one of your idioms that isn't strictly kosher."

Quinn smiled, but Rachel's face remained serious. "*How* hog wild?" she asked.

"He sucked up many times more knowledge than any other subject had before. Other than you, he had already been the world's leading authority on the scientific principles of Matrix Learning, but he had every other neuroscience discipline flashed into his brain as well. And not just neuroscience. Physics. Computer science. Robotics."

"Isn't there a limit to how much knowledge you can shove into a brain?" asked Quinn.

Regev gestured toward Rachel with his head, indicating that she was the right person to answer.

"I'm sure there is," she replied. "But the limits aren't precisely clear. With a hundred billion neurons and almost infinite number of possible connections, the brain's capacity is very, very high. Consider a foreign language. Fluency requires a very broad knowledge of vocabulary, syntax, and so on. Yet a cardinal named Giuseppe Mezzofanti, born in 1774, was known to have spoken thirty-eight languages and forty dialects. John Browning, a governor of Hong Kong in the eighteen hundreds, claimed to speak a hundred languages, although I doubt this is accurate. But you get the point."

Quinn nodded. He had taken Spanish in college but was horrible at it. He couldn't imagine being fluent in even two languages, let alone dozens.

"Using this extensive knowledge base," continued Regev, "and with the help of his team, Kovonov went on to make quite a few advances in neuroscience. Advances that could all be used in scary ways in the wrong hands." He gestured at Rachel. "The very ways you lecture about."

The Harvard professor nodded, looking more troubled than ever.

"I must have missed these lectures," said Quinn. "What scary uses are we talking about?"

"If you truly understand the brain there are all kinds of levers to push on," said Regev. "Memory implantation, as you know better than anyone. And memory erasure, of course. But addiction, sex drive, rage, depression, and many others—all can be impacted if you know the right place and manner to push."

"Davinroy mentioned Pandora's box in the vid-meet," said Rachel. "But this is the *true* Pandora's box."

"I'm still not sure I'm grasping the possibilities the way you two are," said Quinn.

"Take sex drive as one example," said Rachel. "Imagine if you could manipulate this. Ratchet it up to obsessive levels. A woman who wouldn't think of cheating on her husband becomes insanely hypersexual and seduces a co-worker. You could use this to ruin people.

Lie in wait and then blackmail them. Sex has brought down empires. The Trojan War, which many scholars believe is loosely based on actual history, was started over the lust for the beautiful Helen of Troy. Bill Clinton almost lost the presidency because he couldn't resist oral sex with an intern. And don't forget the example of the forty-year-old who suddenly became sexually obsessed with children."

"Okay then," said Quinn, putting on a disturbed expression. "Thanks. This does paint a vivid picture."

"Kovonov wanted badly to use these neuroscience advances against Israel's enemies," said Regev. "Forgive the language, but in the Mossad, we thought of these capabilities collectively as *fucking with people's minds*."

Quinn had to admit that as inelegant as this phrase was, it got the point across well.

"Kovonov was zealously patriotic about his adopted homeland," continued Regev. "He argued that Israel shouldn't hold back against the barbaric hordes devoted to our destruction. If we had the upper hand, we should press our advantage. Kish tended to side with him, while *my* boss, Avi Wortzman, was adamantly opposed."

Regev paused. "Wortzman is in a tough business, but he strives to be as ethical as possible. He has Nietzsche's warning framed in his office, the one about not letting the battle with monsters turn you into one. He argued that the fly drone invention, a direct result of the Matrix Learning program, and other tech that resulted, gave Israel more than enough of an advantage. While he supported using advanced technology to defeat our enemies, he drew the line at fucking with people's minds. That was beyond the pale."

Amen to that, thought Quinn.

But while this was his immediate reaction, he could well understand those Israeli factions in favor of using every arrow in the quiver. After more than seventy years of being surrounded by those who had made repeated attempts to destroy them, it would take impressive ethical resolve not to use all the weapons at their disposal. Especially against ruthless groups that wouldn't hesitate to do the same, with no ethical qualms whatsoever. In 1973, Syria and Egypt joined forces to invade Israel on Yom Kippur, the most holy day of the Jewish year, when Israeli soldiers were fasting and in prayer—something Israel would never consider doing in reverse.

"Wortzman also argued there was a logistical hurdle to overcome," continued Regev, "before these neuroscience capabilities could be deployed, anyway. Kovonov would need to invent a way to manipulate brains less invasively. Like Rachel mentioned in her lecture. Not requiring them to plug in like Neo, or even like we were doing, but remotely. Wirelessly. Until this was perfected, mind tampering wouldn't be all that useful. Say you wanted to implant a memory in the leader of Iran. First you'd have to kidnap him, bring him back to our facility, inject implants, and then stick him in a machine. Not very stealthy. You could then make him forget this happened, but still . . . Best case, this would require a lengthy abduction."

"Given Kevin's false memories," said Rachel, "this seems like a hurdle Kovonov was able to overcome. Unless you're suggesting he captured Kevin and transported him to Israel and back."

"No. Kovonov must have found a more portable, less invasive solution," agreed Regev. "But let me go on. We can circle back to this in a few minutes."

"Okay," said Rachel. "I believe you were saying that Kish and Wortzman disagreed over the use of some of these advances."

"Since this disputed tech was used on *me*," said Quinn, "the prime minister must have won the day."

Regev shook his head. "The opposite. Wortzman convinced Kish he was right. Together they made sure the lid to Pandora's box remained nailed shut."

Quinn squinted in confusion, but only for a moment. "I see," he said, as the answer became clear to him. "So Kovonov must have decided to take his toys and leave, refusing to abide by these restrictions. Which means the part of your story about him going rogue was true. But not because he was still loyal to Russia. But because he had lost an argument with Kish and Wortzman."

Regev sighed. "If only it were that simple," he said miserably.

42

"We've been in place for some time now," reported the life-sized floating head of Daniel Eisen in Hebrew.

"How goes the recon of our evangelicals?" asked Kovonov.

"Quite well. We've surveiled the proceedings on our own and have now set up electronic surveillance in key locations. My confidence is high that this will go off without a hitch."

"It had better. This is one reason I chose this group, and this venue, from among all the possibilities. They should be ripe for the taking."

Kovonov told his underling when he planned to arrive and they discussed logistics. "While you're waiting for me," he said, "I want you to locate a Middle Eastern Islamic terrorist somewhere in the States. Preferably one long affiliated with ISIS. Make this your highest priority."

"I don't understand," said Eisen. "Do you have intel that one is planning an imminent attack?"

"One is *always* planning an imminent attack. But no, I have no specific intel."

"And you aren't interested in a *specific* terrorist. Any one will do?"

"That's correct."

"Does it matter if they are at large or in custody?"

Kovonov shook his head. "I'd prefer at large, but either way will work. As long as they're part of ISIS and not an American citizen. A home-grown terrorist is no good to me."

"I'll have to pan through US intel for this," noted Eisen. "Once the Americans become aware of a foreign terrorist within their borders, they usually don't leave them at large for long."

"Understood," said Kovonov, frowning. He had planned to get Azim Jafari to deliver the terrorist they needed, but this was no longer an option. Oh well. Kovonov was smart and had his fingers deep into the US intelligence apparatus. He had no doubt he would find what he needed soon enough.

"Can you tell me *why* this is such a high priority?" said Eisen. "And your plans once such a man is identified?"

"I can't tell you that right now. But I'll make all of my plans clear in due course."

Eisen stared at Kovonov's virtual image for several seconds, not happy about being kept in the dark, but finally nodded. "Okay, Dmitri. I'll get on this right away."

"Good," said Kovonov. "I'll be in touch."

43

Quinn's intuition told him everything the Israeli was saying was the truth, although he had to admit he had thought the same before. Intuition might be more perceptive than conscious reasoning at times, but it was far from perfect.

Still, Regev's answers to questions were quick and well thought out and had an impeccable logical consistency. And how many ways could the explanation of known facts be contorted, tortured, before the truth became the only remaining option with any chance of being believable?

"About two months ago," said Regev, "two researchers on our Matrix Learning team began behaving erratically. And not because their memories were tampered with. What we told your president about that isn't true. We thought it was the best way to convince your people that Kevin had been manipulated. So they would be on their guard and so they would let us recruit the two of you."

Quinn was familiar with the expression *wheels within wheels*, but what the Israelis had done took this to an entirely new level. Without question lying to achieve specific ends took more brilliance and creativity than telling the truth.

"We monitored these two researchers and came to realize that they had become delusional. Paranoid. Megalomaniacal. There was a lot more to the diagnosis, but I'm not a psychiatrist. Let's just say that their grip on sanity wasn't what it used to be. But what was most alarming was that these two were among the first subjects to undergo the Matrix Learning procedure. One had done so two months after the very first test subject, and one three months after. "

"Uh-oh," said Rachel grimly.

"Uh-oh is right," replied Regev. "It would be accurate to say the Mossad was more than just panicked. It threw us into a *frenzy*. We put considerable resources into analyzing what might have happened, and began careful evaluations of all subjects who had undergone the procedure during the first six months of its use."

Regev seemed shaken to the core, even from just the recounting of these events. After several seconds of hesitation, he took a deep breath, gathered himself, and continued. "Then, about a month ago, Dmitri Kovonov did exactly what we said he had. He killed four members of the fly drone team, took their inventory, and destroyed the factory."

"Didn't you say he waited fourteen months after Matrix Learning came online to try it?" said Rachel.

"Yes."

Rachel's eyes narrowed in thought. "But he had crammed in ten times as much knowledge as anyone else," she said, almost as though talking to herself.

"Excellent," said Regev. "You've grasped the situation immediately, of course. Seems the procedure does have one or two problematic . . . side effects . . . after all. As you already deduced, we concluded that Kovonov had gone insane as well, and that his procedure was responsible. Although we didn't see the possibility of the equation you're alluding to—even though we *should* have—until after Kovonov's actions."

"What equation?" said Quinn.

"The procedure eventually leads to insanity," said Regev. "But *when* this will happen depends on a complex combination of two factors. One, the length of time after first exposure to the procedure. And two, the cumulative amount of information implanted. The very first subject this was used on barely had anything implanted, and is still doing fine. Like Rachel deduced, Kovonov, even though he avoided the procedure for over a year, used it extensively, so was impacted earlier than all but two of the rest."

"So Kovonov went rogue," said Quinn, "not because he isn't loyal to Israel. But because he's stark raving mad."

"Yes."

"Well that's *much* better," snapped Quinn sarcastically.

"This is a disaster of epic proportions," said Eyal with a fierce scowl. "Dmitri Kovonov was a fine man. He may have argued for more widespread use of his neurotech, but he wasn't a killer. Quite the opposite. But now, like we told your president, we have a brilliant man wielding a game-changing technology—*more* than one, but we didn't tell that to your people—who is off the reservation. Ruthless, driven, and unpredictable. Almost certainly suffering from paranoia and megalomania."

"Yeah, nothing bad can happen from that combination," said Quinn in disgust.

"He also managed to recruit a number of our best people when he left. Maybe they were enticed by the prospect of finally pulling out all the stops to destroy Israel's enemies. Or maybe he used his tech to, um . . . fuck with their brains." Regev shrugged. "We only know the end result."

"And you have no idea where they went?" said Quinn.

"We're working on it, but with little success. In addition to taking a number of sympathizers with him, we believe he left several behind as well, who are helping him elude us. We've recently taken to trusting only a few handpicked agents with details of our manhunt."

"Let me be sure I have this right," said Quinn. "Kovonov is off somewhere with a group of followers who are brilliant, have more knowledge packed into their skulls than even the most experienced operatives, and are armed with fly drones and numerous other breakthrough technologies. And don't forget, know all of your agents, your methods, and your secrets." Quinn raised his eyebrows. "Not to mention many of *ours*. And you're nowhere close to finding them."

"You forget to mention a group led by a man who is now ruthless and willing to do anything to achieve his goals. And also that his followers will begin their own descent into madness over the months and years ahead."

"Sorry," said Quinn wryly. "I didn't mean to sugarcoat the situation."

"You think you're saying that ironically," said Regev. "But you aren't."

"What does *that* mean?"

"It means that this story gets a lot worse," whispered the Israeli. "Matrix Learning was so effective it was irresistible to the higher-ups in Israel. They used it to flash-educate themselves as well. Wortzman. Kish. Numerous others." He paused, a horrified expression on his face. "The entire upper level strata of Israel's government and military will eventually go mad."

For the first time, Quinn's mouth dropped open.

"Not to mention all the scientists and diamonds in the rough we used this on," continued Regev, "many who are now CEOs of our companies."

"Incredible," said Rachel in dismay. "You've managed to turn scores of the most brilliant, accomplished, and powerful people in your country—with knowledge of the most advanced technology base in the world—into ticking time bombs."

Regev nodded solemnly.

"It's hard to imagine how you could have possibly screwed yourself any worse," said Quinn.

This seemed to shake Regev from his depression. Strength and resolve returned to his features. "When we told your government about how we stopped imminent attempts by Iran and North Korea to use nuclear weapons, this was true. So while things don't look good, we owe our very existence to the Matrix Learning program. Without it, Israel and Washington both would be radioactive wastelands. If we could go back in time, we'd still do the same thing we did. We were enormously lucky to get it to work, and now the universe is evening the scales by hitting us with an enormous dose of *bad* luck."

"How good is your computer model when it comes to the onset of madness?" said Rachel. "Can you get any sense of precision from just three data points?"

"We can't be certain, but we think so. Our model would have predicted the timing of the first three cases with great accuracy. The good news, if there can be any, is that we have about three months before the next of our people go over the cliff. After that it will be a steady drip, drip, drip. Fifteen to twenty months from now, an avalanche of people will be affected, although most of them don't know anything about this yet. We're debating what actions to take as each victim approaches their tipping point. Surveillance, at minimum. Sedation? House arrest? Imprisonment? There are no easy answers."

Regev paused and there was an extended silence in the room as the two Americans struggled to digest the unthinkable.

"There is only one answer that isn't catastrophic on a number of levels," continued Regev finally. "We need to learn why this is happening. We need to find a way to stop it. Reverse it. Everything depends on this. And not just for our country. Even if we discount Israel tearing itself to shreds and the collateral damage that is bound to follow, the threat to the entire world that Kovonov poses, all by himself, is off the scale."

"And you have no idea what's causing it?" said Quinn.

"No. It's subtle, whatever it is. Neurons and brain structure look normal. Our best people are mystified."

"That's why Rachel is so critical to you," said Quinn. "Isn't it? Because she's the only neuroscientist alive more brilliant than Kovonov. Not to mention having the added advantage of being *sane*."

Regev nodded. "We see her as our only real chance. We hoped to convince her to lead a team to find a cure for whatever this is. In a hurry. Secondarily, we hoped she could help find a way to detect when a mind has been tampered with along the way."

The Israeli turned to Rachel. "It is a lot to ask, and the stakes couldn't be higher. That's why I enrolled in your class. So we could get to know each other. So we could increase our chances of successfully recruiting you. Everything depended on it. As important as we portrayed you in our fabricated story to President Davinroy, it turns out you're a hundred times more important in reality."

Rachel blinked rapidly, dumbfounded by these revelations.

"Our intent would be to disclose to you everything we know. How our system works and all of our data. We could leapfrog you many years ahead of where you are now."

"What, using Matrix Learning?" said Quinn in disgust.

Regev nodded reluctantly. "We're running out of time," he explained. "Once we've loaded all the information we have on our Matrix Learning program into her brain, we would plan to load additional fields that she could draw upon for a solution. Computer science, physics, medicine, mathematics. Far lesser scientists than her have made huge breakthroughs after our procedure. The extension of their working knowledge helped to spark unprecedented connections between seemingly unrelated ideas and fields."

Rachel shook her head in disbelief. "So your plan is to hit me with the same tech you know leads to insanity?"

"Believe me, I know how much we'd be asking. But I'm not sure you can fully appreciate the stakes even now. We're desperate. More than desperate. My trip here to begin to recruit you is one of the most important assignments ever given. Maybe a lesser scientist will solve this, but you are our best hope. If you refuse, or if you fail, the world faces catastrophic consequences. But if you succeed, you probably save millions of lives, and perfect a technology that has been your lifelong dream."

Rachel nodded slowly. "Is that everything?" she said. "I want to be sure you've put everything on the table before I tell you what I'm thinking."

"Yes. That's all of it."

"No it's not," said Quinn. "You're close, Eyal. But we're not quite finished yet."

44

In Quinn's opinion, Regev had done a thorough and unflinching job of telling them the hideous truth. He was sure the Israeli wasn't withholding anything on purpose, but had just forgotten that he still knew things that they didn't.

"What am I missing?" said Regev, genuinely confused.

"Current events," replied Quinn. "How did I get involved? Why does Kovonov want to kill Rachel?"

"Right," said Regev, looking a little embarrassed to have left this off. "There is that."

He paused to gather his thoughts. "With respect to you, Kevin, we had heard rumors that Kovonov had managed a less invasive technique for messing with people's minds. Given your case this must be true. A cause for even more alarm. We believe that you are one of his first attempts at implanting false memories. One of his first guinea pigs."

"But why? Why me?"

"When I spoke with Wortzman earlier he had some compelling analysis on this, which makes a lot more sense than I would have guessed. First, Kovonov despises your president. Many in Israel aren't big fans. You aren't aware of Davinroy's interactions with Kish behind the scenes. Even though your president portrays himself as a true friend of Israel, he is not. In many ways the opposite."

"Actually, I am aware," said Quinn. "He sees the drive for a global caliphate as a ravenous beast and wants to placate it in the hope of keeping it calm. Proving he has no clue about its nature. How he can possibly believe it can be reasoned with or appeased is beyond me."

"Which is why Kovonov would love to see him dead. And while Kovonov may be insane, we believe he remains fiercely loyal to Israel. Which brings us to you."

Regev paused. "Wortzman reminded me that you're known to the Mossad as well, for more than your recent attempt on Davinroy's life. You were also the agent who saved the president of Syria a few years back, weren't you?"

Quinn gritted his teeth. "I was," he said bitterly, the mixed emotions he felt over this action not having diminished with time.

Rachel turned to him in surprise. "That was *you?*" she said.

Quinn nodded. His identity as the man who had saved Zahir was never disclosed, but the controversy of the Syrian president's visit to the US was well known, as was the fact that he had been saved by a Secret Service agent who many in America believed shouldn't have done so.

"The assassination attempt on Zahir was *our* op," continued the Israeli, addressing Quinn once again. "It was disguised so it couldn't be traced back to us, but it was ours. One of the few that failed. After the fact, Mossad made it our business to hack into your file. We learned that it wasn't our incompetence that caused the failure, but your proficiency. We learned that you were very good at what you did."

Regev pursed his lips, remembering. "Our decision to mount the op in the first place was highly contentious. Almost as many were against it as were for it. All agreed Zahir was a monster. But history has shown that the removal of a monster in our part of the world can lead to even worse outcomes."

"How has it come to this?" mused Rachel. "When did keeping a genocidal mass murderer in place become the *best* outcome we can conceive of?"

"When hordes of people passionately believe their god has called on them to destroy the world," replied Regev. "When this happens, rational options go by the wayside. I was in the camp who opposed the assassination attempt," he added, nodding at Quinn. "Those of us in this camp believe we owe you a debt of gratitude for stopping it. Others in my country will never forgive you."

"Let me go out on a limb here," said Quinn dryly, "and guess which camp Kovonov is in."

Regev smiled. "Let's just say that you aren't his favorite Secret Service agent."

"We had the same two factions in the US when it came to Zahir," said Quinn. "About half would have seen me as a hero, and half a villain. To avoid backlash from this second half, we decided to keep my name out of it."

"Good choice," said Regev. "Did you also believe that removing Zahir would have made things worse in the region?"

"To be honest, I wasn't sure. I was only certain of one thing: I had agreed to do my best to protect him. So I did."

Regev nodded. "I admire that, I really do. But getting back to current events, Kovonov must have figured that by turning you into the instrument of Davinroy's death, he got to kill two hated birds with one stone. And what a great experimental test of his capabilities, both the memory implantation and his new less-invasive technique."

"It's hard to imagine I'm the first person he used this on," said Quinn.

"We aren't sure," said Regev. "But you were *among* the first, that much is clear. And you would have been the sternest test of his capabilities. You're a highly trained agent. Smart. Confident. Strong-willed. So he programmed you with memories that were so far-fetched, so improbable, that if the procedure wasn't absolutely flawless it would never work."

"He definitely didn't shy away from extreme field conditions," said Rachel, almost approvingly.

"No he didn't," agreed Regev. "And don't forget that Kevin had also sworn to protect the president with his life. So Kovonov's tampering had to be powerful enough to overcome even this. To transform Kevin from a protector to a killer using false memories that Kevin should have found absurd."

"His technology worked like a charm," said Quinn, disgusted with himself for not being stronger, not being smarter. "Except that Davinroy got lucky. I failed. As it turned out, *I* got lucky, although that's not what I thought at the time."

He paused. "So why did Kovonov come after me later?"

"As you discovered, he had a fly drone watching his weapon—you—in action. He must have been furious when he saw you fail. On the other hand, I'm sure he was thrilled when you accused Davinroy of the exact atrocities he had implanted in your mind. Regardless, he expected you'd be caught or killed afterward. When you escaped, this opened attractive possibilities."

"Like what?" asked Quinn.

"Like obtaining additional data," said Rachel, answering for the Israeli. "Irresistible to the scientist in him. I'd be just as eager to get my hands on you."

"If you were ruthless and psychotic, you mean?" said Quinn.

Rachel allowed herself a smile. "Of course," she replied. "But Kovonov must have been eager to interview you about what you remembered—or thought you did. Before you escaped from his men you never guessed these memories were false. He could find out what percentage of his implanted memories took, how cleanly, how well connected to your rage centers, and so on. Then he could put you in an MRI. After that he'd probably . . ."

Rachel trailed off and Quinn realized she had no plans to finish the thought. "He'd probably what?" he prompted.

"Well, given his disregard for life, he'd probably, you know . . . dissect your brain."

Quinn raised his eyebrows. "Then all things considered," he said, "I'm glad I escaped. You know, as fun as brain dissection sounds."

Rachel laughed.

Quinn faced the Israeli once more. "But if I wasn't the first subject," he pressed, "couldn't he have done these experiments on someone else?"

"All of this is guesswork," said Regev, "but I suspect he needed any others he was manipulating alive. You were expendable. And he really, really isn't a fan. In his condition, I wouldn't be surprised if he was looking forward to torturing you to death—very slowly. You know, before he removed your brain for further study."

Quinn shuddered. "Have I mentioned I'm glad I escaped?"

Regev nodded.

"Good," said Quinn. He paused in thought. "Okay, this explains me. But what about Rachel? Why would Kovonov try to kill the scientist he worshiped?"

"We can't be sure," replied Regev, "but we think he guessed how badly we wanted her."

"But she's his only hope for a cure," said Quinn.

Rachel shook her head. "That's probably the *last* thing he wants. Despite global changes to his personality he's almost certain to be quite happy with the new him. Many psychopaths *know* they're psychopaths, for example, but would never want to be cured. They see themselves as superior. Unshackled from the ethical bonds that hold others. It's likely Kovonov feels the same way."

Quinn eyed the Israeli. "So he's trying to kill her *because* she might cure him?" he said.

"That's our guess," said Regev. "And also because she has the best shot at developing countermeasures against the neurotech he plans to deploy. But after he went rogue, we failed to predict Rachel would be on his radar, or that he would make the effort to eliminate her."

"No kidding," said Quinn. "Which is why you were caught so off guard."

"You're right, of course," said Regev. "As embarrassing as it is, if you hadn't been able to escape from the two mercenaries to warn her—and us—they probably would have succeeded."

"You're welcome," said Kevin evenly. "I could sense your gratitude when you tried to kill me."

"Like I said, we still thought you might be dangerous to Rachel. Once you proved otherwise, you became very important. Kovonov might have made a critical mistake leaving you alive. Rachel might be able to use you to reverse engineer his new technique."

Quinn considered this for several seconds. "Why did you suddenly decide to make the disclosures you made during our recent vid-meet with Washington?" he asked. "To have a better chance to recruit Rachel?"

"When you burst onto the scene we realized Kovonov had improved his neurotech, making him even more dangerous. As if just having the fly drones wasn't bad enough. When I leveled with you—*partially*—in the neighbor's basement, and disclosed that the fly drones were ours, you admitted you had sent one to Cris Coffey for analysis. These two new factors made the decision easy. We would have needed to get the US involved soon, anyway, but given that the fly drone game was up this was the perfect time."

"And your execution was flawless," said Rachel.

Regev issued a short, self-critical laugh. "Not quite," he said in disgust. "None of us had any idea Kovonov had taken an alias, not to mention one representing the exact number of neurons in an apparently famous *worm*."

Quinn looked amused. "We have an expression, *the worm has turned*. Seems to me you're living it."

"If not for this one flaw," said Regev with a frown, "it would have worked. Nothing could have convinced Rachel to join our efforts more than the events of the past few days, especially seeing living proof of memory implantation and having the president bless this assignment. She would have joined us in Israel. She would have come to know and trust the team while we determined the best way to ease her into the deep end of the pool."

"You did succeed in enlisting US help in hunting down Kovonov," noted Quinn. "Given he has sympathizers in *your* camp, this is an important step."

Regev didn't respond.

"And now it's clear why you insisted Kovonov be killed at first sight," continued Quinn. "If he was captured and had the chance to talk, Israel would have some explaining to do."

"Having the US involved in the manhunt is critical," said the Israeli, "but it only addresses the symptom—and only one of many. Nothing we achieved is nearly as important as persuading Rachel to join our efforts."

Regev turned to the brilliant neuroscientist. "Rachel, you spotted our attempted deception, but it all would have come out soon anyway. Maybe it's for the best it happened this way. When I said I would give my life to protect yours, I wasn't being gallant or heroic. I honestly believe that you could help stave off massive destruction and bloodshed. Prevent the misuse of game-changing technology that you lecture about. And help prevent my country from tearing itself to pieces as its leaders go mad."

Regev gazed deeply into her eyes. "So what do you say?" he continued. "I'm *begging* you. Not only on behalf of my country, but on behalf of America and the entire world. This will impact you, I promise. Your president should already be dead because of Kovonov. And his grand plans are sure to be massively destructive. Come to Israel with me. We can share our neurotech advances. Give you time to fully digest the implications of what is happening. Then you can decide if you're willing to help us. Since we need your best work, your *willing* work, we can't coerce you. If you refuse, you refuse."

Rachel snorted. "I have to give you credit, Eyal," she said, "that's your first lie since agreeing to be straight with us. *Of course* you can coerce me. Just force me to undergo your Matrix Learning procedure multiple times. The equivalent of injecting me with a poison so I'll be motivated to find the antidote, even if only to save my own sanity."

"Yes," said Regev with a sigh. "I guess we *could* coerce you. But we *wouldn't*. That's not our way."

"Easy to say that now," she pointed out. "But high-minded ethics have a way of disappearing under utter desperation."

Regev looked uncertain. "I don't know how to respond to that," he said. "I suppose what you say is true. All I can tell you is that this couldn't be more important. Your chance to save the world, and change it forever. Your chance to perfect your dream technology. You'd be taking a risk, but think of the *reward*."

Rachel shook her head. "I understand every action you and your government have taken now, Eyal. To be honest, I'm not sure I would have done anything differently if I were in your shoes. I do think you're one of the good guys, as is your government—in general," she hastened to add. "But I can't come with you."

"Because of fear of coercion?" said Regev.

"No. Because you admitted yourself you aren't sure who you can trust back in Israel. Your country spawned this technology and a rogue Kovonov. You've admitted he has comprehensive knowledge of your agency and that it could be riddled with moles. And you can't even trust those who oppose him. Who's to say he hasn't tampered with their minds? Who's to say he hasn't created more unwilling human weapons like he did with Kevin? Traps ready to spring now or at some unknown time in the future? Kovonov will learn I'm working with you and determine my location. Are you really sure you can stop him from killing me if he unleashes his full bag of tricks?"

Regev wore a pained expression, and his lack of an answer spoke volumes.

"I didn't think so," said Rachel. "I haven't ruled out undergoing your Matrix Learning procedure. I have to weigh this further. But for now, my answer has to be no. I won't go with you. Not because I don't appreciate the mess you're in, or want to help. But because I want to be alive, and feel safe, if I ever do decide to take you up on your offer."

Regev smiled weakly. "You make some valid points," he said. "You do. But Kovonov will still be coming after you. We would get a team of handpicked men from outside the Mossad to protect you. I still think you'd be safer with us than on your own, despite the risks you've mentioned."

"I know I'm still being hunted," said Rachel. "That I have to abandon my old life, at least for a while. So I will dedicate myself to finding countermeasures against Kovonov's neurotech. But not in conjunction with the Mossad."

"And will you keep what I've told you confidential?"

Rachel and Quinn exchanged glances. They had promised not to share what he told them as long as it didn't conflict with the interests of the US. So how dangerous was it for their country if they kept this to themselves? The US government was aware that minds could be tampered with, and that a man named Kovonov possessed dangerous technology and had to be stopped. Were the details of Matrix

Learning and the impending psychosis of the entire upper echelon of an ally critical at this moment?

"To be honest, Eyal, I don't know," answered Quinn finally. "I have to give it a lot more thought."

Rachel nodded her agreement.

"I appreciate your honesty," said Regev softly.

The Israeli tilted his head in thought for several seconds, sighed, and then faced the woman he would have given his life to recruit. "Okay, Rachel. Do it your way. I won't try to stop you. I'll even agree to actively help you evade my agency. But I do have one condition. Of Kevin."

Quinn raised his eyebrows as the Israeli turned toward him.

"I want your word that you'll stick to her like glue," said Regev. "Until this is over. Help her. Protect her with the skill and tenacity of the Secret Service agent that you are."

Quinn didn't need to think about this for even an instant. "You have my word," he said.

"*Thank you*," said Regev in relief. "Kevin, I honestly believe you're one of the most impressive operatives in your country." He smiled. "If you were just a bit more impressive, you might even rate being an operative in mine. You know, at a low level," he added, his grin widening.

Quinn laughed. "Wow, what an honor," he said dryly. "But I have a request of you, also."

"Go on," said Regev.

"I'd like for my people to think we're working with you as planned."

"Interesting. Do you have reason not to even trust your own people?"

"Not a specific one, no. But the fewer people who know where Rachel is, the better. Regardless of how much I might trust them. I'm sure you would agree."

Regev nodded. "Absolutely. I couldn't have said it better. You're like the less-talented, lighter-skinned Christian brother I never had."

"I take it then that you'll do it."

"I will," said the Israeli. "But I'll have to trust *someone* at Mossad to make this work. My every instinct says that Avi Wortzman is a good man. Not a saint, by any means, but incorruptible."

"Unless he's been manipulated," said Quinn.

Regev sighed. "True. But my gut says he's a man I can trust. And if we want to throw off your people into thinking you're working with us, we'll need him. He'll be able to come up with something that will keep you off the radars of both sides."

"That would be appreciated," said Quinn. "And worst case, if you're wrong about him, at least he won't know where we are."

"That's true also," said Regev. "You'll be on your own. But if the two of you ever need us, or want us, I'll give you a means to contact us that will be manned 24/7. If you and the Lord Almighty call at the same instant, we'll put *you* through first. And, of course, Rachel, if you succeed with countermeasures or decide to undergo Matrix Learning and lead our efforts, we'll see to your transportation immediately."

"Thanks, Eyal," said Rachel. "But there is one more thing you can do."

Regev studied her with great interest.

"Give me the passwords to get into wherever in your agency's databanks you keep the specs and experimental data on your Matrix Learning system. I'd like to start understanding the advances you made the old-fashioned way. It may not be flash-fried into my head, but I'd like to think of myself as a quick study."

Regev thought about this for an extended period, and Quinn couldn't blame him. The granting of high-level passwords into the Mossad's inner sanctum wasn't something done lightly.

Finally, Regev nodded. "I'll do that," he said. "And if you let me use my phone, I'll buy you time in case others don't agree that I've done the right thing. I'll tell my people that we've been delayed and will begin our flight to Israel tomorrow. Then Kevin can shoot me with a tranq gun I saw in his borrowed rucksack and you can be on your way."

He smiled. “Not that I want to be shot, but just to give you absolute peace of mind that I won’t try to follow, or tell Wortzman about this too early.”

Rachel caught Quinn’s eye. “Do you trust him enough to let him talk to his people?”

Quinn thought it through. Regev must realize that Rachel was trying to help, just not in the way he had hoped. But also that there was a great chance she was right, and that she *was* safer on her own. If Quinn were the Israeli, he would genuinely try to help them at this point.

“I do trust him,” replied the Secret Service agent evenly. “Let’s cut this man loose and get him a phone.”

PART 3
Belief

"Do I contradict myself?
Very well then I contradict myself,
(I am large, I contain multitudes.)"

—Walt Whitman, *Song of Myself*

"What is 'real'? How do you define 'real'? If you're talking about what you can feel, what you can taste, what you can smell and see, then 'real' is simply electrical signals being interpreted by your brain."

—Morpheus, *The Matrix*

"The Caterpillar and Alice looked at each other in silence for some time; at last the Caterpillar took the hookah out of its mouth, and addressed her in a languid, sleepy voice.

'Who are you?' said the Caterpillar.

Alice replied rather shyly, 'I—I hardly know, sir, just at present—at least I knew who I was when I got up this morning, but I think I must have been changed several times since then.'"

—Lewis Carroll, *Alice's Adventures in Wonderland*

45

Dmitri Kovonov had a cab drop him at the Cockaponset Lodge and hiked two miles through the woods to the GPS coordinates he had been given. He could have had his underlings pick him up but he wanted some time for reflection, and picking his way through trees and undergrowth in a section of the forest without a preset hiking path focused his mind and got his heart pumping.

It was three hours before sunset and the forest was cool and dry, and the higher oxygen levels provided by the foliage invigorating.

After almost an hour of being immersed in the beauty and serenity of nature, he came to a small clearing and saw his associates' rented Land Rover, his preferred vehicle, which had certainly been earning its off-road stripes on this operation. He joined the two men inside, Daniel Eisen and Yosef Mizrahi, and the three shared greetings in Hebrew.

"I trust you both enjoyed your stay in Chicago," said Kovonov wryly. "All two hours of it."

"It's an interesting city," said Mizrahi, playing along, "but it's no Cockaponset State Forest."

Eisen smiled. "Exactly. Chicago is popular with gangs. Not so much with bible study groups."

"Good thing we're here, then," said Kovonov. He turned to his right-hand man. "Before you begin your situation report, Daniel, have you had the chance to search for the terrorist I'm looking for?"

"I have. Once we set things up here we had plenty of downtime. I ran an AI program through all US intelligence computers I could access."

"You could have just said *all* US intelligence computers—period," said Kovonov with a superior smile. "Same thing."

Over the years the Mossad's fly drones had managed to spy on endless passwords being entered by American intelligence personnel. This, along with advanced hack-ware developed by flash-educated geniuses had allowed the Mossad to breach the computers of the entire US intelligence apparatus.

"Unfortunately, no success yet," reported Eisen. "But there are a few leads I'm exploring. Detention of terrorists in the mainland is still very touchy here, so they hide detainees even from themselves."

"Then searching through the data generated by our flies on the walls might be the better option," said Kovonov.

"About that," said Eisen, looking distinctly uncomfortable. "I'm afraid I have some bad news. It looks like the failure of our White House flies wasn't a random glitch." Eisen swallowed hard. "We've lost a number of our best drones."

"What do you mean, *lost*?"

"They've been discovered and disabled. Not all, but enough to matter. Which means that Kish and Wortzman must have decided to tell the Americans about these drones and how to find them."

Kovonov's expression darkened. "Shit!" he bellowed. "Shit, shit, shit. I didn't see that coming."

He choked down his anger and forced himself to think analytically. "It's the smart thing for them to do, I suppose. But I really didn't think they had the balls," he added, although the Hebrew word he used for balls, *baytseem*, translated literally into *eggs*. "What are the chances they told the Americans about *me*?"

Eisen gritted his teeth. "A hundred percent. They're ramping up a massive operation to find you. If I had to guess, I'd say it's among their highest priorities. The good news is that we still have a large number of drones operational, and I've changed them up to make them harder to detect. We also maintain our backdoor computer access. Their net will have holes plenty big enough for you to waltz through without breaking a sweat. No way they find you."

Kovonov nodded. "I agree," he said.

What his underlings didn't know—yet—was that if they did their job right, the Americans would have much more to worry about than just him. Soon, with any luck, he wouldn't even be an *afterthought*.

But he would have plenty of time to ponder the implications of these new developments later. For now, he needed to focus on the task at hand. "So where do we stand with our church group?" he asked.

"The twenty members of the Danbury Evangelical Fellowship are staying three or four miles north of here," replied Eisen. "Twelve women and eight men. Most between the ages of twenty and thirty-five, but a few older. They're lodging at a campground owned by the Holy Church of Christ, also, not coincidentally, out of Danbury, Connecticut."

"Weapons?" said Kovonov.

Eisen shook his head. "Not unless they plan to chuck their bibles at us. They all arrived in a church minibus, which we've disabled. The retreat consists of ten cabins—each capable of sleeping eight, and each with adjoining bathrooms and showers—a storage shack, and a mess hall that looks like it can hold almost a hundred. They disperse to take advantage of various recreational options, individually and in groups, but they all return to the mess hall at seven for dinner, followed by bible readings and discussion. If tonight follows the pattern, this will take place outside, around a fire, and will last until about ten."

Kovonov shuddered. "Can I assume this includes prayers and the singing of inspirational songs?"

"Yes," said Mizrahi with a grimace. "And we listened to it all."

"It was torture," said Eisen, and then breaking into a grin added, "In fact, I think we deserve hazard pay."

He went on to describe the area surrounding the campground and the surveillance they had established, and gave his assurances that the likelihood of interruption was very low.

"And you used standard cameras?" said Kovonov. He had been clear he wanted the fly drones reserved for the most challenging uses, even before the recent unfortunate losses, and just about any use would be more challenging than spying on a church group.

"Of course," replied his second-in-command.

Kovonov gestured in the direction of the campground. "So I assume we strike when they're all together in the mess hall," he said.

Eisen nodded. "That's right. I have an electronic eye watching the one door into this building. After I've counted twenty bodies entering, we can make our presence known."

"Good. I'm eager to learn the exact . . . greeting, you have planned."

"Let's just say there won't be a lot of singing tonight," said Eisen.

"I'm sure the woodland creatures around here will be forever in our debt," said Kovonov dryly.

46

Daniel Eisen and Yosef Mizrahi managed to corral the twenty members of the Danbury Evangelical Fellowship inside the mess hall well before dusk, confiscating all cell phones and other electronic devices.

The structure had a rustic, unfinished appearance, but it was spacious and vaulted—plenty large enough to house groups many times this size—with a steeply pitched roof and three sets of handsome wooden beams forming giant As inside.

The church group put up no resistance, as expected. Given they were all unarmed inside a building with only one entrance and up against two men clearly comfortable with automatic weapons, Eisen would have been surprised if a group of twenty Navy SEALS would have done anything more than surrender.

He and Mizrahi demanded silence from their prisoners. When a few failed to get the message they underscored their seriousness by shooting off a few rounds from a Maxim 9—the first semiautomatic handgun with a built-in silencer—inches from their heads.

"Anyone else want to speak?" barked Eisen. "Because our next shots won't miss. Nod if I've made myself clear on this."

Twenty heads bobbed up and down in unison, and the room fell silent, other than a few sobs and the sound of panicked breathing.

Mizrahi proceeded to link each of the twenty prisoners together in a loose chain of over a hundred zip-ties, providing a few feet of slack between each of them to allow for movement, but no chance for escape. Twenty people linked together was such an unwieldy jumble of humanity that as long as they were kept away from knives and other sharp objects they could use to free themselves they barely needed watching.

Finally, the two men took turns raiding the bunk beds in surrounding cabins for mattresses, hauling twenty into the mess hall—although calling them mattresses was being generous. Thin plastic cushions would be a better term. They tiled one corner of the mess hall with the light blue pads, each slightly longer and wider than a grown man.

Sleeping would be awkward, but there was enough play between each person that they should be able to manage it—low quality though it might be.

When these preliminaries had been attended to, Eisen and Mizrahi alerted Kovonov, who had waited in the Land Rover, working on his laptop supercomputer. Kovonov calmly sealed this revolutionary device, invented by a team at Mossad and unavailable outside of the corridors of power in Israel, inside a cushioned clamshell case and strode into the mess hall like the CEO of a top technology company taking the stage for a product launch.

He stood silently before the prisoners for several minutes, projecting command and building their anticipation. Finally, he walked in front of one outgrowth of this twenty-celled organism, a young, frightened woman wearing jeans and a yellow T-shirt.

"What's your name?" he said softly, knowing everyone would strain to hear.

"I'm Jeanine," she croaked out. "Jeanine Farrar Bubick."

Every man and woman in the room was transfixed by the scene playing out before them.

"Are you scared, Jeanine?"

She nodded, and several tears escaped the corners of her eyes.

"Don't be," said Kovonov, his voice now louder and more definitive. "I can't tell you details of what's going on here, but you have nothing to worry about. I promise you. Who is in charge here, Jeanine?"

She looked uncertain. "Ah . . . you are."

Kovonov laughed. "I should have seen that coming," he said. "Good answer. You're right, of course. But I mean, who's in charge of your group here?"

"I guess it's Pastor Lewan," she replied. "Rich Lewan."

"Which one of you is the pastor?" said Kovonov calmly while his two associates stood guard near the door, not even bothering to raise their weapons at this point.

A man in his late forties with thinning hair and a kind face raised his hand. "I'm Lewan," he said softly.

"Hello, Pastor," said Kovonov, retreating from the woman named Jeanine and locking his eyes on the group's leader . "Sorry to interrupt your retreat, but I'm afraid it had to be done. Let me explain what's going to happen here. In a moment I'm going to give each one of you a very small injection. A pinprick really. I know this sounds scary, especially since I won't be telling you what it is. But I can assure you it's totally harmless. You have more of a chance of getting sick from a vaccination."

From the fearful expressions around the room, this assurance was not effective.

"After that, we'll be administering questionnaires to each of you, one by one, in the nearest cabin. We'll cut you loose one at a time, and I'll have you wear a skull cap I've developed, with leads that will rest on your skull and forehead. Again, this is harmless. It's basically a lie detector. Not perfect, but better than the current state of the art."

Kovonov smiled. "Not that I'm worried. You really won't have any reason to lie, since we'll be asking routine questions. No secrets or incriminating information. Nothing more than details of your backgrounds and your opinions on a range of issues.

"Then we'll reintegrate you back into the chain," he continued. "While this is going on and after, we want you to be as comfortable and happy as possible. I understand these aren't the best circumstances, but I know if anyone can make the best out of them, this group can. So we're going to kill all Internet signals and give you back your phones, Kindles, and other electronic devices. As well as your bibles and any other physical books you might have brought.

"Then we're going to sit tight for two days, during which time we hope you can relax and enjoy yourselves as much as circumstances will allow. We'll cut you lose and reinsert you periodically as your need for bathroom breaks arise. But you'll be left alone as much as possible. We've brought plenty of very good food—so no one has to be on cooking duty. I'm sure it's better than what you've been eating.

"Finally, at the end of this period, we'll question each of you again. Same skull cap, same questions. Cooperate and we'll be on our way. Don't cooperate and we won't hesitate to kill you all. Sorry to have to be so blunt. I know you are all good people, but the stakes are high here, and we're fully prepared to do what we have to do."

Pastor Lewan's face maintained a remarkable serenity. "We're a peace-loving group," he said evenly. "And since you've given us no choice, I can assure you that we'll all cooperate." He shook his head sadly. "But it's not too late to change your ways. Leave now and we'll forget this ever happened. But continue on this path, and you'll have to answer to a higher power than just us."

Kovonov smiled wearily. "Maybe so," he replied. "But I'm prepared to cross that bridge when I get to it."

47

The next day, Mizrahi relieved Eisen and assumed his colleague's post near the mess hall door. It wasn't exactly guard duty, since the door was chained and padlocked, and they had set an AI to alert them if the surveillance videos of the inside showed anything potentially worrisome. But Eisen had thought it prudent to have one of them close enough to act in seconds, if necessary, if an escape plan did suddenly materialize.

Eisen found Kovonov sitting in front of the farthest cabin from the prisoners, on one of the many wooden folding chairs the church group had brought with them. He was drinking a glass of wine and watching a red squirrel cling to a nearby tree as if defying gravity.

Eisen unfolded one of the chairs leaning against the cabin steps and sat facing Kovonov, while his boss poured him a goblet of his own.

They sipped wine and discussed strategy and the latest intelligence gleaned from their searches of US databases, and finally got around to the virus Kovonov had obtained.

"I have to ask," said Eisen, "how did you manage it? How did you get Dr. Acosta to engineer the virus for you? I know you're the master of neurotech, but even so, it doesn't seem possible."

Kovonov considered how much he should say. Eisen was the only high-level player on his new team whose loyalty hadn't been elevated using his neurotech advances, who hadn't been turned into the ultimate fawning sycophant. Kovonov had wanted to leave him untouched, to see what level of loyalty he could command without manipulation.

And Eisen had *earned* special treatment. The man had originally come to *him*, long trying to convince him to go rogue, to ignore

Wortzman and Kish when they refused to unleash every tool at their disposal to defeat their enemies.

At the time Kovonov had been weak. Even though he shared Eisen's views, he had been too loyal to his superiors, too afraid to take steps he knew in his heart were required. Ironically, before his weakness had suddenly changed to strength, his fear to courage, *he* had refused *Eisen's* entreaties.

Now he had concerns that *Eisen's* resolve was weakening. He feared that his most senior lieutenant might now be unwilling to take the steps that Kovonov had identified as being vital to a full victory.

The evangelicals talked about being reborn, and Kovonov had personal experience in this regard. But he had not been born again into the service of Jesus Christ. He had been born again into strength and pragmatism.

He knew that Mossad agents back in Tel Aviv thought he had gone mad. And he couldn't deny that this designation might be technically accurate. But so what? The fear and empathy embedded in "normal" human wiring were nothing more than shackles, preventing men from reaching their potential, from doing what needed to be done.

But now he was free, his regulator blasted open.

He wasn't delusional, he knew that. He wasn't even paranoid, since the threats he was now addressing were all too real. So let those with lack of vision, *weaklings*, think he was crazy. He preferred other terms. Superior. Revolutionary. *Evolutionary*.

So should he tell his secrets to Eisen? To a man who had been ahead of this curve, at least at one time.

Why not? he decided finally. He had perfected Matrix Learning, cracked the brain's code, and developed the ultimate neurotech toolbox. So Eisen was well aware of his genius. But he was also justifiably proud of the brilliant and creative way he was able to deploy these new tools to achieve his ends. So why not gloat? Why not put his full superiority on display?

"All right, Daniel, I'll tell you," said Kovonov finally. "But don't repeat this to anyone else." The others didn't know they had been manipulated, and he didn't want them to have reason to suspect they might have been.

"Of course."

Kovonov had strengthened the loyalty of his followers back in Switzerland before they had left Israel, using the original technique, under the guise of Matrix Learning. But he had only tested his new, more portable approach on a small handful of subjects: two men in Switzerland, Yosef Mizrahi, Dr. Carmilla Acosta, and Kevin Quinn.

When Quinn had escaped from the mansion in Princeton, Kovonov had been eager to capture him. Not only to extract a painful revenge on the man responsible for saving a monster from a well-earned death, but to gather the kind of data the living weren't quite ready to provide. But as disappointed as he was that Quinn had managed to dodge his experiments, Carmilla Acosta was proving to be quite a valuable case study in her own right.

"Dr. Acosta was one of the few researchers who had the bandwidth and expertise to be able to do what I needed," began Kovonov. "Since I've been flash-educated with a PhD level of genetic engineering, I knew it was possible, but it would take someone truly gifted in the field. Since Carmilla had also developed a revolutionary DNA synthesis technology, and was at least marginally screwable, she was the obvious choice."

Kovonov was pleased by Eisen's attentiveness and eager expression. The man seemed well aware he was getting rare insight into the thought processes of a true virtuoso.

"Once the smart dust was in place three weeks ago," he continued, "I began. First, I implanted a set of strong false memories in her mind. Memories of knowing me for almost two years. Memories of my generosity, good humor, and how she had sought me out, rather than the other way around."

Kovonov paused to watch the red squirrel he had spotted rush down the tree trunk and scurry off into the undergrowth. "Turns out the mind has a sort of filing system," he continued. "A specific person becomes associated with a specific neuron, or neurons, which fire whenever this person is considered. Think of these as neuronal addresses. I found the Dmitri Kovonov address in Carmilla's brain and linked any firing at this location to the reward centers of her brain. In a nutshell, I caused her to become powerfully addicted to me.

"I also implanted memories of times we were together that never happened. Of romantic walks on the beach. Of me engaged in selfless sex, relentlessly committed to satisfying her needs before my own. Memories tied into the same regions of her brain that are triggered when she has a powerful orgasm.

"At the same time I mimicked the brain structure of those in romantic love. A time when passion becomes an irresistible force, and lovers are willing to walk off a cliff for the objects of their obsession, can't stop thinking of them."

"Impressive," whispered Eisen, only now getting a sense of what was truly possible.

"Once you've cracked the brain's code, human beings are nothing more than puppets. After one session of manipulation she was convinced she had known me for years and was in love with me to the point of obsession. The few times I did screw her during the past three weeks, for my own enjoyment and to add reinforcement to the virtual memories, I upped her sex drive to ridiculous, insatiable levels."

"The dream of mankind throughout the ages," said Eisen wryly.

"You have *no* idea," said Kovonov, looking shell-shocked just from the memory. "Not recommended for anyone with a heart condition."

Eisen grinned. "Okay, so you make her obsessed with you," he said, getting back on track. "She worships you. But what about the virus?"

"I implanted memories of multiple conversations we had over the months about a sister of mine who doesn't exist. A sister suffering from ever-worsening, inoperable epileptic seizures. I had Carmilla remember that she had come up with an idea that might help this poor girl. That she could construct a virus capable of seeking out and interacting with exquisitely specific neurons and brain regions, the epicenters of the seizures."

A broad, self-satisfied smile crossed Dmitri Kovonov's face. "She wasn't suspicious of my motives because she remembered it being *her* idea, that she suggested to *me*. Then I provided an electronic file with the exact specifications I wanted to achieve, and had her remember she had gotten this after consultation with my sister's physician."

Eisen shook his head. "Truly brilliant, Dmitri. Seems I haven't fully appreciated the potential of the technology."

"The obsession she had for me drove her harder to perfect the virus than any other motivation ever could. She told me she worked on it around the clock, abandoning almost everything else."

"Well done," said Eisen.

Kovonov nodded. He took a sip of wine and reflected on where things stood. Dr. Carmilla Acosta had done well. But assuming the virus performed as he expected, he had to decide how to clean up after himself. He could have her killed, but then there would be an investigation. She was too high profile, with a big discovery about to be released. Why take any chances she left something behind that led to him? Something he had missed.

The simplest solution was to erase all of her memories of him, the ones he had implanted and the ones that had been formed the old-fashioned way. But as he considered this further, inspiration struck.

Because there was another option he could try first. One that had great appeal to him.

One that would allow him to discover just how powerful his tampering had really been.

48

Yosef Mizrahi was tall, athletic, and handsome, with thick raven-black hair and masculine features that drove women wild. Yet he could honestly say that the time he spent in Cockaponset State Forest was more pleasurable than any weekend he had ever spent in the arms of a beautiful woman.

Not in a sexual way, of course. But in a way that enriched his very soul.

And this was due entirely to Dmitri Kovonov. Mizrahi basked in the presence of the great man, barely able to keep his star-struck awe to himself during their interactions, only managing to do so after Kovonov had chastised him repeatedly for gushing and had insisted he keep this adulation more hidden.

What a priceless opportunity Mizrahi had been given. One he would be telling his grandchildren about someday.

He had always had a deep admiration for Kovonov and shared his views that neurotech should be deployed against Israel's enemies, who wouldn't hesitate to treat Israel a hundred times more harshly if given the chance. But ever since joining this inspirational leader on his exodus from the Mossad, Mizrahi's admiration for the man had deepened, had grown to stratospheric levels. He now saw Kovonov as not only a genius whose discoveries would catapult the human species to new heights, but as a father figure, a sage.

Mizrahi sat quietly on a bunk inside the cabin Kovonov had turned into an interview and lie-detector center. He watched the great man as he finished interviewing the last of the twenty prisoners, a pretty young blonde, reveling in how smoothly he did so, how at ease he put each churchgoer. Kovonov had been so elated by the results he could barely contain himself.

History would show that the ultimate game changer had been tested in these woods and that Yosef Mizrahi had been right there to witness the dawn of a new era. He didn't have a ringside seat on history, he was actually *in the ring*, in the corner of the boxer destined to beat the limitations of the human species into submission.

"Yosef," said Kovonov, breaking him from his reverie, "take Linda here back to the mess hall and tie her back in."

"Right away," said Mizrahi, fighting for all he was worth to keep his response subdued.

"Once you've finished," continued Kovonov, "return here for further instructions."

Mizrahi nodded. Given they had now achieved their goal, he suspected what these further instructions would entail: the release of the prisoners. They would need a plan for doing so that would give them an ample head start. Mizrahi had no doubt that Kovonov had come up with one that was as brilliant as usual. He was eager to find out.

"Tell Daniel to give us ten minutes alone and then join us in this cabin," continued Kovonov.

"You're okay with leaving the door to the mess hall unattended?" said Mizrahi, glancing at the prisoner named Linda who had heard this last instruction.

"I am," said Kovonov. "It will be locked and I'll keep my eye on the monitors." He waved a hand toward the prisoner. "And I'm sure no one will attempt to escape now that they're so close to being released," he added pointedly. "Will they?"

The woman shook her head rapidly, as if this was the last thing in the world she would ever consider.

"I'll give Daniel the message," said Mizrahi.

Kovonov nodded curtly and went back to studying a computer readout and making entries into his laptop.

Mizrahi led the prisoner away and reinserted her back into the human chain. He then carefully relayed Kovonov's message to Eisen before eagerly returning to the cabin to learn what else he could do for the great man.

He entered and approached Kovonov, whose back was to him and the door. "So what is your plan to release the prisoners?" he asked.

Kovonov turned, revealing a gun in his right hand that was extended toward Mizrahi. Such was the trust Mizrahi had in this man that it never once occurred to him he was in possible danger, or that he should attempt to protect himself.

He opened his mouth to ask why the great man was pointing a weapon his way, but speech never came. Instead, Kovonov pulled the trigger and Mizrahi's world was instantly plunged into darkness.

* * *

Kovonov was in great spirits as he awaited the imminent arrival of Daniel Eisen. His plan was proceeding flawlessly.

He had even learned that morning that Rachel Howard was dead after all, which had given him great satisfaction, icing on his cake. Perhaps he had judged his second set of mercenaries too harshly. Before they were killed, they had managed to take the professor with them.

Interestingly, Wortzman had gone to great lengths to get the Americans to believe she was still alive and working with the Mossad in Israel. Then he had made sure her location in Israel was a closely guarded secret. A secret that Kovonov's moles managed to learn.

Kovonov had been considering sending in a team to dispose of her once and for all when it occurred to him that this had all played into his hands a bit too easily.

Wortzman was a clever bastard, but Kovonov knew how he thought. One didn't get to the top of the Mossad unless one had a talent for deep deception. He began to suspect that Wortzman had wanted his moles to learn where she was located, hoping that they or their boss would go after her. It was a trap.

When Kovonov had insisted that his operatives peel back further on the onion, they had found the truth: the professor had been killed in Waltham, after all. Wortzman may have deceived the Americans and his own people, but his attempt to flush out Kovonov had failed.

Kovonov's thoughts were interrupted as Eisen entered the cabin, right on schedule. His lieutenant was quick to react to the figure of his colleague sprawled out on the floor. "What happened?" he asked Kovonov who was standing near the body.

Kovonov shrugged. "I shot him," he said calmly, raising a gun at the same instant and providing Eisen with a reenactment of this event.

Eisen collapsed to the ground beside Mizrahi.

Satisfied, Kovonov walked to a bunk on which an assault weapon was resting, an H&K UMP 45, long used by US Customs and Border Protection, a lighter successor to the MP5. He picked it up and pocketed an extra magazine that was sitting beside it.

He made his way to the door of the mess hall and unlocked it, entering as he had any number of times over the past few days. The prisoners were spread across the back corner of the room on the platform of thin blue cushions. Some were reading quietly, others were engaged in conversations, and still others were playing cards.

All eyes turned to him as he held the H&K loosely in his right hand, the muzzle pointed straight down at the floor.

An unearthly quiet and stillness overcame the room.

"Have you come to set us free?" asked the pastor after several seconds, piercing the silence. He eyed the UMP 45 in Kovonov's hand warily. "We've cooperated. We've answered your questions and done everything you've asked."

"You have all been wonderful," agreed Kovonov. "May you spend eternity in heaven with your loved ones."

With that he lifted the submachine gun and began to spray the prisoners with .45 caliber rounds.

It was absolute *carnage*.

Blood and flesh splattered into the air as helpless, unsuspecting men and women were turned into Swiss cheese, to the accompaniment of screams of death and terror that would haunt a medieval torturer.

When the magazine had emptied, Kovonov replaced it with the spare and set the weapon to single shot, this time taking careful aim and making sure to put a round through the forehead of each and every member of the Danbury Evangelical Fellowship. He did so with a ruthless, clinical efficiency and thoroughness, ensuring that none had any hope of revival.

While this resulted in the spilling of additional quarts of slick, bright blood, turning the mats a mixture of light blue and bright red, at least the screams had now died out along with the screamers.

Kovonov had considered letting them know that they would be dying for a greater purpose. That sometimes sacrifices had to be made. Reminding them that even God had allowed his only son to be tortured and killed for the right reasons.

But he knew that this would do nothing to ease their journey into oblivion.

Kovonov calmly checked the monitors and was pleased to see that while the thick wooden structure of the mess hall hadn't fully suppressed the racquet he had made, the noise hadn't traveled far enough to attract attention. The many cameras his underlings had installed earlier indicated that the nearest park visitors were many miles away and going about their lives in blissful ignorance.

Perfect.

Kovonov removed a paintbrush he had shoved into his back pocket. He carefully picked his way between the corpses, minimizing the gore that ended up on his shoes but not avoiding it entirely.

He stopped a few feet in from the back corner of the room, next to where a particularly large pool of blood had gathered, and dipped his brush into the vivid crimson liquid. Carefully, painstakingly, he proceeded to write an Arabic phrase across the entire back wall of the mess hall, coming back for more red ink on numerous occasions.

When he was finally done, he stepped back to admire his handiwork.

Ash hadu an laa ilaaha illallaah he had written: There is no God but Allah

wa ash hadu anna Muhammadan rasool-ullaah: And Muhammad is his Messenger.

It was the Muslim *shahādah*, their most profound statement of faith. In some sects the recitation of this phrase was the first of the Five Pillars of Islam and was the only formal step required for non-Muslims to convert into the religion.

Kovonov surveyed the grisly scene one last time and was struck by the fact that it didn't trouble him. He had previously abhorred violence. Just a month or two ago, not only would he have been appalled by the idea of hurting a single one of these men and women, he would have been vomiting at the sight of the carnage before him.

And yet now that he had changed, he found that he was actually enjoying himself. He found pleasure in his lack of weakness, pride in his thoroughness. He found a certain fascination in the grisly ballet of death, a poetry in the patterns the flesh-and-blood splatter had made on the floor and walls.

A slow, satisfied smile crept across his face.

Perhaps he was not yet done evolving.

49

Yosef Mizrahi's eyes fluttered open and the world gradually swam back into focus. He felt as if he were having an out-of-body experience. He vaguely noted that Daniel Eisen was sitting beside him on a bunk, awake and alert. Both were handcuffed with zip-ties, and both also had their ankles cuffed to the bunk bed, which itself was bolted into the cabin wall.

Kovonov was seated across from them in a folding chair, watching them intently.

"Dmitri?" said Mizrahi weakly.

"Glad to see you're awake," replied Kovonov.

"Now that he is," said Eisen, "are you ready to tell us what this is about?"

Kovonov nodded. "I shot you both with a tranquilizer dart," he said. "Very short acting. You've only been out about an hour. And let me say I'm really sorry about having to do this. You've been loyal and you've performed brilliantly."

"Good to know our work is appreciated," said Eisen with a scowl.

"It truly is," said Kovonov, not responding to the irony. "I felt the need to restrain you for a while because I haven't been completely honest with you about my plans. I wasn't sure how you would take them. I need to be sure that you're with me."

"We'd follow you to hell and back," said Mizrahi, sounding hurt that Kovonov might doubt this for even a moment.

Eisen eyed Mizrahi and shook his head in disgust. "So what *is* the real plan?" he asked Kovonov warily.

"First, with regard to the current op, I know I told you we'd be sparing the prisoners—but we can't. Sacrifices have to be made. We can't take any chances. In addition, if we play our cards right we can pin their deaths on jihadists."

"What?" whispered Eisen in horror. "You can't mean that."

"Of course I do. But I'll make their deaths as quick and painless as possible."

"So you want to just butcher them like cattle in a slaughterhouse?" demanded Eisen. "They're *helpless.* Haven't we hurt them enough already? And we promised to let them go. Are we really going to slaughter helpless innocents?"

Mizrahi found himself agreeing. He had never thought ill of Kovonov before, but he couldn't help but find this a troubling development.

"When you signed on for this project," said Kovonov, "you knew I planned to change the world. Don't tell me you're getting sanctimonious all of a sudden?"

"*Sanctimonious?*" shouted Eisen. "*That's* what you call objecting to the slaughter of innocents? Yes, I signed on to change the world. But with a *virus.* Already a horrific solution, but one that I believe our survival might depend on. But I never signed on for *this*! How are we any different than the Islamists we're fighting?"

"Shit, Daniel! Are you really going to start quoting Nietzsche like you're Avi Wortzman? His *battle not with monsters* shit? In every war civilians are killed. It's called collateral damage." Kovonov shook his head in disgust and disappointment. "I thought you might balk at the next step in my plan, but not this one."

Mizrahi's face had turned into a tortured mask of conflicted emotions, but he remained silent.

"You can't do this, Dmitri, " said Eisen.

"The Americans dropped two atomic bombs on Japanese cities to end a war," said Kovonov. "Do you have any idea how many innocent civilians were killed? How many children? The tens of thousands who were vaporized instantly were the *lucky* ones. An even greater number survived the initial blast and went on to die slowly and horribly from radiation poisoning. The Americans didn't *want* this to happen. But they calculated this action would save millions of lives by ending the war. Would stop the kamikaze-deploying Japanese who were so relentless and unyielding they refused to surrender even *after* Hiroshima."

Kovonov's lip curled into a snarl. "And what was the ultimate fallout from this?" he demanded. "I'll tell you what: Japan and America are now close allies."

"You're going to compare ending WWII to shooting helpless evangelicals like fish in a barrel?" shouted Eisen, so incensed he looked like a rabid dog. "You've observed and questioned these people. On the whole they're a decent, well-meaning group. Maybe we find the bible study thing a little hokey, but it helps *them*. They don't deserve this. And we wouldn't be killing them to end a war or prevent casualties on our side. You and I both know there is no need for them to die."

"Not a direct need," said Kovonov, "but killing them reduces the risk that we'll be caught or found out, which could ruin everything. Could prevent us from ending a war on terror. A trans-generational battle against foes who make the Japanese seem as relentless and unyielding as a *teddy bear*. As a small bonus, the massacre of twenty innocents, if unambiguously tied to jihadists, will continue to prod America out of its reluctance to truly engage. A small prodding, yes, but a tiny step in the right direction."

"No!" said Eisen. "I won't be a party to this! Watching them through the monitors, watching their resilience, I've found a renewed faith in humanity. I'm not sure I even support the *original* plan any longer. But I know I don't support this!"

Kovonov shook his head. "I thought after I revealed my true plans I'd have to question you with the lie detector. Make sure you were telling the truth when you said you supported me. I never thought you wouldn't at least *pretend* to support me."

"Well think again!" said Eisen. His eyes widened as a new thought struck him. "Wait a minute. If this was supposed to be the part of your plan you thought wouldn't trouble us, what's the *next* part like?"

Kovonov told them, quickly and efficiently, with no punches pulled.

This time even Mizrahi whitened in horror.

"You've gone totally fucking mad!" said Eisen. "I was told you had, but I never believed it. I thought it was propaganda from Wortzman to rein you in. But he was absolutely right!"

"What I'm doing is the equivalent of killing one innocent man to save a thousand."

"Spoken like a true psychopath," spat Eisen.

Kovonov turned to Mizrahi. "Yosef?" he said, almost plaintively. "I know I can count on you. You're still with me, right?"

Mizrahi's face was contorted as an absolute war raged inside his mind. Thoughts and emotions vied for prominence, waging a pitched battle with sharp daggers.

He loved Dmitri Kovonov. This man had become almost a god to him. But the atrocities he was contemplating were just too great.

Mizrahi finally decided that Kovonov was still a god, but one who had fallen ill. One he would dedicate his life to curing.

"It pains me to side with Daniel on this one," he said. "But I have no other choice."

And it *did* pain him, not just psychologically but physically as well. His entire being protested the decision to go against Kovonov's wishes, like the body of a transplant recipient rejecting the heart he needed to survive.

Kovonov leaped to his feet in a fit of rage and flung the folding chair toward the far wall of the cabin with all of his strength. "Are you kidding me?" he screamed at Mizrahi as the wooden chair struck the wall like an oversized hammer, shattering into pieces.

He clenched and unclenched his fists and a maniacal look remained on his face. "Do you have any idea how much I've molded you?" he bellowed. "I've turned you into a loyal puppy dog! Your admiration for me has been ramped up so high it's amazing it hasn't shot through the top of your head," he screamed, spittle flying from his mouth. "*So what happened to following me into hell?*" he demanded.

Kovonov took several deep breaths and the fire in his eyes subsided, his tantrum over. "This tells me a lot," he said evenly, the scientist once more. "Even the best of humanity, even manipulated relentlessly, doesn't have the iron stomach to do what is necessary. This is such a disappointment."

"Are you saying my admiration for you isn't real?" said Mizrahi stupidly.

"You fucking idiot! I understand being clueless when you had no idea I tampered with you. But now? A light bulb should be going off in your head, right? I fucked with your brain! Of course I did! That's what I *do*! You followed me from Mossad so I could do this to our enemies, remember? You didn't *always* slavishly worship the urinal I pee in, remember?"

Mizrahi thought his brain was exploding as the dam protecting his psyche from this realization burst open. Gorge rose in his throat.

He had agreed to follow Kovonov initially, had genuinely respected and admired the man, but knowing that he had since been turned into a human puppet was a shock to his system that was nearly debilitating, a lead-fisted sucker punch to his gut.

"As disappointed as I am," continued Kovonov, "I can't afford to lose you both. So I'll still need to salvage you, Yosef. Daniel is smarter and more competent, but I'm forced to make this choice. Your brain has been raped repeatedly and is set up for easy manipulation going forward."

"What does that mean?" said Eisen. "That you're going to kill me? Your friend? The man who stood at your side when Wortzman tried to limit you? Your greatest ally and top lieutenant? If that isn't proof that you've lost your mind, nothing is."

Eisen took a deep breath and softened his voice. "I can still be an ally, Dmitri. Still help you change the world. Just abandon these plans. The virus will be enough. Let these people go."

"Let these people go?" repeated Kovonov in disbelief. "You're starting to sound like Moses."

He raised a gun, this time one that fired bullets rather than tranquilizers. "I'd consider your offer, Daniel, except for two things. One, you've already admitted to having second thoughts about even deploying the virus. And two, the Danbury Evangelical Fellowship is already extinct. I butchered them like hogs while you were out cold," he added with a cruel smile.

Eisen issued a primal scream that Kovonov ended almost before it had begun, calmly pulling the trigger and drilling a hole through the forehead of the man who had been his closest friend and confidant.

"I am so sorry it's come to this," he whispered as Eisen's head slumped forward against his chest.

But rather than sorrow, his face reflected nothing but self-satisfaction.

50

Mizrahi's eyes fluttered open and it took him several long seconds to get his bearings. He was seat belted in on the passenger's side of the Land Rover with Dmitri Kovonov at the wheel.

"What happened?" he said, still feeling groggy.

Kovonov smiled warmly. "You were exhausted. Maybe you need more vitamin C, Yosef. Or caffeine at any rate. Anyway, I insisted you take a nap."

He looked around. "Where is Daniel?"

"You really are tired," said Kovonov.

Mizrahi searched his memory and recent events slowly came back to him. They had left the twenty members of the church group behind, all relieved that their ordeal would soon be coming to an end. He remembered that Kovonov had asked Eisen to watch the group for another five hours before releasing them. Given that the US was ramping up a manhunt to find Dmitri Kovonov, he was vulnerable, and it was important that he be given a head start.

The rest of the recent past began to seep into Mizrahi's brain as he awakened more fully. Before he and Kovonov had left, the great man had asked to speak privately with Eisen, to give him a new assignment after he finished babysitting the evangelicals. Mizrahi hadn't been told the nature of Eisen's new assignment, but he knew it must be important. He wondered when he would see his colleague again.

A sheepish expression came over Mizrahi's face. "Dumb question," he said. "Daniel's back at camp, of course, waiting to free the prisoners. How could I have forgotten? I must have been groggy from the sleep."

"Must have been," agreed Kovonov sagely.

51

In addition to funding civilian scientists at top universities to conduct research in their own labs, the United States government and military maintained secret laboratories throughout the country, working on advanced weapons, computers, drones, satellites, aircraft, nanites, and just about every other area of science and technology in existence. Rachel Howard had received grant money from the government in the past, but she never imagined her results might be funneled into a secret netherworld where brightly lit labs existed in the figurative shadows.

Now that she was actually *in* one of these secret labs, it was a lot easier to imagine.

And not just any secret lab. A notorious one. She had not known this offhand, but even the simplest online query was enough to reveal an avalanche of infamy extending back many decades.

Plum Island was three miles long and one wide, not far from New York City and quite near the Hamptons, a famous seaside resort. Owned by the government for over half a century, most recently the Department of Homeland Security, it was the known site of labs working on biological warfare—defense only, if the military was to be believed—and the suspected site of considerable additional secret biological research.

The island was rumored to have been the site of work on so many esoteric and lethal microbes, including those engineered by its scientists, and the subject of so many lapses in containment, it was widely considered a toxic cross between Area 51 and Three Mile Island.

What Rachel had learned from Cris Coffey—while being whisked to the island with Kevin Quinn like so much illegal black market cargo—was that the military had been responsible for these very rumors, borrowing from a playbook that had long served it well. If you wanted to discourage curious reporters and civilians from trying to breach the robust security on your secret base and gain entry, ensuring they were terrified of being exposed to lethal contaminants was a good way to do it.

In 2020, with great fanfare, DHS had announced they had sold Plum Island to a reclusive Internet billionaire, but Coffey explained this was also a ruse. Ownership had changed hands all right, but only from one shadowy government organization to another: from DHS to a Black Ops group that had not only assumed command but had upgraded the facilities with the most expensive equipment and the latest breakthrough tech coming from other government labs.

The military man running the advanced neuroscience lab on the island, Major Roger McLeod, had once reported to Coffey, and had agreed to ensure that no one on Plum Island would disclose the identity of their honored guests, even to the president or Greg Henry. Coffey had fully briefed him, explaining that the stakes were so high they couldn't afford to have even a single person in the loop who didn't absolutely need to be.

McLeod had simply laughed and reminded Coffey that he had been out of Black Ops too long, and that they weren't in the habit of reporting their activities to the president and DHS anyway.

Coffey had been amazing and Rachel could see why Kevin thought so highly of him. He was taking a big risk keeping his superiors in the dark, a risk that could end up costing him his job—or worse. He had supplied her and Kevin with untraceable phones and laptop computers designed for the leadership of the NSA, with more speed and power than was yet available on the market, the equal of the best mainframes only a few short years earlier.

They had confided in Coffey to a large extent, telling him about Israel's Matrix Learning program and that Kovonov was behind it, determined to deploy advanced neurotech. But they had not let him know that Matrix Learning had ultimately driven Kovonov mad, or that there were ticking time bombs in the minds of untold members of Israel's upper echelon: scientists, military, and politicians. For now, they would keep this to themselves, out of respect for the wishes of Eyal Regev.

While Coffey was pulling strings to make things happen, he put his two wards up at a bed-and-breakfast hotel in the Hamptons. Quinn under the Kevin Moore identity and Rachel under the name of Angie Helms Loftin.

True to his word, Eyal Regev had provided Rachel with the passwords she needed to access the Mossad's entire database on Matrix Learning, and Coffey had made sure she could do so in a way that couldn't be traced back to her location. When she wasn't watching a movie in the hotel with Kevin, or sharing a meal, she was poring over this data like a kid in a candy store, twelve to fourteen hours a day.

She and Quinn developed an easy rapport and an undeniable chemistry: the bad boy whose life had been shattered and the geek genius scientist too busy changing the world to maintain a serious relationship. On paper, it shouldn't have worked, but in reality it did—only too well.

Finally, when it became clear they were falling for each other on any number of levels, they had discussed it openly. Both had acknowledged the elephant in the room, and both were determined to ignore it—for now. Rachel could be the key to preventing widespread chaos and destruction, at minimum. Under the circumstances, giving in to her attraction to Quinn would be a distraction she couldn't afford.

He agreed and also thought it unprofessional to have relations with a woman he was protecting. He joked that he needed all of his blood flowing to his brain when he was with her, and he was afraid that might not be the case if he got any closer. She could have taken this declaration any number of ways, but their relationship had evolved to a point that she took it as he had intended, as amusing and flattering.

After three days of this they had arrived on the Island and to a large five-story building overlooking the Atlantic that had been designated the *Advanced Neurotechnologies Laboratory*. Since this abbreviated to ANL, or Anal, the building's inhabitants referred to it as *The Anus*. This had been an irreverent joke in the beginning but had become so commonly used the scientists there rarely considered its anatomical meaning anymore.

Living quarters had been made available to the two guests on the Island, with Kevin's quarters right next to Rachel's. While they didn't reside with the rest of the Anus personnel, the major made sure to tie Rachel into the lab's computers and equipment.

With this complete, the major decided it was time to introduce them privately to the scientific head of the lab, Dr. Karen Black, who was exceedingly familiar with Rachel Howard and her work.

The major escorted Dr. Black to Rachel's quarters, and her eyes bulged from their sockets when the Harvard professor came into view. "*Rachel Howard?*" she said in disbelief.

She stared at Rachel for several long seconds and then, deciding this wasn't an illusion, extended her right hand. "It is a true honor, Professor Howard."

"Thank you," replied Rachel simply, shaking the woman's hand.

The head of the lab introduced herself and they quickly agreed to use first names. Even if this hadn't been Rachel's habitual choice, it was standard practice for scientists working together to eschew titles, as they added an unneeded level of formality and all of their MDs and PhDs tended to cancel each other out, anyway.

"I can't tell you how often I've fantasized about getting the chance to consult with you," said Karen Black, and although Quinn had shaken her hand as well, Rachel doubted she was even aware any longer that he and the major were still in the room.

"You should have," said Rachel. "I would have been happy to help out."

Karen shook her head wistfully, her short brown hair barely moving. "I know you would have. But when these type of research facilities decide they want someone with a particular expertise, they tend to recruit right out of graduate school. And they can be more persuasive than you'd imagine. They offer futuristic resources to draw on and funding that never runs dry. The chance to work on important, leading edge science right out of grad school. And compensation triple what you could have gotten elsewhere." She frowned. "But there is a catch."

Rachel nodded. "Let me guess," she said. "It's harder to consult with people like me. And you can't ever publish your findings." She was at least somewhat familiar with the work of every scientist in the field, and hadn't heard of this woman, so she was sure her assessment was correct.

"Exactly. You become invisible as a scientist."

"Regrettable," said Major McLeod, "but necessary. But I can tell you, Professor, Dr. Black has done some brilliant work. If she were in academia, I'm sure you would find her a peer."

"Thank you, Major," said Karen. "I am proud of the work I've done. But the professor here is in a league of her own."

52

Rachel had been told by Karen Black that the Anus housed sixteen PhD or MD neuroscientists and an army of fifty-nine subordinate lab technicians. Since she had not become acclimated to this nickname for the Advanced Neurosciences Laboratory, she found this highly amusing at a sophomoric level she had thought she'd long outgrown.

But apparently not.

If the question, "What's inside the anus?" ever did arise, she had been quite sure the correct answer would never be, "sixteen neuroscientists and fifty-nine lab techs."

Which just went to show how dramatically her life had changed.

They had also learned that a team of six ex-special forces commandos handled security on the island. Quinn had commented dryly that after surviving a number of years in the special forces, joining the Secret Service or defending Black sites like Plum Island was considered light duty.

To extend the childish scatological humor further, the security team had taken to calling themselves Prep H. When Rachel had asked why this was, they had grinned and told her it was short for *Preparation H*. In their view a fitting designation since they and this product had both been tasked with protecting the Anus.

Again, Rachel couldn't help but smile. On an island full of stir-crazy scientists and soldiers, naming the primary facility ANL was just asking for trouble. She had considered advising them to change it to *Progressive Neurological Sciences*, or PNS, and had laughed out loud at the thought of the penis jokes that would soon follow.

The Prep H group had been ordered to make protecting her their highest priority until they were told otherwise, so she knew that they would be patrolling outside of her quarters and giving her their every attention. She had felt guilty about this and had suggested Kevin

Quinn was protection enough, but they had told her politely that this decision wasn't up to her, and they would make sure she was protected whether she liked it or not.

She had begun her research right after meeting Karen Black, with the scientific head of the laboratory happily conducting experiments at her request, dropping her own projects and giddy at the opportunity to work with one of her scientific idols.

The head of the lab and Major McLeod were the only two on Plum Island who had been fully briefed on everything Rachel and Kevin knew, other than the fact that Matrix Learning eventually led to madness. Since Rachel couldn't allow herself to be seen by others in the Anus who might recognize her, she worked from her residence a short distance away.

The progress Rachel made in just a few short days was nothing short of breathtaking. First, she had climbed the learning curve on Kovonov's original Matrix Learning procedure in record time while still at the Hamptons. The Mossad's data was quite comprehensive and well laid out, and she had spent many years thinking about the problem. But more importantly, Kovonov had used *her* insights, *her* ideas, for ninety percent of what he had done.

He had made a few lucky guesses that did extend the work, but he would have been nowhere without her theories, which she had formulated just out of grad school. He was only able to perfect the technique because Israel had poured so much money for so long into this research that they had developed specialized technologies to accomplish it.

No wonder he worshiped Rachel, who had been an unknowing collaborator. He could never have succeeded without her.

She felt like Alan Turing, a man whose vision had outrun the state of technology in his era, who had developed sophisticated concepts for modern computers that he didn't have the means to turn into reality.

She had been working for years on ways to get Matrix Learning to work remotely, bypassing the more limited method the Israelis had developed, not content to get there in stepwise fashion. She had no interest in working toward technology that would require multimillion dollar MRI-like equipment, subjects to have electronics surgically implanted, and the need for them to be tethered to the equipment for the knowledge download to occur.

So after coming up to speed on Kovonov and his team's original process, she began working to understand the new, more mobile process he had developed, which had given him the tools he needed to go rogue. Despite this being the area of her greatest expertise, Kovonov had hidden his notes and data from the Mossad, so she would normally have had no way to make progress on this front.

Except that a way had been handed to her in the form of a Secret Service agent named Kevin Quinn. A priceless tool that had magically fallen into her lap from out of nowhere—or into the back of her SUV in any case.

Quinn had been tampered with remotely, seamlessly. She was certain that the evidence of how this was accomplished had been left behind inside his brain, and she quickly discovered she was correct.

Again, Kovonov had built on *her* work, using her theories, thoughts, algorithms, and experimental protocols. Much of it material that she had yet to publish. He had clearly used fly drones or hack-ware to get her passwords and steal her most innovative work.

She felt totally violated, but at the same time she was flattered and gratified that he had gotten her ideas to work. She couldn't wait to study what he had done.

On the third day of her stay on Plum Island, Rachel asked the major to set up a meeting so she could provide a status update. She hadn't even had the chance to discuss her findings with Kevin Quinn, her primary research tool. She was working so hard she had temporarily become a recluse, unaware the outside world even existed. The few times she had tried to catch the news online or on TV, one story dominated the coverage, about a massacre at a place called Cockaponset State Forest in Connecticut, the latest of a long line of horrific terror attacks carried out by Islamic extremists.

The meeting took place in Rachel's quarters, which the major had ordered modified on her first day there. Contractors had cut an opening between her and the apartment to her north, which had been transformed into an office fitted with expensive computers and monitors. Quinn, still to her south, teased her about her decadent quarters and royal treatment, but she reminded him that as her personal bodyguard he benefited from guarding her in larger environs.

When those attending physically—Kevin Quinn, Roger McLeod, and Karen Black—had seated themselves around a glass table on the office side of her twin dwelling, vid-meet software created a virtual table and integrated Cris Coffey's 3-D image into the meeting.

Rachel sat at the head of both the virtual and real tables and welcomed all participants.

"Thanks for accommodating my schedule," said Coffey before they began. Since he hadn't told his superiors about this project he had very little flexibility.

Rachel smiled warmly. "For you, Cris, anything."

"If only my wife would say that once in a while," said Coffey dryly.

There were smiles all around. Rachel waited a moment for them to fade and then began. "As you all know, Karen and I have been working around the clock for the past three days trying to understand how Kovonov was able to do what he did. With the goal of finding a way to stop him."

She didn't mention her other goal: learning why the process ultimately led to madness.

"In the days before I arrived," she continued, "I studied the Mossad's files on Matrix Learning. So I first want to bring everyone up to speed on my progress." She gestured appreciatively toward Karen Black. "On *our* progress," she amended.

"How far over our heads will it be?" asked Coffey.

"It won't be. I know you aren't trained in neuroscience. I'll be giving you simplified explanations and I'll try to focus on the big picture."

She went on to explain how the Israeli Matrix Learning technology worked as best she could for twenty minutes.

"Rachel makes it sound simple," said Karen when she had finished her summary, "but believe me, it isn't. Turns out the Israelis based most of this technology on her theories. I've worked in the leading edge of this field for many years and *I* still have a long way to go to truly understand this, even with the professor's tutelage."

Rachel nodded to acknowledge the compliment. "Understanding stationary Matrix Learning with the help of copious data files is one thing," she said. "But as you all know, Kovonov has now advanced beyond this technology. No more plugging into pricey machinery. Now he can manipulate minds on the go. This is a more challenging problem that wasn't outlined in any Mossad database."

"Were you able to get anywhere?" asked Coffey.

"Yes. Because of Kevin. Without someone Kovonov had manipulated I'd have some guesses, but I'd never know for sure what approach he was using."

Rachel shook her head. "Ironically," she continued, "if he hadn't been so set on killing me, I'd never have known about any of this, or made any of the progress I've made."

She had become convinced that this obsession with ending her life was a byproduct of his madness rather than any rational thinking.

"And maybe someone up there is looking out for us," said Rachel. "Kevin Quinn alone doesn't pose any danger to Kovonov. My work alone wouldn't either. But the two of us together at this research facility is his worst nightmare. Doesn't mean I can figure out what he's doing and stop him. But not only did he fail to kill us, he actually provided the catalyst that drove us together. This was a big mistake on his part, and at least gives us a *chance*."

"So what have you found?" asked Coffey.

"Let me start by explaining *how* I found it," said Rachel. "I began by taking a sample of neurons from Kevin's brain."

"She assured me I wouldn't miss them too much," said Quinn good-naturedly. "But if I ever say or do anything stupid in the future, just know that this is the reason."

"Glad I could give you an excuse," replied Rachel, breaking into a smile.

She touched the screen of a tablet computer and a four-foot by four-foot image of a small group of neurons appeared above the center of the virtual table and began to slowly rotate. The 3-D image was almost neon blue in color, shining from an inner glow, and displaying a number of what looked like misshapen octopi with far too many over-elongated tentacles.

"This is an image from ANL's electron microscope that Karen was kind enough to generate," explained Rachel. "Depicting eleven neurons from Kevin's brain."

"Neurons that no longer have to fear being killed by alcohol," added Quinn wryly.

Rachel smiled and continued. "Notice that they've been dyed blue for better clarity."

She pressed another button on the computer and red circles now appeared around two distinct neuronal structures, which both resembled barren shrubberies.

"These are dendrites," she said, pointing at the branches of a circled shrub that extended from a main cell body. "They receive impulses."

She pointed at the other circled shrub, which extended from the end of a long octopus arm. "And these are axon terminals. Which send impulses. But for the sake of our discussion, their identities and roles aren't important. There won't be a test."

She touched her tablet again and the image of one of the circled dendrites exploded in size, while the rest of the image disappeared. "I've magnified a dendrite extending from one of the cell bodies. Note that even at this magnification nothing appears amiss. But if I zoom in even farther," she said, making this happen as she spoke, "you can see a disk clinging to the main branch. Notice that this disk is perfectly circular."

"I take it that this is a structure that shouldn't be there," said Quinn uneasily.

"No it shouldn't. Extrapolating from our small sample, Karen and I calculated that there are about two hundred billion of these in your brain. And they are perched on every important neuron you have, like small birds clinging to telephone lines. But birds capable of affecting neuronal transmission. We've studied several of these at great length under the electron microscope."

"What are they?" asked Coffey.

Rachel touched her tablet and the image disappeared entirely. "Collectively these particles are called *smart dust*. They're designed and deployed using specifications that *I* came up with," she said in frustration.

"Think of them as nano-electronic devices, smaller than bacteria," she continued. "Nanites for short. So small they would make a particle of talcum powder look like Mt. Everest. Yet each has enough intelligence to know where they are within the brain, and also in relation to their brethren. And they can react to external commands—induce the firing of a neuron, block the firing, and so on. Think of each as having an individual IP address."

"External commands from where?" asked Quinn. "And how?"

"In this case, radio waves. Information sent this way would have to be tightly compressed, but it could all be carried by a radio broadcast of the right length, and with the right supercomputer guiding it, using the right algorithms."

"If this system is based on your design, does this mean you've come up with something similar?" asked Major McLeod.

Rachel frowned. "No. I had the concept, but not the means. The Israelis are at least a generation ahead of us in nano-electronics. They developed this capability for their fly drones, and then Kovonov used it to perfect what I could only dream about. Even with these nanites in hand it would take a team years to reverse engineer the technology, at minimum. Worst case, it might *never* be possible."

"How did Kovonov get them into my brain?" asked Quinn.

"A simple injection would do it. Once in the bloodstream they make their way through the blood-brain barrier and take up residence."

"But wouldn't Kevin know he had been injected?" protested the major.

"Maybe," said Rachel. "There are some new techniques becoming available that almost sneak injections through the skin. But even if Kovonov used a painful horse needle, he could have programmed the particles to erase the past few minutes of memory. Imagine Kevin is walking along and some stranger plunges a syringe into his leg. But twenty seconds later he's forgotten this ever happened. The stranger, the pain, everything. Now billions of nano-particles are swarming in his brain, awaiting instructions."

Quinn shuddered. "Instructions like, 'Lay down memories of a murder that never happened?"'

"Yes. But memory erasure or implantation are only one set of possibilities, " said Rachel. "There are many more, as we've discussed. Once these nanites are resident in a brain, Kovonov can make a victim dependent on him. Addicted to almost anything he chooses. Elated or depressed. Calm or filled with rage. Delusional. Paranoid. Terrified. The sky's the limit."

"But how can he have such fine control?" asked Coffey.

"Technology can perform miracles," replied Rachel. "We can sequence billions of bases of DNA in hours, with no mistakes. If I wrote a million-page book, a standard desktop computer could save it to a flash drive in less than a second, and when I called it up again not a single letter on a single page would be out of place or incorrect. I don't want to get down into the weeds technically, but the radio signals can instruct the smart dust to establish a precise matrix, and to affect precise neurons. Much the same way a copy machine or laser printer sets up an electrostatic matrix before printing."

There were blank looks all around. Even Karen Black seemed not to know what Rachel was talking about.

"Sorry," said Rachel. "I forgot not everyone knows how laser printers work. I studied this technology to get ideas for non-invasive Matrix Learning techniques. Just to give a quick overview, the toner you put in your printer is electrically charged powder that contains pigment. The powder is composed of very fine particles. And the industry has found ways to keep shrinking these particles over the years."

"For better resolution?" asked Karen. "Or better quality?"

"Both," said Rachel. "Today, toner particles average just under a micron in diameter."

"And a micron is . . . ?" prompted Coffey.

"A millionth of a meter," said Rachel. "To put this in perspective, there are over twenty-five thousand microns to an inch. A piece of paper is about a hundred microns thick."

"I knew it was microscopic," said Coffey, "but this is helpful. Thanks."

"So let's imagine you send a document to your laser printer," continued Rachel. "A document with a thousand letters typed in a tiny font. So what happens next? Your computer sends detailed instructions to the drum of the printer, basically calling for it to lay down a precise pattern of negative electrical charges, exactly matching every letter in your document."

She paused to let this sink in. "So your document has now been copied to the drum, only with electric charge rather than ink. But then the drum gets coated with toner. Since the toner is positively charged and the pattern laid down on the drum is negatively charged, the toner clings to this pattern. The toner on the drum is then transferred to a piece of paper rolling through the printer, and is instantly fused to the paper by a pair of heated rollers." She paused. "Just like that, you have a precise copy of every last letter."

Quinn looked intrigued. "Sounds deceptively simple. Impressive that anyone could get a system like that to work so perfectly and so quickly."

"I agree," said Rachel. "As I mentioned, one of my big ideas, which Kovonov adopted, was to do something similar with neuronal dust. Think of the nanites as neuronal toner. In this case, instead of setting up a complex pattern using electric charge, you'd use something like radio waves. You could lay down precise instructions for billions of particles at once, which could then activate or block individual neurons."

"So how would you zap a chemistry course into someone's brain?" said Quinn, and then frowning added, "or a false memory?"

"That's where the weeds come in," said Rachel. "The difference between saying, 'just charge the drum in the exact pattern made by a thousand letters' and actually pulling it off. But with enough knowledge, enough cleverness, and enough computing power, these nanites make it possible. And with enough sophistication under the hood, the user no longer has to care about how his or her instructions are implemented."

She paused, searching for a good analogy. "When I type a sentence into the computer it magically appears on my screen. The technology that goes into converting my key strokes to electricity that can alter the polarity of liquid crystals inside my monitor—in just the right way to display what I write—is extraordinarily complex. But once perfected this miracle is taken for granted, never given a second thought—or even a *first* one."

"So is the Israeli neurotech—Kovonov's neurotech—at that level?" asked McLeod.

"It would have to be," said Rachel. "Otherwise it could never be as effective as it's been. Implementation would be impossibly unwieldy. I'm sure it's been perfected to a level where the user simply has to script out the memories to be implanted, and a supercomputer crunches a universe of data and instructs the nanites to lay down these tracks. The computing power to do this didn't exist in even the best supercomputers until about 2019, and now there are *laptops* that could do the job. Not in wide use, but they exist. I have one. And you can bet Kovonov has one that is much better even than mine. Because Israel's Manhattan Project yielded a technology that helped their scientists improve *all other* technologies."

"If I have this right," said McLeod, "Kovonov injects the nanites, enters what he wants done into his laptop, and it calculates the precise instructions necessary to manipulate minds to his specifications."

"That is my guess, yes," confirmed Rachel.

"And the radio source?" asked the major.

"He'd just have to tie his computer into a cell phone, possibly one with an internal booster added."

"And then convert it into a radio transmitter?" said Coffey.

"No conversion needed," said Rachel. "A cell phone already *is* one. It's basically a two-way radio: a receiver and a transmitter. Put it in proximity to the neural dust you want to control, link it to the laptop, and it should transmit radio signals more than strong enough to do the trick, especially with an internal signal booster added. For very simple instructions, you wouldn't need the laptop. The computing power resident in just the phone would be enough to direct the manipulation all by itself."

Rachel paused in thought. "Right now I'm guessing extensive manipulation still requires a stationary, plugged-in system. So for Matrix Learning, during which enormous amounts of knowledge are layered into the mind, Kovonov would still need the MRI-like device and electronic implants. But a juiced-up laptop and a phone, or even just a phone by itself, are capable of doing smaller, less complex manipulations."

"Like the memories implanted in Kevin?" said Coffey.

Rachel nodded. "In the work I've been doing over the past eighteen months—largely unpublished," she added with a scowl, "I've made a strong case for using radio waves for this very reason. Cell phones are indispensable, and untold billions of dollars are being spent to improve them every year. I argued that by the time the neural smart dust was perfected—in five or ten years I had *thought*—cell phones would have enough computing power to implant even the most sophisticated and exhaustive Matrix Learning programs all by themselves."

"So instead of downloading a movie about World War II onto your phone," said Quinn, "you could use your phone to download the entire history of this war into your brain?"

Rachel sighed. "Yes. This was the idea."

There was a long silence in the room as everyone stopped to assimilate all she had told them.

"Absolutely mind-blowing," said Quinn.

"I'm not even sure that's a powerful enough word to cover it," said Coffey. He paused for several seconds in thought and then blew out a long breath. "So what now?"

"I'd like to see if I can learn how to use this system myself," said Rachel. "At least at a rudimentary level."

"Didn't you say that even reverse engineering the nano-electronics would be all but impossible?" said Coffey.

"I did. But that's not what I meant. I didn't say learn how to *do* this, just learn how to *use* it. I don't have to know how to construct a computer to be able to use one. Although it isn't that simple in this case. In this case, the computer is built, but I have to find a way to create a keyboard from scratch. An interface that will allow me to access the guts of what someone else provided."

"Why do I have a sinking feeling that I'm the computer in this analogy?" said Quinn uneasily.

Rachel laughed. "If you could find others who have these nano-particles implanted in their brain, I'd love to work with them. At the moment, though, you're the only game in town."

"Will you need more of my brain cells?" asked Quinn.

"No. I'll be trying to crack the code Kovonov is using to control the dust. I'll have to try thousands of different radio frequencies and instruction sets, different algorithms, and all of my intuition. If I can implant a single false memory in your mind, even of a single word—which might take a day, or might take a lifetime—this would begin to open the floodgates. Although at best my abilities to use his tech to manipulate you will pale in comparison to his."

"I'm not sure if that's a bad thing or a good thing," said Quinn with a shudder. "I'd prefer women to manipulate me the old-fashioned way."

Rachel laughed. "Then you might be in luck," she said. "Because there's no certainty that I can do this."

Her features hardened. "But it won't be for lack of trying," she vowed.

"Even if you succeed," said Coffey, "I'm not sure how much this will do for our cause."

"I'm not either," said Rachel. "But at minimum, it will allow us to detect who has these nanites implanted. Right now they are much too small to be detectible by sensors. And we don't want to have to forcibly remove neurons from the brains of anyone we suspect and then find the nearest electron microscope. But if I could implant rudimentary memories, I could get victims to reveal themselves."

The major rubbed his chin thoughtfully. "Interesting idea," he said. "When can you begin?"

"The moment this meeting is over," said Rachel eagerly.

53

Every major erogenous zone on Carmilla Acosta's body was on *fire.*

She hadn't seen Dmitri Kovonov in two agonizingly long weeks. But this was about to change. He would be here in minutes. For the first time visiting her at her home.

Taking her at her home.

Her husband, Miguel, had left on a business trip two days earlier and wouldn't return for another week.

She had prepared as usual, spending hours at Victoria's Secret until she found flimsy yet still flattering lingerie, not a simple task for a world class scientist who spent far too much time at a desk or a lab and not nearly enough time on a stationary bike. After this she had scrubbed her house clean from top to bottom, being sure to hide any photographs in which her husband appeared, whether with her or alone.

She would expunge his image from her home, and days later she would expunge the man himself from her life.

Carmilla and Miguel lived in a small red brick home nestled between a smattering of other residences, twenty miles from Princeton University, mostly surrounded by the farmland that had persisted stubbornly in the area for over a century. Each day on her way to work she passed black-and-white splotched Holstein dairy cattle, along with their more unfortunate relations, the Black Angus variety. This breed would ultimately be required to give more of themselves than simply milk, but farms had recently begun to reduce their numbers as genetic engineers got closer and closer to growing steak in the lab that was indistinguishable from the real thing.

She missed Dmitri so much it hurt, and his line of work meant he was out of touch for long periods, which had become intolerable.

But now that he was returning to her at last, she would never let him go for this long again. She wouldn't wait another day to start divorce proceedings, to do whatever it took to have Dmitri in her daily life. The divorce was long overdue. She couldn't take any more of these absences. They affected her, not just psychologically, but physically.

But now that Dmitri was on his way this was shaping up to be one of the best days of her life. Just an hour earlier she had learned that she was clean as a whistle genetically. No ticking time bombs in *her* DNA.

And she couldn't imagine Dmitri's genes could be anything less than perfect, although it didn't hurt to find out for sure. To be confident that they would live happily into their eighties and nineties and even beyond.

The scientist in her might have known that the romantic phase of love didn't last more than a few years, but this voice was drowned out by the lovestruck woman inside who refused to even consider the possibility that she and Dmitri wouldn't be blissfully happy forever. No two people were ever more perfect for each other. True soul mates.

A week earlier she had plucked a hair from her head, affixed it to a piece of Scotch tape, and mailed it to GeneScreen Associates, a company specializing in whole genome sequencing and analysis. And just last night a representative of the company had left a message for her, letting her know the results were ready and giving her a number to call to have them explained by a trained consultant. She had memorized the simple number, 1-800-DNA-TEST, erased the message, and called back just an hour earlier, more nervous than she cared to admit.

But her nerves were unwarranted. The results had been *spectacular*. The consultant had told her it was rare to see a genome this clear of genes known to be potentially troubling down the road, that Carmilla had truly been blessed genetically.

Everything seemed to be going her way. Maybe after she and Dmitri made love, she should go out and buy a lottery ticket. It was that kind of day.

Just as this thought was crossing her mind there was a knock at the door. She checked to be sure it was Dmitri and then threw it open, wrapping herself around him in greeting. He pushed her away sooner than usual and picked up a brown, soft leather briefcase he had set down, bringing it inside.

Carmilla sensed something wrong in his demeanor but decided she was being overly sensitive. She took him by the hand and led him directly to her bedroom, disappointed that he brought the briefcase along in tow.

"I've missed you *so* much," she said, her words filled with aching emotion.

The man of her dreams simply nodded in return.

"What have you been up to?" she asked.

He looked almost put off by the question, as though she were invading his privacy. "Right after I saw you last I spent a few days in the woods," he replied finally. "At sort of a . . . company retreat. What I've been doing since would just bore you."

Something wasn't right, she decided, more certain than ever. *Everything* wasn't right.

"Guess what?" she said, nervously attempting to engage him in further conversation as her unease continued to grow. "I just spoke to someone at GeneScreen Associates. They did a genome analysis on me. Turns out the results couldn't have been better."

Again, Dmitri seemed not to care in the least. How could he not be excited for her? Excited for *them*? Had he told her the same she would have been thrilled.

"Why did you use a company to get your genome sequenced?" was all he said in response. "No one in the world has better tools to sequence DNA than you do."

She had asked herself this same question, wondering if this had been foolhardy. And it probably was. But love prompted people to do things they wouldn't ordinarily do, like shop at Victoria's Secret for lingerie, which before Dmitri came into her life she hadn't done in over a decade.

"True," she agreed, "but I'm busy and this is very inexpensive. So I thought, why not? You've made me so happy, Dmitri, I wanted the chance to clear away any genetic landmines that might be in my future. *Our* future. Besides," she added, "scientists are identifying so many genes linked to rare diseases that even I can't keep up. So better to leave the analysis to specialists."

He shrugged, not really interested in her rationale. She had brought this up thinking she could convince him to get tested as well, just in case, but sensed that now was not the time for this discussion.

"No more conversation," he insisted, pushing her down on the bed and proceeding to force himself on her in ways that he had never done before. He had always been a fiery lover, but gentle and attentive at the same time, as interested in her needs as his own.

This time it was all about him. And he was savage, not caring how aggressive he became or even if he was hurting her.

The act seemed to Carmilla to be closer to rape than to lovemaking.

Still, she loved him enough to understand that moods could vary, *needs* could vary. He deserved to think only of himself on occasion. And there was nothing she wouldn't do for this man.

Seconds after his climax, he rolled away from her and started dressing.

Carmilla's heart raced and she began to panic. Was he leaving? It was as if he was treating her like a whore. Like he was about to leave money on the dresser and go. A wild look came to her eyes.

"Bear with me, Carmilla," he said, sensing her reaction. "I just have some pressing work I need to do. Don't go anywhere."

That had to be it, thought Carmilla. He was stressed out. He had work that couldn't wait.

He pulled a hard clamshell case from his bag and removed a laptop from it, unlike any model she had ever seen. It was constructed out of blue stainless steel and looked like something a futuristic alien might use. Without giving her another glance he attached his cell phone to the computer with a thin cord. Wi-Fi had advanced so much lately she couldn't imagine what application required his phone and computer to be tethered together in this way.

His fingers flew over the holographic touch screen for several minutes as if she wasn't there.

As he worked she became more and more anxious, more and more depressed. What had been euphoria prior to his arrival had turned entirely to despair. She tried to fight through it, to retain perspective, but she found it impossible to do.

So he was out of sorts. It happened. But she had a feeling of dread like she'd never experienced, totally disproportionate to what she knew her reaction *should* be. She felt as if her life was spinning out of control.

Five minutes later Dmitri unhooked his phone and returned his computer to its hard protective shell. He stood up from the bed and turned to face her still-naked form. But instead of the love she had come to expect, his face held nothing but contempt.

"Carmilla, it's been fun," he said dismissively. "But I'm afraid we're through. If I have to spend another minute with you, I swear I'll slit my wrists."

Carmilla whitened, almost matching the sheets on her bed. "I don't understand," she whispered, stunned by not just his words but his venomous tone. "Dmitri? What's going on?"

"How can I be any clearer?" he snapped. "This is over! *We're* over. Are you getting it now? I came here to end things. But I thought I'd fuck you one last time. You know, as a going away present."

Tears began streaming down her face. Was this really happening? *How* could it be happening?

"Stop sobbing you fucking bitch!" he demanded cruelly. "You don't think I ever really cared about you? I was using you for sex. Anything positive I ever said to you was a lie. My job doesn't take me out of touch, I just never wanted to deal with you unless I was screwing your brains out at the time."

Carmilla's face was now a rictus of horror, a ruddy pool of makeup and tears as she continued to take body blows from the man she loved and worshiped.

"While I've been screwing you," he continued, "I've been screwing a dozen others, in a dozen different towns."

The walls of Carmilla's world were now crashing down upon her, battering her psyche into a bruised and bloody mass of raw, open flesh.

"Why would you hurt me like this?" she whispered through her tears.

"Because you're *useless*. And this has just been a game. To get you to fall in love with me. Thank you for playing, but the game is now over." He glared at her. "And you lost, bitch! If you ever try to contact me again, I'll issue a restraining order. Got it?"

Without saying another word, Dmitri Kovonov stormed from the room and out the front door, slamming it behind him.

Unable to move from the bed, Dr. Carmilla Acosta continued sobbing, drawing in on herself in an involuntary attempt to shrink into a fetal position, shattered in every way.

54

Dmitri Kovonov pulled away from the brick house in a black Ford sedan, rented under the name Randy Bork. This was the last time he planned to ever be in Princeton, and it wasn't lost on him that he was less than twenty miles away from where that despised Secret Service agent, Kevin Quinn, had failed to terminate a president who had doubled down on a twisted and dangerous US policy of sucking up to enemies and alienating allies.

Kovonov pushed this failure from his mind as Carmilla Acosta's home receded in his mirror.

His visit couldn't have gone better. Surprisingly—although he shouldn't be surprised by this sort of thing anymore—he had found himself enjoying every minute.

For most of his life it had been sheer agony to break up with a woman. He would stay with them and suffer for months before he finally could take no more, and then he would blame himself and apologize to them over and over, twisting himself into a pretzel to soften the blow. Even so, the guilt he felt at having to lower the boom, no matter how gently, would stay with him for weeks.

Not this time. He was a new man, a better man.

And this time his goal hadn't been to soften the blow, but to do just the opposite—to generate maximum anguish—and he doubted he could have done this any better. Instead of wiping his existence from Carmilla's memory to protect himself, or having her killed, he had decided to try an experiment. To see if he had such a stranglehold on her psyche that he could push her into a state of despair and suffering that only suicide could remedy.

What a test this would be of his neurotech capabilities. Could he take a brilliant, well-adjusted scientist, a woman who was the personification of level-headedness and rationality, self-confident and self-possessed, and send her into a tailspin from which she would never recover?

Losing the object of one's obsession during early stages of romantic love was already debilitating, more jarring psychologically than a cold turkey cessation of heroin was physically. But when the love of one's life ended things in such a cruel and brutal fashion, the effects on the brain were even more devastating.

Even so, Kovonov hadn't left it at that. He had directed the nanites to trigger high enough levels of depression and despair within her brain to cause a squad of *cheerleaders* to commit suicide. He would be astonished if this didn't work.

Not that there still wasn't a chance of failure. It was an experiment, not a certainty. And he had been shocked and disappointed that his tampering with Mizrahi's brain hadn't had the effect he was after. He had turned the man into a loyal slave, but it was apparent that certain moral principles could trump loyalty and devotion in some cases, despite what the results of the Stanley Milgram experiment would suggest.

If he was wrong and Carmilla hadn't ended her life in two days, he would come back and remove all traces of himself from her memory.

He had been driving for an hour when a call came in. He hit, *accept as virtual presence,* on his dashboard and a virtual image of Yosef Mizrahi materialized in the passenger's seat beside him, although he was actually in a hotel room on the east side of Lancaster, Pennsylvania, where Kovonov had left him.

"Hello, Dmitri," said Mizrahi in Hebrew, "I have to say, you look content."

Mizrahi had quickly returned to being an adoring and slavish follower once the memories of Kovonov's disclosure in the Cockaponset cabin and his execution of Daniel Eisen had been expunged.

"I am. My errand went well."

"How long until you arrive?"

"I'm almost to Philadelphia now," said Kovonov. "Say another few hours."

"Great. I've found another property I want you to see. I think you'll like it."

Kovonov nodded. They had spent almost four days familiarizing themselves with the deep woods and farmlands of Pennsylvania, looking for a cabin or farmhouse for sale that fit Kovonov's needs.

It was annoying not to be able to share and discuss his true plans with Mizrahi, but Kovonov had learned his lesson. Mizrahi would follow all orders well and blindly, and wouldn't ask questions, but rubbing his nose in what he was planning was a mistake.

He had explained that they were looking for a place to lie low, to hunker down for a few days to a few months. Somewhere in a cabin deep in the woods, or a farmhouse, surrounded on multiple sides by woods. A place that surveillance could ensure could not be surprised, where food could be stockpiled so they could keep to themselves until they were ready to return to their home base in Switzerland.

When Mizrahi had asked why they weren't ready to return now, Kovonov had simply said that they had more work to do, and reminded him that he was now being hunted by the US military and couldn't risk international travel. Being captured now would ruin everything.

What he didn't tell him was that once his plan had succeeded, and commercial flights had resumed, he would become such a low priority he could walk through an international terminal on fire and not get any notice.

"Farmhouse or cabin?" asked Kovonov.

"Farmhouse."

"Let's plan to visit it right after I arrive. You can tell me why you like it so much when I get there."

There were six properties within a hundred-mile radius of Lancaster, Pennsylvania—Amish country—that had made their short list, and they had nine more they still wanted to inspect. Given that they had plenty of time, at least until they found the terrorist Kovonov was after, it paid not to leave anything to chance.

"I have more good news," said Mizrahi enthusiastically. "I think I've found the guy you've been looking for."

Kovonov stopped at a red light and turned to study his virtual subordinate. He had also tasked Mizrahi with monitoring the various fly drones still in operation at sensitive intelligence facilities within the US, continuing the hunt for the man he needed. A number of their precious drones had been found and destroyed, but he had changed the settings on the rest, and many of these had yet to be discovered.

"Tell me about him," said Kovonov.

"I don't have perfect information. He's a high-ranking lieutenant with ISIS. Haji Ahmad al-Bilawy. Don't know what he was planning in the US, or how he was captured. But I do know he's been taken to a secret detention center in Knoxville, Tennessee, which has been disguised as a civilian facility."

Kovonov raised his eyebrows. Tennessee was the last place he would expect to house a secret detention facility, which is probably why it did.

"Knoxville?" he said. "Is that one of Tennessee's major cities, or in the middle of nowhere?"

"Both," replied Mizrahi with a smile. "Population of about two hundred thousand. Near the Great Smokey Mountains."

Kovonov shook his head. "That doesn't help," he said. He now possessed fifteen PhDs worth of knowledge and expertise, but US geography hadn't been on the menu.

"It's in the northeast corner of the state. Just to the west of North Carolina."

This still didn't help him, but he would go online and come up to speed the way Mizrahi had obviously done. "Tell me about this detention facility," said Kovonov.

"It's being run, temporarily, by a PsyOps lieutenant colonel named Stephen Hansen, an expert interrogator. He's been assigned to squeeze intel out of al-Bilawy, but he has a three-day leash. After that al-Bilawy will be transferred to a Black site out of the country for further handling."

"Perfect!" said Kovonov.

Mizrahi beamed, a dog whose master had patted its head.

Kovonov couldn't believe how well everything was coming together, and how quickly. He had gone from having all the time in the world to having no time at all. Now he had to squeeze a week's worth of activities into a few days.

First, he would make a final decision on a property and acquire it. Then he would finalize the hiring of numerous mercenaries he would soon need as security and extra muscle. And this was only the beginning.

"Great work, Yosef. But given this discovery, I need to change plans. Leave me the info on this property you've identified and I'll check it out myself. I want you to leave now and get your ass to Tennessee. Learn everything you can about Colonel Hansen and this detention facility, starting with a search through Mossad databases."

Kovonov had copied almost the entirety of Mossad's electronic files before he had left for Switzerland, and someone like Hansen rated his own dossier if anyone did. Wortzman had once boasted that the fly drone and hack-ware programs at the Mossad were so good they had better files on American agents than did the Americans themselves.

"I want Hansen's background, habits, tendencies, whatever you can find. And why he's with PsyOps and not their High-Value Detainee Interrogation Group. Since it's not a military base he probably mingles in the community as a civilian when he isn't on duty. Find him. Follow him. Study him. I want to know how the facility is set up, how prisoners are transferred, the chain of command, security—everything."

"I won't disappoint you, Dmitri," said Mizrahi.

You already have! he thought bitterly. *You just don't remember.* "I know you won't, Yosef," he said aloud. "I'll join you in, ah . . . Knoxville, as soon as I can. Probably before noon tomorrow."

As soon as the call ended, Kovonov dialed up a covert communications expert he had identified weeks before. A freelancer whose work was as good as his price was high. He would have him go to Knoxville immediately and purchase a home within a two-hour drive of the city, on the secluded and defensible side if possible. But given that the man would need to complete the transaction within a day or two, Kovonov couldn't afford to be choosy.

Then this freelancer would work his magic on the site, setting up phone and video lines in such a way that they would remain untraceable, thwarting even the most sophisticated military technology.

Kovonov felt electrified. He was in the home stretch now.

He had been painstakingly twisting and turning the faces of a Rubik's cube this way and that since he had fled Israel. But in less than a week, perhaps much less, all of the faces would have uniform colors, the complex cube finally aligned to perfection, finally solved.

55

Carmilla sobbed for almost three hours until she couldn't sob any longer. She struggled to think clearly but couldn't push out the overwhelming despair that engulfed her like a Dementor from a Harry Potter movie, draining her of all hope, happiness, and will to live.

She told herself she was one of the most accomplished scientists in the world, destined for a Nobel Prize. But this didn't help. She felt worthless, suffering wounds so deep they were beyond healing, disillusionment the only possible reprieve.

But why was the chilling touch of the Dementor so effective? Dmitri had revealed himself to be a monster. She had done nothing to bring this on herself. He had used her like a dishrag and disposed of her with utter malice. Wasn't she better off that she had learned his true nature? Hadn't she dodged a bullet? Didn't she still have *everything* to live for?

But somehow the answer to these questions was *no*. Hope had been drained from her, and along with it, all interest in life. She had to end it all. It was the only way.

A memory of a train ride she had taken with her parents as a little girl found its way into her consciousness. They had been headed to New York, a city she had never visited before. Halfway there the train had stopped on the tracks for seemingly no reason. After fifteen minutes the conductor had finally come on the loudspeaker, explaining they would soon be on their way and asking passengers not to look out of the windows on the left side of the train.

Carmilla had been astonished by how quickly every passenger on the train stampeded to the left side to do exactly what they had been told not to do. It was a wonder the train didn't capsize.

Carmilla had learned two important lessons about human nature that day. The first was that curiosity was overwhelmingly powerful, and by leaving his instructions vague, by creating an unanswered mystery, the conductor had guaranteed a response that was the exact opposite of what he was trying to achieve.

When Carmilla had looked out her window, she had learned the second lesson. That suicide happened. That sometimes human beings could lose so much hope, could so drown in despair, they would put themselves in the path of a moving train.

Out of her window she had seen police cars and an ambulance, and a gurney on which pieces of bloodied roadkill were being assembled, only the shape of a pulverized head indicating that this mass of flesh had once been a human.

The enormous power of the train would not be denied. The rare man could survive a fall from a great height, a gunshot wound to the head, or a stomach full of pills.

But no one who had picked a fight with a train had ever lived to tell about it.

Carmilla's thoughts returned to the present and she asked the AI program on her phone for the most lightly traveled road in the area with a railroad crossing, and the next train scheduled to traverse it.

Her phone indicated that the train she was after would arrive in thirty-five minutes, and she could make it in twenty. She waited ten minutes and then shuffled to the garage like a zombie, hopeful for the first time as she imagined the release that suicide would finally give her.

She drove to the indicated intersection, an access road through farmland, and noted that no one else was in sight. She heard the faint sound of the train off in the distance, and decided she didn't have the strength to face it by herself the way the man in her youth had done. She could only bring herself to do so inside the illusory protection of a steel cocoon.

But this was an acceptable alternative, she knew, as recent advances had come about that prevented derailments except in the most extreme of circumstances.

She allowed herself to be mesmerized by the steel behemoth racing along the tracks, bellowing louder and louder as it approached. Finally, even though the train was still twenty seconds away, she pulled across the main track and cut the engine. She knew that at this point the millions of pounds of steel hurtling toward her could not be stopped in time, even if she were spotted immediately,

She closed her eyes tightly. It would be over soon.

The train had become so loud it seemed to be charging through her head, and this was now mixed with an ear-shattering screech of metal on metal as the conductor braked in a futile effort to avoid a collision.

She braced herself for impact.

Her car was slammed into with bone-jarring force.

But this had come almost ten seconds too soon. And from an entirely unexpected direction.

Instead of the train goring the side of her car, lifting it with its horns and sending it flying, she had been rammed from *behind*.

Her car lurched forward from the impact and her head slammed into the side window with a loud crack, missing the now-deployed air bag entirely.

In her last instant of consciousness her mind held only curiosity.

What would death be like?

And why would someone try to kill her seconds before she managed to kill herself?

56

Kovonov made it to Knoxville by noon the next day, pleased with the progress he had made on any number of important fronts. The city turned out to be quite appealing, with modern architecture, lush green areas throughout, and the Tennessee River, which sliced through downtown, complete with four different vehicle bridges that crossed the river at different points.

He joined Mizrahi on a park bench in direct line of sight to the secret interrogation facility, designed to look like a small manufacturing site, with its own loading dock where prisoners were no doubt dropped off and picked up in industrial trucks designed for this purpose.

Mizrahi wasted no time beginning his briefing. He explained that he had, indeed, found a file on a lieutenant colonel named Stephen Hansen, complete with his habits, where he fit in the chain of command, as well as information about the off-the-books interrogation facility.

Hansen was a rising star within PsyOps and had a record of achieving better interrogation results than anyone else, including the High-Value Detainee Interrogation Group, or HIG. This group had been created by a Barack Obama executive order in 2009, which was seconded by Congress in 2015. It was a small interagency group tasked with secret interrogations using methods based on the latest psychological research. While it was under the auspices of the FBI, it drew on elite interrogators from the bureau, Defense Department, CIA, and other agencies.

According to Mossad analysis, though, certain intelligence shops preferred to keep their top people to themselves, sending along second-tier interrogators to join the HIG. Once again, human nature had corrupted what would have otherwise been a highly effective organization.

Hansen's record spoke for itself, and Mizrahi conjectured that the powers that be were well aware that he was the man to go to with the highest value prisoners. A high-level official had almost certainly arranged for Hansen to get the first crack at this prisoner, behind HIG's back, and this latter group wouldn't be brought into the loop until Hansen's allotted time had expired.

"Hansen reports to a full bird colonel," said Mizrahi. He quickly consulted his phone. "By the name of Jeffrey Siperstein."

"And Siperstein's superior?" said Kovonov.

"The head of PsyOps. General Angela Reader."

Kovonov nodded. "Go on."

"The file suggests Hansen's major weakness is an addiction to Starbucks. Prefers the Iced Caramel Macchiato. Tends to drink at least one a day, two or more if he can manage it."

"Did he have one this morning?"

Mizrahi nodded. "He did. And as luck would have it," he added, brightening, "there is a Starbucks within a half mile of the interrogation facility."

Kovonov rolled his eyes. "I'm pretty sure there's a Starbucks within a half mile of every location in this country. But why is that lucky?"

"Because he can indulge his craving easily. He can take a twenty-minute coffee break anytime he wants."

"I see. So you expect him to get another of these iced drinks later today."

"I wouldn't be surprised. That's why we're here. Think of this not only as a briefing, but also a stakeout."

Kovonov was clearly pleased. "Excellent work, Yosef," he said. "I have plenty of work to do on my computer anyway. So I think I'll go ahead and get myself a coffee and settle in. If he does show up to get his fix, we'll be ready for him."

57

Colonel Stephen Hansen neared the entrance to Starbucks in a foul mood. He needed this pick-me-up more than usual.

He had used all the tricks he knew of and was getting nowhere. Haji Ahmad al-Bilawy was smart and tough, and Hansen could tell already that success was unlikely. He would complain to Siperstein that he had only been given three days, not nearly enough time, but the truth was he doubted if he could get anywhere with al-Bilawy if he had three *years*.

He hated his job with a passion but couldn't bring himself to battle for reassignment. First, he was very good at what he did, which was a curse. The more competent you were, the more work you got. And he knew what he was doing was critically important. So he had found a way to suck it up for the past two years and travel to sites like this one when the need arose.

But very soon this would change. At minimum he would insist he be assigned to training *others* how to extract information from these rabid extremists. He couldn't take it anymore. And by training others, extending his reach, he was arguably doing an even greater service to his country.

The Starbucks store was a hive of activity, having become as much a social destination in the area as a retailer. Hansen was reaching for the door, calculating how quickly he could expect the line inside to move, when a tall stranger crashed into him from the side, as though Hansen had been in his path but temporarily invisible.

Both men grunted from the shock and physical impact of the collision. The incoming human battering ram, who had been walking briskly with his eyes glued to a phone, had jet-black hair and moved like an elite athlete.

"Sorry," he said in an accent Hansen couldn't quite place after both had recovered their composure.

Hansen's hand shot up to inspect his own neck as if it had a mind of his own. Had he been stabbed?

If he were anyone else he wouldn't have even noticed it, given the distraction of the man plowing into him like a football lineman, but he was one of the few people to have experience taking injections using a microneedle array. This was fairly new injection technology that used hundreds of nearly microscopic needles, each filled with drug, so small that they penetrated the skin too shallowly to trigger a pain response.

His neck had felt a tingling sensation for just a moment. Not pain, but something that reminded him of how he felt after previous injections with a microneedle array.

"Hold on!" he said immediately to the man who had slammed into him before he could move on, reaching out and seizing his arm. "Don't move!"

Something wasn't right. Hansen was sure of it. And until he got to the bottom of it this man wasn't going anywhere.

He checked to be sure he hadn't been pick-pocketed. A purposeful collision was a classic technique for separating a mark from his watch or wallet, but Hansen confirmed that both were still in place.

The man waited patiently, not seeming to take affront at having his arm held and in no hurry to leave the crime scene, if that's what this was. And he didn't ask why Hansen was delaying him, which he should have done no matter what, guilty or innocent.

As Hansen was considering this strange behavior he lost his train of thought. In fact, he lost all trains of thought, almost as if he had blacked out for a fraction of a second. He blinked rapidly in confusion and disorientation. For a moment he wasn't even sure how he had come to be just outside the Starbucks door.

A blank look spread across his face. He felt certain he had been considering something important, but whatever that might have been refused to come to him. He shook his head to clear it, realizing he was holding on to someone's arm.

"Thanks," said the arm's owner. "If you hadn't caught me, I might have done a faceplant on the concrete."

Hansen immediately released the arm, as confused as he had ever been. He must have caught this guy out of instinct, because he couldn't remember the stranger stumbling or beginning to fall, or that he had reached out to prevent this from happening. Hansen had been lost in thought before, but never *this* lost.

"Glad I could help," mumbled the PsyOps colonel, and then shaking off the entire strange experience, entered the shop.

He ordered his usual caffeine delivery system and sat at one of eight outdoor tables to enjoy it before getting back to his duties. A man three tables down was working on the most futuristic-looking laptop he had ever seen, connected to his phone. Hansen tried to catch his eye to ask him what kind it was, but the man seemed to be in a fugue state, utterly focused on whatever work he was doing.

After five minutes the man finished and left, never glancing back.

Hansen, still sipping at his coffee, turned his thoughts to Haji Ahmad al-Bilawy. Was there an angle he had failed to consider? One that could somehow create even the tiniest of cracks in the terrorist's dike?

Hansen shook his head vigorously as he realized he was due at Volunteer Landing Park at five thirty to meet with a mysterious Black Ops operative. How had this slipped his mind for even a moment? Wow, forgetting the only order he had ever been given personally by the head of PsyOps would have been career limiting. This should have been the *only* thing he was considering.

But it had suddenly all come back to him. General Angela Reader herself had called him earlier in the day. The head of PsyOps had bypassed the chain of command, purposely as it turned out, not wanting anyone in the loop, including Colonel Siperstein.

Now that this had become top of mind again, he remembered the exact words of the conversation with unusual clarity.

"I've never contacted you before, Colonel Hansen, as you know," she had said, "so take this as a measure of the importance of this communication."

"What can I do for you, General?" he had responded.

"To be honest, *I'm* not even sure. I hate to be so cloak-and-daggerish, but I need you to meet with a man who goes by the alias of Darryl Dorton. A high-ranking Black Ops operative. Be at Volunteer Landing park at five thirty. I assume you know the place?"

"I do."

"Good. Appear to be enjoying the park and before too long this Dorton will approach you and introduce himself. After that the first thing he will say is that I sent him. Provided that he does this and then gives you his alias, I need you to follow his orders as if they were my own—whatever they are."

"And you have no idea what these orders might be?"

General Reader had smiled. "I have an idea, but not a certainty. I think some other hotshot within a Black Ops research group has come up with a superior interrogation method, and wants a crack at al-Bilawy before HIG gets its hands on him. But whatever he wants, do it, and tell no one of this. Not of my call, the meeting in the park, or Dorton's orders. And I mean no one. Even Colonel Siperstein. Understood?"

"Understood, General," he had said as the call ended. "You could not have made this any clearer."

58

Consciousness slowly returned to Carmilla Acosta along with her memory.

She was alive, she realized. Lying on her back on something soft, her eyes closed.

How could this be?

She still felt devastated by the loss of what she had been certain was the love of her life, but the effect wasn't quite as suffocating as before, perhaps because she felt so weak. Confusion and disorientation had replaced some of the anguish that continued to torture her.

She opened her eyes and waited as they adjusted to the light.

She was in what looked like a makeshift hospital room, with an infusion pump on a pole beside her bed, the plastic tubing of an IV line snaking into her arm and held in place with tape, and bandages wrapped around her head. She was vaguely aware of an assortment of other cuts and bruises along her entire body, but the pain was almost entirely muted, meaning the IV must be delivering a potent opioid.

And her hands had been strapped to poles running along the bed. Was she now a prisoner?

"Thank God you're awake," said a petite young woman, startling her. She had been seated about six feet from the bed, reading something on a tablet, and must have realized Carmilla had awakened when she had tried to free her hands, rattling the poles. "How are you feeling?"

"Where am I?" said Carmilla, ignoring the question.

"You know what, I'm going to get two people in here who can answer all of your questions. All I can tell you is that you're safe here, and you're going to be okay."

The woman proceeded to text someone on her phone while she watched Carmilla. "I'm not authorized to give you any information," she said when she had finished, "but I am trained as a nurse, so while we're waiting for this pair to arrive, I'd love to know how you're doing."

Carmilla looked into the woman's eyes and saw genuine concern. So she told her what she wanted to know. They discussed how she was feeling and her level of pain while the nurse changed her bandages.

Ten minutes later a man and a woman entered and asked the nurse to free Carmilla's hands. Once this was done the nurse wished her patient well and left the room.

"My name is Rachel Howard," began the woman who had just arrived. "I'm a neuroscience professor at Harvard." She gestured to the man beside her. "And this is an associate of mine, Kevin Quinn."

"Okay . . . Rachel. I assume you know that my name is Carmilla Acosta."

"We do."

"The nurse said that you would be able to answer my questions."

"That's correct," said the woman, one who was almost surely pretending to be a Harvard professor, although her reasons for doing so were entirely unclear.

"Then where am I? Why am I here? How am I still alive?"

"I promise we'll tell you everything," said the woman, Rachel. "But this will take a while. The situation is somewhat complicated. And there is a lot you don't know."

"Like what?"

"Like *everything*," said the man named Quinn.

"We can tell you that you've been unconscious for over fifteen hours," said Rachel. "It was touch and go there for a while, but you're going to be fine. At least physically. How are you feeling emotionally?"

Carmilla suddenly understood why the young nurse wouldn't leave her until these two had arrived, and why her hands had been immobilized. The nurse had been on suicide watch. For obvious reasons.

"I honestly have never felt more miserable," she replied. "The greatest sense of loss and despair I've ever experienced. But I don't think I'm suicidal anymore."

Rachel blew out a relieved breath. "That's good to hear. We've given you pain killers, along with a cocktail of antidepressants and other pharmacological agents I put together that I thought might at least take the edge off."

"At least tell me how I'm alive. How did I survive a train collision?"

"Because you weren't in one," said Rachel. "Your injuries are from a car collision. Kevin here had been following you. When your intention became clear he closed the distance between the two of you and rammed you off the tracks with his own car. You have him to thank for saving your life."

"Or to blame," said Carmilla, not sure yet if she meant this or not. "It all depends on your perspective." She nodded toward Quinn. "So how did *you* survive? I take it your car replaced mine on the tracks."

Quinn nodded grimly. "Pretty much. I survived because I was eager to *avoid* the train. The moment your car was clear of the tracks I dived out of my own. I had so much adrenaline on board I might have been able to fly out. I made it clear in *plenty* of time," he added wryly. "You know, with as much as a second, maybe even two, to spare. I only wish someone had caught it on video."

"We'll tell you the rest," said Rachel, "but before we do, we need to know everything about your experiences. First, do you recognize this man?" she asked, manipulating her phone to project a 3-D image at Carmilla's eye level.

"*Dmitri!*" she whispered, shrinking back.

Several tears began to slide down her face as though a light switch had been thrown.

Her two visitors exchanged meaningful glances.

"Can you tell me where he is?" said Quinn gently, trying to hide his eagerness.

"He was at my home three or four hours before you rammed me on the tracks. I have no idea where he is now."

"So you know that his first name is Dmitri," noted Quinn. "Do you know his last?"

"Carston."

Quinn nodded. "Interesting," he said. "His real last name is Kovonov. Dmitri Kovonov."

"Why would he lie to me about his name?"

"I need you to tell us everything you know about him," said Quinn, ignoring her question. "And every experience you've had with him—or at least *think* you've had."

"*Think* I've had? What is *that* supposed to mean?"

Quinn ignored her yet again. "Please. Dr. Acosta. You can't imagine how important this is. I promise everything will be made clear to you. Very soon. Tell me about him."

Why not? thought Carmilla. Who cared at this point? She had kept her emotions bottled up for so long, afraid to tell anyone about Dmitri because she was still married, and because she had promised him she wouldn't breathe a word to anyone.

So she told them. She detailed her entire two-year association with Dmitri. No audience had ever been more attentive, or had hung on her every word more completely. On occasion they exchanged knowing or worried glances, but they didn't interrupt.

She finished by sharing the brutal manner in which Dmitri had ended things, how he had turned into such a monster that she had become so distraught, so drained of hope, that killing herself had become her only escape, shedding additional tears as she did so.

"Thank you," said Rachel softly when her story had ended.

Quinn nodded his thanks as well.

"I know that couldn't have been easy to tell," said Rachel. She paused for several seconds. "And what I'm about to tell you won't be easy for you to hear. But you need to know who this Dmitri Kovonov really is, and what he's been up to."

For the next thirty minutes, Rachel Howard spun a tale that was beyond belief. A tale of Dmitri being an accomplished neuroscientist who had perfecting Matrix Learning, who had used it on himself and others, and who had then perverted it into a method of tampering with minds by injecting victims with billions of nanites that took up residence within their brains. A tale of a man who had gone insane, and who was now wanted by multiple governments for crimes he had already committed and to prevent those he was certain to commit in the future.

It was utterly preposterous. All of it.

Except that it was also clear that this Rachel was a brilliant scientist. Her answers to Carmilla's questions displayed a level of expertise that was staggering, that could not be faked, especially since she had considerable knowledge of Carmilla's own field. They had also allowed her to Google *Rachel Howard* on a tablet. Sure enough, the image of the woman speaking to her came up on Harvard's neuroscience faculty page along with articles in scientific journals describing her as likely the most accomplished neuroscientist of the age.

"So do you believe us?" said Rachel when they had finished.

"I'm not sure," said Carmilla honestly. "I believe that *you* believe it. But let's say I do. What then? Are you suggesting that this Dmitri Komo . . ."

"Kovonov."

"Right. That this Dmitri Kovonov implanted false memories in my mind?"

"I'm not suggesting it," said Rachel. "I'm stating it as a fact. For all but the last month of the time you think you've known him, he was never even in America, let alone Princeton. So all of your memories of him prior to this time must have been implanted, and quite recently."

Carmilla struggled to grasp what Rachel was saying. How could this be so? Her memories of their meetings were crystal clear. "I've loved this man for almost two years," she said. "Now you're telling me I never even *met* him until this month." She shook her head. "It just can't be true."

"I know how you feel," said Quinn grimly. "I know better than anyone."

For the next ten minutes he described his own experiences. He told her how Dmitri had programmed his memory so he would be desperate to kill the president. She had gasped when she realized she did recognize his face. He was the Secret Service agent she had seen on TV who had tried to kill Matthew Davinroy and who had later died in an accident in a Cincinnati suburb called Finneytown.

When Quinn had finished describing his ordeal and his own realization that his memories were not his own, Carmilla was too stunned to speak. She broke eye contact and turned toward the IV tubing in thought, as though mesmerized by the steady flow of fluid still entering her arm. Both of her visitors waited patiently for her to come to grips with what had happened to her.

"So what *is* real?" she said finally. "If he can do this, how can I know *anything* is real? How can I know I'm actually having this conversation?"

"You can't, I'm afraid," said Quinn. "As you probably know, Descartes wrestled with this same problem, before anyone with Kovonov's capabilities was around. He concluded the *only* thing one could be certain of was one's own existence."

Carmilla nodded, but this was something she hadn't known. She was well-versed in all aspects of molecular biology but remembered almost nothing from her philosophy class.

"But for the sake of your sanity," continued Quinn, "I'd encourage you to accept everything you experience or remember as real. All except the memories you have of Kovonov that date back prior to a month or so ago, which we're certain never happened."

Carmilla considered this as she gingerly adjusted her position on the hospital bed.

Rachel gazed at her with palpable concern. "You told us you were drawn to Dmitri at first because your husband was unfaithful," she said softly. "But I suspect this isn't true. I suspect you just have a memory of catching him with another woman. A false one. Think hard about when this happened. *How* it happened. Is there texture? Does any of it make sense in a broader framework?"

As Carmilla replayed these events out in her mind and really focused on the logic, it all began to break down. How could she have gone almost two years without ever confronting Miguel? There were other memories she should have had, that should have arisen as she decided what to do about his infidelity. But it was all a house of cards, a western town built on the lot of a Hollywood studio. Seen from the front it fooled the eye beautifully, but peek even a millimeter behind the facade and there was nothing there at all.

She hadn't been certain this was really possible until this exercise. But now she was a true believer. Poor Miguel. She had treated him so badly recently, and he had never deserved any of it.

Quinn could tell she was now fully on board. "Lack of texture is the key, isn't it?" he said. "I was certain I had a pregnant wife. Until I realized I didn't have any memories of the wedding, of the pregnancy—of anything. It's a jarring realization."

"Yes it is," said Carmilla.

"So Kovonov manipulated your wiring so you thought you were in love with him," said Rachel. "Which means you *were* in love with him. Unfortunately, you still are. He modified the connections in your brain, your memories, your brain's reward system. And he probably did actually sleep with you and interact for real during the last month to bolster the artificial implanting."

As horrified as Carmilla was by this intellectually, the thought of sex with Dmitri began to arouse her against her will.

"I can soften what he did to you with drugs," continued Rachel, "but I can't reverse it. The brain is plastic and reshapes itself. So even though the nanites trigger neuronal pathways artificially, once they've been triggered they strengthen connections and build new ones. And these can't be so easily undone, although they will fade through time and inattention. I'm also confident that as I get a better and better handle on the technology I'll find ways to at least weaken them. Hopefully, knowing these feelings for Kovonov aren't real can aid you in your recovery, along with copious feel-better drugs. But I really don't know."

Carmilla sighed. None of this helped as much as it should. The drugs were a godsend, but the knowledge of the manipulation not as much. She still felt keen loss and despair. The man of her dreams had shaped her unconscious in such a way that it refused to listen to headquarters when it reported her love was a facade.

But she shouldn't be surprised in the least, she realized suddenly. How many men and women throughout history had known intellectually that the object of their romantic love was wrong for them? But the inner mind could be impervious to reason. It wanted what it wanted, immune to rational thought.

"Once he decided he didn't need you anymore," said Rachel, "he must have wanted to see if he could drive you to suicide. There is no reason to end the relationship with such over-the-top cruelty otherwise. He's a scientist, so it's no surprise that he wants to test the limits of his new toy."

"And it worked," said Carmilla. "I became suicidal just like he wanted. If not for Kevin I'd have succeeded." Her face twisted in confusion. "But how is it that Kevin was there? How did he know about this? About me?"

"As you know, Kevin has been injected with nanites also," said Rachel. "So using him as a guinea pig, I've been able to decipher how Kovonov is able to do what he does."

"Most of it is based on her ideas anyway," pointed out Quinn.

"The important thing," said Rachel, "is that I was able to figure out how to usurp Kovonov's nanites to implant simple memories of my own choosing. It's painstaking, rudimentary, and clumsy, but with enough brute force work and Kevin to guide my efforts, I can manage it. An analogy would be that Kovonov is using an elegant and sophisticated programming language, while I'm entering ones and zeros by hand—with mittens on. And blindfolded. I'm very limited in what I can do, and it takes orders of magnitude longer to accomplish than it would for him."

"Still quite an accomplishment," said Carmilla. "Congratulations." Her eyes narrowed. "But how does this apply to me?"

"As I said earlier," replied Rachel, "Kovonov programs these nanites using radio signals. I realized I could take advantage of this to reach people he's manipulating."

"Her brilliance really knows no bounds," said Quinn, shaking his head in genuine awe.

"Take advantage how?" asked Carmilla.

"Cell phones work on radio waves. Cell towers are powerful radio broadcasters. I wondered if I could press them into service to send out the instructions for a simple memory implantation. See if I could get his victims to contact me."

Using cell towers for this task was quite inspired, but Carmilla still wasn't sure where this was going.

"Unfortunately, because my ability to use Kovonov's system is still so clumsy," continued Rachel in obvious frustration, "I need to broadcast for an extended period. We could blanket the entire country with a signal and find anyone in America that Kovonov has manipulated, but that would require taking down the nation's entire cell network for about an hour. Well, not taking it down, just borrowing it for our purposes. But the effect to cell phone owners would be the same. No service. Despite our military and government connections, and the critical nature of what we're doing, we weren't able to get permission for this."

"Not surprising," said Carmilla.

Rachel frowned. "It's maddening, but there isn't anything we can do about it. Those with the keys to the system won't allow hundreds of millions of cell phones to be simultaneously turned into paperweights, even if only temporarily. Not under any circumstances. We were able to get permission—barely—to do this quadrant by quadrant. Disruptive for an hour to cell phone users within the quadrant, but the overwhelming majority of the nation's system would still be effective."

"How long will it take to sweep across the entire nation?" asked Carmilla.

"At the rate we're going, almost three weeks. And that's if our permission isn't revoked, which could happen at any time. Let me tell you, it's taken some high-up, shadowy, powerful players in Black Ops calling in favors to even make this happen."

"We started with the Eastern Seaboard," explained Quinn. "We hit your neck of the woods yesterday morning."

Carmilla shook her head. "I don't mean to seem slow, but I'm still not quite getting your strategy. What memory did you try to implant?" she said.

"Not try to implant," said Quinn with a smile. "Succeed in implanting. You're living proof—and I stress the word *living*, since you wouldn't be if it had failed. The program Rachel devised and sent out causes anyone hosting nanites to remember having sent a DNA sample to a company called GeneScreen Associates for a full genome sequencing and analysis."

Carmilla gasped. "Of course," she said, her eyes now as wide as half dollars. "That *is* brilliant. And it worked like magic. I remembered sending in a sample. And you implanted a memory of a phone message stating that the results were in and that I needed to call an 800 number to get my results. This was crystal clear. I knew something was a little off about this. Sending out for a genome analysis wasn't something I would ever do. I was puzzled by it. But since I remembered already having done it, I chalked it up to the effect that Dmitri was having on me."

"That's the beauty of this ruse," said Rachel. "The conscious mind is expert at fooling itself. No matter how strange an action seems, if you have a firm memory of having taken it, your mind will invent a reason for why you did."

Carmilla nodded. "In retrospect it is remarkable that I didn't question it more than I did."

"We asked the Prep H guys to man the 800 number 24/7 in case anyone called," said Rachel. "And gave them precise instructions what to say if someone did."

"Prep H guys?"

Rachel smiled. "Long story. Our security team. Anyway, I can't tell you how amazing it was when they told us you had called. Even though I had tested it on Kevin, who now also falsely remembers sending his DNA out for analysis, you were the ultimate confirmation that we were on the right track."

"But why be so indirect? Why didn't you implant memories directly into Dmitri's mind instead of mine?"

"Couldn't," replied Rachel. "Only works on those with nanites in their brains, and he doesn't have any. He has electronic implants, and his neurons can only be manipulated if he's plugged in, so to speak, to an expensive MRI-like device. This system is much more of a hassle, but it's far more powerful. In hours, or even minutes, it can download a field of knowledge into his mind that otherwise would have taken him many years to learn on his own."

Carmilla considered this for a moment. "I see," she said. "So you were just hoping that someone close to him did have these nanites onboard."

Rachel nodded.

"And when I called with my name, the man who answered asked for my address to verify that I was really me, since genome information is private."

"Exactly," said Quinn. "But it wouldn't have mattered, even if you didn't give an address. Calls to that 800 number are tracked using the most sophisticated methods known to the military. Even if you had a phone that couldn't be tracked, this wouldn't be true anymore once you actively connected to this number. At that point, the system is able to trace back your location instantly. Unless you're ultra advanced and run the line through decoy systems and dummy routers."

"The moment you got off the phone," added Rachel, "Kevin and two members of our security team took a helicopter to Princeton, where they had cars waiting for them. The idea was to stake you out. Learn if you were working with Kovonov. Ideally, we were hoping you could lead us to him."

"We had one member of our team stake out your lab," said Kevin, "and two of us were on your house. When you left, I followed, and my colleague stayed behind to keep watch on your home."

"But why did *you* go on this mission in the first place?" said Carmilla. "Weren't you Rachel's only guinea pig? And wasn't this potentially dangerous if I did lead you to, um . . . Kovonov?"

Rachel grinned, immensely pleased by this question. "Exactly!" she said. "Spoken like a true scientist and a rational, thinking human being. I had no idea Kevin planned to be in on this."

She turned to Quinn. "That was so reckless—and stupid!" she added, unable to help herself, but Carmilla could tell she had enormous affection for the man and this was out of concern rather than malice. "How could you not realize that you're indispensable? Or did you think *indispensable* and *expendable* were the same thing?"

"We've been over this already," said Quinn. "You're right. It won't happen again."

"Well, at least now you have another subject," offered Carmilla.

"Thank you," said Rachel. "This will be helpful. But it only means that both of you are indispensable."

"To get back to what I was saying," said Quinn, "I followed you, hoping you were driving to meet with Kovonov. I hung back so you wouldn't notice you had a tail. When I realized what you were doing I barely had time to ram you off the tracks."

"You took a huge risk for me," said Carmilla gratefully.

"As much as I'd like to appear heroic, the truth is I wouldn't have taken such a crazy risk for a stranger. I did this only because you were a possible connection to Kovonov, our only lead, and I wasn't about to let you get turned into paste."

"Thanks anyway," said Carmilla. She tilted her head in thought. "Have any other victims phoned your GeneScreen hotline?"

"So far only you," replied Rachel. "Which brings us to the heart of the matter. Kovonov didn't just do this to you for kicks. He had to have chosen you because you're one of the most accomplished molecular biologists on the planet. So there's something you left out of your story. Namely, what did he want from you? You must have done something for him that involved your expertise?"

Carmilla didn't need to think about this for even a moment. She sighed, embarrassed by how easily she had allowed herself to be used. "I engineered a designer virus for him," she said. "His sister has epilepsy."

She shook her head and frowned deeply. "Well, the implanted memories I have tell me his sister has epilepsy. And now that I think about it, his sister probably isn't real either. I constructed the virus to exact specifications to help her. I thought I'd gotten the specs from his sister's doctor, but they must have come from him."

"And what does this virus do?" asked Quinn.

"It's designed to attack exquisitely precise regions of the brain. Regions I had thought the doctor wanted knocked out because they were the epicenters of his sister's seizures. I was too blind with love to even question any of it."

"What regions?" said Rachel.

"I don't recall offhand. I know they meant nothing to me." She raised her eyebrows. "But I kept the specifications, which have the targets listed. It would be a simple matter to pull them from my cloud account."

Rachel Howard could barely contain herself. "Please do that," she said. "Right away. Because I'm certain they'll mean something to *me*."

Her lip curled up into a scowl. "Let's find out what this twisted bastard is up to."

59

Volunteer Landing Park was situated on the banks of the Tennessee River and offered visitors a picturesque stroll near the tracks of the Three Rivers Rambler, a steam engine powered train that took passengers on a lengthy journey along the Tennessee River to the Three Rivers Trestle, where two other rivers joined to form the Tennessee.

Colonel Stephen Hansen arrived at the park just before five thirty and sat on a bench near a busy playground. Toddlers and gradeschoolers in brightly colored clothing were squealing in delight as they splashed through several fountains and a man-made waterfall, while their parents either assisted or looked on in amusement. A college-aged woman wearing a white backpack squirted by on a unicycle, and Hansen shook his head and smiled. As unlikely as this was, it was nothing compared to being ordered by the head of PsyOps to meet with a Black Ops operative at this ridiculous location.

The man he was to meet, going by the name Darryl Dorton, had doubtlessly staked out his arrival and knew exactly where he was, probably pissed off that he had parked himself on a bench rather than wandering aimlessly through the park. Hansen wondered how long Dorton would make him wait, either for silly cloak-and-dagger reasons or just because he could.

Ten minutes later a man approached him and sat down on the bench by his side. "Colonel Hansen," he said by way of greeting, "I'm Darryl Dorton. Angela Reader sent me."

Hansen appraised him carefully. The man's pronunciation was a little off, like he was a foreign actor trying to put on an American accent, but Hansen couldn't quite place it. "You were at Starbucks earlier today," he said, having recognized him immediately. "Working on a laptop. Why were you spying on me?"

Now the man's futuristic laptop made sense. It must be an advanced prototype only available to elite members of the military.

"I assume the general made it clear that this is my show, not yours, correct?" said Dorton, shooting him a look of contempt.

Hansen frowned. "She did."

"So my taste in coffee is not your concern."

Hansen took a deep breath. "Okay. I'm sure you had your reasons." He paused. "So what can I do for you . . . Darryl?"

"As you've probably already guessed, I want al-Bilawy. An off-the-books transfer. Can I assume you have prisoner transport vehicles with commercial markings?"

Hansen nodded. "One at the moment. A ten-foot moving truck with U-Haul markings. Indistinguishable from the actual vehicles from the outside, but with untraceable plates. Reinforced body, bulletproof windows, and four seats bolted in with secure restraints."

"That will do fine," said Dorton. "You've done some excellent work, Colonel. But now it's time to demonstrate some . . . advanced interrogation techniques. I want you to secure al-Bilawy in the transport and drive—alone, of course—to an unpaved road within Cherokee National Forest. I'll send you the GPS coordinates later this evening."

"What timing do you have in mind?"

"I'll meet you there at midnight," replied Dorton. He raised his eyebrows. "And pack a bag for up to a week, since we'll be working together for potentially this long."

"So you can teach me these advanced techniques?"

"That's right. Leave al-Bilawy unsedated. Note in the log that you have reason to suspect a security breach at the Knoxville site and you'll be taking the prisoner alone to an unspecified location until you can investigate this suspicion further. Disable any means of tracking the transport vehicle. Don't mention this to anyone, not even General Reader. She ordered you to follow my instructions, not to report the content of these instructions back to her."

"Understood," said Hansen.

Dorton stood, pausing to watch a mom scoop up a toddler who had been scurrying in their direction for reasons that only the toddler understood. "I'll see you at midnight, Colonel."

"Roger that," said Hansen, wondering what Angela Reader had gotten him into.

60

The instant Rachel Howard learned the precise regions Kovonov wanted targeted with his designer virus she knew what he had in mind. This time Quinn called for a vid-meet, which Coffey's duties delayed until eight at night.

At the appointed time the participants seated themselves around the glass table on the office side of Rachel's extended quarters and waited for a virtual Cris Coffey to join them.

For this call the Plum Island contingent had grown by one, and Quinn knew he would have some explaining to do. He was in attendance along with Rachel Howard, Roger McLeod, and Karen Black. But this time, Carmilla Acosta had also joined the proceedings, wearing a soft blue bathrobe they had provided to maximize her comfort since she had been stitched and bandaged in a number of places.

When Coffey did beam into the proceedings his expression revealed just what Quinn had expected it would: anger. "I see we have a newcomer," said Coffey immediately in clipped tones. "Quite a surprise," he growled through clenched teeth.

"This is Dr. Carmilla Acosta," said Quinn, "the Princeton molecular biologist—and Dmitri Kovonov victim—we told you about."

"Yeah, the robe and the bandage on her forehead were big clues," said Coffey. "You do remember bringing me up to speed on her and the whole train track thing, right?" he added.

"She's here at my request," said Quinn, holding his ground. "As a passive observer rather than a participant for now. Not because we don't value her input, but she really should be resting in a hospital bed right now. We made her promise not to tax herself."

Coffey turned to face the newcomer. "I understand that you've been helpful to our efforts," he said, "and I thank you for that. I don't mean to be rude, and don't take anything I say personally, but

I'm going to need to discuss this situation with Kevin as though you aren't in the room."

He turned and stared sharply at Quinn, not waiting for a response. "Since she's here, I have to assume you've read her in completely."

"She's as up to speed as you are," said Quinn, an accurate statement since Coffey wasn't as fully briefed as he believed.

"And you did this under whose authority?"

"My own. We have a fluid, fast-moving mission objective and I made a call."

Coffey shook his head. "So I'm risking everything keeping this from President Davinroy—at your request—and you decide, unilaterally, to read in a random civilian?"

"You and I decided that Kovonov was so dangerous," replied Quinn, "and the mission so important, we should keep it on a need-to-know basis. Well, Davinroy and Henry don't need to know. Not yet. And they also could have been compromised. Unlikely, but in this case, possible. Kovonov managed to get to me, after all."

"So your argument is that Dr. Acosta has a need to know?"

"Yes," replied Quinn. "Kovonov put Carmilla right in the center of this."

"On a related note," said Rachel, "I think it's time to begin thinking about bringing Davinroy and Henry into the fold, after all."

"Why the change of heart?" said Coffey.

"We've learned more and could use even higher level resources and string-pulling," she said. "Not that you and the major haven't come through beautifully," she added with heartfelt appreciation. "But the president and head of DHS do add some pull, you have to admit."

"You argued earlier that these were the very men Kovonov would most want to manipulate."

"They still are, but I'm making enough progress that I should soon be able to know for sure if someone has been tampered with. Right now I can only tell with a convoluted memory implantation scheme. But I think I'm close to figuring out how to stimulate the nanites to broadcast their presence back to me. Maybe a week. Maybe less."

"Bringing the president and Greg Henry into the loop will take some delicate maneuvering," said Coffey, "because they can't know they were ever *out of* the loop."

"I agree," said Quinn. "We can talk more about this later. But Davinroy and Henry think Rachel and I are in Israel working with the Mossad. So we can schedule a vid-meet after Rachel has declared these men free of nanites and keep that facade going. I know the Israelis will agree to it. We'll bring the president fully up to speed on our results, telling him we didn't want to report on our progress piecemeal, or waste his time on preliminaries."

Coffey paused in thought. "We'll need to think through all the angles very carefully," he replied. "But like you said, that's a discussion for another time. So let's get back to your decision to bring a civilian into this."

"The truth is I pushed hard for this course of action as well," said Rachel. "Carmilla *does* need to know. And she's a world-class genetic engineer, which we can use. She's also loaded with nanites, someone else that Kovonov has manipulated, and she's volunteered to be a test subject alongside Kevin."

She paused and stared deeply into Coffey's virtual eyes. "But most importantly, sending her back to Princeton right now is a death sentence."

"In what way?" said Coffey.

"I'm administering a sophisticated treatment. She'll continue to be in a state of severe depression for some time, but she shouldn't be suicidal. At least as long as I'm involved. I know what's been done to her and the best way to help."

"You really think she'd still try suicide if not in your care?" said Coffey in disbelief. "Even knowing what she knows?"

"Yes. Kovonov's turned her unconscious brain against her. She can't reach it to reason with it. But even if this wasn't a concern, Kovonov clearly wanted her dead. We shouldn't even be calling what happened attempted suicide. It was attempted *murder*, plain and simple. If she pops back up in Princeton, I think he'll send some mercs to finish the job."

"She's already called in and is arranging for a sabbatical," noted Quinn. "Like Rachel did. The authorities found her car at the edge of the tracks, but Major McLeod managed to have some strings pulled so they wouldn't pursue her for a statement. The official line is that a maniac tried to ram her car onto the tracks, but he overshot the mark."

"And the perpetrator got his just reward when he ended up on the tracks instead," added Rachel, "and was pulverized by the train."

"Since Carmilla is the victim, the investigators have agreed to keep her identity confidential," said Quinn.

Coffey considered for several long seconds. "Okay," he said finally. "You've sold me. We can't put her back in harm's way, and she may be able to help." He turned to Carmilla. "Apologies for talking like you aren't here. Welcome to the team. My name is Cris."

"Carmilla," she said. "Nice to meet you."

"How are you feeling?"

"Really, really crappy," she said with a weak smile. "But I'll survive."

"We made sure her communications were untraceable," said Quinn, letting Carmilla go back to being a passive observer. "We then had her text colleagues and family members that she decided to take an unplanned sabbatical. But we've also planted a story online. If you Google *Dr. Carmilla Acosta* and *suicide*, you'll find a story indicating that she succeeded in killing herself."

"Smart," said Coffey. "Kovonov is the only person likely to ever search using these terms."

"That was our thinking," said Rachel. "So the story is there if he uses the Web to learn if his plan succeeded. If he falls for this, so much the better. She's off his radar. But if he doesn't and learns she's still alive, at least he won't know where to find her."

"Good thinking," said Coffey. He spread out his hands, palms up. "So what have you learned?" he asked. "Last I heard you discovered that she'd engineered a virus for him. Any idea what it might do?"

"We know precisely what it does," said Rachel. "Carmilla provided the exact specifications of what he wanted." She blew out a long breath. "I suspect you'll find this hard to fathom. Are you ready?"

Coffey visibly braced himself. "Go for it."

"Basically," said Rachel, "to put it in its simplest terms, the virus is designed to wipe religious belief off the face of the Earth."

61

Cris Coffey was sure he hadn't heard right. Ever since he had learned that Kevin Quinn's memory had been tampered with the world had continued to get more bizarre by the day. This must have been how Alice felt after falling through the rabbit hole. His forehead wrinkled in dismay. "*What?*"

"Kovonov wants to destroy religion," replied Rachel, like this was something that could actually be done. "Or more accurately, religiosity. Spirituality. His virus is designed to erase these beliefs in whoever it infects. He's almost certainly concluded that the global Islamic caliphate could be reversed if fundamentalist religious passions were annihilated."

"I have so many questions I don't even know where to begin," said Coffey. "First . . . *what*? How can you erase spirituality? That's the most absurd thing I've ever heard."

The hint of a smile appeared on Rachel's face. "Like many behaviors that have been found to have an unexpected genetic origin," she said, "religiosity is baked into our genes. Prewired into our brains. Those who are more spiritual than others just respond to these genes, this wiring, more profoundly. And environmental factors do come into play, triggering this wiring more potently in some than in others."

"So you're suggesting religious belief is like *hair color*?" said Coffey skeptically. "Just another genetic trait?" He shook his head adamantly. "I find that very difficult to believe."

"The evidence is irrefutable," replied Rachel. "Clear even before modern neuroscience and genetics came along. Although these tools have confirmed and bolstered the case."

"Not clear to me," said Coffey. "If it's common knowledge that religion is prewired, I must have missed that class. How long has this been known?"

"A century," said Rachel. "Maybe more. The trick is to ask yourself, what does prewired behavior even mean? How do we know what is prewired versus what is learned?"

Coffey didn't respond, deciding she really wasn't looking for him to answer.

"Behavior is wired in," she continued, "if it's exhibited by all humans across the globe, across all societies. The suckling reflex is wired in. All newborns can find a nipple and know what to do with it. Facial expressions are prewired. All humans cry when we're sad and laugh when we're happy. Even blind people who have never seen a smile, on themselves or anyone else, smile when something strikes them as humorous. This behavior is involuntary. A genetic reflex. The same expressions occur in every society, and are unchangeable. Try to train someone to laugh in response to sadness and see how much luck you have."

"Are you saying that religious beliefs are like facial expressions?" said Coffey.

"That's exactly what I'm saying. No human culture has ever been found without supernatural beliefs. Man is a spiritual animal. There is not a single civilization known to us that didn't have a belief in one or more gods. Over a hundred years ago, the Swiss psychiatrist Carl Jung studied the mythology of hundreds of cultures. He was stunned to find so many common themes among them, which he dubbed *archetypes*. He concluded that the only way this could be the case was if these archetypes stemmed from some inherent psychic substrate shared by the entire species. Something he called our collective unconscious."

Coffey found himself fascinated. He had heard these terms before, but never knew how they had arisen.

"Jung called this our *natural religious function*, long before neuroscience would confirm it. He wrote that our religious function influences us as powerfully as sexuality and aggression. That man throughout the ages had been as preoccupied with religion as in acquiring food and fulfilling other basic needs."

"Then how would he explain atheism?" asked Coffey.

"Good question," said Rachel. "The propensity for religious belief is wired in, but that doesn't mean it can't be actively ignored. Catholic priests choose not to have sex, and no one would argue that *this* impulse isn't prewired. But when all is said and done, there really are no atheists in a foxhole. When facing death, even atheists tend to plead with some higher power."

"But isn't organized religion in decline around the world?" said Coffey.

"I thought so too," said Quinn. "But after I learned what Kovonov was up to, I spent some time before this meeting brushing up on the subject. Since 2005, Gallup has conducted a survey of religiosity across a large number of countries around the world. Turns out that, collectively, organized religion is growing. And even those people who don't believe in standard religions tend to believe in the supernatural. Sweden and Iceland are often held out as examples of places where reason has triumphed over religion. Church attendance is very low in both countries. But over a third of Icelanders believe in reincarnation, and more than half believe in elves and trolls. A majority of Swedes believe in mental telepathy, or reincarnation, or healing crystals, or even ghosts."

"I really thought religion was on its way out," said Coffey, "but I'll take your word for it. But all of this aside, *why* would we have a religious function?"

"Because religion must have a survival benefit," said Rachel, "like sex and language. Lucretius said, 'fear begets gods,' and he was right. Humans evolved consciousness, intelligence, and this gave them a huge advantage. But at the same time we became smart enough to realize that death was inescapable. No matter what we do, the sword of Damocles is dangling above us."

She paused. "Primitive man faced death every day. Harsh conditions, short lifespans, no medicine. An anxiety function is built into every animal to help them survive, us included. But once we became aware of death, this function would have become overwhelming if not counterbalanced with something hopeful. Life is useless, meaningless. Why struggle to survive when it's only a matter of time before you fail? Spirituality allows us to *know* we're going to die, but to *believe* we'll still survive this event. Even with our religious function, awareness of death has made mankind hopelessly unstable psychologically. Turned us into what Freud called *the neurotic animal*."

Coffey made a face. "Great," he said sarcastically. "How lucky for us." He paused in thought. "You said earlier there was also more modern evidence that religion was prewired. Like what?"

"Religiosity has been studied in thousands of pairs of identical twins," replied Rachel, "who were separated from each other at birth and reared apart. Imagine one is raised by an atheist and the other by the pope. Turns out the likelihood that they both go on to be religious, or both go on to be *areligious*, is greater than it is with non-identical twins reared together."

"Just to be certain this point is clear," said Karen Black, jumping in for the first time, "identical twins have identical genes. So this result shows beyond a doubt that the genes you carry play a clear role in your propensity to embrace religion. Not the only role, by any means, but a clear role."

"And with respect to the wiring of our brains," said Rachel, "the evidence is just as conclusive. Parkinson's can cause people to lose their faith. Head injuries have been known to do the same. Individuals with passionate religious beliefs have lost all interest in religion after a head injury. Others who were areligious have suddenly become hyper-religious after a head injury."

"Hyper-religious how?" asked Major McLeod.

"Obsessive praying," responded Rachel. "Religious urges. Intense religious passion. A feeling of certainty about one's beliefs."

"Go on," said Coffey.

"As I'm sure you're aware," continued Rachel, "any number of drugs can induce mystical, transcendent, spiritual experiences in people. Epileptic seizures can also lead to hyper-religiosity. Seizures have also been known to cause a condition called religious hypergraphia, which is an obsessive urge to write about religion and God."

Coffey tilted his head in thought. "So you're saying that if religion, if belief, can be ramped up and down by natural causes, by trauma to the brain, it can be manipulated *unnaturally*."

"Exactly," said Rachel. "There is a growing sub-field of neuroscience called neurotheology. Very recently, scientists have been able to unravel this system, to identify interactions of over a dozen pinpoint areas in the brain required for spiritual belief."

"The virus Carmilla designed," said Karen, "targets these precise regions. The chance that Kovonov chose these neuronal clusters randomly is infinitesimally small. So it is absolutely clear that the abolition of religion is his endgame."

"I am so sorry," said Carmilla as a tear escaped her left eye. "I can't believe I let him use me like this."

"You didn't *let* him," said Quinn quickly. "You had no choice. We all know that. Hell, I almost killed a president I took an oath to protect."

Carmilla nodded and dried her face with the back of one hand.

"But aren't these findings you've spoken about conclusive proof that God isn't real?" said Coffey. "That religion isn't real?"

"Depends on who you ask," said Rachel. "Some think so. Others don't. If you believe a Creator designed us, then this Creator designed *these* regions of the brain as well. Perhaps to make it easier for us to have faith. Let's face it, for the most part we're a very skeptical species. We don't believe anything we can't see for ourselves."

She raised her eyebrows. "Except when it comes to the supernatural, which is prewired in. If I claim that an invisible giant hamster is hovering above me, I'm a lunatic. If I sense the spirit of God hovering above me, I'm simply a spiritual being."

"Are you saying God might have baked in this religious function to overcome our skeptical natures?" said Major McLeod. "So we can still choose to believe in an unseen Creator if we want?"

"It does make sense," said Quinn. "If there is a God, he would need to do that. One part of the Moses story from the Old Testament always bugged me. If I have this right, Moses brings down ten plagues on Egypt. After each one he asks Pharaoh if he's ready to let the

Jewish people go. But each time, God hardens Pharaoh's heart, so that he refuses, when he might otherwise have agreed."

Karen nodded appreciatively. "I never thought about that," she said. "But you make an interesting point."

"Hardly seems fair, does it?" said Quinn. "If God forces you to refuse, how can he be justified for punishing you when you do? You have to have free will. So it makes some sense that—if there is a God—he would give us a genetic God-function, which we can either cultivate or ignore."

"That's exactly how believers explain our predisposition to spirituality," said Rachel. "Non-believers continue to think these findings provide absolute evidence that religion is all an illusion."

"This is fascinating," said Coffey. "But given what we're up against, this debate is irrelevant. Because Kovonov's virus will kill off this religious function no matter *how* it came to be there. Right?"

Rachel nodded. "That's right," she said. "But weren't you the one who said the idea of a virus wiping out religion was absurd?"

"It is absurd," said Coffey. "But you've also convinced me it's possible." He paused. "But does Kovonov really think this will slow the jihad? These terrorists are just using religion as an excuse to destroy the West, aren't they? They are radical, no doubt. But is what they do really about religion? Seems impossible that it is."

"Some are just *using* religion to achieve their goals," replied Rachel, "but many are inspired by it. Many wouldn't do what they do if not for their religious passion. You've been trained in the Judeo-Christian ethic. So you imagine if someone is truly spiritual, truly religious, they would be like Gandhi. But this is the opposite when you are truly spiritual and you believe your god and prophets want you to wipe out all infidels, engage in global genocide."

"But most Muslims who are truly religious don't subscribe to this part of the religion," said Major McLeod.

"That is true," said Rachel. "There are all different levels and interpretations. Just because most jihadists are hyper-religious doesn't mean that all Muslims who are hyper-religious are jihadists. But

Kovonov doesn't care. If he succeeds, the global caliphate will die out as a threat, and ultimately even a concept."

"But his virus won't discriminate," said Coffey. "It will take down all the world's religions."

Quinn nodded grimly. "Speaking of which, it occurs to me that we should reassess the recent Cockaponset massacre. These evangelicals were wiped out soon after Carmilla gave the virus to Kovonov. In my view, this is too much of a coincidence."

Coffey considered. "Are you saying that it wasn't Islamic terrorism? That Kovonov was behind it?"

"I am," said Quinn. "They were a secluded group of true believers. What better group to test his virus on? As you said, the virus won't discriminate. It will work the same on Christians as it will on Muslims. So I'll bet he exposed them to the virus, waited for it to do its thing, and then tested them to see if they suddenly lost their religious passion."

"Makes sense," said McLeod. "We just have to hope that his field test failed."

Carmilla Acosta shook her head. "Rachel is certain the regions targeted are those needed for religious belief," she said weakly. "And I'm certain the virus will do its job. I'm sure the test was successful."

Coffey frowned deeply. "I'll try to pull strings to get one of the bodies from the massacre," he said. "Rachel, if you had one of the victim's brains, could you confirm this happened, and if the virus worked or not?"

Rachel didn't hesitate. "I'm sure I could. If I remember right, they were all shot through the head. So all of their brains will be . . . compromised. But I should be able to find pinpoint ablations of the religious centers within otherwise undamaged brain tissue. I don't have to verify every last one has been hit. Two or three would be more than enough confirmation."

"Given that we're certain it will work," said Karen, "is this worth doing?"

Coffey nodded. "I think so, yes. For good measure. And in case others in the future require more convincing than we do."

"But don't we have to face the fact we might already be too late?" said Major McLeod.

"We're not," said Quinn. "Carmilla assured us that the current version of the virus isn't contagious. No matter how manipulated she was, Kovonov could never have supplied a plausible reason to engineer *this* in."

"Can it be *made* contagious?" asked Coffey.

Rachel turned to Carmilla. "Do you feel up to fielding this, or do you want me to?"

"You," whispered Carmilla, her energy having faded even since the meeting had begun. They needed to get her back to her room.

Rachel turned to address the gathering. "I'll just parrot what Carmilla told us earlier today," she said. "The answer is *yes*, it can be made contagious. Hypercontagious. But Kovonov will need to have extensive modifications done. It will need to be inserted in a hyperinfectious carrier, which won't be simple. But if done correctly, she estimates it could infect every man, woman, and child on Earth within six months."

"No virus ever gets *everyone*," said Coffey.

"This one could," said Rachel, "because it will be insidious. No one will know they have it. No one will seek treatment. Carriers won't stay at home or be put into quarantine. A number of seizure victims over the years have shown us what to expect. Those true believers who are infected will suddenly stop being true believers, without having any idea this is due to an outside agent."

"How long will it take Kovonov to make the needed modifications?" said Coffey.

"Carmilla thinks it will take at least a few months," replied Quinn. "But she's convinced he can't do it himself, even if he had genetic engineering implanted using his Matrix Learning system. It can only be done by the best in the world."

"So what's our play?" said Coffey.

"Carmilla is putting together a list of maybe twenty to thirty scientists in the world capable of pulling this off," said Quinn. "Rachel will race to find a simple method to confirm that Davinroy and Henry haven't been compromised. Then we can bring them on board."

Coffey nodded thoughtfully. "And once this happens, they can activate more than enough resources to put surveillance teams on every last scientist on Carmilla's list."

"That would be the goal," said Quinn.

"Then maybe it's a good thing Carmilla is on the team, after all," acknowledged Coffey with a smile.

62

Quinn stayed behind in Rachel's apartment after the meeting disbanded and the participants had gone their separate ways. Their mutual attraction had continued to grow, and Quinn couldn't help but wonder if this, too, was simply their genes, neurons, and unconscious minds giving them no choice in the matter.

They had agreed to keep their relationship platonic, to resist the magnetic pull their personalities and presence seemed to have on one another. Yet the more they fought to ignore this pull the more it seemed to intensify. Was this just human nature? Quinn wondered.

If something was forbidden, did that necessarily make it that much more appealing? Or was this effect like that of hunger? The longer you denied yourself food that was sitting right in front of you, the greater your hunger would grow, eventually becoming irresistible.

Quinn could tell that Rachel Howard was just as susceptible to this effect as he was, whatever the cause.

In addition to a natural attraction, they found they made a great team, and had made great progress together. They had managed to chip away at the secrets of Kovonov's neurotech advances, and they were now beginning to get a handle on the man himself.

They had been on the couch for forty-five minutes, engaged in effortless conversation, as usual, punctuated by long bouts of laughter, when Kevin decided he couldn't take it any longer. If he didn't have Rachel in his arms he would burst.

Judging by the look in her eyes as he inched ever nearer on the couch, she felt the same.

He leaned in closer to her face, slowly, and she didn't pull away. She closed her eyes as his lips neared her own, and he longed to feel their softness against his.

"Incoming call from Major McLeod," announced her phone, breaking the spell when his lips were but millimeters away from their destination.

Rachel's head jerked back and her eyes shot open.

"Accept the call," she called out, and instinctively Quinn slid a foot or two farther away from her on the couch.

McLeod's head floated in front of them and his enthusiasm was unmistakable. "Good, you're together," he said by way of greeting. "We just got another bite on your 800 number."

Quinn was immediately alert. Finally, another of Kovonov's neural nanite victims had identified themselves. "Tell us about it," he said.

"Male caller." The major raised his eyebrows. "Israeli accent."

Rachel inhaled sharply. "Are you sure?"

"I took the call myself. I worked with a few Israelis on a joint project years ago, and I know the accent well."

"What name did he give?" asked Quinn.

"He didn't. It was a very short call. He said that he remembered sending some hair in for genome analysis, but that he hadn't been thinking clearly. He said he had no interest in the results, and insisted that we not call again." McLeod grinned. "He was quite agitated by the whole thing, as you can imagine. I told him we couldn't take him off our call list if we didn't know who he was."

"Nice touch," said Quinn.

"Thanks. He still didn't give a name, but he gave his cell phone number so we could remove it. Then he threatened to sue if we ever called again and ended the call abruptly."

Even after having personal experience with the implantation of false memories, Quinn continued to be impressed by just how powerful they could be. The Plum Island team never had this guy's number in the first place because no message had ever been left. He just *remembered* having listened to a message, which he *remembered* having deleted.

"I assume you were able to trace him," said Quinn.

"We were. I've scrambled two of the Prep H team, Lieutenants Gene Bowen and Dave Zerkle. They're in the air now. Their helo will land at Fort Drum in New York and take a faster aircraft to this new lead. They should be at their final destination in just over an hour. Once they are, given we now have this guy's cell number, they'll be able to pinpoint his exact location. I have a few items to attend to, but I'll be leaving in a hour myself to meet up with them. Captain Stagemeyer—Brian Stagemeyer—will be in charge of the Prep H team while I'm away. So you'll still be well protected."

"I never doubted that for a moment," said Rachel.

"Same plan as with Dr. Acosta?" said Quinn. "Wait to move in, hoping this guy will lead you to Kovonov?"

"Yes. Maybe the second time will be a charm."

"So where was he calling from?" asked Rachel.

"Just outside of Knoxville, Tennessee."

Quinn thought for a moment and then frowned. "What's in Knoxville, Tennessee?" he asked.

"Hopefully, Dmitri Kovonov," replied the major. "But whoever this guy is, and whatever he's doing in Knoxville," he added, "you can bet your ass we're going to find out."

63

Dmitri Kovonov waited calmly in the deep darkness of Cherokee National Forest. He was lurking just inside the tree line beside a narrow road, with a small rucksack resting on the ground near his feet. It was ten minutes until midnight and he knew that Colonel Stephen Hansen would take great care to arrive for their rendezvous precisely at the appointed time, parking a few minutes away, if necessary, to ensure he arrived not a minute too early or too late.

Earlier that day, just after Kovonov had left the Starbucks, he had sent Mizrahi to help his freelance communications expert ready the new home they had acquired nearby. When this was completed, Kovonov had sent his underling on another important mission, one designed to take advantage of a strategic opportunity he wanted to exploit.

Kovonov loved midnight. It held a unique place in the collective imagination, had become synonymous in literature and mythology with evil and dread. The stroke of midnight, the precise moment separating one day from another. In ancient times called the *witching hour*, when black magic was at its zenith and witches, demons, and ghosts roamed the Earth at their most powerful.

And in modern times, when experts wanted a way to represent their assessment of just how close humanity was to self-destruction, they settled on something they called *the doomsday clock*, with midnight representing the global apocalypse, of course. Currently, the clock was set to its latest point ever, 11:58, but Kovonov thought these so-called doomsday experts were idiots. In his opinion it was 11:59:59. And then some. If not for Israel's efforts at thwarting the plans of Iran and North Korea, midnight might have already arrived.

But he was determined to usurp the witching hour. Instead of the global apocalypse Islamic extremists longed to bring about, he would use the stroke of midnight to mark the beginning of the end of this malignant threat. The precise moment that he had single-handedly begun to reverse the tide.

Several minutes later a pair of headlights lit the dark night, perhaps a quarter of a mile distant. The headlights continued to work their way closer until the ten-foot truck to which they were attached pulled up to within yards of Kovonov's position and stopped.

Right on schedule.

Kovonov noted the truck had U-Haul markings, as expected, although the telltale colors of orange and white were impossible to make out in the dim moonlight. He hadn't seen another vehicle since he had arrived thirty minutes earlier and didn't expect to see another one for at least as long.

He emerged from behind the tree line with his rucksack in hand and approached the driver, motioning for him to lower the window. "Glad to see you, Colonel," he said by way of greeting. "I assume al-Bilawy is inside," he added, nodding toward the back of the truck.

"That's correct, ah . . . Daryl," replied Hansen, rolling his eyes. "I don't suppose you want to tell me your real name since we're going to be working together."

"Not yet," said Kovonov.

He moved to the opposite side of the cab, pulled open the door, and seated himself. He directed Hansen to drive along a dirt road that twisted deeper through the woods, ensuring even greater seclusion and privacy.

After about ten minutes of this Kovonov called a halt. "Let's get out," he said, "and you can introduce me to our prisoner."

"Right here and now?" said Hansen in disbelief. "Can't this wait until we're at our destination?"

"If I thought it could wait," growled Kovonov, "it would wait! I don't expect my orders to be questioned again!"

Hansen glared at his temporary superior. "Your show," he said through clenched teeth, bristling at the entire bizarre situation he was now in and the need to answer to a stranger he knew nothing about.

Kovonov followed the colonel to the back of the truck through a blanket of darkness, taking a moment to gaze at the glorious star field above, which he rarely took time to appreciate.

Hansen opened the back of the truck and climbed inside, with Kovonov close behind.

The prisoner was restrained in one of four chairs bolted securely into the vehicle's frame. His loathing of the two men who had entered was etched into every line in his face. He had all the markings of a zealot, a true believer, for whom the assertion that America was the *Great Satan* wasn't just a rhetorical flourish.

"Haji Ahmad al-Bilawy," said Kovonov in delight, still holding his ruck. "Am I ever glad to see you."

Al-Bilawy glanced back and forth between Hansen and Kovonov. He looked confused by Kovonov's obvious enthusiasm. Interrogators had often tried to establish rapport with him, but had never acted as though he were a long-lost uncle.

Hansen looked equally confused. More so when Kovonov removed a silenced pistol from his bag.

"What are you planning to do with that?" demanded the colonel.

"Shoot you dead," said Kovonov calmly, raising the gun in one smooth motion and pulling the trigger. Hansen's head exploded like a pumpkin dropped from a skyscraper. Blood and brains sprayed outward, splattering the prisoner and much of the inside of the truck.

Al-Bilawy's eyes widened and he shouted into the duct tape covering his mouth, which muffled his words.

Kovonov ripped the duct tape free.

"*What is going on?*" demanded the prisoner, having no idea what to make of what he had just witnessed.

Kovonov didn't reply. Instead, while al-Bilawy was pinned to his seat with no range of motion, he reached up and injected him in the neck with a microneedle array.

"Is that truth serum?" spat the terrorist in disdain. "If it is, it won't work. Besides, you American *pigs* don't believe in truth serum, or in torture."

Al-Bilawy glanced at Hansen's bloody corpse on the floor of the truck and his smug expression vanished. Americans didn't believe in executions of this type, either. "*What have you done to me?*" he shouted in alarm.

"First, I'm not an American," replied Kovonov, reverting back to his Russian accent. "Second, have you ever considered that if America truly were the Great Satan, it would revel in torture, not outlaw its use? Or is Satan a pacifist in your religion?"

"What?"

"I'm saying, shit-for-brains, that you possess a psychotic ideology that is as stupid as it is evil. But I'm not here to debate theology. In answer to your question, I injected you with many billions of nano scale electronic devices. They are already making themselves at home in your brain."

Al-Bilawy shrank back in horror.

"This nanite infestation won't hurt you," continued Kovonov. "But it will allow me to implant complex memories, and perform other manipulations. This will take some doing, since the memories I plan to implant are fairly extensive. But the bottom line is this: I'm going to turn you into a puppet. Into my *bitch* as the Americans would say. You're going to do exactly what I want you to do, and you'll think you're carrying out orders from your own leaders."

"I will never do anything for you!"

"Were you not listening? It won't be for me. It will be for your superiors. You'll think the orders came directly from that psychopathic asshole, Walid Abousamra."

"Do your worst!" bellowed al-Bilawy. "I am a loyal servant of Allah. He will either protect me or I will be happy to become a martyr in his service."

He shook his head and his eyes burned into Kovonov's. "And very soon Allah will help his pious followers smite you dead, along with all other infidels on Earth."

"Yeah, yeah . . . smite us dead. I get it."

Kovonov pulled a standard syringe from his bag and injected al-Bilawy in the arm. "You really need to relax," he said. "This will help.

In fact, you'll be going to sleep now. For a long time. It's easier to manipulate you with the proper precision when you're unconscious, and I don't need you just yet."

"I'm going to kill you," whispered the prisoner, already fading away.

"No you're not," said Kovonov, looking amused. "Because when you awaken, you won't remember that we ever met, and none of what I've told you."

The Israeli smiled. "Sweet dreams, you demented piece of shit!"

64

McLeod's call the night before had brought great news, but had spoiled the mood Quinn and Rachel had been in. Once the call had ended they both managed to find their restraint once again and Quinn had retired to his own apartment next door. Alone.

The next day was all about work. Rachel bent herself to the various tasks she was pursuing with her usual insight and stamina, most of the time in close consultation with Karen Black. Quinn joined them for dinner and Captain Brian Stagemeyer also dropped by to provide an update.

According to the captain, McLeod and the two others with him, Lieutenants Bowen and Zerkle, had found the man they were after and had run an exhaustive facial recognition search. And they had located an exact match.

His name was Yosef Mizrahi and he was known to have worked extensively with the Mossad, but was thought to have been killed in action a month earlier. This made sense. The Israeli intelligence agency was trying desperately to conceal how many of their men had left with Kovonov, even from its own government.

But the fact that Mizrahi was almost certainly in league with Kovonov was a lucky break. Whether or not this was a voluntary association was unclear. Rachel and Quinn both suspected the man was unaware that microscopic guests had set up shop in his head. Regardless, the chances that he would lead them to Kovonov were excellent.

McLeod and his fellow soldiers had been following this Mizrahi for an entire day, but they had yet to see any sign of the Russian-born Israeli. Still, Quinn was as optimistic as he had been in a long time.

Later, when he retired for the night, he rolled onto his back in bed to consider all that had transpired since the fateful day in Princeton when he had tried to kill Davinroy, and examine events from as many angles as he could.

But try as he might, all he could think about was the woman who was in the bed next door.

And how irresistible the impulse to join her there had become.

65

Haji Ahmad al-Bilawy could barely contain his excitement. His blood felt like rocket fuel coursing through his veins, energizing him like never before. Allah had blessed him like few others in history, had chosen to turn him into an instrument of destruction, who would deal the Great Satan a devastating blow.

He stroked his thick, billowy black beard absently as he considered the glorious afternoon and night to come. The fruition of planning and sacrifice that had taken years to accomplish. While he was to be the designated face of ISIS in America, others had performed brilliantly to make sure everything was in place.

His excitement was so great that everything that had come before this day now seemed like a fading dream. Being summoned by the esteemed leader of ISIS, Walid Jassim Abousamra, and told of the glorious task he had been chosen to perform. Working out the details and the scripts he would use, planning for every contingency. And coming here, to a house that had been set up for him an hour outside of Knoxville, Tennessee. It had all been a whirlwind that was now nothing more than a blur.

But while he could recall almost nothing of the last few months of his life, he could recall every detail of the plan in nearly photographic detail. His preparations and rehearsals for this day must have been all-consuming, so much so that they ran together in his mind in such a way that he couldn't remember a single one. But the results spoke for themselves, and he had never been more prepared, more ready, for anything.

He picked up the phone that had been left for him and dialed the number of the Secretary of Homeland Security. The call was answered on the third ring.

"Who is this?" demanded Greg Henry, obviously miffed at his phone's inability to identify the caller. Al-Bilawy had been assured that all the phone numbers he had memorized were up to date, and no communication from his phone, or from the video hookup in this home, could be traced or identified.

"You are speaking with Haji Ahmad al-Bilawy," he said proudly. "Calling on behalf of Walid Jassim Abousamra and the glorious members of what you call ISIS. And in service to the almighty Allah."

"Is this some kind of joke?" said Henry, unimpressed. "How did you get this number?"

"Not a joke," said al-Bilawy. "Retribution for your sins. Punishment for your evil."

"Al-Bilawy has been captured and is in a detention facility. Who is this?"

"You mean the detention facility in Knoxville?" said al-Bilawy smugly. "You'd better check again. But first put this call on video so we can see each other. That way you can run my image through your facial recognition software."

A moment later virtual images of both men were staring at each other. Al-Bilawy grinned fiercely upon seeing Henry's face. He was clearly shaken from the mention of Knoxville.

"What's this all about?" said Henry uneasily.

"First verify my identity," said al-Bilawy. "I'll call you back in five minutes," he added, ending the connection.

Five minutes later Henry's image floated once again before the ISIS soldier, his face now ashen. "I've confirmed that you're al-Bilawy. How did you get my personal number? And what do you want?"

"What I want is for every non-believer to die a horrible death!" snapped al-Bilawy. "But for now I'll settle for the seven or eight million people living in the Bay Area of California."

He shot Henry a cruel smile. "Although *living* will soon be the wrong word to use."

"What's that supposed to mean?"

"It means that there is a nuclear device embedded in the foundation of a building in downtown San Francisco. There are additional devices in other major cities, but let's begin with San Francisco."

"You're bluffing."

"And you are all too predictable. Do you think we are children? Calling you with idle threats we can't make good on. Of course we're prepared to demonstrate our claims."

The terrorist paused. "I'm sending a file to your phone now," he said. "It's locked, but it will open for you on its own at four p.m. It provides the name of the building and instructions for how to verify the existence of the device. This includes drilling into the foundation. It specifies precisely where to do this. You can then snake a detector down to get clear video of the device and measure its telltale radiation signature. The file will also detail the various booby traps that surround the device. Any attempt to remove the bomb, disarm it, remove any surveillance sensors, or remove any wireless signal sensors will cause it to detonate."

"Why not let us access the file now?"

"We want to give you time to verify what you're up against. But not too much time."

"The Bay Area has one of the highest Muslim populations in America. You expect me to believe you'd kill hundreds of thousands of your own?"

Al-Bilawy laughed. "I envy them," he said passionately. "They are the lucky ones who will get to die gloriously in service to Allah."

Henry swallowed hard. "Assuming this isn't a bluff," he said. "What do you want?"

"Oh, there will be plenty of time for further discussion. For now, just wait until four and then verify there is a nuclear device where I say it is. I'll call you again at seven. This will give you three hours to confirm it's real. Did you get the file yet?"

Henry glanced down for several seconds and then nodded. "I did."

"Good. When I call back, you had better accept it as a video call. And your despicable President Davinroy had better be on the call, as well. Do I make myself clear?"

"You know you're signing your death warrant."

"Don't try to cheer me up," said al-Bilawy. "Unfortunately, I am not in the Bay Area myself, so I will be denied the honor and the glory of becoming a martyr for Allah in this attack. But after this is over, I plan to gun down as many people as I can in a crowded movie theater. So rest assured, I will still soon be able to join Allah and thank him personally for allowing me to be his trigger."

66

Rachel was taking a break for a late lunch and Quinn decided to join her in her apartment. She was having an especially productive day in the lab and the lunch was even more lively, and more fun, than usual. She told Quinn that she and Karen had been working with Carmilla Acosta, who had been more helpful than they had expected. Carmilla was still deeply scarred by what had been done to her, but Rachel was convinced that in a few weeks' time she could cut back on some of Carmilla's meds without fear she would take her own life.

Once again Quinn found himself pulled irresistibly to the Harvard Professor, but once again the mood was spoiled, this time by an incoming call from Brian Stagemeyer.

A moment later his virtual presence was with them in Rachel's apartment.

"I'm really beginning to hate you guys," mumbled Quinn under his breath.

"What was that?" said Stagemeyer.

"Nothing," said Quinn with a sigh. "So what's up, Brian?"

"Lieutenant Bowen just contacted me."

Quinn's eyes narrowed. "Bowen?" he said worriedly. "Is the major okay?"

"He's fine. Just preoccupied. But I have some great news."

"They found Kovonov, didn't they?" said Rachel excitedly.

"They did. He's holed up at a farm about an hour out of Lancaster, Pennsylvania. The major is busy staking him out and setting up an attack plan, so he sent Bowen to relay some orders to me. Namely, he wants the rest of the Prep H team on-site as soon as possible. He doesn't think we'll be necessary, but Kovonov is a high-value target and not someone who should be underestimated."

"Amen to that," said Quinn. "Glad to hear it. I'd love to come along also, but Rachel would kill me before I got on the chopper."

The captain laughed. "We won't need you. Bowen says Kovonov looks like a squirrel settling in for a long winter. He'll be a sitting duck. But the major will wait until we arrive to strike. By then he'll have studied the survey of the property, the electronic blueprints to the farmhouse, and observed our target for an extended period."

"Make sure Kovonov doesn't have any of his mercenary friends protecting him."

"He does. Bowen says they've spotted three. Given that we got the drop on them, they shouldn't be a problem to take out. Don't worry, Kevin, we're going to get this bastard."

"Have the major call us the second you do," said Quinn.

"I will. Bowen also told me McLeod scrambled a temporary security team to the island from a base in New York. My team and I will be in a helicopter waiting to take off. As soon as this New York team lands—which should be in about an hour—we'll check them in and join the major. But the point is, even though this op requires all of us, we aren't about to leave you unguarded for even a minute. So rest easy."

"Thanks," said Quinn. "But I wasn't worried. Especially since you've got eyes on Kovonov."

He paused, and his voice became more somber. "One last thing. Remind the major that this is not a capture mission. We promised the Israelis that we'd kill Kovonov on sight. He's too dangerous to take any chances with."

"Don't worry. The major doesn't need a reminder. And Kovonov won't live out the night."

"I've never believed in the death penalty," said Rachel. "Even after someone is convicted in a court of law and given this sentence by a judge. I should be outraged by what's about to happen. But I have to admit that when it comes to Dmitri Kovonov, I'm prepared to make an exception."

She sighed. "Good luck, Captain."

* * *

The moment the call ended Quinn could tell that an elephant-sized weight had been lifted from Rachel's shoulders. She was still carrying considerable psychological baggage as she raced to learn why Matrix Learning led to madness and tried to reverse it in time to stave off catastrophe, but at least she would soon be able to do this without fear of the Kovonov bogeyman.

Quinn broke out champagne he had been saving for just such an occasion. They had Kovonov dead to rights and the Prep H team was very good. The team would still need to recover the virus Carmilla had constructed, but given it wasn't contagious, even this wasn't critical as long as they returned with Kovonov's head on a platter.

As he and Rachel celebrated, the dam between them finally burst, and they found themselves in a passionate embrace without quite knowing how this had come about. Not only were they more than ripe for it, one of the main reasons not to fraternize in the first place was about to be removed.

They began kissing on the couch like they were in junior high school, but they quickly graduated to Rachel's bed, with most of their clothing not making the entire trip, ending up as a haphazard trail on the floor behind them. Their session of lovemaking was as passionate and mind-blowing as any Quinn had experienced.

He decided that if a starving man denied himself cheesecake day after day, when he finally did take a bite the taste would be enhanced to extraordinary levels. This was the first time Quinn had been forced to deny acting on a mutual attraction for this long, and while he never wanted to repeat the experiment, the payoff for doing so was one for the record books.

Perhaps it was the epic sex talking, but Quinn decided that the total destruction of his old life may have been for the best, his emergence as Kevin Moore from the ashes of Kevin Quinn. Until Princeton happened, his life had been largely empty—he just hadn't realized it.

He had some friends and felt a kinship with his fellow Secret Service agents, but he had been empty inside. He had slept with too many women to count, but his relationships were shallow and he had avoided commitment like the plague.

Rachel was different. She wasn't after him just for a one-night stand. She had more substance than any five of the women he usually dated, and more intelligence than ten. She was someone so out of his league academically he still couldn't believe he enjoyed spending time with her. But he did. Immensely. Who knew that sex was so much better when the relationship had nothing to do with sex?

And while protecting the president had been meaningful, working with Rachel and the Israelis to perfect a revolutionary technology and prevent disaster was more challenging, and certainly more important, than anything he had ever done. He could make a profound difference in the world.

He had found a purpose, and a woman he respected more than anyone he had ever met, of either sex. She was an egghead professor who had been thrust into his world and was managing herself with grace and a remarkable competence.

Quinn was about to share these thoughts with the woman resting contentedly in his arms when there was a knock at the door. He shook his head in disbelief. Were a few hours of privacy really too much to ask? He decided that he should look on the bright side. At least they hadn't been interrupted while making love.

Rachel turned to face him and gave him a quick peck on the lips. "I'd better see who it is," she said miserably.

He nodded.

"Activate intercom feature," she ordered her phone. "Audio only."

"Activated."

"Who's there?" she said.

"Sorry to bother you Dr. Howard; Mr. Moore," said a deep voice coming through her phone. "But we've been assigned temporary security duty, and we wanted to introduce ourselves."

Quinn frowned. "We'd better let them," he mouthed, "or they'll never leave us alone."

"Can you give us just a few minutes?" said Rachel into her phone. "We were just, ah . . . finishing up an experiment."

"Sure. Take all the time you need."

They kissed a final time and dressed, so content they almost floated to the door as though on a cloud.

Four men entered calmly and the first extended a hand. As Quinn went to take it he found himself facing three drawn guns.

"What's going on?" he said.

"Resist or call out and you're dead!" said the man.

Quinn didn't doubt his sincerity for a moment. The group looked deadly serious, and deadly competent. They quickly cuffed his and Rachel's hands together with zip-ties.

"Okay," said the leader. "Now we're going to duct tape your mouths shut and escort you out of here. We'll be flanking you so no one can see the tape or restraints. If any of your colleagues do become suspicious, they'll end up dead. So it's in your best interest to see to it that we remove you from the island with no fuss."

"Who sent you?" said Rachel just before black duct tape was pulled across her mouth. "And where are you taking us?"

"We're taking a trip to Pennsylvania," he replied. "And I don't know the name of the man you'll be going to see. All I know is that he told us to call him 302."

PART 4
Endgame

"Knowledge is the food of the soul."

—Plato

"The predisposition to religious belief is the most complex and powerful force in the human mind and in all probability an ineradicable part of human nature."

—E. O. Wilson. Professor Emeritus, Harvard University, and Father of Sociobiology.

"Your mind is software. Program it. Your body is a shell. Change it. Death is a disease. Cure it. Extinction is approaching. Fight it."

—Peter Thiel, Billionaire Venture Capitalist

67

The E-4B jet lifted off at 8:00 p.m. with its precious cargo, just forty-five minutes after Matthew Davinroy and Greg Henry had ended the call with Haji Ahmad al-Bilawy. Davinroy preferred this plane to any of the five underground bases that had been established to ensure emergency command and control and the continuity of government during a crisis.

E-4Bs were specially modified aircraft that had been at the ready since the early '80s, but this was the first time Davinroy had set foot in one. Also known as the Advanced Airborne Command Post, the plane was a militarized version of the Boeing 747-200, designed to provide the president, Secretary of Defense, and the Joint Chiefs of Staff a survivable command, control, and communications center to direct US forces and civil authorities.

The plane could be refueled in flight, was shielded from nuclear and thermal effects, including an electromagnetic pulse, and had been designed to support advanced electronics and communications equipment.

Davinroy had summoned key members of his National Security Council to join him. The vice president was out of the country and several others were too distant, or weren't able to commandeer a helicopter in time to join them, but he had waited to take off until the personnel he deemed most critical were on board. Greg Henry, of course, but also his Director of National Intelligence, Andrea Hardie, his Secretary of Defense, Ryan Hardcastle, and the Chairman of the Joint Chiefs, Admiral Tony Loro.

As soon as the plane leveled out these four men and one woman met in the forward conference room, which was surprisingly spacious and boasted a table that could have sat five or six more in comfort around it. Davinroy could have chosen to have others attend virtually, but he wanted to keep this meeting small.

"I know you're all eager to learn why you're here," he began without ceremony. "So I'll turn this over to Greg Henry, who was the first person contacted."

Henry took the floor and recounted the call he had received around noon from Haji Ahmad al-Bilawy.

"I assume his nuke checked out," said Andrea Hardie, "or we wouldn't be in this plane."

"It did," replied Henry. "In every particular. It's embedded in the foundation of the Champion Tower in San Francisco, just as his file specified. He claims he has the detonation codes and can set it off remotely."

Admiral Loro frowned. "He claims?"

"We don't have absolute proof," said Henry, "but there is no reason to doubt him at this point. There are electromagnetic conduits to the device embedded in the concrete, which lead to the surface. Any one of these can carry a remote signal if he has the proper codes, and we have no reason to doubt that he does. Uprooting any of these conduits will set it off."

"Can't we block electromagnetic signals?" asked Tony Loro.

Henry shook his head. "My experts have read the file he sent to me. They tell me it is very precise and very credible. The device was set up so that any attempt to block his specific signal—which we don't have the specs on anyway—will set it off. I'm told it is a very impressive, foolproof design."

"He wouldn't have directed us to it if he thought we could stop him," pointed out Hardie.

"He also has surveillance cameras everywhere," continued the Secretary of Homeland Security. "If we remove them, he can set it off. If we try to dig the bomb out, he can set it off."

"I'm no technical genius," said Admiral Loro, "but if I'm understanding your experts correctly, *we're totally fucked*. Is that about it?"

"Elegantly said, as always," muttered Hardcastle.

"But essentially correct," admitted Henry. "He followed up with a call to me and the president about an hour ago. Insisted on audio and video. During the call he threatened to set off the device at the stroke of midnight tonight, Eastern Standard Time."

The Director of National Intelligence looked confused. "He's called us *twice* already?" she said. "So why haven't we found him yet?"

"We've activated every resource we have," said Greg Henry, "but whoever set up his communications was a magician. I'm told we'll eventually be able to find him, but the chances of doing so before midnight tonight are very slim."

"Which al-Bilawy must know," said the admiral.

"Are we certain this guy is a lieutenant with ISIS?" asked Andrea Hardie.

"Yes," said Henry. "We captured him and sent him to an interrogation facility in Knoxville, Tennessee. A few days ago he disappeared, along with the PsyOps colonel who was charged with the interrogation. The log says he was worried about a security breach and moved the prisoner, but we think ISIS managed to free him somehow."

Ryan Hardcastle nodded grimly. "Defense is quite familiar with this asshole," he said. "He's a member of ISIS's military council. An ethnic Chechen Georgian national of all things, who rose to the rank of colonel in Georgian military intelligence. He recently commanded ISIS fighters in Edlib, Aleppo, and the mountains of Lattakia. Known to be ruthless and to be a true believer, even among true believers. If the rest of ISIS leadership is drinking the Kool-Aid, he's a Kool-Aid alcoholic."

"Perfect," said Hardie, chewing on her lower lip. "So what are his demands?"

"He didn't make any," said Davinroy. "Not yet. He says he will at 11:30 tonight. He knows we won't have enough time to follow through on them, but if we agree to do so later, he won't detonate the device."

"That's a bluff," said Admiral Loro immediately. "To mute our actions now. The demands will either be ridiculous, like surrendering our country, or he won't make them. I have no doubt he won't miss his chance to wipe the Bay Area off the map."

"Why give us a heads-up, then?" asked Davinroy.

"To get his jollies, for one," said Henry. "I agree with the admiral. You heard this asshole, Mr. President. He was in his glory. And this also allows him to maximize our terror."

Admiral Loro shook his head in disgust. "This is also a propaganda bonanza for ISIS. You say he insisted his call with you be both audio and video?"

Greg Henry nodded.

"Why do you think he did that?" said the admiral in contempt. "Because now he has footage of a US president and head of Homeland Security at his mercy, pleading with him not to detonate, offering to negotiate. He'll have this footage sent out around the world right next to that of a crater where San Francisco used to be. So in addition to striking a horrible blow, killing millions, he can further embarrass us. The footage will make us look weak, show that we were powerless to stop him. I'm sure he'll include a standard ISIS rant about the death of infidels, the inevitability of the global caliphate, and so on."

"Which will also ensure that ISIS gets unambiguous credit around the world," said Hardie. "Talk about driving panic. Not to mention being the ultimate recruiting video."

"He claims there are more nuclear devices buried throughout the country," said Henry. "Which may be another reason he's notified us about this ahead of time. So we know for certain he's responsible. If his negotiating position is strong now, think how strong it will be if this goes off."

"Do we believe him when he says there are more?" said Hardcastle.

"Our experts are doubtful," said Henry. "But they also would have bet their lives there couldn't be a nuke in the foundation of the Champion Tower."

Davinroy blew out a long breath. "Recommendations?" he said.

There was an extended silence.

"We only have one hope," said Loro finally. "We stab ISIS in their heart. We scramble the entire might of the country. We use overwhelming force so we can have a knife at their jugular before midnight. A nuclear knife. We tell them if they don't call al-Bilawy off, the caliphate ends today."

"So play a game of nuclear chicken with ISIS?" said Davinroy.

"What other choice do we have?" said the admiral.

"And if they refuse?" said the president. "Maybe this is exactly what they want. We nuke ISIS and they don't go through with San Francisco. We'd never be able to convince the Muslim world that the threat to our city was real, that a preemptive strike of this magnitude was justifiable. We'll look like monsters, killing untold innocents along the way."

"You really think getting themselves nuked is their grand plan?" said Henry dubiously.

"It's possible," said Hardcastle, defending the president's position. "They don't think like we do. We can't comprehend a religion that glorifies death for a cause. It doesn't compute. But they strap bombs to their kids. They launch rockets from elementary schools, praying those fighting against them will kill kids while trying to take out the launchers so they can score a public relations coup. Militaries around the world have reported that putting women and children purposely in harm's way for the cause has become standard practice for the jihadists for decades."

"I don't care if it's their grand plan or not!" said Loro. "It's something we have to do. And we're running out of time."

"They didn't have to give us warning," said Henry. "So they must be prepared for whatever we throw at them, threats or otherwise. I hate to say it, but I can't imagine them not detonating, no matter what we do."

"I already told you why they gave us the warning they did," said the admiral. "So they could get our president on video. Even so, they've still managed to tie our hands brilliantly. Al-Bilawy pretends we have a chance to get out of this at 11:30, giving us no time to do anything if this is a lie. They know you won't do anything preemptive if you believe a peaceful solution is possible," he added, addressing the president. "And if you do, they get the ultimate public relations coup. But I say, fuck them! Let them have their virgins in heaven! Let them have their PR coup! If we throw everything we have at them right now, believe me, they'll call al-Bilawy off."

"I don't know," said Hardcastle grimly, "I agree with Greg. I think we lose San Francisco no matter what we do."

"Either way, we're running out of time!" said Loro. "We need to mobilize now! Let them know what's in store if they don't call this off."

Hardie frowned deeply. "I have to agree with Tony," she said.

"Well I don't!" said the president. "I'll agree to whatever al-Bilawy demands at 11:30 to buy us time. I've been told there is some chance we'll be able to get through his firewall before midnight anyway. But if I can delay him even twelve hours, I'm told tracing his calls and finding him becomes almost a certainty. I've also been given to understand that nukes like this fail to go off about five percent of the time. I'm confident that we can stop this. *Without* having to start a global war with the Muslim religion. And let me remind you all that this is a religion practiced by a quarter of the world's population."

"Wake up!" shouted Loro. "And get your head out of your ass! We're in a global war *already!* Is it going to take watching San Francisco turn into a sun and millions of people being vaporized before that's going to sink in?"

"Good thing I'm still commander in chief, then, isn't it Tony?" shouted an enraged Davinroy. "And one more outburst like that and you won't be Chairman of the Joint Chiefs anymore."

Loro fumed but didn't respond.

"Do we at least warn the Bay Area?" said Andrea Hardie, trying to move on and break the tension.

"No," said Davinroy. "Because it's not going to end up happening. We'll find al-Bilawy or I'll delay this until we do. And when the nuke *doesn't* go off, I don't want to be responsible for panicking an entire country and causing hundreds or thousands of deaths as these people trample over each other to get out of the blast zone. Which they wouldn't be able to do anyway if word got out. Highways and airports would become parking lots."

Tony Loro was the picture of contempt. "And what if you can't stop it?" he said, not shouting but with acid dripping from his every word. "Please tell me you'll at least let me mobilize the military to be in the best position to strike back. Do it because it's good politics if for no other reason," he added, and of those in attendance only Davinroy didn't realize that this was the greatest insult he could ever deliver.

"If you are wrong and San Francisco is hit," continued the Chairman of the Joint Chiefs, "what do you want to tell a devastated public? A public in a state of shock a hundred times worse than after 9/11? That you knew about it ahead of time and did nothing? Or that you stand ready to avenge the loss of San Francisco and wipe ISIS off the face of the earth? If it's the latter, we should make sure our forces are moving into place so they can be unleashed without delay."

Davinroy nodded. "Get a plan together and tell me when such an attack can be launched. If events play out the way you believe they will, we'll do exactly as you say. But I'm confident San Francisco is going to be just fine."

Loro had won this argument, but his face was still a seething mask of rage and resentment. He had won the right to shut the barn door, but only after the horse had already bolted. Or in this case had been incinerated. Not nearly good enough.

"You have no idea how much I pray that you're right, Mr. President," he said bitterly. "But I feel certain that you aren't."

68

Rachel Howard and Kevin Quinn were brought to a cabin deep in the woods somewhere in the vicinity of Lancaster, Pennsylvania. Night had fallen and clouds blotted out the moon and stars, leaving the area not in proximity to the cabin as dark as a cave.

They were forced inside and tied with plastic strips to chairs bolted into the floor of the main room. Quinn tested his bonds, which held as he expected. He and Rachel had been affixed to their chairs by experts, and there would be no escape.

He took a practiced survey of his surroundings. The room was barren and had no books or knickknacks or plants to suggest it was someone's home, vacation or otherwise. It had a couch, a few chairs, a table, and a monitor, but that was all.

A polished stainless steel container sat alone on the table, about the size of a paperback book, but there were no knives or other weapons in sight, and nothing Quinn could see that could be used as a weapon. A key fob hung from a small hook set into the wall next to the front door. The fob was a black oval emblem with the words *Land Rover* spelled out in silver lettering, matching these words spelled out on one of the two vehicles parked outside.

Quinn's survey was interrupted as his captors ripped the duct tape from his mouth, and then from Rachel's, and proceeded out of the cabin, most likely to man a security perimeter.

"Where do all these guys come from?" said Rachel when they were alone. "Mercenaries-R-Us?"

Quinn couldn't help but smile, despite their grim circumstances. "Pretty much," he replied.

How could he not be impressed with this woman? She had been ripped forcibly from her former life but she never complained, and she was able to maintain her sense of humor in the teeth of danger and adversity.

"The legitimate warriors for hire work in organizations called Private Military Corporations," he explained, "which are paid to conduct much of the actual fighting around the world. But any number of the ex-soldiers employed at these PMCs are only too happy to work for scumbags for the right price. Like strippers earning extra money by turning tricks."

Dmitri Kovonov entered the room just as Quinn finished, clutching a goblet of red wine in his left hand. He walked over to Rachel, beaming. "Professor Howard," he said in delight, "what an honor. Welcome to my little hideaway."

Kovonov slowly turned to Quinn, shook his head in disgust, and then turned back to Rachel. "But you really do need to hang out with a better class of people," he added, setting the goblet of wine down on the table nearby.

He closed the few yards that separated him from Quinn and drove his fist into his helpless prisoner's stomach. Quinn doubled over. When he lifted his head once again, Kovonov hit him with a right cross to the face, his ring tearing a gash in Quinn's cheek that quickly began to leak bright red blood.

"Never interfere with the extermination of a monster!" hissed Kovonov, still incensed over Quinn's role in saving the Syrian president years earlier.

Quinn glared back, his stomach and face still stinging from the blows they had taken. "You can bet I won't interfere with *your* extermination," he said defiantly.

Kovonov laughed. "Please don't tell me you think the cavalry is outside, Agent Quinn. Major McLeod and his hemorrhoid team? You *have* noticed we're in the woods, not at a farmhouse, right?"

Quinn's heart pumped madly against his chest. "Where are they?" he demanded.

"You thought they had the drop on me, didn't you? Here's the thing. None of this was your plan in the first place. It was mine."

"What are you talking about?" said Quinn.

Kovonov ignored the question, turning to Rachel Howard instead. "I bought that Agent Quinn had been killed in an auto accident, of course. But I really thought you were dead, too. Avi Wortzman outdid himself. He made it clear you were alive, but in such a way as to arouse my suspicions. When I dug further and found evidence he had planted that you were actually dead, he knew I'd buy it, congratulating myself for my thoroughness. I had no idea there was yet another layer of deceit, and that you were alive after all."

Kovonov studied her expression for several seconds. "Not even you knew about this, did you?" He shook his head. "But of course you didn't. Because you chose not to work with Wortzman. Instead, you decided to freelance on Plum Island."

He lifted the goblet of wine from the table and drank from it once more. "Which brings me to how I learned you were alive. And how I was able to capture you so easily. As much as I hate to admit it, turns out I got a lucky break. Of course, no one else could have taken advantage of it nearly as well as I have."

"Are you going to congratulate yourself all night," said Rachel, "or are you going to actually tell us how you found us?"

"I wouldn't miss telling you for the world. Turns out my lucky break came from the good Dr. Acosta. While I was visiting her to crush her soul and further program her brain, she happened to mention she had sent away for a genome analysis. Seemed funny to me, because she could do this herself, and she didn't seem the type. GeneScreen Associates," he added with a smirk. "Ever heard of them?"

Quinn noted approvingly that Rachel didn't give him the satisfaction of a response, answering his taunt with nothing but a look of contempt.

Kovonov continued. "Imagine my surprise when my associate, Yosef Mizrahi—the recently deceased Yosef Mizrahi I might add, since I finally don't need him anymore—later confessed that *he* had sent his DNA out for analysis also. To an outfit called GeneScreen Associates. I was driving when he told me about it. Almost drove off the road I was so stunned."

He shook his head. "First Carmilla and now Yosef? This GeneScreen outfit must have a very persuasive advertising program, don't you think? I got a kick out of how upset Yosef was by it all. He remembered getting a call that the results were ready to review, and he remembered having sent away for them, but admitted it was a severe lapse in judgment he couldn't explain. He assured me he wouldn't call back. He apologized profusely for his carelessness, saying he had no idea what had come over him."

Kovonov raised his eyebrows. "But *I* had an idea what had come over him," he said. "I knew exactly what it was."

He nodded at Rachel, a look of admiration on his face. "Someone had found a way to use my nanites for their own ends. Even more remarkable, this someone had found a way to do this remotely, over vast distances. Must have used a cell tower. This was just so ingenious. There is only one person in the world who could have pulled it off. Not the using the cell tower part, the knowing what to broadcast part. Only you, Professor Howard. I already knew you were brilliant, but you really outdid yourself this time."

He paused to take another sip of wine. "But even if you were alive, you couldn't have done this if Agent Quinn wasn't alive also. So the reports of *both* of your deaths must have been greatly exaggerated."

Quinn couldn't believe it. What were the chances that both Carmilla and Yosef Mizrahi would mention GeneScreen Associates in Kovonov's presence? Once again he thought of Adolf Hitler surviving so many assassination attempts due to blind luck. It seemed a cruel irony that people as despicable as Kovonov would catch this kind of break.

"And once you figured out we were still alive," said Quinn, "you found a way to set a trap."

"Very good," said Kovonov. "Maybe you're not as stupid as I thought."

He turned back to Rachel. "My sources were certain you weren't in Israel, so I knew where you'd have to be to make the progress you've made. Plum Island. I didn't even need a fly drone to spy on activities there. The Mossad hacked security on the island years ago, allowing us to get the feeds from your own surveillance cameras."

"Why?" said Quinn.

"Maybe you *are* as stupid as I thought," said Kovonov. "Because Plum Island is the center of America's secret neuroscience research program. Of course we were keeping tabs on US efforts. How could we not? When the American government was engaged in its Manhattan Project, you'd better believe you were paying close attention to Nazi efforts to build a nuclear bomb. Why would we do anything less? We needed to see what the competition was up to."

"In case you got tired of stealing *my* work," said Rachel.

Kovonov smiled icily. "You had the theory, but I did the implementation. And this was the more difficult achievement. But I do give you some of the credit for my breakthroughs."

He drank the last of the wine and set the goblet down on the table next to him. "But back to Plum Island," he said. "I took a long look at their security feeds. The Island is covered in video and audio, with the exception of the inside of living quarters. Which I'm thankful for," he added, making a face. "I've put you on a bit of a pedestal, Professor Howard. Seeing you go at Quinn like a porn star would really tarnish the image I have of you."

"If you had no eyes in my apartment, what makes you think we had sex?"

"Give me *some* credit for knowing how to read body language," he said, shaking his head in disappointment at her behavior.

He paused to gather his thoughts. "So after confirming where you were and getting the lay of the land, I had Yosef call the GeneScreen number and allow himself to be found. Your men took the bait right away as expected. While *they* were following Yosef, all five of my mercenaries were following *them*."

"What have you done with them?" snapped Rachel.

"You know the answer, you're just afraid to admit it to yourself. They're dead. All of them. I did spare one in the first batch temporarily, a Lieutenant Bowen, so I could erase his recent memories and implant those of my own choosing. Memories of a routine surveillance of a farmhouse. Memories of orders from Major McLeod to contact Plum Island to bring the rest of the gang along for the slaughter."

Quinn wanted to scream, wanted to spew molten hatred from his eyes strong enough to melt Kovonov where he stood, but he forced himself to remain calm. Giving in to his rage wouldn't help him, or Rachel.

"As part of the orders Bowen *remembered* receiving from McLeod, he also made sure that before your hemorrhoid guys flew off, they put out the welcome mat for my team, so we could waltz onto the island and remove you." Kovonov grinned, quite pleased with himself. "And, finally, I had two of my men lying in wait at the landing coordinates he provided to his comrades, about fifty miles from here. The last members of your security team were gunned down while you were on your way here, I'm afraid."

As sick as Quinn was about these revelations, there was no denying the effectiveness of Kovonov's strategy. In one fell swoop he had effortlessly managed to kill off the entire Prep H team, have his own team invited to the island, and get Quinn to lower his guard to such an extent that he was, literally, caught with his pants down.

"Not bad, right?" said Kovonov. "The file on you, Agent Quinn, says your instincts for avoiding a trap are legendary. But apparently not as good as my instincts are for *setting* one," he added with a superior smirk. "My men told me there was a champagne bottle on the table when they entered. Let me guess. You were celebrating that you had found me and that I was a sitting duck?"

He shook his head in mock regret. "Sorry to have ruined your party, but your celebration may have been a bit premature."

Quinn saw that Rachel was fighting to keep a cool head as well. Instead of cursing him for butchering good men she had come to care for, she took the opposite approach. "You know you haven't been yourself," she said, her tone displaying nothing but concern. "Your colleagues told us you were a good man. Before the change brought about by Matrix Learning. You can fight this. Remember who you were."

Kovonov laughed. "I do remember who I was. I *was* a good man. Now I'm a *better* one. I like the new me. I have no interest in going back to the sniveling existence I had before, when I was incapable of being bold. But no danger of that. You're the only person alive who has a chance of reversing what happened. And you won't be allowed to . . . proceed."

"Allowed to proceed or allowed to live?" asked Rachel.

"I'm not sure yet. With proper programming even you should be controllable. And what an addition you'd make to my brain trust." Kovonov winked. "And you aren't half bad looking, either. Holing up here is sure to get lonely. It would be nice to have some female companionship, if you know what I mean."

"Not if my life depended on it."

"Come now, Professor Howard. We both know that you wouldn't have a choice. I could make you forget everything you know about me. Replace your contempt with memories of adoration. Turn you into a Dmitri Kovonov *addict*. Given who you are there are risks involved, but I just might do that." He glanced at Quinn in disgust. "Although the idea of sloppy seconds makes this much less appealing."

Quinn's jaw clenched so tightly his teeth were in danger of breaking.

"Either way," continued Kovonov, "I don't want a cure and I don't need one. This change has freed me to do what needs to be done without a conscience screwing up the equation."

"What needs to be done!" said Rachel. "What, like wiping religion from the human race?"

"You're quite the detective," said Kovonov in amusement. "But I'm not surprised you knew about this. I did happen to notice Carmilla was on the island with you. Apparently, whoever was manning the GeneScreen hotline got to her in time to disrupt my little experiment."

He reached toward the table next to him, carefully avoiding the empty goblet he had set there, and lifted the rectangular stainless steel container from its surface. He pressed a small indentation on one edge and the lid slowly slid open, accompanied by an electric whirring sound.

"The case may be a little excessive," he said, "but it is protecting precious cargo."

He reached inside and removed a small stainless steel vial, about the size of his thumb, from a cushioned cavity, and held it up to his eye. "This is it," he announced proudly. "The virus Carmilla fabricated for me. She truly is a rare talent. Almost in your league, Professor Howard. Before too long I'll be able to make it contagious."

"You tested it on those evangelicals in the Cockaponset woods," said Quinn, "didn't you?"

"Very good," said Kovonov, genuinely impressed. "I'm surprised you made this connection."

"So why kill them afterward?" pressed Quinn. "You'd already stripped them of their belief. Wasn't that enough damage?"

"With this much at stake, I couldn't take any chances. I had kept them as prisoners for days, and they had all seen my face."

"You can't do this!" said Rachel. "The eradication of religiosity is a bridge too far. Even you must know that."

"I *can* do this!" replied Kovonov. "And I *will!* You understand better than anyone how effective this virus will be. All twenty evangelicals exposed to it lost their faith. The interviews were fascinating. Even those who pretended to still have a strong belief at the end were called out by my lie detector. When pressed, they admitted they were having significant second thoughts about it all. Each fooled themselves into believing this change of heart had been the culmination of thoughts that had been brewing just under the surface for years. As you well know, Professor, if the unconscious mind makes a decision, the conscious mind strives to find a way to make sense of it, to take credit for it. Just because my virus forced their unconscious into losing faith, it worked the same way. I thought you would appreciate this finding."

"Well you were wrong!" said Rachel in disgust. "What you did is *unforgivable*. And when I said *you can't do this*, I wasn't speaking literally. Of course the virus will work. I was saying you can't do this because of its impact on humanity. You know it will affect all religions, all supernatural beliefs."

"Of course I do," he replied, returning the small vial to the case and setting it back on the table.

"Do you have any idea what that might do to our species?" she said. "The unintended consequences? The scientist in you knows this propensity is there for a reason. We evolved it. It's an integral part of the human condition."

"I agree it's an evolved feature," said Kovonov. "But so what? It's vestigial. We evolved tonsils, an appendix, and wisdom teeth. These are no longer needed. Same is true of religion."

"You couldn't be more wrong," insisted Rachel. "Our fear of the unknown is as great as ever. Our need for religion as great as ever. It's a tenet of human nature as fundamental as sex or hunger. And you're just going to rip it out by its roots? Erasing these areas of our brains might ramp up the neuroses of our species to unsustainable levels. Do you really think this is a good time to take that chance?"

She forced her expression to soften. "I get your frustration with religion," she continued more calmly. "It *has* caused a lot of harm. But the importance of spirituality in human existence can't be overemphasized. Only when this spirituality impulse becomes entwined with a restrictive and dogmatic religious creed are we threatened."

Rachel paused, deciding on the best way to press her argument further. "Do I wish there weren't extremists who interpreted their religion as a call to send civilization into the Dark Ages, to kill all non-believers, to bring about the Apocalypse? Of course I do. And I wish I didn't have to go through long lines at airports, or learn about a terror attack somewhere in the world almost every day. But what you're planning isn't the answer. Religion can become bastardized, but so can *everything*. Islamic extremism is a cancer on religion. But if you can't excise the tumor, you don't vaporize the entire patient. You contain the tumor and wait for an immune response to kick in."

"This isn't just about a too-literal interpretation of Islam," said Kovonov. "Throughout history *every* religion has been antagonistic to every *other*. Because if one divine faith is true, every other must be a lie. The history of our species contains endless examples of religious tribalism, of conquests justified in the name of a Creator, spurring on our violent tendencies and leading to massive bloodshed. Do you know how many millions of people have been murdered in the name of Christ? In the name of a savior who preached love and compassion and turn the other cheek?"

"The crusades and pogroms were many hundreds of years ago," said Rachel defiantly. "The Christian religion has now become the peaceful religion its deity intended. Through time, the same will happen with Islamic extremists. If you could limit this to only the most rabid extremists, stripping them of their core beliefs, of their passion for jihad, this would be one thing. But you can't. And I promise you that removing all religiosity from the human species will only end in disaster. It will leave a gaping hole in the human psyche that can never be filled."

Kovonov smiled icily. "I guess we'll soon get to find out."

"Even if you strip religious belief from the jihadists," said Rachel, "this won't stop the jihad. Not anymore. It's been set in motion. For many it's all about their faith, but for many others it's come to be about more than this. About revenge, and hatred, and power. Once there is death and destruction on both sides, it becomes self-fueling, the reasons that it began not important anymore."

"Now *this* is something I can agree with," said Kovonov. "Which is why the virus is only step *two*. Step one is to wipe out the current generation of jihadists like so many cockroaches. Wipe the slate clean. Then introduce the virus to prevent this cancer from ever growing back."

"How do you plan to exterminate all jihadists?" said Quinn.

"I don't. I plan to leave that to the most powerful military force the world has ever seen. It's *your* country that will end this worldwide threat, once and for all."

"Not a chance," said Quinn. "Our people—our leaders—haven't shown an appetite to devote the boots on the ground and financial resources needed to even dent this threat, let alone eliminate it."

"They just haven't been properly motivated yet," said Kovonov ominously.

Quinn had a sick feeling in the pit of his stomach. "Are you saying *you're* going to supply the motivation?"

"I am, indeed," said Kovonov smugly. "In just about two hours from now, the instant the clock strikes midnight in your nation's capitol, the San Francisco Bay Area will no longer exist. It will suffer a nuclear detonation. For a brief instant, it will become hotter than the sun, with only a mushroom cloud to mark where a thriving city once stood."

He stared at Quinn with a grim intensity. "How's that for proper motivation?"

69

Quinn was reeling. Could it be? Was this madman's true plan even worse than the elimination of all religious belief? It was too horrible to even contemplate.

Just a short time earlier he and Rachel had thought they were on the brink of stopping Kovonov cold. Now Quinn knew his own life expectancy could be measured in days, at most, and that not only was Kovonov untouched, he was crazier and more dangerous than ever.

Quinn shook his head as he came to his senses. What was he thinking? Of course this last threat wasn't true, regardless of how resourceful and formidable Kovonov had shown himself to be.

"You've finally gone full bore delusional," he said. "Just getting a nuclear device into San Francisco would be all but impossible. But you're asking us to believe that you not only managed this, but also orchestrated events so ISIS will take the fall for it?"

"Believe what you want," said Kovonov. "But that's exactly what is about to happen."

"How?" said Rachel.

"Glad you asked," replied Kovonov. "Remember Kim Jong-un? He may have been a psychotic imbecile, but he had some people working for him who were exceedingly competent. You'll find this hard to believe, but they managed to sneak nuclear devices into six of your cities several years back. Israel learned about this at the eleventh hour from our fly drones. We were just able to stop them in time. And then we killed Kim Jong-un. You have Israel to thank for averting a catastrophe and removing an enemy from the board. But these nuclear devices remained in place."

Quinn whitened. This threat had suddenly become much more believable.

Kovonov studied his prisoners with great interest, noting that both of them now looked like they had seen a ghost. "Wortzman disclosed this to you already, didn't he? I can tell from your reaction."

Quinn nodded woodenly. "He did."

"Interesting," said Kovonov. "I never guessed my old boss would come clean about so much. Good. Now you know I'm telling the truth. To continue, we only managed to stop North Korea because we were able to get the detonation codes and change them at the last moment. We later managed to remove five of the six devices in secret and transport them back to Israel to add to our own arsenal. Which took some doing, I might add."

He raised his eyebrows. "The sixth, in San Francisco, had been embedded in the foundation of a skyscraper that was being constructed at the time. There was no way for us to remove this one without being obvious. Wortzman was adamant that we not tell your government about stopping North Korea, which meant we couldn't say anything about the device. If we did, Wortzman worried it would raise too many questions about our capabilities that he didn't want to answer."

"So you just left it there?" whispered Quinn, feeling hollow, sickened.

"Why not? We were the only ones with the activation codes and we wouldn't use them under any circumstances. Only a few people in all of Israel knew that this was the case, and the codes were deleted from every database we had. All except one."

"Which you found," said Quinn.

Kovonov nodded. "I've had them for some time now. But very recently I freed a member of ISIS's military council who was being held here in America. A man named al-Bilawy. He's still in this country, and I've programmed him to set off the nuke. But before he does this, he'll make it absolutely clear to your government that he and ISIS are responsible."

He paused, seeming to enjoy the horrified reaction of his audience.

"Not that he wouldn't have been thrilled to do this without any programming," continued Kovonov, "but I wanted to make sure he got your attention in the proper way. In just a few hours, he will kick awake a sleeping giant. I'll admit, the kick will be much more painful than I would have liked. But then again, the giant is in a *coma*."

He nodded proudly. "Once America is awake, your country will flip on the light switch to reveal the full extent of the cockroach infestation, and you will exterminate them once and for all. You will finally worry more about the future of civilization than about political correctness or possible collateral damage. America will turn its awesome might to a scorched earth campaign deploying every missile, plane, and pair of boots on the ground available to it."

He paused for several seconds as if visualizing this glorious future in his mind. "Then, once you've wiped the slate clean and destroyed the caliphate, I'll release my virus and make sure this tumor never grows back."

Kovonov nodded slowly. "And it all begins in just a few hours in the City by the Bay."

Tears welled up in Rachel Howard's eyes. "How can you do this?" she whispered, barely managing to get the words out. "How can you kill millions of innocents like this?"

"If that's what it takes to wake the US up to the threat, I'm doing you and the world a favor. Believe me, if not for Israel, San Francisco would have already been lost. Along with five other American cities. And if I didn't initiate this, the real jihadists would very soon. The global caliphate has been allowed to grow too strong and too bold. Your leaders have their heads buried so deep in the sand it's inevitable. I know you think I'm a monster, but I'm just speeding it along, amputating an arm to save a life. Like Hiroshima, I'm taking innocent lives to spare even more."

"Yeah, you're quite the humanitarian," spat Quinn.

"Just so you know, I did set this up to give your country an out. But Davinroy failed to take it, as I knew he would. He's a jackass and a weakling. I made sure al-Bilawy gave him plenty of notice. I made sure Davinroy knew that he couldn't stop the detonation. In this case, the only option he had was to begin a preemptive strike against ISIS. Throw everything at them, including nuclear weapons, until they agreed to call off their dog."

"But this al-Bilawy *isn't* their dog," said Quinn. "He's yours."

"True, but your president doesn't know that. Had he acted quickly with a preemptive strike, I would have stopped al-Bilawy myself. But of course Davinroy did nothing. He continues to live down to my every expectation. And San Francisco will have to pay the price for his incompetence, his inaction."

"You will go down in history in the same breath as Stalin and Hitler," said Quinn.

"I don't care how history judges me," said Kovonov. "These other men sought global domination. I do what I do to *prevent* global domination."

He shook his head. "As much fun as this has been, Agent Quinn, it's time for you to leave. While I prefer to have companionship while I await America's awakening, Dr. Howard will do just fine. And with you here, I can't help but feel like a third wheel. I'm sure you understand."

"Fuck you!" spat Quinn.

"No thanks," said Kovonov. "But when Dr. Howard makes this same offer, you can believe I'll take her up on it."

Quinn fought against his restraints, even knowing it was useless, but retained just enough presence of mind to stop before he injured himself.

Kovonov waited patiently for him to settle back down. When he had, Kovonov reached into Quinn's front pocket and removed his cell phone. "While I was spying on Plum Island I heard McLeod tell his men that the phones he issued to you were untraceable, even by him. I asked my men not to destroy your phones when you were captured so I could study them. Just curious how these compare to Israeli models." He smiled. "In case you didn't know, I happen to have a PhD level of knowledge in electronics, cryptography, and counter-surveillance."

"Of course you do," said Quinn.

"I also want to study you, Agent Quinn. So I set up a makeshift lab a half mile from here. I'm going to have one of my hired guns take you there now so I can complete a few choice experiments."

"Do these experiments include torturing me to death?"

"Maybe," said Kovonov with a shrug. "I guess we'll just have to see how cooperative you are."

* * *

Kovonov sent a text to one of his mercenaries and a few minutes later left the prisoners alone so he could meet with the man in the pitch-darkness beyond the cabin.

"I want you to come inside and remove Kevin Moore from the premises," he explained. "I told him you'd be escorting him to a separate lab facility. So pretend that's what you're doing. If he thinks he'll be allowed to live he won't be inclined to try something desperate."

"What do you really want me to do with him?"

"Take him to the banks of the river. To the grave your men dug for my, ah . . . fallen comrade earlier today. Then kill him. The hole is big enough for them both. I didn't have you fill it in earlier for a reason."

"Any other reasons to leave it open I should know about?"

"None," said Kovonov. "Finish burying the bodies and make sure the gravesite blends in with the surroundings."

He paused. "On another note, I trust everyone on your team is currently manning their posts?"

"Of course."

"Good. I don't expect any trouble, but I tend to be overcautious. I need you and your men on high alert until midnight. After that you can get by with a single sentry while the rest of you get some sleep."

"Understood," said the mercenary. "But back to this execution. You do realize that every kill triggers the hundred grand bonus, even if the target is wrapped up with a bow. You can do this yourself if you want to save the money. Your call."

"I'm aware of the terms of our agreement," said Kovonov. "If I wasn't planning to pay your bonus, I wouldn't have given you the assignment. Just get it done as soon as possible. No hesitation."

"That won't be a problem."

70

As the mercenary led Quinn away from the cabin the darkness became a living entity, enveloping and relentless. The man became impatient as his prisoner's pace slowed to a crawl, the lack of even starlight forcing Quinn to pick his way forward like a blind man without a cane or guide dog.

The merc finally shoved a penlight into Quinn's hands, which were cuffed tightly together with a zip-tie. "Use this," he instructed, backing up and continuing to keep a gun pointed at his prisoner's back. "We don't have all night."

The man Kovonov had assigned to take Quinn to an offsite lab was wearing the latest night vision goggles, so advanced they were no longer bulky but looked like goggles a swimmer might use, not to mention being more effective than past models at turning the night into a neon green day.

"Stay close," he told Quinn. "If we get separated by more than two yards you'll be killed. And not by me."

"What?"

"Never mind. Just stay close."

They continued walking through the woods, the night air a perfect temperature. Quinn shined the penlight on the terrain in front of him as he picked his way between trees and over aboveground roots that bulged up from the dirt like giant worms. The buzz of insects and the hooting of an owl punctuated the silence, and Quinn thought he could hear the faint rush of a river from the direction they were heading.

"What's your name?" said Quinn after several minutes had gone by.

"Why? So we can become buddies?"

"So I don't have to address you as *hey fuckhead*."

The mercenary couldn't help but smile. "I'm Daniel Bell."

Quinn wasn't sure this was his real name, but it was as good as any. "Thanks, Daniel. How much do you know about your boss? The man you call 302?"

"I know he pays ridiculously well. That's all I have to know."

"Actually," said Quinn, "you need to know more. I assume you aren't aware that he's about to nuke San Francisco. In just under two hours it will be slag, and millions of people will be dead."

Bell laughed. "Sure they will. He's going to nuke California from his cabin in the Pennsylvania woods. Let me guess. He'll be launching an ICBM from his bedroom."

"I know how it sounds. But it's true. Why do you think he wouldn't let any of you in the room while he was talking with us? So you wouldn't know what he's really doing. The device is already there, and he has a guy who can set it off remotely. At midnight our time. But your boss knows where to find this guy, so it isn't too late to stop him."

Quinn halted and turned to face the merc. "Help me," he pleaded. "Help save millions of lives. Help *yourself*. What do you think the US government will do to reward you for saving *San Francisco*? I promise you at least ten times what your boss is paying you. Not to mention you get to save more lives than any man in history."

Daniel Bell shook his head in contempt. "That's really the best story you can come up with?" he said, gesturing for Quinn to resume walking. "You should have told me my employer was an alien from the planet Jupiter. Now *that* I might have believed," he finished, laughing at his own joke.

"You're right. I could have made up a hundred stories more believable than this one. Why do you think I didn't? Because this one is the truth!"

"Save your breath. There's no way I'll ever believe you."

Quinn realized his efforts were futile. There was no chance he could convince this man to help him save San Francisco. But perhaps he could salvage a minor victory. "After midnight, you'll learn I was telling the truth," he said, his voice hollow. "You'll learn you could have averted the most horrific event of all time but chose not to. When this happens, at least take out your boss. Promise me that you'll kill him for committing this atrocity."

"Sure," replied Bell. "If San Francisco is vaporized exactly at midnight, I'll take him out. Free of charge. Satisfied?"

"You think you're humoring me. But just remember your promise."

The sound of rushing water had become louder and louder as they proceeded and they finally reached the banks of a river. Bell led his prisoner to a ditch. Quinn trained his penlight on the open gravesite and made out a body that couldn't have been there long, one that had belonged to Yosef Mizrahi.

"There is no lab, is there?" said Quinn. "I can't say I'm surprised. So what, you're just going to kill me now?"

"I'm afraid so," said the merc, backing away a few more feet to stay out of range of a possible desperation attack. "My employer doesn't seem to like you."

"Shoot me, then," said Quinn in resignation. "At least I won't have to live to see the coming horror. Just remember your promise."

"I will," said Daniel Bell pleasantly, giving no indication that he was seconds away from gunning down a man in cold blood.

Quinn shut his eyes tightly and braced for the end, wondering if there really was an afterlife, and if there was anything more he could have done to prevent a cataclysmic event that was now unavoidable.

71

A deafening shot exploded throughout the woods. Quinn fell to his knees, surprised that the bullet that killed him had brought no pain in its wake.

He heard a thud behind him and his eyes shot open. He was still alive!

He pointed the penlight toward the sound. The mercenary who had called himself Daniel Bell had fallen to the dirt, a river of blood spurting from a gaping hole in his chest.

A man emerged from behind a tree holding an automatic pistol and wearing night vision goggles of his own. "Jesus, Kevin, how many times am I going to have to save your life?"

Quinn's eyes widened. "Eyal?" he said in disbelief. "Eyal Regev?"

"I'm touched that you remember," said the Israeli, producing a combat knife and cutting Quinn's hands free.

"How are you here?"

"Rachel is critical to us. I knew you had Black Ops connections, and figured she might end up on Plum Island. After I confirmed this suspicion, I've been living in the Hamptons in case I was needed. I hired three mercenaries to stay close and on call."

"And I'm guessing you've been watching us through Plum Island's own security feeds."

"Yes. The Mossad's kept a close eye on this facility for years. How did you know?"

"Kovonov. He spied on us the same way."

"I told Wortzman where you were, but he's the only one," said the Israeli as he began to frisk Bell's corpse. "He agreed that until he could root out any moles in the Mossad, keeping Rachel's whereabouts between the two of us would better ensure her safety."

The Israeli handed Quinn the dead mercenary's gun and night vision goggles and pocketed his cell phone for future intelligence gathering. "I have no idea how Kovonov learned you were alive," he said. "Shocked the hell out of me when he moved on you. Sorry it took us so long to get here. We had to land the helicopter farther out than Kovonov and be more careful in our approach."

"We?"

"I brought my guns for hire."

Quinn nodded. "Well, for my money, your timing couldn't have been better," he said, sliding the goggles over his eyes. "Kovonov has Rachel in the cabin east of us. Just the two of them. She should be fine for at least the next few hours." A haunted look came over his face. "And we've learned what Kovonov is up to."

"Yeah, I caught that during my surveillance," said Regev. "An anti-religion virus. I never would have believed it."

"More than that, Eyal. Much more. You guys didn't happen to leave a Korean nuke in San Francisco, did you?"

"No!" said Regev in horror, understanding the implications immediately. "It can't be!"

"It *can* be. Kovonov got the detonation codes. He's orchestrated things so the blame goes to ISIS, to galvanize America into wiping them out. It goes off at midnight. We can still stop it, but we need Kovonov alive to do it."

Regev waved his arms in a prearranged signal. Seconds later three men emerged from the woods, each having been completely concealed by the darkness and the trees, and joined Quinn and Regev by the open grave.

"The good news is that your pay just doubled," began Regev, addressing his three hires. "The bad news is that we have a tough mission ahead of us. One that couldn't be more important."

He turned to Quinn. "We're not sure how far out from the cabin you were when we began following you, but we didn't see anyone else. How many men are protecting Kovonov?"

"Kovonov mentioned five, and this was my count also. The men who brought us from Plum Island and the guy you just killed. So now we're down to four."

"Good," said Regev. "Our odds are excellent. Five of us. Four of them. And we'll have plenty of cover and the element of surprise."

"Can we still surprise them?" asked one of the mercenaries. "They'll have heard the gunshot."

"They were expecting that," said Quinn. "With me as the target." He gestured toward Bell's body. "Assuming he was planning to fill in the grave when he was done, they won't be expecting him back for a while."

"But from now on," said Regev, "we need to limit ourselves to silenced weapons. We should be able to take the rest of them out and get to the cabin without too much trouble. But here's the tricky part. Once we do, we have two mission parameters that absolutely have to be met. The cabin contains one man and one woman. Dmitri Kovonov and Rachel Howard. First, we have to take Kovonov alive. Second, we have to do this while making sure he doesn't kill Rachel Howard. Both are equally critical."

"You think he'll try to kill her as a last-ditch act?" said one of the mercs.

"Very possibly."

"What if taking out Kovonov is the only way to save the woman?" asked the same man.

"Just make sure it doesn't come to that!" barked Regev.

Realizing this wasn't helpful he paused for a moment and then added, "Capture him alive without Rachel being harmed and your pay will be *quadrupled*."

"That's a generous incentive," said the merc. "But what if it does come to that, *despite* our best efforts?"

Regev and Quinn exchanged pained glances. Quinn was falling in love with the Harvard neuroscientist and Regev was convinced she represented Israel's best hope for avoiding a meltdown. But they had to prevent the nuclear device from being detonated. This was the coldest of equations, but the answer to this question was clear.

"Kovonov must remain alive," spat Regev bitterly, disgusted by a universe that would force him to speak these words. "Even at the expense of Rachel Howard."

72

"Are we ready to do this?" said Regev.

The four men with him made it clear that they were.

"Let's make this count," he said. "I'll take point. Kevin, you take the rear. The rest of you fan out behind me, but not so far as to lose sight of anyone. Far enough apart that if one of us is spotted, we aren't all spotted, but close enough that we don't risk friendly fire."

Regev paused in thought. "We'll pick them off one by one. When all four are down we'll regroup outside the front door of the cabin and I'll give you further instructions."

These orders were acknowledged and the group set off through the woods with Regev in the lead. The Israeli moved like this was an exercise he practiced twice a day. He glided silently through the woods like a panther, his night vision goggles replacing gleaming eyes, every bit as stealthy as this masterful predator.

When Regev got to within fifty yards of the cabin he identified the first of Kovonov's mercenaries and fired a silenced round. Even though a silencer interfered with accuracy he managed a clean head shot and his target collapsed to the ground.

One down. Three more to go.

Regev began to advance toward the cabin once again when he heard screams behind him. He whirled around to witness all hell breaking loose.

Bright ropes of laser light seared the night sky, their origin unclear, and skewered the three mercenaries multiple times. Two were killed instantly by tunnels that were burned straight through their bodies, the diameter of quarters. The third had been severely wounded and tried to run from this unseen enemy, but he managed only a few steps before a blinding laser pierced his chest and he fell to the hard soil.

All three had been killed in seconds.

Quinn, watching this carnage from the rear, rushed forward to take cover behind a tree when one of the beams found him, boring a large hole through his left arm. His instinct was to run to get out of danger, but as he began to move Regev launched his body at him and he was driven backward, away from the cabin.

So much blood poured from his limp arm that he was already growing weak as Regev quickly rolled off of him and pulled them both behind a cluster of trees.

"Shit!" whispered the Israeli, still out of breath from sprinting to tackle Quinn. He reached into one pocket and removed a full aerosol can of wound sealant, along with a sterile package that contained a combination of wound dressing and bandage, and went to work on his American friend to staunch the flow of blood.

"He's deployed Lase-Net," said Regev, speaking rapidly and barely loud enough for Quinn to hear. "A tech our learning enhanced scientists just perfected. It's a set of self-installing drones the size of your hand that contain advanced AI. Release dozens of these around a perimeter you want protected and they disperse into trees. They scan for human heat signatures. When they find one in range they check if it's friend or foe. If foe, they laser it to death."

"How do they know the difference?" whispered Quinn as Regev continued to administer first aid.

"One way is to set the system to recognize friendly phones."

Quinn thought about this for a moment. "Which is why you were immune," he whispered. "You had Bell's phone with you."

Regev nodded. "The system can be set to ignore someone moving in close conjunction with a friendly, in case you want to escort a prisoner through the kill zone. If the prisoner tries to escape, he gets fried."

Quinn realized this explained Bell's warning not to get more than two yards ahead of him. He vaguely recalled the US was working on something similar, but it was a number of years from being realized. Once again, Israel had eaten America's lunch technologically.

The reason Regev had tackled him was now clear. When the Israeli had realized what was happening, and that Quinn was the only one who hadn't entered the laser kill zone, he had raced back to make sure he stayed out of range.

"What now?" whispered Quinn. "Now we're outnumbered, three against two. Or maybe three against one and a half," he added, nodding toward his injured arm.

"Wait here," said Regev under his breath. "These mercs won't venture beyond the laser perimeter and give up their advantage. I'll take one out and bring you back his phone as soon as I can, so we're both immune."

Regev unscrewed the silencer from his gun, since surprise was no longer an option, and disappeared without another word, as catlike as ever. Less than a minute later gunfire could be heard in random locations as Regev fired, moved quickly to another location, and fired again, trying to confuse his foes about his position and giving them a sense they were up against a greater force than they actually were.

This strategy was working beautifully as far as Quinn could tell. Regev seemed to be in five places at once. Shoot, move, shoot, move—he circled around and doubled back like a deft boxer in a two-acre ring.

Five minutes later he returned, hopping on one leg and using trees to steady himself. He had successfully downed one of the mercs, but one of the other two had gotten the drop on him while he was retrieving the fallen soldier's phone for Quinn. His advanced body armor had protected his torso but he had been hit twice in the right leg, and much of this limb now looked like hamburger.

Regev tossed a phone to his American partner.

"How many down?" whispered Quinn as he pocketed the phone and joined the Israeli.

"Just one, I'm afraid."

"Can you apply wound sealant and bandages on your own?"

"Yes," whispered Regev. "Go!" he added, knowing that since he was now the more injured their roles had reversed.

Quinn cut through the trees, his left arm hanging uselessly by his side. He paused to wait out a brief bout of dizziness brought on by loss of blood, which had been slowed considerably but not completely stemmed, and then continued. As he did so he picked up the faintest sound of movement to his right as one of the remaining mercs attempted to outflank him, and caught the neon green image of the man ducking behind a tree.

Quinn rushed away from the cabin and to his left, putting a number of trees between him and his adversary. He circled back silently and threw a pebble to the right of his quarry, a tactic as old as time yet almost always effective. The mercenary instinctively swiveled toward the sound and as he did so Quinn emerged from behind a tree and put a bullet into his head.

He was rushing back to Regev, who was just completing his self-administered first aid, when the last mercenary emerged from a tree behind the Israeli.

"Eyal, dive!" screamed Quinn frantically.

Regev used his good leg to launch himself five feet to the left, crashing into the hard soil as a shot missed him by inches. Quinn rolled, firing three times as he did. Only one of the shots hit the target, but it did so with deadly effectiveness.

He raced to the fallen merc, kicked his gun away, and then checked for a pulse.

"He's gone," said Quinn. "That's all of them."

He held out his right hand to pull Regev up. "I guess we're even now."

"*Even?*" rasped Regev weakly, managing the faintest of smiles to go along with his feigned outrage. "I saved you three times. You saved me once."

"Well, if you want to get *technical* about it," said Quinn wryly as he finished pulling Regev to a standing position.

The Israeli may have managed to seal and bandage his wounds while Quinn was gone, but he was in bad shape. "Put your arm around me and use me as a crutch," said Quinn. "On my left so I can still shoot."

The Israeli did as he was instructed and Quinn pulled him along to the cabin, the dizziness returning. He whispered his plan to Regev as they moved. He led the Israeli to the front window and left him there to use it as a crutch while he returned to the front door, approaching from the side.

Quinn drew in a deep breath and signaled to Regev. The moment the Israeli acknowledged the signal he shot through the lock and dived away from the door, an instant before a volley of automatic fire emerged from the cabin that would have turned him into a sieve if he had remained where he was. A moment later Regev shot the window, shattering it, and dropped to the ground as a volley of bullets was sent his way, also.

"Come in here and Rachel Howard is dead!" shouted Kovonov after all gunfire had ceased. As Quinn had hoped, when Kovonov realized there were at least two men outside, men who had somehow defeated both his laser perimeter and mercenaries, he had given up trying to fight his way out.

The Israeli had pulled himself to a sitting position but he looked to be on the verge of losing consciousness. Quinn didn't think he would last much longer, which was a big problem.

"Your plan has failed!" shouted Quinn with all of his strength. "Tell us where to find your puppet in time to stop him."

"That's never going to happen!" shouted Kovonov. "No matter what."

"There are four of us out here who know you're responsible," said Quinn. "So you've failed. Millions will die, but *you'll* be blamed. Not ISIS."

With his last vestiges of energy, trying to sound strong, Regev shouted two sentences. The first was in Hebrew, but then realizing it might be important for Quinn to know what he was saying, he switched over to English. "Tell us how to stop this, leave Rachel in peace, and we'll let you escape."

"Agent *Regev?*" said Kovonov in shock. "Is that really you?"

Kovonov laughed. "You're out there with agents of the *Mossad*, Agent Quinn?" he said derisively, his tone now suggesting he felt he had regained the upper hand. "Do you really think your new friends are going to tell the world an *Israeli* was behind this?"

Quinn glanced over at Regev who now appeared to have finally lost consciousness.

"Why not?" shouted Quinn. "Israel won't be blamed. We'll make sure they know you were acting alone. That you had become insane."

Kovonov laughed. "You can't really be that naive. Israel gets blamed for *all* the ills of the world. We've saved you from six nuclear detonations, but that won't matter. Even knowing I went rogue, Israel will get blamed, and Davinroy will let it happen. Scapegoating Israel has become an international sport. You aren't even Jewish, Quinn, but surely you must know this is true."

Quinn did know. Kovonov was right. It was impossible to miss. Radicalized Muslims cut off heads, burned people alive, and treated women like vermin, even killing them for trying to go to school. But the UN—packed with Islamic countries—spent all of its time condemning *Israel* for human rights violations, ignoring atrocities committed in Muslim nations hundreds of times worse than any supposed Israeli offenses.

"So my plan goes forward," shouted Kovonov with absolute conviction. "And you can choose. You can tell the truth, and blame me. Or you can let ISIS take the fall, and let this be a catalyst to eliminate a threat you know has to be stopped before it destroys civilization."

Quinn was fading fast. Given this turn of events, he was now certain he had no chance to stop the nuke from detonating, no matter what he did. His best bet was to try to at least save Rachel before he collapsed. If he didn't resolve this soon he and Regev were both dead, and Rachel was lost.

"Okay, you win!" he shouted as the world continued to spin around him. "You're right. We can't let Israel take the fall. But here are *your* choices. We can storm in and fill you with holes, risking that Rachel will be hit in the crossfire. Or you can leave her and your virus behind and exit through the back door. We give our word we won't follow."

"How do I know I can trust you?"

"You don't. But it's the truth. And if you want to live it's your only choice. We're breaching in exactly one minute, regardless."

A minute passed without a response.

It was now or never, Quinn decided. He could well be walking into a curtain of bullets, but he had run out of options. He stumbled through the door, expecting to be cut down like a weed, but no gunfire came.

Kovonov had left through the back door. Rachel was still zip-tied to the chair, her mouth once again sealed with duct tape, but very much healthy and alive. His eyes welled up with tears upon seeing her.

The Land Rover keys were still on the hook by the door, and Quinn noted that the virus container was still on the table. Kovonov had decided to trust that Quinn would honor his word if he stuck to the bargain.

He cut Rachel loose as the last bit of adrenaline he possessed shot into his depleted bloodstream, allowing him to remain conscious for just a few minutes longer.

73

Rachel drove away from the cabin and followed her phone's directions to the nearest grocery store twenty minutes away, which had closed more than an hour earlier. After Quinn had rescued her, he had managed to help her load Regev into the Land Rover and had seatbelted himself in before finally blacking out.

Kovonov's stainless steel container was on the floor of the passenger's seat and she had confirmed that the vial of virus was still snugly inside.

When she hit a main artery that would take her most of the way to her destination she instructed her phone to sync itself to the car's speaker system and call Cris Coffey's emergency number. The call went directly to voice mail.

"Cris, call me back immediately!" she said, unable to keep the panic from her voice. "I promise this is the most urgent call you've ever gotten."

Shit, shit, shit, shit!

Two men she cared deeply about were dying beside her and San Francisco was about to be vaporized, and no Cris Coffey. Without him she couldn't reach the president, and without this there was no hope.

She made it to the grocery store in fifteen minutes, just after eleven. Time zero was in less than an hour.

She pulled into the dark, empty parking lot. Just as she was shutting off the engine the phone rang.

"Rachel, where are you?" blurted out Coffey when she had accepted the call. "I heard you were taken from the island. Are you okay?"

"I'm at the Healthy Foods Grocery on Elm Street," she replied, relieved that he had finally gotten back to her. "Near Lancaster,

Pennsylvania. First things first: Kevin Quinn and Eyal Regev are both with me. Badly injured. Can you scramble a Black medevac helicopter to get these men medical attention and get us out of here?"

"Eyal Regev? What is *he* doing there? How badly is Kevin wounded?"

"No time for questions, Cris. Can you get us a medevac?"

"Yes. Hold tight. I'll be back on the line shortly."

Three minutes later Coffey returned. "Your ride will land in the parking lot in about an hour. It's the best I could do. It'll have a doctor on board and will be prepared for incoming wounded."

"Thanks, Cris. Now I need Davinroy. Immediately! San Francisco is about to be destroyed, but I think I can stop it. Get me through to Davinroy!"

"How do you know about San Francisco?"

"Long story, and we may be out of time already. Get me Davinroy!"

"I can't. He's on board a specialized aircraft for use during a nuclear threat. I wasn't on duty at the time or I'd be up there, but they've battened down the hatches. Full-on emergency mode. No way I get through to him now. Last I heard, hours ago, was that he had a call scheduled with the terrorist at 11:30 and was confident he could buy a reprieve. But Davinroy only sees the distorted view of reality he wants to see, so I doubt this is true."

"You're right. The attack is going forward no matter what he does. Do you have any contacts who *could* break through to him?"

"I'm sorry, Rachel, but no power on Earth will get you Davinroy's ear before midnight."

"Okay Cris, I'm forced to try plan B. Gotta go."

"Good luck," said Cris Coffey solemnly.

Rachel took a deep breath and called the emergency number Regev had given her before they had parted ways in Waltham. It was picked up by a woman on the first ring, answering in Hebrew.

"Do you speak English?" said Rachel.

"Of course. You've reached the Jerusalem Trading Company. How can I help you?"

"My name is Rachel Howard. I was told to call this number in an emergency. I need to speak with Avi Wortzman right away."

"Please hold," said the woman. She came back on the line only a few seconds later. "Yes, we have you on our list, Dr. Howard. Can you tell me the nature of the emergency? It's six fifteen in the morning here."

"I don't care what time it is! Get me Wortzman! Wake him and get him on the line! I was told I rated top treatment. This is the mother of all emergencies."

"Please hold for Avi Wortzman," said the woman evenly.

Two minutes later Wortzman was on the line. "Rachel? Are you okay? Where is Eyal? I've been up for hours, waiting to hear from him."

"He and Quinn are injured, but they got us away from Kovonov."

"Thank God."

"Were you aware Kovonov has a puppet about to blow the Korean nuke you left buried in San Francisco?"

"*What?*" replied Wortzman in dismay. "No," he mumbled. "I had no idea. This is worse than I feared. Davinroy boarded an E-4B and is in the air, so I knew something big was brewing. But this is *unspeakable*. What could he be thinking?"

"It's set to go off at midnight, in about forty-five minutes. His plan is for ISIS to get the blame so the US will wipe them out. I might be able to stop it, but I can't get through to Davinroy."

"At this point, even I can't help you with that."

"I know. But I believe you can do what I needed Davinroy to do. I need you to take over the US cell phone grid."

"What makes you think we have this capability?"

"Can you or can't you? No bullshit. Millions of lives are at stake. Don't tell me about political fallout, or strained relations. You guys all spy on each other and play stupid games. I'm sure you know how to screw with each others' electrical and communications grids, even though you're allies."

There was a long pause, during which Rachel held her breath.

"Yes," said Wortzman finally. "I can do that."

Rachel threw her head back over the car's headrest in relief, exhaling loudly. "Awesome!" she said to the Land Rover's ceiling. "How long will it take?"

"Probably under an hour."

"That's not good enough. Get it done in thirty minutes. I'm sending a short file to you now. Once you have control of the grid, ramp up the transmission strength to its highest level and broadcast the signals specified in the file right away. Repeat it over and over until just past midnight in Washington DC. Understood?"

"Why?"

"Too long to explain. But there's a chance it can save San Francisco. Promise me you'll get it done."

"I will," said Wortzman solemnly. "In thirty minutes or less," he added as he ended the call.

Rachel remained in the parked Land Rover and immediately called Karen Black, waking her from a sound sleep.

"Rachel, are you okay?" she mumbled, the third person in a row who had asked this same question. Her voice strengthened as adrenaline drove her fully awake. "I heard you and Kevin had disappeared. What happened?"

"No time to explain. I need you to get Carmilla and take her to the MRI room. Close it up and stay with her there until 12:15."

"What?"

"Please! Just do it! Trust me. Get her inside, close the door and don't let her out for any reason until 12:15. I'll explain later, but this could not be more critical."

"Okay. I'll do it."

"Thanks, Karen!" she said. "I'll explain soon," she added as she ended the call.

With this done, Rachel exited the vehicle and popped the hatch. She opened a recessed compartment and unscrewed a tire iron attached to a spare tire. She approached the glass entrance to the grocery store, using her phone's flashlight app to light the way, and stood to the side, swinging the tire iron for all she was worth.

The glass was largely shatterproof, but after five or six blows she managed to forge a hole large enough for her to get through. She braced herself for the earsplitting sound of alarms, but none came. Much to her great relief the dark night remained quiet.

Rachel rushed through the store searching for the kitchenware aisle. Being in a grocery that was as dark as a cave was unsettling, but no more so than anything else she'd been through that night.

She found the aisle she was looking for and illuminated the aluminum foil offerings with her phone. She chose the widest roll available—eighteen inches—and noted that it was twenty-five feet long. More than enough for her needs.

Clutching her bounty, Rachel Howard returned to the car, dropped the tire iron to the pavement, and managed to slide Quinn to the ground beside it. She began to wrap aluminum foil over every square inch of his head, lifting it gently when necessary, and continued this process all the way to the bottom of his ribcage, turning his upper half into a silvery mummy. She repeated this procedure a second time for good measure, making sure to provide enough ventilation for him to breathe.

With this completed she sat on the pavement beside a man she was coming to love and stared at the night sky.

How had it come to this? Two men she cared about deeply were dying nearby and all she could do was wait for Armageddon, dependent on the head of the Mossad to seize control of America's cell phone infrastructure, at her insistence, to have any chance at heading it off.

And she had thought calling her new lab the Anus was surreal.

She broke out laughing from the ridiculousness of it all. She considered checking on Avi Wortzman's progress, but forced herself to leave him alone, since another call would only cause a further delay. All she could do was sit in a dark parking lot and watch over an aluminum mummy.

A bright light appeared from out of nowhere and blinded her.

"Freeze!" said a male voice.

Rachel almost starting laughing again when she saw it was a young police offer, scared out of his mind, pointing his gun at her. After facing scores of mercenaries with automatic weapons, a baby-faced rural cop who looked to be fresh out of the academy wasn't all that frightening. She realized that just because she hadn't heard an alarm when she had broken into the store didn't mean a silent alarm hadn't sounded.

She held up her hands.

The cop gestured at the tire iron beside her. "You're under arrest for breaking and entering," he said. "You have the right—"

He stopped in mid-sentence when he noticed the wrapped body next to her for the first time.

Alarmed, he swept his flashlight in a broad arc, gasping when he spotted yet another lifeless body in the vehicle. He shined his flashlight through the window, illuminating the blood-covered Israeli in the backseat.

The cop's naturally pale face whitened further. "Did you *kill* them?" he asked in dismay.

Rachel sighed. "No. They're badly injured, but I'm trying to save them."

"Sure you are. I guess someone else broke into the store and left these bodies and a tire iron next to you, right? This is just an elaborate frame up."

"No, I admit to breaking into the store. But if you'll check, the cash register wasn't touched. I'll pay for the door and the aluminum foil."

"Who are you?" he said as if he had come across a unicorn.

"Would you believe a world-renowned neuroscientist?"

The cop shook his head. "You are one sick puppy."

He gestured to Quinn. "Uncover him. I want to verify that he's still alive."

Rachel's face became panic stricken. "I can't do that," she said. "You got me. I destroyed a door and stole some aluminum foil. And I'll accept the consequences. But just let me leave this foil in place for another few minutes and I'll do anything you ask. I'm begging you."

The cop crouched down while still holding a gun on her. "If you won't do it," he said, reaching for Quinn's head, "I'll do it myself."

Rachel snatched the tire iron from the pavement and lunged. The young cop's eyes went wide, but he didn't get off a shot as the tire iron came crashing down on his right arm, sending his gun flying.

He grunted in pain and reached for his gun, but Rachel kicked it ten yards farther away into the darkness as though the parking lot were a hockey rink. The cop rushed off, frantically searching for the weapon with his flashlight.

Rachel didn't hesitate. She fell back beside Quinn and removed the gun he had been using from his pants, being careful not to disturb the foil.

She rose from the pavement with her arm extended. "Freeze!" she screamed, unable to believe she was actually doing this. "Take another step and you're dead! Try to shine that light in my eyes and I'll shoot!" she added.

The cop stopped in his tracks and slowly turned to face her, careful to train his light at her knees, which provided enough illumination to verify that she had a gun pointed at him, one more lethal than his own, which was still five feet away.

"Do what I tell you and you're in no danger," said Rachel. "This will be over soon. In about twenty minutes or so a helicopter is going to land in this parking lot. The people inside are going to take me and these two men with them, and you'll be free to go. You're perfectly safe. I'm sorry that I hurt you, but I didn't have a choice."

The cop's eyes remained wild, certain he was about to be killed by someone who had escaped from the psychiatric ward at a hospital. "So we're just waiting for your helicopter?" he said in an obvious attempt to humor her. She could almost hear the word *imaginary* inserted before the word *helicopter*.

"You think I'm totally out of my mind, don't you?"

"Not at all."

Rachel laughed wildly, which didn't help her cause. *Of course* he thought she was crazy. She was holding him at gunpoint in a dark parking lot waiting to see if the world would end.

"Maybe I am crazy," she said with a heavy sigh. "Either way, we're both going to find out soon."

74

Haji Ahmad al-Bilawy was *euphoric*, a feeling beyond any he thought he might ever experience. He was but minutes away from plunging a knife deep into the eye of the Great Satan. And he had just ended a call with the President of the United States.

Davinroy had been pathetic, and al-Bilawy had strung him along, made him squirm. By the end the president was begging, offering anything al-Bilawy wanted to call it off, or even delay the strike for half a day.

Al-Bilawy had taken great pleasure in teasing Davinroy, toying with him, making him grovel, pushing him into utter embarrassment and beyond, and finally, with ten minutes left on the clock and the United States powerless to stop him, he had cut Davinroy off at the knees. He had figuratively spat in his face, displayed his contempt, and made sure the president knew that this was just the beginning. That Allah had no mercy for the infidel, and this would be but a taste of things to come.

Al-Bilawy had a video ready to go just after midnight, to be sent to YouTube and media outlets around the world. It would show the strength of ISIS, the greatness of Allah, and the weakness of the United States. It would make it clear for all the world to see who had been responsible for this heroic deed, and how Davinroy had pleaded like a little girl. It would be ISIS's finest hour.

He checked the device that would detonate the bomb and carefully entered the codes that he had committed so firmly to memory they seemed carved into his brain. He waited eagerly to press the button, to send the world into a new age, and the caliphate on its way to a new glory.

Six minutes to go.

He desperately wanted to jump the gun, the wait for the ecstasy to come now seeming eternal. But he owed it to those who had sacrificed to make this happen, who had planned this to perfection, not to deviate from the plan by even an instant.

He had tapped into an atomic clock on his phone so he could be as precise as possible. He would wait until the stroke of midnight in Washington DC, the center of power of this corrupt country, and do what he now knew he had been put on this Earth to do.

"All praise to Allah," he said aloud in Arabic.

A triumphant smile began to spread across his face but stopped abruptly of its own accord. Just as he realized his face was frozen, an overwhelming smell of burnt rubber assaulted his nostrils. He turned to see what might be causing the pungent odor when his sight stopped working. He blinked several times, but this did nothing to relieve his sudden blindness.

His euphoria of a moment earlier turned to pure, unreasoning terror.

This, too, was short-lived as his entire body started convulsing and he crashed to the floor in agony. He bit down so hard on his tongue it began pouring blood into his mouth, mixing with copious amounts of saliva to produce a red foam that slithered down his face. He lost bladder and bowel control at the same time and both systems voided explosively into his pants.

His heart beat erratically and he gasped for breath before his respiratory system shut down entirely, followed seconds later by his heart.

During a period of only twelve seconds so many of al-Bilawy's systems broke down or malfunctioned that he died a horrible death many times over. What had once been a zealot dedicated to bringing about an apocalypse was now a dead husk lying in a pool of his own saliva, blood, urine, and excrement.

As close as al-Bilawy had been to fulfilling his life's purpose, he had expired far too quickly to have any understanding of what was happening to him, or to regret that he hadn't chosen to detonate the nuclear device a few minutes early after all.

75

Andrew Danson doubted he would live out the night. The crazed woman holding him at gunpoint had made him move another ten yards away from his gun, and she had likely broken his arm with a tire iron, although he couldn't be sure if the blinding pain he was feeling was simply due to blunt force trauma brought on by her savage blow.

He had only been a cop for six months, so of course he had drawn night duty. He hated the graveyard shift because of what it was doing to his natural sleep rhythm, making him feel like a vampire, out all night and sleeping all day. But more than this, he hated it because of the unrelenting boredom. Other than having to check out the occasional false alarm generated by a residential home security system or help out with a rare predawn auto accident somewhere, there had been as close to zero excitement during the past half year as it was possible to get.

Suddenly he longed for this lack of excitement.

Decades of television dramas had convinced the public that cops always worked with partners, but this was often not the case, especially when it came to night duty in low-crime areas. But he should have called for backup, even before arriving on the scene. He had been a fool.

He had accepted the risk of being killed in the line of duty, but he had always imagined if this ever did come about it would be a result of him intervening in a bank robbery or terrorist attack.

Not like this.

Not at the hands of a crazed woman who killed people, covered them in foil, and ranted about helicopters. People this deranged were impossible to predict. She might let him go as she had promised or might just as easily decide to turn his skull into a coffee mug.

The woman never took her eyes from his, her gun never wavering as she stood guard over her foil-covered prize, a silent vigil that had gone on now for quite some time. Her left arm hung down by her leg, a phone loosely clutched in her hand.

Finally, she broke the long silence. "What time is it?" she asked her phone, as though not having the strength to lift it to her face to see for herself.

"Three minutes past midnight."

The woman winced as though she were in pain. She shot a glance toward the western sky, as if searching for an answer there, and looked to be on the verge of vomiting.

"Are any restaurants in San Francisco open at this time of night?" she asked. Her voice was strained, and it seemed to Danson she was choking back tears.

"Hundreds. San Francisco is on Pacific Standard Time," pointed out the AI function of her phone, "so it is now only three minutes past nine o'clock there."

"Oh, right," croaked the woman. "Call the first restaurant on your list within city limits."

Danson looked on in disbelief. Sure, why not? Maim or kill two men, attack him, hold him at gunpoint, and then order takeout from a restaurant three thousand miles away. No crazier than anything else she had done.

"Calling *Aaron's Sea and Wind Bistro* on Market Street," announced her phone.

The call was answered after three rings. "Aaron's Sea and Wind Bistro," said a man's voice through the speaker, with the typical clamor of a busy restaurant in the background.

The woman become weak in the knees and stumbled, barely avoiding falling to the ground next to her foil-covered victim. "Please tell me you're in downtown San Francisco," she pleaded, her voice thick with emotion.

"We are. We're located at the north end of Market Street."

As Danson looked on in wonder the woman before him underwent a complete transformation. Her mouth dropped open and she whimpered as though a crushing weight had been lifted from her soul. While the gun remained steady in her right hand, her phone slipped from the fingers of her left and dropped to the pavement, while tears began streaming down her face.

Should he say something? Should he try to be sympathetic, or try not to attract attention to himself?

While he was deciding the woman began to hum the unmistakable tune of "The Star Spangled Banner" through her tears, just barely loud enough to be heard. She was dazed, and sounded completely cut off from reality, humming like a woozy fighter hit one too many times in the head.

"Gave proof through the night," she sang faintly under her breath, "that our flag . . . was . . . still . . . there."

She stopped abruptly and tears began to roll down her cheeks even faster.

How was it possible for anyone to be this messed up in the head? wondered Officer Danson.

"Are you okay?" he said finally, hoping this wasn't a mistake.

She nodded, still sobbing and still holding a gun on him. "Oh yeah," she said exultantly. "Everything is great."

As he was wondering what to do next, a helicopter abruptly appeared in the distance from behind a hill, racing at breakneck speed in their direction. In less than a minute, churning through the night air and creating an unmistakable din, it dove like a hawk and settled abruptly fifteen yards away in the empty parking lot.

This time it was the rookie police officer whose mouth dropped open.

And for the first time, Andrew Danson began to wonder if this weeping woman was insane, or if *he* was.

76

It was just after 2:00 a.m. and the militarized 747 rolled to a stop on the runway. Matthew Davinroy had just lived through the most brutal night of his life, and while he had thought of himself as an atheist—pretending to believe in God for political expediency—he had found himself praying as midnight approached.

And perhaps his prayers had been answered. He had dodged a bullet the size of an asteroid. Either al-Bilawy had been bluffing or the bomb had been a dud, as he had been told was a possibility.

Either way, all that mattered was that he had come through this crisis intact. Had the device gone off, the impact it would have had on his presidency, on his legacy, would have been *incalculable.*

Perhaps God had been looking out for him, after all.

77

It wasn't until four in the afternoon, almost sixteen hours after the helicopter had lifted off from the Healthy Foods Grocery parking lot, that Rachel was allowed into the room in the Plum Island infirmary that housed her two favorite men. They had been given blood and meds and had been patched up in flight, a testament to the skills of both the pilot, who had kept the helicopter perfectly level, and the doctor, who had hands as steady as a slab of granite.

After landing on the island they had been rushed to beds, IVs still attached, and had received additional treatment. Regev, who had been shot twice in the leg and who had lost even more blood than Quinn, was still being sedated, but Rachel had been assured he would pull through and eventually regain full use of his leg.

Quinn was weak, but now fully conscious. He had been told the still-unconscious Regev would make a full recovery and that San Francisco was doing fine, but he had no idea how this latter could be possible. He couldn't have been more eager to learn what had happened after he had blacked out.

Rachel described how she had raced to the Healthy Foods Grocery before Cris Coffey had finally returned her call. How he had agreed to send a medevac but had been unable to put her through to the president.

"I don't understand," said Quinn. "What good would Davinroy have done at that point? And how is it that the bomb didn't go off?"

"Not to be immodest," she replied happily, "but you have me to thank for that. And Avi Wortzman."

"Doesn't seem possible," said Quinn, trying to make sense of this. "I don't see any way you could have stopped al-Bilawy." He paused in thought. "Unless . . . did you trick Kovonov into giving you his location?"

"Not a chance. But I knew that al-Bilawy must have been injected with neural nanites. I also knew that he was hiding somewhere in the country. So I wasn't searching for a needle in a haystack. You know," she added with an impish grin, "I had it pretty much narrowed down to the continental United States."

Quinn laughed and then immediately groaned in pain as he realized this wasn't a good idea in his current condition.

"So I thought about my trick with the cell towers," she continued. "How we had reached out and touched Carmilla Acosta and Yosef Mizrahi. We had no idea where they were, but we were still able to manipulate their nanites. I knew I could do the same with al-Bilawy."

"But you'd have to take over the cell grid of the entire country. In record time. And even if you managed that, what memory could you implant that would get him to call it off? Besides, I thought it took you half a day to develop instructions to get the nanites to lay down even the simplest of memories."

"All great points," said Rachel, beaming. "The first part, taking over the cell infrastructure . . ." She shrugged. "Well, that's where Avi Wortzman came in."

Quinn tilted his head in thought, trying to reconstruct what must have happened. "You used the emergency number Eyal gave us to get through to him. You must have guessed Israel had the capability to take control, didn't you?"

Rachel nodded. "I figured I had some pull. Israel is racing toward a catastrophe and Eyal did tell me they think I'm pretty much their only chance to avert it. Not that Wortzman wouldn't have helped under any circumstances, but he asked fewer questions than he would have otherwise. And he did come through with flying colors."

"Have I ever told you that you're brilliant?"

"Actually, yes, several times. But you know, it never really gets old."

"You are absolutely brilliant," said Quinn. "So what memory did you implant? And how did you manage to come up with the required instructions so quickly?"

Rachel shook her head. "Nothing as subtle as a memory. You're right, I couldn't have programmed one in time. But there is one command that is so simple it can be written on the head of a pin. Memories require a complex construction of pathways, a subtle excitation of neurons. But an epileptic seizure is nothing more than the *uncontrolled* firing of neurons. So I transmitted a command to the nanites to cause every single neuron in al-Bilawy's brain to fire at the same time. No finesse, no subtlety—a command that was as basic as it got. But one designed to cause the ultimate seizure."

"Which would do what, exactly?"

"Kill him in seconds. Cause a total meltdown. Al-Bilawy would be unable to control his muscles or his autonomic nervous system. He'd go blind, salivate uncontrollably, lose bowel and bladder function, and his heart and respiration would shut down." She shuddered. "It truly is a horrible way to go."

"Remind me not to piss you off," said Quinn.

Rachel laughed. "If this technology is ever perfected enough to come into use, we'll really have to install a fail-safe so what I did to al-Bilawy can never be repeated."

"Wait a minute," said Quinn, blinking in confusion. "How is it *I'm* not dead? You sent this command across the entire nation. Shouldn't I have had one of these death seizures also?"

"You *should* have," said Rachel. "But I've become very fond of you. So I decided it would be better if you took a pass on the whole, *every neuron firing at once* thing. Which brings me to why I was driving to the grocery store in the first place."

"Yeah, I was getting around to asking about that. It just seemed less important than how you managed to save San Francisco."

"It's how I managed to save *you*. I wrapped your head completely in aluminum foil, and even your upper body."

"You what?"

"First I broke into the store to get the foil, and then I wrapped you like a mummy. I'm not sure that reflective aluminum is your color, but it did block the signal from the cell tower so your nanites stayed calm."

"Aluminum foil is a real thing?" said Quinn in astonishment. "I thought wearing foil headgear was something done by lunatics. Delusional conspiracy theorists who thought it could keep their minds from being taken over by outer space aliens or some other nonsense."

"This is true. But it's also true that nothing blocks radio signals better. Next time you're in a kitchen, use a landline to call your cell until it rings. Then put a single layer of aluminum foil over your cell phone and call again. It won't ring this time."

"No kidding?"

"No kidding. You're living proof that this works."

"I'll be damned," said Quinn. "So I was blacked out in the parking lot of a grocery store covered in aluminum foil." He grinned. "I can't say this is the first time that's happened. But it's definitely the first time it happened when I was *sober*."

Rachel laughed.

"Anything else I should know about?" asked Quinn.

"Well, I did attack the cop who tried to remove your metal helmet. With a tire iron. To save your life." Rachel shrugged. "You know, that's what I do," she added, fighting to keep a straight face.

She went on to describe what had happened in the grocery store parking lot in great detail.

"Wait a minute," said Quinn in alarm when she had finished. "What about Carmilla? Is she okay?"

"She's fine. I thought of her too. You don't have to sleep with me to get my protection."

"Yes, but it is the *best* way," said Quinn with an impish grin. "So how did you save her?"

"I made sure she stayed in the MRI room while the signal was being sent out. Radio waves can ruin the results of an MRI, so MRI rooms are built to block them out. Microwave ovens are too, but I figured the MRI room was the better choice. Not quite as cramped."

"Good call," said Quinn with a smile. "But I bet she's jealous she didn't get the foil treatment," he added wryly.

"How could she not be?"

"That was quite a night," said Quinn.

Rachel leaned forward and kissed him gently. "Yes it was. Glad you made it."

"Thanks to you," he said. "You saved millions of people. It's just too bad that the world will never know what you did."

"I'm okay with that," said Rachel. "I mean, it would probably get me a few free rides on the cable cars, but I'm okay toiling in anonymity. And the truth is," she added more seriously, "it wasn't just me. If you and Eyal hadn't managed to fight your way through a gauntlet, Kovonov's plan would have gone off without a hitch. And I'd either be dead or his toy right now."

"We have Eyal to thank for that. If not for him, I'd be in a ditch by a river."

"Don't downplay your own heroism. How about you thank Eyal, and I'll thank you?"

"Now that sounds like a good plan," said Quinn. "And when I've recovered, I have an idea of how I'd like you to show your gratitude."

"Does it involve a bed?"

"Lucky guess," said Quinn with a broad grin.

78

Two days later Prime Minister Ori Kish sent a private plane to transport Quinn, Regev, and the esteemed Professor Rachel Howard to the Holy Land.

Carmilla had steadily improved. She had become fascinated by the application of advanced DNA synthesis techniques to neuroscience, which helped occupy her attention.

Her strength of will and level-headedness also allowed her to counteract the damage Kovonov had done better than most would have managed, and while still suffering from loss and depression she was holding up well. Her husband, Miguel, was now staying with her on the island for an indefinite period, although not permitted to venture into secure areas.

She had told him how her mind had been tampered with, how memories of an infidelity he hadn't committed had been implanted, and how intense feelings of depression had been triggered. But she had left out her physical encounters with Kovonov. She had been manipulated into sleeping with him, mentally raped, and saw no reason to burden her husband with this knowledge, especially now that the prospects for their marriage were stronger than ever.

Eyal Regev was recovering, but would need to use crutches for some time to come, and Quinn's arm would take time to fully heal as well. The two men, who had hit it off so well and so quickly in Waltham, continued to grow even closer, and were well on their way to building the strongest friendship either had ever experienced.

During the flight to Israel, Rachel completed the programming for a new set of implantable memories, tailored to Avi Wortzman's specifications. The Mossad leader then used these false memories to cause four moles that Kovonov had manipulated to self-identify, so he was now confident his organization was clean once again.

The morning after Kovonov had bolted out of the back door of his cabin, Wortzman had alerted the American team hunting for him that a Mossad agent, now injured, had located Kovonov in the woods of Pennsylvania, and had given them exact GPS coordinates. To prevent additional lives from being lost, he had made sure they were also warned to be wary of a new automatic perimeter protection technology that Kovonov had been rumored to have developed.

Wortzman would have liked to wait until he could have had a team retrieve this technology, but Kovonov's elimination was too important for any further delay. Even so, somehow, *inexplicably*, the Americans had failed to find him. Wortzman had been furious, not understanding how they could have possibly let Kovonov slip through their net, but there was nothing he could do about it.

Seven days after al-Bilawy had been stopped, Ori Kish, Avi Wortzman, Greg Henry, and Matthew Davinroy met around a virtual conference room once again, at the request of the president.

"How goes the hunt for our Russian-born rogue?" said Wortzman when pleasantries, brief as they were, had been dispensed with.

"Not well," said Henry. "It's possible he never made it out of the woods alive. He could have gotten hopelessly lost and starved to death. He could have fallen over a cliff or into a river. Or maybe he lost a skirmish with a wild animal. We don't know. All we know is that we haven't found him."

"Well, thanks for the effort," said the head of Mossad. "Keep us posted if anything turns up."

"I will," said Henry.

"I trust our fly-drone experts have all now arrived in America and are bringing your scientists up to speed," said Prime Minister Kish.

"As far as I know," said Davinroy, clearly not intending to elaborate further.

"Any word on your team's assessment of the technology?" pressed Kish. "Do they seem enthusiastic?"

"Not really," said the president. "But I'm sure they're learning a few new tricks."

A few new tricks? Wortzman wanted to strangle the smug bastard, but he decided he shouldn't be surprised by how far Davinroy went to downplay what Israel was providing. The tech was five to ten years beyond what the American team could do. And as far as not being enthusiastic, Wortzman's people had reported that the American scientists were wetting their pants, in awe of the breakthroughs his scientists were sharing.

"How goes the initiative that your Agent Regev is leading?" said Greg Henry. "Any progress in understanding how false memories might have been implanted in Special Agent Quinn? Or who might be responsible?"

"Professor Howard has made excellent progress," said Wortzman. "Special Agent Quinn has been key, as well. Thank you again for loaning them to us. I'd like to schedule another meeting very soon so they can present their findings to you."

"We'll put something on the calendar," said Henry.

"I don't know if Special Agent Coffey has mentioned it," added Wortzman, "but since this is a joint US/Israeli operation, he's shared some research from one of your Black Site neuroscience teams. He didn't disclose its location, of course."

"Of course," repeated Henry.

"Rachel Howard was very impressed with the work of the head of this lab, a Dr. Karen Black. Apparently there is another woman who is consulting there, Dr. Carmilla Acosta. Anyway, we probed to see if they might be amenable to being part of the Regev task force, and they seemed eager to join up. I assume you're okay with that?"

This time the president fielded the question. "If Professor Howard is happy," he said, "and the scientists in question are happy, I can't imagine why they shouldn't all work together."

"Excellent," said Ori Kish. While he had been content to let Wortzman respond to Henry, he preferred to respond to Davinroy himself. "I know Rachel will be excited to hear the news."

"Speaking of Rachel Howard," said the president, "has she left Israel at any time during the past few weeks?"

"She hasn't," said Kish. "Why do you ask?"

"I'm sure you're aware we had a scare a week ago today, and were forced to briefly board our command and control aircraft."

"Yes, we had heard, ah . . . rumors to that effect," said Kish. "I don't suppose you'd care to share what that was all about?"

Davinroy smiled humorlessly. "Not really, no. But it was a very strange night. You know we found a cabin, dead bodies, and an automated laser defense system very near where your man spotted Kovonov. But later it came to our attention that a woman had broken into a grocery store on the night in question, very near this location."

He paused and searched the two Israelis for any reaction.

"Go on," said Kish evenly.

"Apparently the woman and two wounded men flew off in a helicopter," said Davinroy. "The thing is," he added, raising his eyebrows, "no one seems to know whose helicopter it was or what it was doing there."

"That is strange," said Kish.

The president's face flashed his hatred of the Israeli Prime Minister for just a moment before becoming neutral once again. "Our people ran the store's video footage of the break in," he said. "The woman stole a single roll of aluminum foil. That's it. The footage wasn't as clear as we would like, given it was very dark and the camera didn't have high-end nighttime imaging, but we ran it through our software anyway. Came back with an eighty-seven percent likelihood of being a match to Rachel Howard. "

"Wow," said Wortzman, "that's even stranger. Wasn't her though."

"Right, because she's been in Israel the whole time?"

"Exactly."

The president studied the Mossad leader for several seconds. "Then another strange thing," he added. "That very night, our nation's cell phone grid was taken over for a few minutes. Just before midnight."

"Your entire grid?" said Kish in apparent alarm. "Do you think the Chinese were testing their capabilities?"

Davinroy glared at him. "No, my best people tell me the signature of how this was accomplished was wrong for the Chinese. They told me the approach smacked more of being something the *Israelis* might do."

Kish shrugged. "That is odd. It wasn't us, of course, but if you send over the data, we'll be happy to help you identify who it might have been."

"No need," said Davinroy caustically, "I wouldn't want you to go *too* far out of your way to be helpful."

"Let us know if you change your mind," said Kish. "Anything else?"

"Yes," said Greg Henry. "We also found an ISIS soldier. High level. Name of al-Bilawy. He was in a home outside of Knoxville, Tennessee, with an airtight communications firewall. Turns out he had suffered a seizure the likes of which our doctors had never seen before. Massive. His brain was fried from the inside, and his body didn't make out all that well either."

"Difficult for me to grieve too hard for a man like that," said Kish. "There are those who might argue that his death is probably for the best."

"*Definitely* for the best," said Henry. "But due to some circumstances we don't want to get into, we can pinpoint the time of his death very accurately. We know he was alive at 11:49 and that he died before midnight. We believe he died right within the narrow window that our cell grid was seized and used by some other party. We've studied the signal that was broadcast during the siege, but it's nothing but harmless noise."

"Very bizarre," said Wortzman.

"And you know nothing about this?" said the president dubiously.

"Should we?" said Kish with a shrug.

Wortzman knew the Americans were almost certain they were lying, but he was confident they wouldn't push it. Israel was transferring game-changing technologies to them, useful for much more than just drones, and their crisis had magically resolved.

To borrow an American idiom, Wortzman felt sure they weren't about to look this gift horse too hard in the mouth.

"Getting back to the emergency you had that same night," continued the prime minister, "I trust everything turned out okay. Whatever it is that had your top people so . . . excited."

"It all turned out very well," said Davinroy.

The president paused and glanced at Henry, seemingly reluctant to continue. "But I should tell you that I've decided to use the bully pulpit to drum up greater public support for a more aggressive anti terror campaign. I plan to lean hard on ISIS and other jihadist movements. This will consist of a far greater deployment of resources, looser rules of engagement, and even boots on the ground. It's time to clean out the swamp."

The hint of a smile passed over Ori Kish's face. "I consider this very good news," he said. "As you know, Mr. President, I have long advocated for this type of strategy. Israel will, of course, support this effort with intelligence and in any other way that we can. You can count on us."

"Good to know," said Davinroy dryly. "I had a feeling that I could."

79

After the meeting with Davinroy and Henry ended, Rachel Howard, Eyal Regev, and Kevin Quinn were escorted into the conference room. A selection of ice-cold drinks was brought in, including several bottles of Snapple peach tea, Rachel's favorite, which was no accident.

Wortzman quickly described how the call with the president and the secretary of DHS had gone, including the latest on the hunt for Kovonov, and answered their questions.

When this was done, the prime minister got down to the most important business he had ever conducted. He locked his gaze on Rachel Howard as though she were the only one in the room. "So you've now had several days to meet the key players on our neuroscience team," he said to her as she swallowed a mouthful of peach tea. "How has that gone?"

"It's been great," she replied. "You have some wonderfully impressive people, and they couldn't have been nicer."

Kish laughed. "Good to hear. They really are nice. Truly. But they've also been told to treat you like royalty. To throw themselves on broken glass and let you walk on their backs so you don't scuff your shoes."

Rachel smiled. "You've definitely made no secret that you want to keep me happy," she said. "I'll give you that. My quarters are spectacular. The personal shopper, maid, and chef are nice touches also. And the freshly cut flowers every morning. But none of this is necessary."

"It is," said Kish. "You know we're doing it for selfish reasons. Well, not entirely selfish. As Eyal explained, having our top people go mad will have worldwide repercussions."

"You mean many hundreds of additional Kovonovs?" said Quinn wryly. "Yeah, I think we get how the possible repercussions could spread beyond Israel's borders."

Rachel swallowed hard. Even *one* Kovonov had almost proven too many, although he was especially talented, even among the talented bunch to come. He was also potentially still at large.

The last Korean nuke left in America had now been removed and defused, and Kovonov no longer had his virus, but it was still unsettling to know he might be out there somewhere.

"The upcoming crisis will be bad," said Wortzman, "but it won't be like having multiple Kovonovs running around. We're now fully prepared for the personality changes that will come over our people. We aren't about to let those affected out of our sight. And we'll most likely put them under house arrest when they're approaching their sell-by date. But there are many powerful people involved, and this will be a disaster no matter how you slice it."

Rachel nodded. Regev had already told her that two of the people who would be affected were sitting right in front of her, the prime minister and the head of Mossad. Both had found the use of Matrix Learning too tempting to resist, although, according to Regev, neither had indulged all that much, meaning both would retain their sanity for at least the next year.

"But let me get back to why we feel it's necessary to pamper you," continued Kish. "While the tipping point of this crisis is still a ways off, every second counts. We know you need rest and recreation. But our goal is to see to it that you're either working on solving this problem, resting, or enjoying yourself. We want to take every chore off your hands. Anyone can cook and clean and do laundry. Only *you* can get us out of this mess."

"I'm flattered," said Rachel.

"As I told you before," said Regev, "it isn't flattery. It's honesty. *Reality*. I *know* you can solve this," he added with such conviction it was as if the matter had already been settled.

"Several of the scientists I've met this week seem to me to be more capable than I am."

"I explained why that might be the case in Waltham," said Regev.

Rachel smiled. "I know you did, Eyal. And I wasn't pointing this out because I lack confidence. I was pointing it out because it demonstrates the truth of what you were telling me."

"I'm not sure I'm following," said Wortzman.

"I told her that far lesser scientists than her had made major breakthroughs after undergoing Matrix Learning," explained Regev. "After loading several other disciplines into their minds."

"Which brings us to the crux of the matter," said Rachel. "The elephant in the room. What you really want to know. Am I willing to undergo Matrix Learning myself? For the cause?"

"Yes," admitted Kish. "Knowing that if you don't solve it in time, you'll follow the rest of us over the cliff."

This was something Rachel had been pondering since Regev had first proposed it back in Waltham.

"My interactions with your people have been eye-opening," she said. "I've been able to witness just how much of an advantage an encyclopedic working knowledge of neuroscience and all related fields can give someone. Your scientists possess knowledge it would take me thirty years of study to learn on my own."

Rachel decided that Matrix Learning truly was the ultimate capability. She had familiarized herself with the work of the scientists she had met, before and after their use of this technology, and it was night and day. The tremendous additional working knowledge they had downloaded allowed them to catapult beyond her current capabilities. She had been five lengths ahead of the pack, and now they were one length ahead of *her*.

But if she were to undergo this flash education, she could only imagine where she might end up, what she might be able to accomplish. If it had even half the effect on her that it had on the others she had met, she was as confident now as the Israelis that she could solve their problem. She wondered what problems in neuroscience she *wouldn't* be able to solve.

Rachel had known that if Matrix Learning could give her any added chance to avert the coming disaster, she had to undergo the procedure no matter what. The stakes were too high to worry about her own future. And how could she not try it out, anyway? She had spent the bulk of her career working toward this technology. You didn't spend your life designing rockets only to refuse to travel in one because of the risk.

But the past few days had impacted her attitude dramatically. Having the chance to meet those who had benefited from this technology had changed everything. Where she had been reluctant to go forward, even fearful, she was now giddy at the prospect. The potential of Matrix Learning was greater even than she had imagined. Rachel was now eager to see what she could accomplish, convinced she could find the antidote to the poison she was choosing to ingest in time to save her sanity.

She had discussed her decision with Quinn prior to the meeting, and his reaction had surprised her. He told her he believed their relationship was evolving into something special. And while he agreed she had no choice, he feared what might happen to their relationship if the knowledge gulf between them grew even larger.

So if she was going to take this risk, he insisted on doing so as well. He would see to it he was programmed with a PhD level of neuroscience education. This would still leave a massive gap between them, but at least it wouldn't be the size of the Grand Canyon.

Rachel was optimistic by nature, but she felt more hopeful about the future course of her life than ever. If a genie had offered to conjure up her ideal man, she would never have been so audacious as to ask for a handsome Secret Service agent who could be her close friend, confidant, lover, and protector, and who also possessed an advanced knowledge of neuroscience—not to mention having technology in his head she couldn't wait to study further.

There had been a long silence in the conference room as everyone waited for Rachel's next utterance. She decided she had made them sweat long enough. Now it was time to use her power to do a little arm twisting. *A lot* of arm twisting.

She faced the Israeli prime minister. "You've said you think I can avert your crisis if I cram more knowledge into my brain," she said. "Well, with all due modesty, I've come to believe you're right."

The three Israelis in the room brightened enough to light a cave. "Does that mean you're in?" said Kish excitedly

Rachel nodded. "I'm in. But I do have some conditions," she added quickly. "Maybe *demands* would be the better word."

"Anything," said Kish, his enthusiasm not diminished in the slightest.

"We'll see. I plan to drive a hard bargain. And this isn't about me. I won't be asking for something easy like having a chocolate placed on my pillow each night."

"Which we're glad to do also," said Kish with a smile. He quickly became serious once more. "All right, then. Tell me what you want."

Rachel decided to start with a demand she knew Kish would meet. They had already assured her she could choose her own team, from both the Mossad group and the group on Plum Island, and that Regev and Quinn would be key players, in security and other capacities.

But Quinn felt they owed their favorite Israeli even more.

"I want Eyal Regev promoted," she began. "Without him Kevin and I would be dead several times over and San Francisco would be devoid of all life. He performed brilliantly and heroically. I want you to award him your country's most prestigious medal, whatever that is. And I want his salary doubled."

The blood drained from Regev's face and he held out his hands helplessly. "I didn't put her up to this," he said to Wortzman and Kish, clearly embarrassed. "Honestly."

Wortzman looked amused. "First of all," he said to Rachel, "we're well aware of Agent Regev's contributions. His skills have not gone unnoticed. Which is why he was sent on a mission to recruit you in the first place. His promotion and medal are already in the works. I was going to tell him about them by the end of the week. Thanks for ruining the surprise," he added with a smile. "The salary thing we weren't planning on, but consider it done."

Regev looked like he wanted to crawl under the table. Quinn had told her he wouldn't be happy about being part of her negotiation, but she felt confident he'd get over it when the first of his new paychecks arrived.

"What else do you need?" said Kish.

"I need your word that once I've solved this problem, you'll put Matrix Learning in the private sector, agree to disclose it to the world."

Kish's face fell. This one wasn't so easy. "You know we can't do that. And why. You better than anyone."

"I've given this *extensive* thought," replied Rachel. "In fact, I've thought about this—lectured about this—for many years. Eyal was in one of these lectures, and I understand that Avi Wortzman was attending . . . remotely. Here is the bottom line. This technology is disruptive. No doubt about it. And I know the dangers as well as anyone. Dmitri Kovonov provided quite a case study for what bad actors can do with this capability. But while I'm working to reverse the insanity effect, I want to direct half of the vast neuroscience team you've assembled to come up with countermeasures to *prevent* this misuse."

Wortzman nodded slowly. "Yes, I remember these discussions from your class."

He turned to the prime minister. "It was an impressive lecture. She pointed out that for too long scientists have failed to prepare for the misuse of transformative technologies. Early computer scientists not only didn't spend any time trying to prevent the future use of computer viruses, they never even considered these might come into existence. She urged her students to consider tackling this end of the spectrum, which she argued might be even more important than the innovation itself."

"We happened to discuss Matrix Learning during the class," said Rachel. "We explored any number of ways this technology could lead to trouble. But if we can find a way to ensure brains are protected from unwanted memories, unwanted tampering, this alone would be enough to warrant giving this to the world."

"I have no problem working to counteract possible misuses," said Kish. "It's an excellent idea. And of course you should be in charge. I'm happy to let you control the most highly resourced program in my country, Rachel. You can deploy our scientists—*your* scientists—any way you like, and I can promise you a nearly unlimited budget for additional people and equipment."

The prime minister shook his head. "But we really can't give this to the world. No matter how many countermeasures we come up with, there will be misuses we can't predict, disruptions we can't predict."

"As long as we're able to develop countermeasures against the most severe misuse of the technology," said Rachel, "we have to just let the cat out of the bag and let the chips fall. Let's face it, these capabilities will be developed someday soon, somewhere, by some person, or group, or country. It can't be stopped. At least this way Israel can reap the credit and the financial rewards."

She paused for a moment to let the prime minister consider her arguments.

"No technology in history will be more disruptive, more transformative," she continued. "I get that. But we can't flinch. Humanity is already at a severe inflection point, just starting up the handle of the hockey stick. There's no turning back. The risks of self-destruction are very real, but this train has left the station and there's no stopping it."

"But the longer we delay disclosure," said Kish, "the more time we have to perfect countermeasures."

"Secrecy is the *problem*," insisted Rachel, "not the solution. We have to open source it. If you're the CEO of Apple and you want to provide scores of innovative apps for your new cell phone offering, you don't hide the source code in-house. You let it out. You let the entire world work on it."

She paused to take another drink of peach tea. "Civilization will adapt. Or it won't. But we can't hoard what we all know is a development as important as fire, the wheel, or agriculture."

Kish considered. "It's a scary prospect," he said after a long silence. "If we set it loose, the world will never be the same. And there will be no turning back."

"It's an *extremely* scary prospect," said Rachel. "But I believe this technology will end up solving more problems than it will create. Imagine everyone on Earth having the same universal language implanted in their minds along with their native tongues. Just like that, every person in the world would be able to hold a conversation with every other. Think of all the problems, technological and otherwise, that quick and easy education could help solve. If the inventors of farming had kept this advance to themselves, the human race would have likely gone extinct long ago. Either that, or the few people remaining would be in small clans, still hunting and foraging with simple tools."

Kish nodded thoughtfully but didn't respond.

"These are my terms," said Rachel. "I'll undergo Matrix Learning. I'm confident I'll find a way to solve your problem and perfect the technology. In exchange, I get to direct work on finding countermeasures for the most dangerous misuses. The moment I solve both problems, you agree to let the technology see the light of day." She stared intently at the Israeli prime minister. "I need your word."

Kish paused for almost a full minute in thought. Finally, he nodded. "It's a deal," he said. "You have my word. And not because you have us over a barrel. But because you're right. Perfect the technology, and I'll see to it that this is disclosed. Better yet, *you* can see to it."

"I'll support this decision as well," said Wortzman. "You make a lot of sense, Rachel. I've been battling with monsters a long time. Might be nice to do something to actively better humanity."

Rachel sighed. She had been confident she would eventually get agreement, but there was part of her that worried about the old adage, *be careful what you wish for*. This could be the biggest mistake ever made. She was rolling some very powerful dice.

On the other hand, she believed in what she had argued. There was no turning back. Knowledge was the key to success, to happiness, to progress, and it would soon be available in nearly unlimited quantities to every single person. Illiteracy and ignorance would be wiped from the planet. And while knowledge and wisdom were not the same thing, perhaps one could eventually lead to the other for the human race.

"Great," she said. "Let's do this thing. Load me up so we can get to work finding solutions."

Rachel Howard seemed to glow from within as a dazzling smile erupted onto her face. "And then let's go change the world," she added with absolute conviction.

From the Author: Thanks for reading *Game Changer*. I hope that you enjoyed it. As always, I'd be grateful if you would rate the novel on its Amazon page, as a high number of ratings really helps drive the success of a book.

Also, feel free to visit my website at www.douglaserichards.com (where you can get on a mailing list to be notified of new releases), Friend me on Facebook at *Douglas E. Richards Author*, or write to me at doug@san.rr.com.

***Game Changer*: What's real, what isn't, and a few personal anecdotes**

As you may know, I conduct fairly extensive research for all of my novels. In addition to trying to tell the most compelling stories I possibly can, I strive to introduce concepts and accurate information that I hope will prove fascinating, thought-provoking, and even controversial.

Game Changer is a work of fiction and contains considerable speculation. I encourage interested readers to read further to get a more thorough and nuanced look at each topic, and weigh any conflicting data, opinions, and interpretations. By so doing, you can decide for yourself what is accurate and arrive at your own view of the subject matter.

The genesis of the overarching plot: I've long been fascinated by neuroscience and human behavior, and wanted to do a novel that could extrapolate from current breakthroughs in these fields and examine future possibilities from every angle. The more research I did, the more fascinated I became. But I soon discovered that neuroscience offered an embarrassment of riches. How could I possibly narrow it down to a single novel given all the possibilities that a true understanding of neuroscience, and the manipulation of the human mind, could bring about?

Plots swirled around in my head. What if you could control addiction? The sex drive? Religion? Memory? Aggression and rage? Depression? What if you could implant ten years of knowledge into someone's brain in days?

Unable to decide between these possibilities, I finally decided to touch upon them all, with what I call Matrix Learning as the central driver.

At some point soon thereafter, while I was researching the science of memory, a scene materialized in my brain. I imagined a Secret Service agent trying to assassinate the president for the crime of torturing and killing his wife, only to learn later that he had been manipulated. Before I had any idea of the characters, the story, the background, or the settings, I knew one thing: the first section of the novel would end with someone saying to this Secret Service agent: "How do I know the president didn't torture and kill your wife? Because you never married. You never had a wife."

It was a scene I couldn't get out of my head, and I knew I had to write it. In some ways, the entire novel was built around these few sentences.

So with this brief explanation of how *Game Changer* came to be, I'll go on to detail some of the science behind it, along with some personal anecdotes. This field is producing so many astonishing results, and it has grown so rapidly, that I regret I can only provide the slightest taste within these pages.

Finally, I had to cram the information I needed to write this novel into my head the old-fashioned way. By reading books and studying. If only Matrix Learning were real, I could have finished months sooner. What a wonderful advance this technology would represent.

Although, as we have seen, it would not be without its dangers . . .

Matrix Learning: This topic deserved to come first, but it is a bit long, so if you find yourself losing interest in this or any other section, I encourage you to skip ahead to whatever sections interest you the most (I tried to restrain myself and keep each one short, but some are longer than others).

Here is a list of topics that I covered, in their order of appearance:

How often are we sure of memories that are wrong?

The pace of technological advance

The San Diego fire of 2007, cows, and suicide on the tracks

Neuroscience—what makes us tick?

Addicted to Dmitri Kovonov?
Plum Island
Neurotheology—God on the brain
Aluminum foil and laser printers
The BRAIN Initiative
A sleeping giant
Fly drones and fly catching
Israel, the Mossad, and US Intelligence
Neuroscience and the law
Miscellaneous

Now on to Matrix Learning. This is a term I made up, but I have read articles referring to Matrix-*style* learning, and I wouldn't be surprised if this becomes a shorthand for the technology someday. While scientists are a very long way away from achieving Matrix Learning like that depicted in the novel (or in the movie), they are making progress on a number of fronts. This progress includes the implantation of false memories (and knowledge would be just another category of false memory), and the use of smart dust and other technologies that could evolve into the nanites described in the novel.

I've included passages from four lay articles that I found intriguing below. Again, while these only scratch the surface, interested readers can readily find additional information online.

1) Scientists Give Mice False Memories (Elizabeth Landau, *CNN*, July 25, 2013).

Scientists say they have, for the first time, generated a false memory in an animal by manipulating brain cells that encode that information. What's more, the researchers say, the cellular events involved in the formation of a false memory resemble what takes place in forming a real memory. This jibes with the fact that humans who have false memories of events that didn't happen firmly believe that those memories are real.

"We should continue to remind society that memory can be very unreliable," said the study's senior author, Susumu Tonegawa, director of the RIKEN-MIT Center for Neural Circuit Genetics.

The lucky mice who participated in this study underwent a brain exploration technique called optogenetics, a means of manipulating individual brain cells with light.

. . . The researchers showed that if you can activate particular brain cells using light, and those brain cells contain memory information, then you have the power to make an animal believe it experienced something that never actually happened.

"The results indicate that the underlying brain mechanisms used in the recall of a false memory are very similar to those governing a real memory," Tonegawa said. "This may be why our memories feel so real to us, even if they have been distorted. It's not that false memory is formed by forgetting, some kind of a simple mix-up, or what we call imagination," Tonegawa added. "No, it really happened in the brain, as far as the brain is concerned."

2) Twenty billion nanoparticles talk to the brain using electricity (*New Scientist*, June 8, 2015)

Nanoparticles can be used to stimulate regions of the brain electrically, opening up new ways to treat brain diseases. It may even one day allow the routine exchange of data between computers and the brain.

When "magnetoelectric" nanoparticles (MENs) are stimulated by an external magnetic field, they produce an electric field. If such nanoparticles are placed next to neurons, this electric field should allow them to communicate.

Sakhrat Khizroev of Florida International University in Miami and his team inserted 20 billion of these nanoparticles into the brains of mice.

Khizroev's goal is to build a system that can both image brain activity and precisely target medical treatments at the same time. Since the nanoparticles respond differently to different frequencies of magnetic field, they can be tuned to release drugs.

"When they are injected in the brain, we can 'see' the brain," says Khizroev, "and if necessary, we can release a specific drug inside a specific neuron on demand."

3) How Smart Dust Could Spy On Your Brain *(MIT Technology Review*, July 16, 2013)

Intelligent dust particles embedded in the brain could form an entirely new form of brain-machine interface, say engineers.

Today, Dongjin Seo and pals at the University of California Berkeley reveal an entirely new way to study and interact with the brain. Their idea is to sprinkle electronic sensors the size of dust particles into the cortex and to interrogate them remotely using ultrasound. The ultrasound also powers this so-called neural dust.

Each particle of neural dust consists of standard CMOS circuits and sensors that measure the electrical activity in neurons nearby. This is coupled to a piezoelectric material that converts ultra-high-frequency sound waves into electrical signals and vice versa.

[Note: this last one is on editing and erasing memory—the flip side of the coin—which is also featured in the novel.]

4) Brain Researchers Open Door to Editing Memory (Benedict Carey, *New York Times*, April 5, 2009)

Suppose scientists could erase certain memories by tinkering with a single substance in the brain. Could make you forget a chronic fear, a traumatic loss, even a bad habit. Researchers in Brooklyn have recently accomplished comparable feats, with a single dose of an experimental drug delivered to areas of the brain critical for holding specific types of memory.

The discovery of such an apparently critical memory molecule, and its many potential uses, are part of the buzz surrounding a field that, in just the past few years, has made the seemingly impossible suddenly probable: neuroscience, the study of the brain.

Now neuroscience, a field that barely existed a generation ago, is racing ahead, attracting billions of dollars in new financing and throngs of researchers. The National Institutes of Health last year spent $5.2 billion, nearly 20 percent of its total budget, on brain-related projects. Endowments have poured in hundreds of millions of dollars more, establishing institutes at universities around the world.

The influx of money, talent, and technology means that scientists are at last finding real answers about the brain—and raising questions, both scientific and ethical, more quickly than anyone can answer them.

"This possibility of memory editing has enormous possibilities and raises huge ethical issues," said Dr. Steven E. Hyman, a neurobiologist at Harvard.

How often are we sure of memories that are wrong?

My own memory is atrocious. I have always been able to learn things very quickly, but I forget them just as quickly. When I'm writing a novel and have an idea, I have to record it somewhere or it will soon be gone forever. I get out of the shower and use my phone to e-mail the idea to my computer upstairs, while I'm still dripping wet, or I pull off the side of the road and send a message to myself. As much as I think I'll never forget an idea, I've done so too many times to take that chance.

The section describing the memory experiment conducted at Emory, comparing students' recollections of the Space Shuttle *Challenger* explosion the day after it happened and over two years later, is accurate—and truly scary. We all know human memory isn't great, but what is jaw-dropping to me is that not only is our memory unreliable, it is unreliable even when we're absolutely certain we've gotten it right.

This really calls into question everything we think we remember. When my version of past events differs markedly from my wife's, I used to be sure that I was right. Now I'm pretty sure that we're both wrong.

In my view, the most entertaining description of the Emory study and its implications can be found in an article that appeared in *The New Yorker*, and which is available online, entitled, "You Have No Idea What Happened" (Maria Konnikova, February 4, 2015).

After I read the Emory memory study, I was still skeptical. I discussed this study with my sister, Pam, and she was skeptical also. We both agreed that for something like the *Challenger* disaster, misremembering was a possibility, but surely not for something as profound as 9/11.

But then Pam had an idea. She had been at a conference with two colleagues on 9/11, giving a presentation. So why not ask them where they were on this tragic date? When they laughed at her for asking, because, of course, they were with *her*—how could she not remember?—she could explain the findings from the Emory study.

Sure enough, the first colleague she asked *did* remember they were together at the conference when it happened.

But the other colleague did not. She remembered being at home, and learning about it there. My sister was flabbergasted. Perhaps the Emory study wasn't so crazy after all. When Rachel Howard describes being at a sleepover with two friends on 9/11, and learning that they have different recollections of even this memorable day, this was meant as a fictional recounting of my sister's experiment.

The pace of technological advance: About thirty years ago I was a grad student in a PhD program in molecular biology, although I finally decided to write a master's thesis and leave, since I didn't have the patience for lab work.

As part of my research project, I mutated viruses, looking for interesting mutant phenotypes (observable manifestations), and then sequenced these viruses to learn what exact changes had taken place at the DNA level.

Sequencing even two hundred bases back then was quite an ordeal, took days, and required working with potentially dangerous levels of radiation. I really didn't enjoy it.

The fact that it is now possible to sequence billions of bases in the time it took me to do two hundred continues to blow my mind. How can this be? If you had asked me back then if this would be possible in 2016, my answer would have been an emphatic NO!

I would have said it would *never* be possible. Not in 2016, not in 22,016.

We are truly living in an amazing age. Every time I write one of these novels, I always come to a point at which I hesitate to push the possibilities of a technology any further. No, this is going too far, I think. My readers will revolt, thinking the technology I present is too far-fetched, too impossible, even for five or ten years in the future.

But then I always come back to DNA sequencing. And cell phones. And computers. And I realize that I'm not being too far-fetched—because a decade or two ago, I would never have had the audacity to suggest we could perfect technological miracles that I now take for granted every day.

The San Diego fire of 2007, cows, and suicide on the tracks:

The San Diego wildfires of 2007 described by Azim Jafari happened, just as described, and the statistics cited are accurate. It did cause the largest peacetime movement of civilians in America since the civil war, with nearly a million residents forced from their homes.

I was one of these residents.

While the fires headed in the direction of my neighborhood, my family loaded up what we could into our car, including photo albums, one dog, and one guinea pig, and I spent fifteen minutes dousing my home with water before we headed downtown. It was exceedingly stressful. Eventually we found lodging at a not-so-great motel, and smuggled in our pets.

Our house was spared, but the entire week was a horror show. Soot rained from the darkened skies and breathing the unfiltered air was dangerous. From the cast of the sky, it did seem like we were living in the aftermath of a nuclear war. It was eerie and creepy and surreal, and deeply distressing.

And as mile after mile of Southern California was consumed, and schools and businesses and the economy ground to a halt, it did occur to me that the region had been brought to its knees without need of a bombing, or a jet crashing into a skyscraper, and that a terrorist could have brought it about with a lighter and few gallons of gas.

So while I was writing *Game Changer* and needing to come up with a terrorist plot for the Mossad to foil—allowing me to introduce Mossad characters and their counterparts in the US—I thought this would be a good, dramatic choice.

Now let me switch gears. I was Director of Biotechnology Licensing at Bristol-Myers Squibb in Princeton, New Jersey, long ago, in a galaxy far, far away. Each day on my way to work I passed farms and many cows, just like Carmilla Acosta. I once knew Princeton well, so I enjoyed setting a few scenes here, even if I didn't spend much time describing the community.

When Carmilla remembers having been on a train that made an unscheduled stop, followed by the conductor asking passengers not to look out of the window on one side, followed by so many passengers rushing to this side to look out it was a wonder the train didn't tip over, this was an event that I experienced personally, on a trip from Princeton to New York. Before this time I had never associated trains with suicide, but after this event it was impossible not to. (I just performed a quick search—and while I didn't find any up-to-date figures, I did find that in 2011, tragically, there were 173 train-related suicides across America.)

Neuroscience—what makes us tick? All of the neuroscience discussed by Rachel Howard and Kevin Quinn, predominantly in chapters twenty-five and twenty-nine, is real, and as accurate as I could make it, although highly summarized and not rigorously presented. Most of this was gleaned from two books written by David Eagleman, a neuroscientist at Baylor College of Medicine, who is a gifted writer and who does a brilliant job of explaining complex concepts in a highly entertaining manner. The books are *Incognito* and *The Brain: The Story of You*. If you had to read just one, I would choose *Incognito*, as it contains more material and is truly captivating (but only after reading all of *my* books, of course, and recommending them to thousands of your friends :).

Some of the material on memory I found in the book *The Seven Sins of Memory*, by Daniel L. Schacter, Chair of Harvard's Department of Psychology, who has done groundbreaking work on this subject.

The Danziger study is real. Apparently a full stomach can influence who gets paroled and who doesn't.

It is also true that damage to different regions of the brain can cause dramatic and specific changes to personality and behavior. The story about Charles Whitman, The University of Texas shooter, is real. He did have a tumor and he did know something was going terribly wrong inside his brain. The same for the man with a brain tumor who began to exhibit pedophilic tendencies.

The link between the physical brain and human behavior, and the implications of this when it comes to the concept of the soul, is fascinating to me, and I attempted to address different views on this subject, although this is all highly speculative and subjective.

As discussed in the novel, human beings are born largely unfinished, and our brains are wired-up as we go, and unconscious subroutines burned into our brains tend to perform better and more efficiently than tasks carried out by our conscious minds.

The unconscious does control our bodies, the random thoughts we have, and far more of our lives than we'd ever imagine. This point is demonstrated repeatedly in the book, *Incognito*, and is truly astonishing to ponder. The unconscious really does run much of the show, and we really have become expert at taking the credit.

The Hess experiment, in which men ranked women whose eyes were slightly dilated as being more attractive, is true. And the unconscious has been shown to be able to pick up on patterns faster than the conscious in a number of experiments.

Emotions *are* important in driving decisions, and those with a certain type of damage to their prefrontal cortex, whose emotions no longer influence their behavior, can largely lose the ability to decide, paralyzed by even the simplest of choices, like what to make for dinner or watch on TV.

With respect to split brain patients, researchers really can get them to act without their consciousness knowing why, and they will fabricate reasons for their actions from whole cloth.

Finally, our memories really can be readily manipulated. The Loftus experiment, in which a memory of being lost in a mall was more or less implanted in subjects, is real, as is our tendency to embellish memories, even those that are false.

<u>Addicted to Dmitri Kovonov?</u> Obviously, the many manipulations Kovonov carried out on Carmilla's brain to get her to fall in love with him, and become addicted to him, are impossible. At least right now.

Kovonov's claim that specific people are represented in the brains of others by specific neuronal addresses, as it were, is accurate. These addresses can be as short as a single neuron, are known as Jennifer Aniston cells, and might potentially be manipulated one day for unsavory purposes, as suggested in this passage from the *New Scientist* article, **New memories implanted in mice while they sleep:**

> Evidence suggests that single neurons can represent specific people in the brain—such cells have been termed Jennifer Aniston cells, after a test subject was found to have one brain cell that only fired in response to images of the actress. If you could identify a neuron that represents you in someone else's brain and then stimulate areas of the brain that create a rewarding feeling every time that neuron fires, you might, in theory, be able to make that person like you more. "The fact that you can do it during sleep is a bit worrying, in that it implies that you could make somebody want something even if they didn't really," says Neil Burgess at University College London. "There are a few ways of thinking about this—there's the medical application, and there's the more Orwellian application, where the government gets inside people's heads and starts to control them," he says.

Plum Island: This is a real island with a checkered history, and the background on it given in the novel is accurate, all except the following sentence: "In 2020, with great fanfare, DHS had announced they had sold Plum Island to a reclusive Internet billionaire." This hasn't happened yet, but check back in 2020 to see if this comes true.

Notably, in the movie *The Silence of the Lambs*, FBI trainee Clarice Starling offers Hannibal Lecter an annual vacation on Plum Island in exchange for helping her track down a serial killer. In response, he scathingly refers to it as "Anthrax Island."

To the best of my knowledge there is no Black neuroscience lab on the island, and if there were, I suspect it wouldn't be abbreviated as ANL. But Plum Island would be a great place to put such a secret lab, in my opinion.

Finally, because the island is a major setting for the novel, I'll leave you with this excerpt from a CBS News story from June 10, 2012, entitled, *Plumbing the Mysteries of Plum Island* (which can easily be found online):

Plum Island sits at the end of New York's Long Island like a question mark. For nearly 60 years, controversies and mysteries have engulfed it.

And no wonder. The island is controlled by the Department of Homeland Security. Its labs are staffed by scientists from the United States Department of Agriculture. They come and go by special government ferries, guarded by armed officers.

We were asked not to film the docks on either side.

So what really goes on here? The USDA says scientists study diseases that can affect livestock, primarily overseas, to develop vaccines.

And although the government says the germs stored on the island affect only animals, that doesn't mean they're not dangerous. And information about them is strictly protected for security reasons.

Neurotheology—God on the brain: I had thought that religion was in decline around the world, certain pockets notwithstanding, but this is apparently not true, as described by Kevin Quinn in chapter sixty-one. The Gallup poll data and the data about the supernatural beliefs prevalent in Sweden and Iceland were taken from the book *The Triumph of Faith*, by Rodney Stark, which has as much data and statistics on the subject as you would ever want to see. In preparation for these sections I also read Matthew Alper's *The God Part of the Brain*, which I found both fascinating and useful.

The evidence presented in chapter sixty-one that a propensity toward religiosity is prewired into the human brain is accurate, including the identical twin studies mentioned, as well as the similarities across virtually all cultures as noted by Carl Jung and others. Also, spiritual feelings can be ramped up or down as a result of drugs, disease, or physical trauma.

Like the discussion about the existence of the soul earlier in the novel, thinking about the philosophical implications of these findings was intriguing to me. The argument about why these findings don't necessarily disprove religion is my own, as far as I know. I wouldn't be surprised if this argument had been made before, but it isn't one that I've read.

I thought it made some sense that if there were a Creator, he would give us this prewired religion function. Faith is defined as belief in the absence of proof. If a Creator made us without the ability to have faith, we could hardly be expected to come to it on our own. But if we were made *with* the ability to have faith, prewired for it in fact, we could always choose to ignore it. (Again, this doesn't mean there is a Creator, just that these findings don't necessarily rule it out.)

Those of you who have read other novels, and other notes, I've written, may know that when I began writing novels I was leaning toward atheism. But the more physics and cosmology I've learned, the more open-minded I've become (which is the opposite of what I thought would happen). This has occurred because, while I find the idea of a omnipotent Creator preposterous, the answers proposed by physicists and cosmologists to explain the origin of the universe are at least as preposterous. The universe is exquisitely fine-tuned for life (Google "The fine-tuned universe" if you're interested in learning more). Scientific theories to explain the impossibly perfect balance of forces that allow life to exist typically involve infinite universes, which sounds cool, but which isn't any easier to wrap one's mind around than the concept of God.

In the final analysis, all that I am sure of is that something amazing is going on, something impossible, and something far beyond my ability to understand, whether this something is God or physics.

The novel describes precise locations in the brain responsible for spirituality. While some progress has been made in unraveling where this spiritual function might reside in the brain, these locations have yet to be mapped out. This being said, I postulated that this would involve multiple locations, rather than a single location, after reading articles like the one excerpted below, from a piece in the *Huffington Post* (April, 2012) entitled, **No God Spot in Brain, Spirituality Linked to Right Parietal Lobe:**

Scientists have speculated that the human brain features a "God spot," one distinct area of the brain responsible for spirituality. Now, University of Missouri researchers have completed research that indicates spirituality is a complex phenomenon, and multiple areas of the brain are responsible for the many aspects of spiritual experiences.

"We have found a neuropsychological basis for spirituality, but it's not isolated to one specific area of the brain," said Brick Johnstone, professor of health psychology in the School of Health Professions. "Spirituality is a much more dynamic concept that uses many parts of the brain. Certain parts of the brain play more predominant roles, but they all work together to facilitate individuals' spiritual experiences."

In the most recent study, Johnstone studied 20 people with traumatic brain injuries affecting the right parietal lobe, the area of the brain situated a few inches above the right ear. He surveyed participants on characteristics of spirituality, such as how close they felt to a higher power and if they felt their lives were part of a divine plan. He found that the participants with more significant injury to their right parietal lobe showed an increased feeling of closeness to a higher power.

Aluminum foil and laser printers: I had fun writing the scene in which Kevin Quinn is turned into an aluminum foil mummy. It turns out that aluminum foil really does block electromagnetic signals. Like Quinn, I had thought this was a myth, but my research indicated it wasn't.

But I had to prove it to myself. So I did the experiment Rachel recommends in the novel. I parked myself on the couch and called my cell phone from our landline. Then I placed a single sheet of aluminum foil over my cell and called again, responding with a triumphant, "Yes!" when the phone didn't ring. My wife, long used to being married to a writer, now takes anything I do in stride, and looked on in amusement.

"Working out a scene?" she asked.

"Yep," I replied. "Did you know that aluminum foil is a real thing?"

With respect to laser printers, when I was an undergraduate at Ohio State, my father owned a company that sold copy machines, faxes, and other business equipment. His biggest client was the General Electric jet engine plant, which was a massive (and incredibly cool) complex of buildings. He had placed over a hundred copy machines there, spread out over many, many acres and many, many giant buildings. The repair technician he sent when a copier had an issue was rubbing many of the GE people the wrong way, and they weren't happy with the level of service.

So during one of my summer breaks from college, he decided to make me his secret weapon to bring his company back into good graces with GE. He gave me a crash course on copy machine repair and sent me to the GE plant every day as the maintenance, repair, and customer good will technician. Most of the tweaks required to optimize copier performance were simple. For anything that wasn't routine, he would send a real repair technician to fix the problem. But I was really there to be charming and polite and helpful and repair the damage to the relationship another tech had caused.

Why do I mention this? Because copiers and laser printers work the same way, and I haven't taken this technology for granted since the days at GE. Both devices lay down an electric charge on a drum in the precise pattern of the document to be printed, and then suck up toner. It occurred to me when writing *Game Changer* that this would be a useful analogy to use when thinking about how the nanites could quickly be directed to assume complex patterns.

The BRAIN initiative: This is real, and the blog post that Rachel read to her class, likening this effort to the NASA moon launch, is also real. As discussed, this was written by Francis Collins, who led the Human Genome Project.

As Collins wrote, the goal of this initiative is to produce the first dynamic view of the human brain in action, revolutionizing our understanding of how we think, feel, learn, remember, and move. This is a massive, expensive project, and a very big deal.

I won't spent further time with it here, but I would direct you to HumanConnectomeProject.org, or you could Google *The BRAIN Initiative*, or these specific articles: 1) *The $5 Billion Race to Map Your Brain*, and 2) *Whole mouse brain mapping within reach.*

A sleeping giant: Kovonov was attempting to motivate America to get off the sidelines and unleash its full might to destroy an enemy.

This is precisely what the Japanese did during World War II, although in this case it wasn't on purpose. America had chosen to sit out this war at the start. But this changed dramatically after Japan's attack on Pearl Harbor. A Japanese admiral, realizing the grave mistake his country had made, was alleged to have said, "We have awakened a sleeping giant, and have filled him with a terrible resolve."

The Kovonov character would no doubt be aware of this history, so I chose to have him call this to mind by characterizing his actions as *kicking awake a sleeping giant*.

Fly drones and fly catching: I put very little material into the novel about the science of fly drones, but the pursuit of Micro Air Vehicles is a real thing, of course. Drones have become impossible not to notice, and before I turned to neurobiology, I had planned to write a novel based on a future in which MAVs had been perfected.

Not only could fly drones and other MAVs be used in surveillance, they could be used to inject poison, could be directed into jet engines to down planes, and could engage in all sorts of other mayhem. I threw myself into the subject for almost two months, during which I read books on the subject and spent many hours attempting to come up with an overarching plot.

But try as I might, I could never find one that really grabbed me. Finally, I gave up, and turned to neuroscience as the basis for a possible novel. But while writing *Game Changer*, I still had drones on the brain, and realized they could work quite nicely in a supporting role, although I chose not to go into any technical detail.

With respect to killing and catching living flies with one's hands, these passages are accurate. I know, because I captured flies this same way as a kid. I'd have other kids try to catch one, which couldn't really be done without the *sliding a hand on a smooth surface* technique. When they were unable to do so, I'd bet them that I could. I won a number of bets this way, and couldn't resist including this in the novel—the technique, not the bets :).

Israel, the Mossad, and US Intelligence: Meir Dagan really was the head of the Mossad from 2002 until 2010, and really did have a framed black-and-white photo of his grandfather, just before he was killed by the Nazis (and the results of the Stanley Milgram experiment that are described are accurate, as well).

Anything in the novel about Israel and the Mossad that wasn't obviously fictional—like their Matrix Learning Manhattan Project, and so on—was factual. Israel is as tiny as described, has as scant a population, and is surrounded by countless larger enemies determined to destroy it. The Mossad has become almost legendary in its excellence as a spy agency, as described. Finally, the country does contain perhaps the most highly educated population, per capita, of any country in the world, and has become a world-renowned center of innovation. I drew on two books for much of this information: *Spies Against Armageddon*, by Dan Raviv and Yossi Melman, and *Start-Up Nation: The Story of Israel's Economic Miracle*, by Dan Senor and Saul Singer.

The US Intelligence Community is as unwieldy of a behemoth as described in the novel, with seventeen separate agencies, almost thirteen hundred government organizations, and two thousand private companies, operating from over ten thousand locations spread across the country. In 2010, the *Washington Post* published the results of a two-year investigation of the US Intelligence Community entitled, "A hidden world, growing beyond control," which is quite eye-opening. Here is how this lengthy story begins:

> The top-secret world the government created in response to the terrorist attacks of Sept. 11, 2001, has become so large, so unwieldy and so secretive that no one knows how much money it costs, how many people it employs, how many programs exist within it or exactly how many agencies do the same work.
>
> These are some of the findings of a two-year investigation by *The Washington Post* that discovered what amounts to an alternative geography of the United States, a Top Secret America hidden from public view and lacking in thorough oversight. After nine years of unprecedented spending and growth, the result is that the system put in place to keep the United States safe is so massive that its effectiveness is impossible to determine.

<u>**Neuroscience and the law:**</u> I touched upon this briefly in the novel, when the decision was made to fake Quinn's death rather than disclose the possibility of false memory implantation, so as not to throw a lifeline to criminal defense attorneys throughout the country. This is another area I find fascinating, but I couldn't spare the space in the novel to address it more fully.

David Eagleman does discuss this extensively in his book *Incognito,* however. In addition to his other duties, Eagleman is also director of Baylor College of Medicine's *Initiative on Neuroscience and the Law*, and has lectured on these issues all over the world. Here is an excerpt from this section of his book:

> The biggest battle I have to fight is the misperception that an improved biological understanding of people's behaviors and internal differences means we will forgive criminals and no longer take them off the streets. That's incorrect. Biological explanation will not exculpate criminals. Brain science will improve the legal system, not impede its function. For the smooth operation of society, we will remove from the streets those criminals who prove themselves to be over-aggressive, under-empathetic, and poor at controlling their impulses. They will be taken into the care of the government.
>
> But the important change will be the way we punish the vast range of criminal acts—in terms of rational sentencing and new ideas for rehabilitation. The emphasis will shift from punishment to recognizing problems (both neural and social) and meaningfully addressing them.

<u>**Miscellaneous:**</u> The information about Alan Turing, his contributions to computer science and the war effort, and his recruitment of non-typical code breakers, is accurate. If you haven't seen the movie *The Imitation Game*, about Turing and his efforts to crack the Nazi Enigma Machine, I can't recommend it more highly. One of the best movies I have seen.

Adolf Hitler did survive multiple assassination attempts over many years. Had just one of these succeeded who knows what the world would look like today.

The transparent roundworm, C. elegans, has played a vital role in neuroscience for many decades for the reasons given, and does, indeed, possess just three hundred and two neurons.

The information about girls outperforming boys when it comes to reading is accurate. Not only this, it is often difficult to get boys to read at all. I've written articles for *Today's Parent* and others on this subject, since my *Prometheus Project* kids series has been touted by both parents and educators for its appeal to reluctant readers (and interestingly enough, gifted students at the same time).

Microneedle arrays *are* being developed for painless delivery of medications.

The information about the Advanced Airborne Command Post (the E-4B jet), and the High-Value Detainee Interrogation Group is accurate.

The information about the vulnerabilities of facial recognition, including CV Dazzle and the use of remote control bulbs to blind cameras, is accurate, as is the discussion of the Chinese torture called *Death by a Thousand Cuts*.

Finally, the symptoms experienced by al-Bilawy after Rachel Howard activated all of his nanites at once are all actual symptoms of what is called a Tonic-clonic seizure (previously called a Grand mal seizure), although these would typically not all occur during the same episode, nor be as severe.

My first responsibility in business development for a biotech company was trying to partner an experimental anti-epilepsy drug, and I gave my first ever presentation in this role to executives of Eli Lilly, in Indianapolis, Indiana.

My guess is that if every neuron fired at once, al-Bilawy would simply collapse, dead, in an instant, but I took a bit of dramatic license, stepping through symptoms sequentially and keeping him alive for a full twelve seconds.

ABOUT THE AUTHOR

Douglas E. Richards is the *New York Times* and *USA Today* bestselling author of eight technothrillers, including *Wired*, *Amped*, *Mind's Eye*, *BrainWeb*, *Quantum Lens*, *Split Second*, *Game Changer*, and *The Cure*. He has also written six middle grade/young adult novels widely acclaimed for their appeal to boys, girls, and adults alike. Douglas has a master's degree in molecular biology (aka "genetic engineering"), was a biotechnology executive for many years, and has authored a wide variety of popular science pieces for *National Geographic*, the *BBC*, the *Australian Broadcasting Corporation*, *Earth and Sky*, *Today's Parent*, and many others. Douglas has a wife, two children, and two dogs, and currently lives in San Diego, California.

CPSIA information can be obtained
at www.ICGtesting.com
Printed in the USA
FSHW020042290119
55312FS